wicked

wicked

Witch & Curse

Nancy Holder and Debbie Viguié

SIMON PULSE

NEW YORK LONDON TORONTO SYDNEY

ʍʍ

SIMON PULSE
An imprint of Simon & Schuster Children's Publishing Division
1230 Avenue of the Americas, New York, NY 10020
Witch copyright © 2002 by Nancy Holder
Curse copyright © 2003 by Nancy Holder
All rights reserved, including the right of reproduction in
whole or in part in any form.
SIMON PULSE and colophon are registered trademarks
of Simon & Schuster, Inc.
Designed by Ann Zeak
The text of this book was set in Aldine 401BT.
Manufactured in the United States of America
This Simon Pulse edition September 2008
20 19 18 17 16 15
Library of Congress Control Numbers:
Witch: 2002106487
Curse: 2002110488
ISBN-13: 978-1-4169-7119-1
ISBN-10: 1-4169-7119-X

These titles were originally published
individually by Simon Pulse.

contents

AUTHOR'S NOTE

In preparation for the writing of this series, I explored one of the Wicca traditions under the guidance of a Wiccan high priest. I am aware that Wicca is not a single faith tradition, but a set of them, and that some magic users and spellcasters dislike the more stereotypical "black magic" of fictive invention. To them, I offer apologies; to everyone else, I offer the hope that the many forms of magic I present in this novel serve to show what a diverse and rich place can be found within a Book of Spells.

—Nancy Holder

wicked

Witch

To my wonderful co-author Debbie Viguié, and to Michael Reaves, with love.

—Nancy Holder

To the three people who have always loved me: my parents, Rick and Barbara Reynolds, and my husband, Scott Charles Viguié.
—Debbie Viguié

ACKNOWLEDGMENTS

Thank you Debbie, for being the great writer and friend you are. Thanks to Lisa "The Termineditor" Clancy and her intrepid Schusterians past and present: Liz Shiflett, Micol Ostow, and Lisa Gribbin. To my agent, Howard Morhaim . . . you're magic. Thanks to David Hahn for the technical assist, and thanks to those who kept it goin'—Melissa, Von, and Jenn. *Mahalo* John and Shannon Tulius and Liz Engstrom of the Maui Writers Conference. You are *no ka oi*! And a big thank you to Christopher Vogler for writing *The Writer's Journey*.

—N. H.

I would like to thank my coauthor, Nancy, whose generosity as a writer and a person has enriched my life. Thank you Lisa Clancy, you are a fabulous editor and your humor and compassion make you a joy to work with. To the organizers of the Maui Writer's Conference I extend my heartfelt thanks. You do so much more than help writers grow in their craft, you provide a forum for forging friendships and alliances. Lastly I need to thank the people who have always believed in me and encouraged me: my grandparents, Harold and Mildred Trent, who encouraged my creativity; Matt Washburn, an awesome writer and encourager; Chrissy Hadley, my number-one fan; Juliette Cutts and Ann Liotta, true friends who have always read what I've written with joy; Michael Mueller, the most loyal friend anyone could ask for. Peggy Hanley, thank you for always being there for Scott and now for me. Thank you to my other writer friends who have patiently waded through hundreds of pages and given helpful critiques: Penny Austen, John Oglesby, and Kelly Watkins. Thank you to Jennifer Harrington for always listening. I love you all.

—D. V.

Part One: Lammas
The Harvesting

(

LAMMAS
"And the ground refused to give up its natural fruits, but instead yielded unholy and unnatural creatures. The dead walked along with those who had never lived."
——Simon the Prophet, 8th century

ONE

BARLEY MOON

☾

Fare ye well, Lord of Light
Thou wilt rule on Yuletide Night
Blackfires burn and scythe the Rows
So crieth House of Deveraux

From out thy Vessel, Lady Faire
Cahors Witches take to Aire
Blood drink of Foe and Blood of Friend
Renew the Earthe with Blood again

Mile 76 from Lee's Ferry, the Colorado River, August 1 (Lammas)

Oh, great. A storm. On top of everything else.

Ignoring for the moment the thick, hot words her parents were exchanging at the bow of the inflatable raft, Holly raised her gaze to the shard of sky between the canyon walls. Nickel and copper sunlight sheered her vision, making her eyes hurt. Clouds like decomposing gray fists rumbled, and the canyon wrens fluttered from their hiding places, cooing warnings to one another.

3

Behind her, the extremely buff boatman who did these rides every summer for his USC tuition money grunted and sighed. Her parents had pushed the guy beyond his "Hello, my name is Ryan and I'll be your river guide" manners, and she didn't blame him. Her mother and father were wearing everybody out—him, her, and Tina, her best friend, who had had the bad luck to be invited on this nightmare vacation. Of course, Tina got invited to everything. Being an only child had its advantages, and both Tina and Holly were onlies.

Tina's mom had dropped out at the last minute, claiming a problem with her schedule at Marin County General, but Holly wondered if the petite, dark-haired woman had known something was up. That would make sense; Barbara Davis-Chin was Holly's mom's best friend, and even grown-up best friends told their girlfriends everything.

Hey, I know the score, Holly thought. *I've seen* Sex and the City.

Five days ago, when Holly had gotten home from her horse stable job, it had been obvious something had been going on behind the closed doors of their classically San Franciscan Queen Anne Victorian row house. Her parents' shouts, cut short by the sound of Holly's key in the front lock, had practically echoed off

4

the white plaster walls. She'd heard the rhythmic sound of a push broom as one of them swept up a mess. Above Holly's head as she stood in the foyer, taking off her jacket, the floorboards of her parents' bedroom creaked with tension.

"Hey, hi, you guys, I'm home," she'd called, but no one had answered. Then after a moment or two, her father had come downstairs, his smile reaching nowhere near his eyes as he said, "Hi, punky. Good day at the stables?"

No one had talked about what had happened. Her parents, Elise and Daniel Cathers, had joined in a conspiracy of polite silence, chilly to each other that night while packing for the trip, with the emotional frost dipping below freezing on the flight to Las Vegas. Thankfully, she'd sat with Tina in another row of the plane, and she and her best friend had had their own room in their suite at the Bellagio.

Her parents had gone out to see Cirque du Soleil, leaving Holly and Tina in their own room to talk about the upcoming senior year and their plans for college— USC for Tina, UC Santa Barbara for Holly. Then the two adults had come back, very late—and drunk, Holly hoped, because she didn't want to think that they would ever speak that way to each other when they were sober. They had flung mean words at each other like knives, words designed and honed to hurt. Holly knew it was wishful thinking that her father was not saying *bitch,* but *witch,* even though it had sounded like that through the closed doors of the suite's second bedroom. That was what Tina had heard too.

In the morning Ryan had met the four of them in the Bellagio foyer and driven them to the raft trip launch site. Mom and Dad had barely been civil to each other during the daylong safety training class.

Ryan got the raft into the water and told them where to sit. Then, as if the swirling waters of the Colorado had driven their tempers, the arguing had begun again, and during the day of white-water rafting it had grown steadily worse.

Now Holly and Tina hunched over their oars, paddling according to Ryan's directions and pointedly trying to pretend nothing weird was going on. They wore bright orange life vests and orange helmets, Tina's hanging low over her black hair, which she had dyed aquamarine in honor of the trip. Holly, her own dark hair a mass of damp, crazed ringlets, was crammed beside Tina in the center of the raft, which resembled a kind of pudgy dinghy. Cold water sluiced at them from every direction as the raft roller-coastered between slick black boulders and tree trunks. As chilly as the environment was, it was tropical compared to her parents' attitude toward each other.

"Dude, what is *wrong* with them?" Tina asked in Holly's ear. "They're going to kill each other. Or us."

"When we get home, adopt me," Holly said miserably.

"We're almost old enough to get married." Tina wagged her eyebrows suggestively. "C'mon, baby, you know you want me." She blew Holly a kiss.

Smiling faintly, Holly sighed and shook her head. "Your mom would love that."

"My mom is a bigger knee-jerk liberal than your whole family put together," Tina retorted. "She'd love to plan our commitment ceremony, *darling*."

Holly grinned and Tina grinned back. The smiles quickly faded, however, as the sound of angry voices rose once again over the rapids' roar.

"—*not* going back early," Holly's father hissed.

"You never told me." That was her mom. "You should have told me . . ."

Ay, Chihuahua, Holly thought. Tension eddied between them, and a fresh wave of anxiety washed through her. Something was basically, fundamentally wrong, and if she got really honest with herself, she knew it had been wrong for over a year.

Ever since I had that nightmare . . .

Her dad broke eye contact first and her mother

quit the field, two territorial animals both dissatisfied with the outcome of their face-off. They were both good-looking people even though they were in their forties. Dad was tall and lanky, with thick, unruly black hair and very dark brown eyes. Her mom was the odd one out, her hair so blond, it looked fake, her eyes a soft blue that reminded Holly of bridesmaid dresses. Everyone always thought they looked so good together, like TV parents. Few besides Holly knew that their conversations were more like dialogue from a horror movie.

"Okay, hang on," Ryan interrupted her thoughts— and for a split second, the arguing. "We're gonna start the Hance Rapids. Remember, stay left." He looked up at the lowering sky and muttered, "Damn."

Holly cocked her head up at him. His face was dark and durable, much too leathery for someone who was only twenty-one. *By the time he's thirty,* she thought, *he's going to look like a statue made of beef jerky.*

"Gonna be a storm, huh," she said, raising her voice to be heard over the rapids and the creaking of the raft's rubber skin.

He glanced at her. "Yeah. We'll stop early tonight." He glanced at her parents. "Tempers are getting kinda short."

"They're not usually—" she began, then shut her

mouth, nodded, and got back to paddling.

White water tumbled ahead like a kettle put on to boil, and she and Tina sat up a little straighter, getting ready for the big, exciting zoom downward. Going down rapids was officially the fun part, the reason they were there. But Holly had had enough. She wanted to go home.

The river currents rushed, threading together and then separating, curling around rocks and boulders and making eddies like potholes in a street. They skidded and slid along, the by-now familiar blend of joy and fear tightening Holly's chest and tickling her spine. "Yee-ha!" she yelled, and Tina took up the cry. They broke into laughter, bellowing "Yee-ha!" over and over in voices loud enough to echo off the canyon walls. Canyon wrens joined in and thunder rumbled overhead, and Holly felt a flash of anger that her parents were too busy being pissed off at each other to share in the fun.

The raft picked up more speed, then more; Holly's stomach lurched and Tina shrieked with fearful delight.

Then the sky rumbled once, twice, and cracked open. Rain fell immediately, huge bucketfuls of it, completely drenching them. It rushed down so hard, it slapped Holly's shoulders painfully. She flailed for her yellow raincoat wrapped around her waist, and the boat pitched and bowed as everyone lost track, startled by the downpour.

Ryan yelled, "To your oars!"

Holly's parents snapped to, guiding the boat the way Ryan had taught them. Rain came down like waterfalls; the river waters sluiced to either side of a giant boulder, and Holly remembered rather than heard Ryan's admonition to stay left of it. *Everything around here, stay left.*

The huge granite outcropping towered above them. Its face was jagged and sharp, not rounded with erosion as one would have expected.

"Wow," Tina yelled, taking a moment to gesture at it.

The rain fell even harder, pummeling them, and Holly worked frantically to pull her hood back up over her head as a bracing wind whipped it off. The torrents blinded her. She couldn't see anything.

"Jesus Christ, *duck!*" Ryan screamed.

Holly ducked, peering through the rain.

There was a millisecond where everyone froze, shocked brains registering what was happening. Then they all scrambled as if responding to an air raid in a World War II movie, grabbing their paddles and fighting the river's determination to slam them en masse against the huge piece of granite.

"*No!*" Tina cried as her oar was almost torn from her hands by the force of a wave. She started screaming as the raft dove down at a 45-degree angle. Foaming angry water rushed over the five passengers up to their waists. Tina screamed again and batted futilely at the water as Holly shouted, "What do we do now? What are we supposed to do?"

"Keep calm!" Ryan bellowed. "Left, left, *left!*"

Holly's oar felt entirely too fragile and slight to make any difference in the trajectory the water was flinging them into; at the same time it was too heavy and unwieldy for her to manipulate.

Then her mother shouted something and Daniel Cathers cried, "*No!*"

The river was a maelstrom now; everything was gray and cold and unforgiving and treacherous; gray stone and gray water, as the raft was propelled toward the boulder with the force of a catapult.

Holly held on to the paddle. It was useless now, but still she held it, hands frozen around it in terror. Someone, she had no idea who, was shouting her name.

Then Ryan's voice rang out. "Jump! *Now!*"

His command broke her stupefaction. As she tried to unbuckle her safety straps and jump, the river crested over the raft, completely engulfing it. Cold, unforgiving water surrounded her, cresting above her shoulders, her head; she waited for it to recede, but it just kept barreling over her. She panicked, unable to breathe, and began pushing frantically at the restraints. She couldn't remember how to undo them.

I'm going to drown. I'm going to die.

The steel waters thickened, becoming waves of blackness. She couldn't see anything, couldn't feel anything, except the terrible cold. The raft could be tumbling end over end for all she knew. Her mind seized on the image of the huge face of rock; hitting it at this speed would be like falling out of a window and splatting on the street.

Her lungs were too full; after some passage of time she could not measure, they threatened to burst; she understood that she needed to exhale and draw in more oxygen. She fumbled at the belt but she still had no clue how to get free. As her chest throbbed she batted at the water, at her lap and shoulders where the straps were, trying so hard to keep it together, so hard.

I'm gonna die. I'm gonna die.

The ability to reason vanished. She stopped thinking altogether, and instinct took over as she flapped weakly at the restraints, not recalling why she was doing it. She forgot that she had been in a raft with the three people she loved most in the world. She forgot that she was a teenager named Holly and that she had hair and eyes and hands and feet.

She was nothing but gray inside and out. The world was a flat fog color and so were her images, thoughts, and emotions. Numb and empty, she drifted in a bottomless well of nothingness, flat-lining, ceasing. She couldn't say it was a pleasant place to be. She couldn't say it was anything.

Though she didn't really know it, she finally exhaled. Eagerly she sucked in brackish river water. It filled her lungs, and her eyes rolled back in her head as her death throes began.

Struggling, wriggling like a hooked fish, her body tried to cough, to expel the suffocating fluid. It was no use; she was as good as dead. Her eyes fluttered shut.

And then, through her lids, she saw the most exquisite shade of blue. It was the color of neon tetras, though she couldn't articulate that. It shimmered like some underwater grace note at the end of a movie; she neither reached toward it nor shrank from it, because her brain didn't register it. It didn't register anything. Oxygen-starved, it was very nearly dead.

The glow glittered, then coalesced. It became a figure, and had any part of Holly's brain still been taking in and processing data, it would have reported the sight of a woman in a long-sleeved dress of gray wool and gold trimming, astonishingly beautiful, with curls of black hair mushrooming in the water. Her compassionate gaze was chestnut and ebony as she reached toward Holly.

Run. Flee, escape, don't stop to pack your belongings. Alors, she will perish if you do not go now. Maintenaint, a c'est moment la; vite, je vous en prie. . . .

Nightmare, Holly thought fuzzily. *Last year. Nightmare. . . .*

The figure raised forth her right hand; a leather glove was wrapped around her hand, and on it perched a large gray bird. She hefted the bird through the water, and it moved its wings through the rush torrent, toward Holly.

"We aren't witches!" her father shouted in her memory.

And her mother: "I know what I saw! I know what I saw in Holly's room!"

Go, take her from here; they will find her and kill her . . . je vous en prie . . . je vous en prie, Daniel de Cahors. . . .

"Je vous en prie," the man in the deer's head whispered heartbreakingly.

It was Barley Moon, the time of harvest, and the forest was warm and giving, like a woman. The man was staked to a copse of chestnut trees, his chest streaked with his own blood.

The Circle was drawn, the tallow candles set for lighting.

"I am so sorry for him, Maman," Isabeau whispered to her mother. The lady of the manor was dressed in raven silks, silver threads chasing scarlet throughout, as were the others in the Circle—there were thirteen this night, including her newly widowed mother's new husband, who was her mother's dead husband's brother, named Robert, and the sacrifice, the quaking man in the dead deer's head, who knew that he would soon die.

The Circle's beautiful familiar, the hawk Pandion, jingled her bells as she observed from her perch, which had been fashioned from bones of the de Cahorses' bitterest enemy . . . the Deveraux. She was eager for the kill; she would snatch the man's soul as it escaped his body, and daintily nibble at its edges until others caught hold of it for their own purposes.

"It is a better death," Catherine de Cahors insisted, smiling down on her child. She petted Isabeau's hair with one hand. In the other hand she held the bloody dagger. It was she who had carved the sigils into the man's chest. Her husband, Robert, had felt compelled to restrain her, reminding her that torture was not a part of tonight's rite. It was to be a good, clean execution. "His wagging tongue would have sent him to the stake eventually. He would have burned, a horrible way to die. This way . . ."

They were interrupted by a figure wearing the silver and black livery of Cahors; he raced to the edge of the Circle and dropped to his knees directly before the masked and cloaked Robert. *Robert's height must have given him away,* Isabeau thought.

"The Deveraux . . . the fire," the servant gasped. "They have managed it."

Pandion threw back her head and shrieked in lamentation. The entire Circle looked at one another in shock from behind their animal masks. Several of them sank to their knees in despair.

Isabeau was chilled, within and without. The Deveraux had been searching for the secret of the Black Fire for centuries. Now that they had it . . . what would become of the Cahors? Of anyone who stood in the way of the Deveraux?

Isabeau's mother covered her heart with her arms and cried, "*Alors,* Notre Dame! Protect us this night, our Lady Goddess!"

"This is a dark night," said one of the others. "A night rife with evil. The lowest, when it was to have been a joyous Lammas, this man's ripe death adding to the Harvest bounty. . . ."

"We are undone," a cloaked woman keened. "We are doomed."

"Damn you for your cowardice," Robert murmured in a low, dangerous voice. "We are not."

He tore off his mask, grabbed the dagger from his wife, and walked calmly to the sacrifice. Without a moment's hesitation he yanked the man's head back by the hair and cut his throat. Blood spurted, covering those nearby while others darted forward to receive the blessing. Pandion swooped down from her perch, soaring into the gushing heat, the bells on her ankles clattering with eagerness.

Isabeau's mother urged her toward the man's body. "Take the blessing," she told her daughter. "There is wild work ahead, and you must be prepared to do your part."

Isabeau stumbled forward, shutting her eyes, glancing away. Her mother took her chin and firmly turned her face toward the stream of steaming, crimson liquid.

"*Non, non,*" she protested as the blood ran into her mouth. She felt defiled, disgusted.

The gushing blood seemed to fill her vision. . . .

★ ★ ★

Holly woke up. As far as she could tell, she lay on the riverbank. The sound of rushing water filled her pounding head; she was shaking violently from head to toe and her teeth were chattering. She tried to move, but couldn't tell if she succeeded. She was completely numb.

"Mmm . . . ," she managed, struggling to call for her mother.

All she heard, all she knew, was the rushing of the river. And then . . . the flapping of a bird's wings. They sounded enormous, and in her confusion she thought it was diving for her, ready to swoop her up like a tiny, waterlogged mouse.

Her lids flickered up at the sky; a bird did hover against the moon, a startling silhouette.

Then she lost consciousness again. Her coldness faded, replaced by soothing warmth. . . .

The blood is so warm, she thought, drifting. *See how it steams in the night air. . . .*

Again, the sound of rushing water. Again the deathly chill.

The screech of a bird of prey . . .

★ ★ ★

Then once more Holly saw the hot, steaming blood—and something new: a vile, acrid odor that reeked of charnel houses and dungeon terrors. Something very evil, very wrong, very *hungry* crept toward her, unfurling slowly, like fingers of mist seeking her out, sneaking over branch and rock to find her wrist, encircle it, enclose it.

Someone—or something—whispered low and deep and seductively, *"I claim thee, Isabeau Cahors, by night and Barley Moon. Thou art mine."*

And from the darkness above the circle a massive falcon dove straight for Pandion, its talons and beak flashing and savage. . . .

"No!" Holly cried into the darkness.

A bird's wings flapped, then were still.

She was shivering with cold; and she was alive.

A brilliant yellow light struck her full force in the face. Holly whimpered as the light moved, bobbing up and down, then lowered as the figure holding it squatted and peered at her.

It was a heavyset woman dressed like a forest ranger. She said, "It's okay, honey, we're here now." Over her shoulder, she yelled, "Found a survivor!"

A ragged cheer rose up, and Holly burst into frightened, desperate tears.

Wicked: Witch

Kari Hardwicke had wrapped herself in a simple, cream-colored robe of lightweight gauze that was totally see-through and that clung everywhere. In her slashed blond hair she had entwined a few wildflowers, and she had bronzed her cheeks and shoulders. Her feet were bare and she had dabbed patchouli oil in all the strategic places.

Spellcasters loved patchouli oil.

Now she curled herself around Jer Deveraux as he brooded silently before her fireplace. He had burst through her door with the storm, fierce and enraged, but he wouldn't tell her what was wrong. He had accepted the glass of cab she offered him and drawn up her leather chair before her fireplace. He sipped, and he fell silent, his dark eyes practically igniting the logs in the fireplace.

Hell hath no fury like Jeraud Deveraux when he's in a temper.

That made her want him all the more. There was something about Jer she couldn't explain. It wasn't simply his air of command, as if he could make one do his slightest bidding merely by raising one eyebrow. Nor was it his sharp wit, or his drive; the pull he had on almost everyone who knew him; the way he fascinated people, both men and women, who would fall to discussing him once he had left a room.

It was all that combined with his astonishing looks. His brown-black eyes were set deep into his face beneath dark brown eyebrows. His features were sharply defined, his cheekbones high above hollows shaded by the soft light in the room. Unlike his father and his brother, he was clean shaven; his jaw was sharp and angular, and his lips looked soft. He worked out, and it showed in his broad shoulders, covered for the moment by a black sweater. Like his family members, he wore black nearly all the time, adding to his allure of danger and sensuality.

But it's even more that that, Kari thought now. *He's . . . how does the old song go?*

A magic man.

Heavy rain rattled the dormer window of her funky student apartment; the storm matched his mood, but she was determined to shake him out of it. It was Lammastide, the witches' harvest night, and she knew he would leave in a while to go perform some kind of ritual with Eli, his brother, and Michael, his father. They were "observant," as he liked to phrase it . . . and she wanted him to take her with him tonight. She wanted to know what they did in secret. Their rites, their spells . . . all of it.

The Deveraux men are warlocks, she thought.

But use that word in front of Jer, and he would deny it.

In the early days of their relationship—a year ago, now, how it had flown!—he had been eager to bring her into the fold. Back then, she was his teaching assistant, and he, a newbie undergrad; after the first time they'd gone to bed together, he had told her he would share his "mysteries" with her. He had hinted about an ancient family Book of Spells.

She was thrilled. She was getting her PhD in folklore, a path she had chosen so that she could investigate magic and shamanism with the full resources of the university behind her. The University of Washington at Seattle treated Native American belief systems with the utmost respect; thus, her field of endeavor was encouraged, and never challenged.

But it wasn't simply Northwestern magic that interested her. She was fascinated by European magic . . . especially black magic. And though, like being a bona fide warlock he denied that his family practiced the Dark Art, she was fairly certain they spent more time in the shadows than they did in the diffuse light of Wicca. Yet she maintained the fiction that he practiced one of the Wicca traditions; it was what he had told her.

"I've dressed like the Barley Maid," she said now,

moving between him and the fireplace and stretching out her arms to him. He looked startled and—she hated to admit it—irritated by her interruption of his reverie.

Jer, you loved me once, she thought anxiously. *You were thrilled that a glamorous "older woman" graduate student wanted you, a mere freshman. What did I do wrong?*

I want you to come back to me. Not just treading water with me, but back into the deluge, the flood that was all that passion you poured into me. We made such waves . . . we drowned in such amazing ecstasy. . . .

"I've read that if we make love tonight, whatever spells we cast will be extra powerful." She smiled lustily.

"That's true," he said, giving her that much. His smile was gentle, tinged with both sadness and great wisdom. "And you've cast quite a spell on me, Kari. You're beautiful."

She let herself believe he was sincere, and he rose from his chair, scooped her up in his arms, and carried her into her bedroom.

TWO

WINE MOON

☾

Wine and wisdom go hand in hand
But not while our foes stand
Lord we beg this humble boon
Let us drink of their blood soon

Let us drink of you, Lady bright
Filling our eyes with second sight
Bring us wisdom and let us know
How to bring great kings to woe

Seattle, Washington, August 1 (Lammastide)

Thunder seized the rafters of the Anderson family's Victorian mansion in the Upper Queen Anne area of Seattle and shook them until the century-old timbers bowed and nearly cracked. Skeletal fingers of cold rain rapped the windows, impatiently demanding entrance.

Death wanted in very badly, and Michael Deveraux,

the reigning warlock of the Northwest, was doing all he could to open the door.

Or rather, to burn that door down, he thought. *By the Horned One, I will burn that sucker down. I threw the runes. I read the auguries. They all said the same thing: that tonight's the night I, Michael Robert Deveraux, will conjure the Black Fire.*

And I'll destroy the House of Cathers with it, once and for all.

Reeling with anticipation, he shut his eyes and made fists against his chest, fingernails gouging his palms. His heart thudded hard and fast like a battle drum; his hot Deveraux blood ran molten through his veins.

It can mean only one thing: It's time for the Deveraux to take over. After centuries of sucking it up and pretending we've accepted defeat, we're going to steal the ball and make that touchdown. We're going all the way. Because baby, we got game.

Oh, yeah—the boys and I got game.

This morning at the Dark Hour—3 A.M.—he had opened his Book of Shadows to the Rites of Lammas Night to prepare for Ritual. Lammas was hallowed; it was the Eve of Harvest. In the old, pagan days, the wheat and grapes had been blessed, the day sanctified to the Goddess. But in the world Michael worshiped—the mystical Greenwood, home of the Horned One—it was a night for harvesting power . . . and the lives and souls of enemies.

Michael's sons were due home at eleven to participate in the Rites. Now it was nine o'clock, two full hours ahead of schedule. Not wanting to tip them off to the fact that there would be no simple Lammastide for them this year and less than eager to have them present for what he was doing in its stead, he had forbidden them to help with the preparations. Eli had been fine with that—he had no problem letting his father and brother carry the burden of magic use, as long as he continued to reap the benefits in the form of money, women, and cars—but Jeraud had thrown a full-blown tantrum. He had argued violently, slammed things around, glowered and sworn and made a lot of very foolish threats that Michael had ordered him take back for fear of suffering the consequences. Then, mustering all his authority, Michael had told him to get out, backing up the dismissal with the threat of more harmful magics than Jer could even imagine—which had infuriated Jer all the more.

Jer knows something's up. I should have given him more credit, made a better attempt to hide my work. I've been keeping lots of secrets. Well, once tonight is done, he'll understand that I had to keep my focus. I don't need any distractions. If only he were more like Eli—just plain greedy and simple-minded. No wonder Sasha tried to take him away with her when she left me.

Michael opened his eyes, smiling grimly at the droplets of blood that had beaded on his palms.

I don't need to share all my power with my ambitious boys. Eli would kill me without a second's hesitation if he thought he could get away with it. Well, the old man's got a lot of years left in him. Centuries, I hope. So watch your back, kids. One step in my direction and I'll annihilate you.

"Are you watching, Duc Laurent?" he said aloud. "You're finally going to get what you've wanted. I'm going to burn the witch tonight. So forgive and forget, all right? Tonight's the night for Black Fire, and I'll need your help. Your *power.*"

There was no answer. The phantom spirit of Laurent de Deveraux, the noble warlord of the family and dead these nearly seven centuries, had not communicated in any way with Michael for nearly six moons. Michael knew the Duke was livid with him for binding the witch to him "in spirit and heart"—in other words, for beginning an affair with Marie-Claire Cathers-Anderson. During the ancient fertility festival of Imbolc, Michael had put her in thrall, the Lady to the Lord as in the old days of witch and warlock together. His hope had been to harness the power that was said to erupt when Cahors and Deveraux were joined.

It was a good idea, he thought. *And it was fun, even if the union didn't result in a magical upgrade, as I'd hoped. So that part of the story must have been simple legend, as Laurent insisted it was.*

He shrugged, wondering if the Duke was watching him. Michael had learned the hard way that his spectral kinsman had his own methods of surveillance. *Too bad she has to die, but at least it'll make Laurent happy. He's been pissed off ever since I started up with her.*

Ten feet away, on a red velvet sofa footed with birds' claws, Marie-Claire lay unconscious. She was sprawled on her back with one arm over her head, her profile silhouetted against the red velvet. She was wearing a black satin bathrobe and bloodred ruby earrings. Her toenail polish matched her earrings, but her mouth was red from kisses, not lipstick. At forty-two, she was still incredibly beautiful, with heavy lashes and full, exquisite lips. *What will it be like to watch her flesh blister and crack, her lips disintegrate, her eyes boil away?*

Enticing Marie-Claire had been easy, and he liked to think he hadn't really needed his magic to accomplish it. Michael Deveraux knew that he was incredibly good-looking. Like his children's, his appearance was exotic, very French, with deep-set, soulful eyes that women loved to gaze into, and a chiseled face with a square, cleft chin. That fact that his nose was a little too narrow made him intriguing—one of his conquests had said it made him look "deliciously cruel." He liked that. A lot of women were drawn to cruelty, mistaking it for strength.

With his loose, black curls, his trim beard, and his lean body, honed to edgy bone and sinew from hours of working out, he knew he had been a temptation to Marie-Claire ever since they had met at their children's preschool. Though her witchly powers had lain dormant then, he had felt the call of blood to blood. He knew at once that there was more to this lady than a pretty face, a French name, and a certain selfish drive that he found utterly charming.

After that first meeting Michael had rushed home and descended into the Room of Spells, the heavily fortified hexagonal chamber he'd had built into the heart of his two-story Art Deco house. He'd put on his sorcerer's robes of red and green and summoned his patron with blood and smoke. First had come the sulfurous odor that always made his eyes water, and then the charnel stench of the grave. Then the cold frost of Charon's ferry, parting the veil, had descended upon the chamber. Michael's breath had joined with the mist that rose from nothing and diffused through the frigid room. The dipping of the oars became his own heartbeat.

From the darkness the phantom had taken shape—the ghostly skull and skeleton at first all that was visible, followed by decayed flesh and dust that hung loosely on bone and leathery muscle as the revenant stepped from an invisible boat. According to his faded portrait, the Duke in life had been even more handsome than Michael. He claimed that once their House was again ascendant he would "carry myself as a full man," as he had said in medieval French—a language Michael had dutifully learned in order to communicate with him. Neither of Michael's sons spoke it . . . because neither of them knew about Laurent.

Laurent, Duc de Deveraux, had declared that he was as intrigued by Marie-Claire Cathers-Anderson as his descendent was, and together they had consulted with various demons and oracles to find out more about her. Michael had asked Jer's help in searching the Net for information on genealogy, heraldry, and French peerage, for he felt certain that the Cathers family had once been noble. It was in her bearing and speech—even, it seemed to him, in her very scent.

Now he walked over to her, looked down at her. He bent, ran one fingernail up the side of her neck, tracing the large vein that he could feel pulsing slowly just beneath her skin. He smiled.

For over a year Michael had investigated this mysterious woman, whose appearance was striking in much the same way as his—ebony hair, black-brown eyes, her face a perfect oval, her skin seashell-smooth and pearly. She was tall and graceful, like the Deveraux men who lived in Lower Queen Anne. Indeed, for a time he wondered if she were a Deveraux herself, the family name perhaps lost through marriage at some point in the past.

During that year—those thirteen moons of the Coventry calendar—Michael had spied on Marie-Claire, had watched her with her daughters and her husband. He sent falcons to circle their gabled rooftop, observing from afar through their eyes with a scrying stone. On his visits to their mansion he had hidden glasses of cursed water in various rooms, through which he could eavesdrop on the family's conversations. He felt he knew them intimately . . . and he wanted to know Marie-Claire even better. And when Michael Deveraux wanted a woman, he usually got her.

Then had come the revelation: After that year, Laurent had told Michael the story of the Cahors and the Deveraux, informing his descendent that he had known before Michael had even met her that Marie-Claire's maiden name, Cathers, was what had become of the ancient French name Cahors. Through time and forgotten family history, the "Cathers" had no idea that they had once been the Cahors, one of the noblest witchly houses in medieval France, and the bitterest enemies of the House of Deveraux.

All the research and spying had been a test to see if Michael could learn the truth for himself. Michael had been embarrassed by his failure, but delighted to discover that Marie-Claire was a bona fide witch. That she had no idea of her powers was obvious, although she proved them time and again—by "knowing" who was going to call on the phone; by being in the right time and the right place in many instances. She found things people lost, and she had incredible magnetism toward money and good fortune. And she aged with extreme grace and beauty.

It was said that warlocks and witches together could create astonishingly powerful magics—and though Laurent had warned Michael not to go near Marie-Claire, he had promised himself he would have her . . . when the time was right.

I didn't know then that he could spy on me. I thought he would never find out.

Michael had bided his time . . . for thirteen long

years. During those years he tried another tack—encouraging his two sons to get involved with the Anderson daughters. Marie-Claire's girls were twins named Amanda and Nicole. Like her mother, Nicole possessed an interior, if unrecognized, spark of magical ability, but Amanda appeared to be a blank—as mousy and passive as her father, Richard Anderson.

Eli had launched himself at Nicole, who, barely fourteen, had not been able to resist his allure. Eli was four years older than she, and when Marie-Claire demanded she put an end to their relationship, Nicole had taken it underground. Maybe the girl sensed the power that swirled just beneath the surface of Elias Alain Deveraux. Maybe being constantly expelled and jailed a couple of times made him exciting and forbidden. Back in the day, all his "crimes" would have been seen for what they were—high spirits and hot blood. But in these times, these overly civilized, unbelievably dull times, Eli had been classified as a "juvenile delinquent."

Now seventeen, Nicole still saw Eli every chance she got.

Michael knew that his son's dubious reputation only added to his own attractiveness—poor Michael Deveraux, a hot-looking, rich, single father whose wife had left him, now trying so hard to manage his career as a very successful architect while providing a home for his boys. It was a challenge to women who imagined themselves becoming his angel of mercy, taking on those motherless kids and spending all that money. . . .

So while he worked his way through the married women of Seattle and coveted the prize of Marie-Claire, mousy little Amanda had gotten the hots for Jeraud. Michael knew it from his constant spying, but Jer was oblivious to her pining. Jer had found passion elsewhere, with that nosy grad student Kari Hardwicke at the university. Michael couldn't stand her. She wanted magical knowledge; she was after power. Besides, she was a slut.

But Jeraud-Luc could not be told what to do, even when it was in his best interests to obey. So he stayed with his grad student while Eli continued to see Nicole, just as Michael wanted him to. Though Eli was far wilder than his little brother, at least he saw the wisdom in doing what Dad said, if it could get him what he wanted.

And Michael saw to it that it always did get Eli what he wanted. Eli stayed controlled. *But Jer . . .*

Et bien, *as Laurent likes to say. All that'll be over as soon as Jer realizes I finally have the secret of the Black Fire. Then there'll be no stopping the House of Deveraux.*

The Cathers witch mother would die tonight, and the girls soon after. Michael's experiment with uniting the two families was over, and the Cathers would soon prove more useful to him as sacrifices to the Dark Ones than as magical helpmates.

So, it's time.

He bent to put on his elaborate hunter-green robe, decorated with eclipsed moons and bloodred falcon's claws. There was power in the velvet and satin, and as he lowered the hood over his hair, his scalp tingled. Surges of what felt like electric shocks skittered from his forehead to his toes and back again. He flicked his fingers, sending luminescent green sparks into the air. An almost subsonic hum enveloped him, a bass backbeat to the driving rain outside. Then he turned to face Marie-Claire.

She and he, the two illicit lovers, had planned this night for almost a month. Her dull, weak husband was out of town and her daughters were both at a sleepover. The fact that the coast was clear was more evidence to him that this was going to be an especially memorable Lammas.

Not that she knew it was Lammas; he had never shared his magic use with her. He had simply tried to draw power from their sexual encounters. It had not worked very well. He had been surprised and disappointed. . . . It was said that in each generation of witches and warlocks, one of each family was the strongest. None of the combinations he had pursued and encouraged—himself with Marie-Claire; Eli and Nicole; Jer and anybody—had yielded a harvest worth cultivating. Michael wondered if, along with forgetting their legacy, the Cathers-Cahors magic had lain dormant for so long that its power had been significantly diminished.

But this night had augured well for bringing forth the Black Fire . . . if he, Michael, presented the God with suitable sacrifices. A witch, no matter how weak, was always a prize. Her soul would certainly be worth something in the underworld. . . .

Warding his Porsche Boxer so that no one saw him drive to her home, he'd listened to the Grateful Dead, drumming his fingers on the dash, loving the irony of "Dead Man's Party"—*"walkin' with a dead man over my shoulder"*—figuring Laurent was somewhere with him, in spirit if not manifestation.

Once through Marie-Claire's front door, he'd swept her into her bedroom—she had had no scruples about the fact that this was her marriage bed—feeling, somewhat to his surprise, remarkably tender toward her. This was their last time, although she didn't realize it. She was going to be dead in a matter of hours, and he wanted to give her something to remember him by as her soul went screaming down into Hell, the home of all unrepentant adulterers.

He'd suggested they go into the living room, and she would have gone anywhere with him by then, even outside into the pouring rain. *I'm that good.* She loved cabernet; he'd drugged her glass of vintage wine while she wasn't looking rather than bother with a spell. If tonight was going to work, he needed to save every bit of magical power he had. He hadn't yet decided if he would let Marie-Claire die unconscious, or if he would wake her up so that she could feel the flames. Laurent would want her to suffer, of course—he could make points with the old boy that way.

Nobody can hold a grudge like my ancestor.

Now, as the storm slammed her house and the angels wept over her morals, he stared at her, stirred deeply by her loveliness. Then resolutely he opened his briefcase and pulled out his athame, handling the dagger with reverence and caution. The double blades were jagged and rough but very, very sharp, and they bore the stains of an enormous number of sacrifices. *If the walls of my spell chamber could scream, that thunder outside would be a whisper in comparison.*

Like all good—or evil—practitioners of the Art, he had forged his athame himself. Once it had been created, he had fed it his own blood. Marie-Claire had cried out in shock when she'd first seen the scars on his chest and upper thighs, never dreaming they had not been caused by falling through a plate-glass window when he was seventeen—which was what he'd told her—but by giving this magical knife the taste for rituals of torture and death.

In medieval French, he murmured, "I open this Rite with Deveraux blood," and ran the left blade of the athame across his left palm. He hissed, drawing in his breath. He didn't like pain, and he had never gotten used to how much pain the dagger could elicit when it was properly used.

As a zigzag of scarlet formed across the lifeline in his hand, a bolt of brilliant lightning lit up the room. Thunder crashed immediately thereafter, shaking the mansion to its foundations. The nightfire clearly illuminated each corner of the large room, showing the fine antiques that Marie-Claire loved to shop for, polishing her cheekbones with a golden sheen as she lay unmoving on the couch. As if she'd been X-rayed, each bone in her skull glowed through her skin. Her fingers became sticks of bone. At the arch of her graceful neck, the vertebrae sat one on top of another, clearly visible.

It's a portent of her death, Michael thought. *The Horned One is accepting her as my sacrifice.*

"Do you see that, Laurent?" he murmured. "We've got the big guns on our side for this."

With his unbleeding right hand, he pulled an ornate wooden box from his briefcase. Demonic faces with outstretched tongues glared at him from the centers of pentagrams, one per side. The Deveraux falcon was carved on top, holding a clutch of ivy in its mouth. Ivy was the living symbol of the Green Man, and of the warlocks who worshiped the Lord in all his guises. Let witches have their Lady, their Goddess. It was a fact of nature that the male was always stronger, always prevailed, no matter the battleground.

Michael carried the box to the empty fireplace—he had had some trouble talking Marie-Claire out of laying a fire, when the night clearly called for one—and knelt. He bowed his head and closed his eyes, silently marshaling his occult strength for what lay ahead.

Behind the bricks and mortar of the fireplace, the body of the falcon he had walled up alive three months ago rustled and stirred. Michael Deveraux was renowned for his tireless efforts to locate and preserve the grand old buildings of Seattle, and of his meticulous attention to period detail when he restored them. Indeed, he had proven to be a marvelous help to the Anderson family when they had decided to tear out the old forties' fireplace that had defaced their Victorian home and return it to its earlier grandeur.

Seizing the opportunity—which he had, after all, helped to create with a few well-dropped hints about enhancing the original charm of their lovely home— Michael had offered to do the work himself. Richard Anderson had promised him a copy of his latest software in return. Michael had pretended to be happy with the exchange, although he couldn't have cared less about data compression or whatever the hell it was Richard's firm bought and sold. But as a result of their bartering, the number of charms and sacrifices Michael had installed inside that fireplace would astound most warlocks if they knew of it.

And Michael's cleverness had certainly impressed Laurent.

Ever since Laurent had told him the story of the Deveraux and the Cahors, Michael had tried to conjure the Black Fire. It was said that the secret of the Fire had died with Laurent's son, Jean, and that if ever the Deveraux retrieved it they would rule all of Coventry, as was their cursed right. Laurent was as eager as Michael to draw forth the secret weapon; they had simply disagreed on the best way to go about it. Michael had been certain that allying their House with Marie-Claire's family once more would unlock the shadowed spells. Laurent, hating whatever remnant of the Cahors the lady and her girls represented, would have none of that. In fact, he was certain that allowing the three women to exist could only hamper success.

We'll find out soon if Laurent was right, Michael thought.

"I call upon my forbears and their powers," he chanted in old French, placing his bleeding left hand over his mouth. "I call upon the Darkness. I call upon the Hunting Hounds to aid me in the chase. *Avantes, mes chiens.*"

The distant moaning of a tempest wind echoed through the room. The tip of the mound of ashes in the fireplace shifted very slightly. Michael continued to kneel, tasting his blood on his lips, and waited.

The keening grew louder. A chill breeze ruffled the hair at the back of Michael's neck, and he smiled with anticipation. The Hunting Hounds had unleashed themselves.

"*Mes chiens, mes frères du diable,*" he said boldly, calling to them. *"Aides-moi."*

Then he lifted his hand from his mouth and held it up, much as one would raise the right hand to swear to tell the truth in court. The faint whistle became the fierce belling of huge canines, animals with devilish cunning and dark senses; were-creatures that sniffed out souls and light and devoured them whole, ripping shreds any protective wards or talismans designed to prevent Michael's ritual from achieving his aim.

A sigh escaped Marie-Claire. To his shock, she shifted on the couch, as if seeking a more comfortable sleeping position.

She shouldn't be able to move at all.

"Marie-Claire?" he asked softly, carefully. She didn't answer, but lay as pale and still as death. He wondered if he'd imagined the whole thing. "Laurent?" Michael called. "Is that you?"

Marie-Claire moved again. Definitely moved.

"Aides-moi!" Michael whispered beneath the supernatural howling, which then erupted into frenzied barking. As he gazed at the unconscious woman, the invisible hounds howled triumphantly. They had picked up the scent of something opposing him and weakening his focus, and they screamed with demonic glee as they coursed the hidden forests of his realm of power. Obstacles had presented themselves before, of course, especially during other spells. No warlock alive was without his enemies, and Michael, being ambitious, had many, many enemies.

Has Sir William heard of the plan to overthrow him? Has one of my allies in the Supreme Coven turned on me?

He would leave trespassers and invaders to the Hounds for now. If they caught something, he would deal with it then. In the meantime, he would try to continue as best he could, to outpace anyone or anything that was trying to stop him. The forces were in alignment *now,* and it wasn't possible to change them.

He scowled in concentration as he held his wounded hand over the ashes. His rich, red blood dripped steadily and his heart caught up the rhythm as he began to chant in the ancient tongue of his ancestors. In his mind, he translated the potent words: *I call up the Black Fire of the Deveraux, I conjure the Burning Night. It is our Hour. It is our Will.*

It is my Destiny.

The paws of the dogs clattered over the freshly waxed wood floors of the Cathers mansion. They began to take form and shape. Vague, blurry shadows darted across the boards, racing through the furniture, pawing at the wallpaper. The elaborate crystal chandelier above the sofa swung back and forth like a buoy on Elliott Bay.

The dogs were definitely after something, and it was leading them on a wild hunt. Whatever it was, it was drawing near. Any moment now, it might materialize in this room.

Michael opened his eyes very wide and pressed his forefinger against the whites, opening his Sight with his blood. His vision swam with viscous pink, and beneath the mounting cacophony he heard the rustle of the dead falcon he had walled up in the Andersons' chimney as it sought to join the fray.

He thought he saw the faint outline of a human figure, but he could not be sure. He squinted hard through the blood as the Hounds tore around the shimmering form, baying and shrieking like banshees. From his hand, his blood dripped steadily onto the wooden floor.

"Get thee from my sight," he said, holding out his hand. "I banish thee. I send thee hence. I abjure thee, by the Hunting Lord."

The figure raised its arms, and new, cold wind shot through the room.

Instinctively, Michael turned protectively toward the pile of ash on the fireplace, shielding it with his hands.

And in that moment, Laurent, Duc de Deveraux, appeared in his advanced state of decay at Michael's side.

The empty sockets bore down on him; the slack mouth hung open in a grimace of fury. The phantom raised one bony arm and struck Michael across the cheek, the fragments of its brittle fingertips slicing open his cheek.

Michael fell back, more shocked than hurt, staring

up at the Duke as the latter reached into the fireplace and grabbed up the handful of ash. The ancient nobleman cradled it against his rib cage, where his desiccated heart hung like a deflated gray beach ball, and shook his other fist at the man on the floor.

"Tu est rien," the Duke's voice echoed from the fleshless jaws. *You are nothing.*

Then, as Michael watched in helpless fury, the Hounds disappeared, the wind died, and the Duke and shimmering figure both vanished.

It was over. His spell would not work this night.

Angrily, he took off his robe and put it back in his satchel.

I'll kill her anyway, he thought savagely. *I'll become the dutiful descendant, atone for my disobedience, and work whatever magic Laurent will show me. I'll find the secret of the Black Fire if it takes the rest of my life.*

I'll strangle her in her sleep. Back in our day, witches who confessed were garroted before they were burned. She's ignorant of her powers, making her somewhat innocent, so that should balance the karmic wheel. She has such a slender neck; it will be easy.

In the sudden silence, the phone rang like the shriek of a bird of prey. Marie-Claire's portable phone had somehow wound up on the couch, though Michael hadn't noticed it there before.

Rousing at once, she sat up and fumbled for it.

"Hello?" Marie-Claire said fuzzily. She glanced at Michael and mouthed, *Did I fall asleep?*

He nodded, holding his wounded hand, balled into a fist, behind himself. Apparently he had recovered his poise sufficiently, because she returned her attention to the caller's voice; first she blinked, and then she frowned. She said, "What? *What?*" in a high, shrill voice. Her mouth worked silently for a few seconds—then her face crumpled, and she burst into tears. With a shaking hand she pressed the phone against her chest.

"My brother's dead," she wailed. "His wife, too. Jesus, Michael. . . ."

"Oh, my God," Michael responded, and in her distress, she couldn't tell that he was faking it. He held out his other hand. She left the couch and sank against him, shuddering, her ear pressed to the phone again.

"Holly. Of course." She nodded as she spoke. "Of course she can. I'll catch a plane." Tears streamed down her cheeks. "Yes, yes, sure." She ran a hand through her hair, and he put his arm around her to keep her steady.

"Let me call you back," she said. "Yes. Thank you. Yes."

She disconnected, then pressed herself against

him, seeking reassurance. "Daniel," she moaned. "Oh, Daniel . . ."

He gentled her; he was good with animals and women. He caressed her back and her wet, cold cheeks and kissed her furrowed brow. He let her sob for what seemed like forever, impatient with her but not showing it. He wondered if his sons were home, wondering where he was. This night was not turning out the way he had expected it to, not at all.

So, should I still kill her? he asked himself, gazing bloodlessly down at the bowed head, the riotous mass of shining curls.

Then she raised her head and said, "They want me to come get my niece. She's an orphan now. She has no one else."

"Your niece," Michael said slowly.

She nodded. "My brother's daughter. Holly."

He showed no outward sign of the shock he felt at this news. He kept his voice low and his expression a model of compassionate detachment.

"I didn't realize there were any other women in your family."

At this, she heaved another sob. "She's not a woman. She's the same age as my twins."

So there's another Cathers—Cahors—female. Maybe she's the one who inherited the family's magical power. And if I ally her with our House, the Black Fire might burn bright for Michael Deveraux after all. . . .

"Then she'll be coming to live with you," he said slowly.

She looked at him in abject misery and said, "They want me to go get her. She has no one else."

"Then you should go. She's family."

Her sigh was ragged and determined and resigned, all at once. "The funeral's in two days. I'll leave in the morning." She raised her tear-streaked face up to look into his eyes. Her lips were moist and her body was pressed tightly against his.

"I'm so glad you're here," she whispered. "I couldn't have handled being alone tonight."

"Ma chere," he said, brushing the damp strands away from her forehead. "Don't worry. I'll take care of you."

And in that moment, he really was glad that he hadn't murdered his mistress.

Yet.

THREE

BLOOD MOON

On kings and saints we gladly feed
And wash their flesh down with mead
We bathe in blood and whittle bone
And dream of all the fear we've sown

By the light of the blessed moon
We hunt again and very soon
We'll catch within our snare
Our greatest enemy's one heir

Canyon Rock Hospital, Arizona

Holly drifted along on a gentle sea halfway between waking and dreaming. Though her eyes were closed, she sensed the brightness of the sun through her eyelids, smiled at the pleasant warmth on her face. Soon her mother would remind her to put on sunscreen, and Holly would, to please her. Secretly, she liked tans and when she was at the stables, she never bothered.

She told herself her cowboy hat was enough, but of course it wasn't.

A shadow moved between her and the sun's nourishing heat; she wrinkled her brow slightly but then relaxed as a large, familiar hand slipped around her own and gave her a squeeze. She tried to say, "Hi, Daddy," but it was too much effort in her deliciously languid state. So she smiled again to indicate that he was welcome, and drifted along, her hand in his, loving her father, remembering all the years of looking up to him and adoring him. Her mom had always said Holly was a daddy's girl, but she hadn't minded. Elise Cathers's own childhood had been a nightmare, and she had told Holly one of the most important gifts she could give her daughter was a good, healthy love and respect for her own father.

"Not being able to love him, not wanting him anywhere near you," her mom had said, "that's the worst thing for a young girl. I'm glad you love your dad so much." That's what she would tell Holly, and then she'd smile a bit wistfully. "It's as that writer says—having a child is another chance to get it right."

It amused Holly that even though her mom repeated those words over and over, Elise couldn't remember the name of the writer who had written them, or where she'd read them. But Holly got the message, and she was immensely proud of her mom; whatever had happened to her as a little girl, it hadn't held her back. She was a skilled, compassionate doctor and a fabulous mother. The only thing she didn't seem to be very good at was being a wife.

Or is all the fighting Daddy's fault?

There would be other times to puzzle over that; for now, she and her father savored the peace and quiet together. It was a gift, this moment. So many of the parents of Holly's friends didn't get that it was about just being together, not overscheduled days and nights saturated with "activities" and expensive presents to make up for absences and missed dance recitals. Tina's mom got it, though. *She's a great mom, too.*

Her father's grip began to slacken, and she heard his voice inside her head: *Time to wake up, punky.*

Then the panic started, because she knew what the dream was. The word *survivor* echoed in her muzzy brain and she knew she was stalling; when she woke up, they were going to tell her about death. Someone had died . . . *no, wait, I don't know that. We could all be survivors. Of course we all survived. Because this is my life and in my life, things like dying don't happen. . . .*

Her father's voice whispered more insistently, *Wake up,* and then she realized that the words were sounds outside her head. That meant he was alive, really there beside her, really trying to rouse her from her dreams.

Her heart beat a little faster and she tried hard to pull her eyelids open. She was incredibly tired. Her head swam as if she were falling; then her left leg jerked, the way body parts sometimes did when one was falling asleep or waking up. From the heat on her face, she assumed she would be staring into the sun, so she tried to turn her head, but she simply couldn't manage it.

"Holly. Wake up."

And then she did, because that was definitely Dad's voice; she not only turned her head but opened her eyes, a smile on her face and—

A scream ripped out of her, tearing up and out from her stomach to the top of her head. She screamed again, and again; because her father was leaning over her, only she had no idea how she knew it was her father, because the face of the figure had been smashed flat, and the flesh was swollen and black. There were no eyes, just compressed eyelids; the nose had been crushed by a head-on collision, the cartilage and bone smeared across the cheekbones. The chin had been cracked in two, and the hinges of the jaw dangled like the wings of a roasted chicken.

A voice echoed from the destroyed mouth, but she was screaming so loudly, she couldn't hear what it was saying. She couldn't hear if it was her father. She shot away from it, arms and legs flailing, scrabbling backward in terror, shrieking. The face moved with her, then glanced in another direction.

Something jabbed into her arm with a painful prick, and the ruined face melted in slow motion. As her shrieks slid into moans and then into whimpers, she was forced to watch the bloated, purplish skin slide down from her father's forehead and cheeks, riveleting down the hollows of his cheeks, taking the rapids of his chin. Then the bones stretched like pliant candle wax, elongating hideously; and then, for one instant, an oval of black stared at her. The shadow mask stared at her, and then it vanished, all at once.

In its place emerged the face of a woman, very lovely and glamorously made up, almost middle-aged, with Dad's dark, flashing eyes and Dad's generous mouth and Dad's dark, wild hair. Holly blinked, too woozy to speak, and the woman raised a hand toward her.

"I'm your aunt," the face said with brilliant red lips, and then Holly went back to sleep.

On a beautiful, gentle sea, she held hands with her father, and—

★ ★ ★

And Holly Cathers's life was about death after all.

She was the only survivor of the rafting trip. Mom, Dad, Tina, and even their guide, Ryan—all were dead.

She was in a hospital near the Grand Canyon, where she had been treated for exposure, and they had sedated her after her freak-out. *But I saw him. I saw my father, all . . . all injured.* The daughter of an E.R. physician, Holly was not squeamish. *But that was Daddy. My daddy. I want my daddy . . .*

Holly began to wail. She shut her eyes and keened like a dying animal, rocking herself. Acid filled her mouth; her stomach burned; she leaned forward and heaved, clutching a wafer-thin hospital blanket as if to protect her hospital gown. Heavy, deep, rolling sobs exploded out of her, breaking her down. All she could do was weep.

Someone spoke with great authority, announcing, "That's okay, Holly. You go right ahead, honey. Get it out."

She didn't know how long she cried until the same someone said to another person in the room, "Jesus. Let's give her something."

There was another jab, and as she began to descend into drugged sleep, she heard a flapping like the wings of a hunting bird. Swooping, diving, careening down the tunnel of blackness with her . . .

. . . and then she realized it was her own heart beating hummingbird fast, then slowing . . . slowing . . .

. . . and a gauntleted hand made a fist, and the bird perched upon it.

Holly woke up again, worn out and sick and numb. The woman who said she was her aunt tried to stop crying. Her makeup was smeared all over her face. She wiped her nose with a tissue from the box on the nightstand and said, ". . . your guardian, in your father's will."

Holly couldn't remember her name. *Daddy never even told me he had a sister.*

"Um, and you'll like the school." The woman swallowed hard. Her eyes darted left and right, as if she were looking for somewhere else to be. She had on a lot of jewelry, and her earrings caught the light as she moved. "My girls like the school."

Holly squinted her swollen eyes, trying to follow. "School?"

"You're going to be a senior, right?" the woman asked.

Years ago, when Janna Perry's brother had died, Janna had been like the star of a movie. Everyone had circled around eleven-year-old Janna at school, treated her carefully, whispered in furtive circles about the poor girl, the poor thing, the one left behind. Janna had been pretty much of a creep, and now she was a saint. She even acted like a saint. She was good. She was kind. She was very, very sad.

Sad kids get their way.

Kids who had been mean to her brought her little presents. Kids she had been mean to took her home to their houses for dinner and sleepovers. She got excused from tons of homework assignments and even though she missed a lot of school, she made the honor roll for the first time in her life. Holly, only nine at the time, had been a little jealous. All the drama, all the specialness, Janna like some mythic tragic heroine dragging around with dark circles under her eyes and going to the nurse whenever she felt like it. Janna had entered the annals of coolness, and for the rest of her life, she would have an unbeatable card to play whenever she wanted attention.

"So, um, we can pack your things and . . ." Her aunt looked momentarily stunned. "Where do you live?"

Holly stared back at her. "What?"

Before her aunt could answer, there was a rap on her hospital room door. Before Holly could say "come in," it opened.

Barbara Davis-Chin, in her corduroy overalls and

Birkenstocks, hippie Barbara with no makeup and her black hair in a bun, stood framed in the doorway for an instant. Then she saw Holly and rushed to her side. Holly's aunt moved awkwardly out of her way and Barbara's arms enfolded Holly, pressing her cheek against Holly's own. She smelled of sweat and perfume, and tears slid down Holly's cheeks.

"Holly, baby," she murmured. "Oh, Holly. Oh." She rocked Holly as Holly grabbed on to her, clinging as hard as she could, shaking and crying.

"Tina," Holly murmured back, holding on hard, grateful to her core that Barbara was here. She was solid and real and maybe it had all been a mistake, and now Barbara would tell her that and everything would be the way it was supposed to be.

I don't care if Mom and Dad fight for the rest of their lives, she thought fiercely.

"It's a mistake, right?" she blurted. "It's not them."

"I saw them, sweetheart," Barbara said firmly, caressing Holly's cheek. "I identified them."

Holly was amazed at the fresh wash of grief and despair that overtook her. She had had no idea that people could hurt this badly. She thought again of Janna and was deeply ashamed of herself.

Maybe God is paying me back for being such a bitch, she thought.

After Holly quieted, Barbara turned to the stranger and said, "I'm Barbara Davis-Chin. Holly's best friend's mother." She was amazingly composed.

"I'm Holly's aunt, Marie-Claire," the other woman said. Her smile was watery weak and sad. "I guess Danny never mentioned me. Apparently he had listed me as next of kin."

Barbara made a moue of apology, then turned her attention to Holly. "Sweetie," she said, "your mom asked me to look after you if anything ever happened to her. Did you know that?"

Holly wasn't surprised, but still she said, "No."

Barbara nodded. She reached forward and trailed her fingertips over Holly's corkscrew curls. "I've watched you grow up," she said softly.

Holly glanced at her newly discovered aunt. "My dad wanted me to live with her."

"Yes, about that . . . ," Barbara began.

The woman stepped forward and cut in, "Holly, if you have someone you want to stay with, that's all right." She smiled at them both. "I certainly don't want Holly to come to Seattle against her will."

For a moment, Holly was stung. It was obvious her aunt didn't want her. Then her more adult self kicked in; who would want a third high school student in the house? Marie-Claire's family had their own lives, and she was a total stranger. Besides, she wanted to stay in San Francisco for her senior year.

"Of course, if you want to come to Seattle," Aunt Marie-Claire added, "you're more than welcome." She laid a reassuring hand on Holly's forearm. "I'd love to get to know Danny's daughter." Her eyes softened. "I missed him, all those years."

"We can talk about all this later," Barbara suggested. "Holly needs to think things over."

"No," Holly said. She colored at the panicked tone in her voice. "I'd like to stay with you, Barbara. If it's really okay."

"Oh, sweetheart, it's more than okay." Barbara put her arms around her. "It's what I'd like, too. That house is going to be awfully empty without . . . without Tina."

"Okay, then." Marie-Claire pressed her hands together. She said to Barbara, "I'd like to go back to . . . home with you both and help with the . . . arrangements."

The funerals, Holly translated, feeling a little sick again. *Oh, my God, I'm an orphan. My parents are dead. I have no brothers or sisters.*

"Holly?" Marie-Claire said.

Both women looked at her. Holly shook her head. "I'm tired." She touched her forehead and sighed. "Just really tired."

"She needs her rest," a nurse announced as she bustled in. "She's had enough visiting for now."

Barbara moved away from Holly's bed. She said to Holly's aunt, "Let's get some coffee, all right?"

In unison, they smiled at Holly, then picked up their purses and walked out of the room. Barbara was very much the counterculture San Franciscan, Marie-Claire the upscale fashion trender.

She must be rich, Holly thought. Then for the first time, she realized, *I'm rich, now, too.*

The nurse said, "You're all wound up. I'm going to ask the doctor to prescribe something for you to sleep."

"No," Holly whispered, thinking of her terrible dream. But as soon as she said it, her eyes were closed, and she was drifting, back to the river and her father and life as it never would be again.

The University of Washington at Seattle

The sweat lodge was filled with sweat and nearly naked bodies. Jer was very quiet, searching for the serenity that had eluded him last night. It had been Lammas, one of the most important Rites of the warlock year, and his father had never showed.

He and Eli had celebrated together, a desultory affair, since neither brother could stand the other. As the younger brother, Jer was obliged to serve as backup during the Rites, fuming as Eli made fun of the entire ritual and finally concluded by intoning in a mock-stern voice, "Go in peace. The Black Mass is ended. *Mwahahah.*"

"So, are you tired from whatever you did or what?" Kari asked. Jer didn't open his eyes. It was bad manners to talk in the lodge, and she knew it. She had been upset last night when he had left because he hadn't invited her.

Does she think I feel guilty, so I'll come across with some information for her? Because I don't feel a shred of guilt.

"C'mon, baby. It's for my paper on harvest folklore," Kari persisted, arching her back and moving her neck, wafting the steam and smoke toward her chest with her hands. It was said to cleanse one of impurities, within and without. Jer resented her trying to manipulate him by drawing his attention to her body, and he was humiliated that it was working. Guys were entirely too much governed by their desires, and girls like Kari knew it.

"Hey," Kialish protested. "No talking." Over time, Kari seemed to have forgotten that she was a guest here; the lodge belonged to Kialish, Eddie, and Jer, if it could be said to belong to anybody besides the University of Washington.

"Sorry," she said, not at all sorry. She touched her forehead. "I'm just too hot in here today. I can't keep my focus."

"Nobody can, if you keep talking," Kialish said firmly.

"Okay. Sor-ry. Look, I'm going to split." She gazed at Jer expectantly, wanting him to go with her.

Jer gave his head a quick shake, then moved his shoulders to show her that even though he wasn't in the mood now, that didn't mean they couldn't hook up later. That mollified her.

I have issues with women, he thought. His father insisted that his mother had been terribly insecure and passive, a very weak person. It had occurred to Jer more than once that leaving someone takes a decisive act of will, which a passive, very weak person would be unable to accomplish. Likewise, he tried to leave thoughts about his mother in the past, where they belonged, but he found that impossible. Since he didn't trust his dad's version of her, and that was all he had at present, he was better off not forming an image of her at all.

Someday I'll have the magic for it, though. And I'll cast a finding spell and locate my mom, see if she's okay. And I'll ask her if she's sorry she left me with him and Eli. . . .

Kari rolled onto her feet and crouched beneath the low, rounded ceiling of the lodge. She gave Jer's knee a caress and said softly, "See you later, babe." Then she opened up the flap and crawled out, careful to refasten the Velcro strips on the outside.

Now that she was gone, Jer refocused his attention on the burning logs. He stared at them, his lids half-closed, lulling his emotions to a passive place; letting his arms and legs slacken, his breathing to slow. He imagined the heat and smoke entering all the cavities of his body and warming them, the herbs in the smoke mingling with his being so that part of him was the mixture created by this place and this moment. Like sips of water, he took in that image, and he began to let go of his other thoughts—about the missed Lammas ritual, his brother and father, school assignments, Kari, what his life would become after college . . . every concern seemed a distant, odd object that he firmly discarded, clearing his mind of clutter and debris.

The fire appeared to grow larger, the rocks more like small boulders; the flames those of a bonfire; the logs were felled trees. As he stared, the smoke whirled and eddied into shapes alien to his culture, more Eddie's and Kialish's totems and icons than his—

salmon and orcas and strangely clawed bears. Ravens flew everywhere, and other birds joined them, wheeling in a sky boiling with fire and smoke. Falcons skyrocketed toward the moon, joined by hawks. The ravens wheeled around the other birds as falcon and hawk squared off, each rushing toward the other, screaming through clacking beaks, wings flapping. *Whum, whum, whum;* the smoky sky vibrated with their great wings' beats.

Whum whum whum . . .

He became aware that his heartbeats matched the rhythm of the wings; and then the sound changed and became what sounded like the beating of a skinheaded drum: *Brum, brum, brum* . . .

. . . and Jer was somewhere else, very different from the lodge; and he was some*one* else, someone not so very different from himself . . . someone named Jean, who was a Deveraux, like him. . . .

The drummers sounded as the Great Hunt trooped through the forest; the rounded, ringing tones reminded Jean of the drumming that preceded an important execution. Dirgelike and purposeful, relentless . . . *death comes for all us, but at this moment we are Death's army,* he thought with amusement.

He was riding Cockerel, his favorite warhorse, at

the head of a phalanx of Hunters. Fantasme, the Circle's falcon familiar, rode on his shoulder like an eager little brother, screeching for his dinner.

The drummers marched on foot several meters ahead. All in all, a glorious sight, the Deveraux on the move through the Greenwood, home of the God in his aspect as King of Nature and of the Hunt. Green and red livery, fine ermine robes, crimson jewels and fine golden cloaks from the Holy Land gleamed and flashed and sparkled beneath the smile of the sun.

Swelling with pride, Jean signaled to the flushers to continue their work. With large wooden canes, they smacked the forest undergrowth, easily driving out the foxes, ermine, bears, and other game, which Jean and the others would happily slaughter, spurs to the flanks of their mounts, swords and hatchets drawn and dripping with gore and blood.

They had been routing out the animals for hours, with great success. Behind the lines of noblemen, servants loaded the carcasses of the animals routed thus far; the scent of blood was intoxicating to the clusters of hunting hounds that strained at their leads beside and around the tumbrels. Their eagerness and bloodlust matched the men's own.

Jean's father, the Duc Laurent de Deveraux, trotted up beside his son and smiled broadly at him.

He tipped his head, swathed in fine velvet and a golden tassel, to Fantasme, who screeched in reply. Laurent was dressed in hunting finery of ermine and leather. Jean was a younger version of the great lord of the manor—flashing, dark eyes and heavy brows, an abundance of dark, shiny hair and beard. Their noses were quite straight, their mouths strong, not too fleshy. Deveraux faces were hard and sharp. Deveraux faces promised no mercy, no tenderness, no warmth. They were warriors' faces. Leaders' faces. Some said devils' faces . . .

"We'll have a magnificent feast," the Duke said approvingly, gesturing with his head over his shoulder at the huge amount of game they had harvested. "We'll show those posturing Cahors how real men make a wedding banquet."

Jean smiled proudly at his father. "And make a wedding bed as well."

The two laughed lustily. The Duke clapped his son on his shoulder and said, "In the old days of the coven, the master took the virgins first, you know."

"*Oui, mon père,* and as I recall, leadership of the Circle was achieved through combat to the death." He slid a sly, somewhat challenging glance at his father.

"*Touché.*" Laurent threw back his head and laughed, clearly amused by and unafraid of his son's mild challenge. The Duke was a lion; Jean knew it would be years before he could hope to inherit the titles, both of their House and of the coven. The prospect did not bother him; his father was a good leader, and Jean profited well from his guidance.

"It's a grand day for us, boy. The Cahors dowry makes us the richest noble family in all of France." His eyes glittered at the thought. "Get Isabeau with child tonight, and I'll make him king by the time he's twelve."

"As you wish, Father," Jean said, sweeping his arm downward like a gallant. His blood stirred at the thought of bedding Isabeau. "I shall do my best."

"With all the spells we've cast, we'll have a boy by Beltane."

"*Certainement,* the Green Man will reward our generosity." Jean jerked his head in the direction of the animals they had already slaughtered. "We're giving him plenty to eat. And soon we'll give him plenty more."

The two smiled at each other. Laurent made a magical motion with his hand and winked at his son. Almost simultaneously with the gesture, a flusher dressed in Deveraux green and scarlet emerged from the thick copses of chestnut trees and shouted, "The first of the prized flesh!"

"Oyez, oyez, the first of the prized flesh!" shouted Compte Alain DuBruque, the Marshal of the Hunt. "This bounty is reserved, *mes seigneurs,* for the bridegroom!"

A roar of approval rose from the lines of the mounted huntsmen. The drums thundered; the hounds bayed and lurched. Jean let go of his reins and held both hands above his head, receiving the approbation of the gathering as his due. Cockerel pranced in a circle and chuffed and Fantasme capered above his head, crying with bloodlust. Jean put his heels to Cockerel's hot, solid flanks, and the fantastic stallion reared majestically. Fantasme landed on his head, riding the horse like its master.

"Release the dogs!" Jean commanded.

Trumpets flared. From the rear of the hunting company, a brace of dogs, made savage from near-starvation, were loosed. Shrieking and baying, they dashed through the ranks of human hunters, dodging horse hooves as they hurtled themselves toward the shadows of the forest. Jean joined the race, Cockerel's mighty hooves narrowly missing the eager curs.

Then the quarry emerged, forced into the open by the threshers. A tall peasant of perhaps sixteen, he was. Jean was pleased; the quarry was a young, vigorous man, capable of many more years of life. It was a good sign; the Green Man would be appreciative of such a fine gift, and surely requite his acolyte's efforts with a male child. The firstborn of the Cahors and Deveraux must be an heir. Laurent and Jean had no idea how long the alliance between them would last; who knew if it would be long enough for him to get a second child on his new wife?

Galloping ahead of the dogs, Jean reached the man, who, seeing him, turned tail and fled. Fantasme screamed with eagerness and flew after him.

Fool, Jean thought with a vicious thrill; *this horse outran a thousand infidels in Jerusalem; does he think an underfed serf can achieve what hardened warriors could not?*

To shouts of encouragement from his men, Jean urged Cockerel forward; then, coming abreast of the man, he drew his sword, let go of the reins, and arced downward at an angle. At that moment, the young serf looked fearfully over his shoulder. He saw the sword headed for him and opened his mouth to shriek. Too late; Jean's sword sliced off his head, very cleanly and neatly. The head shot forward for some distance before it smacked against the earth and rolled.

Jean jerked his right boot out of his spur and hoisted himself over the saddle, so that he was draped at a dangerous angle on the left flank of his charger. Like a wild Arabian, he leaned down, grabbed up the head, and threw his body upright astride his saddle once more. He held it high for all to see while the dogs dove in a frenzied heap upon the headless, still twitching corpse. Blood gushed from the neck, and the horrified eyes stared at Jean for a moment. There were some who said that those who were beheaded lived for a few seconds afterward; in case that was true, Jean laughed at the dying face and said, "Your death brings me a boy child, or I curse your soul to the Devil."

The eyes rolled up in the head. And Fantasme took his share while the assemblage cheered their familiar . . . and the heir of their Circle.

Laurent galloped up and cried, "Well done, my son!" He held out his hands, and Jean tossed the head into his father's arms. Then he waved at his cheering fellows and cantered away to prepare for his wedding, leaving the others to take the rest of the peasants selected for the Hunt.

Moonlight and firelight gleamed across the courtyard of Castle Deveraux. The great stone gargoyles that had haunted Jean's childhood nights stared down at the assembly, fire pouring from their snouts. Torch flames whipped in the warm air, and great bonfires flared from the tunnels leading down to the dreaded dungeons, infamous throughout France as bastions of unspeakable cruelty. *Woe betide him who crosses a Deveraux,* went the saying, and it was true. The Cahors had been wise to entangle their fate with the Deveraux, now that they knew the Deveraux had achieved the creation of Black Fire. They would be loath to have it used against them.

As was the custom of the day, Isabeau joined Jean in front of the closed chapel doors. Men and women married before church doors; thus it was no insult to the Bishop that they did not go inside the church. On this night of the Blood Moon, the two stood facing each other before banks of lilies and twining ivy. Lilies were the flower of the Cahors, and ivy, of the Deveraux. Fantasme and Pandion were present, each preening on a beautifully decorated perch. Loose them, and they would kill each other.

Isabeau was like a fantastic she-dragon, dressed as the mighty lady she was, and would become, in ebony shot with silver thread. But she trembled like a shy virgin, and by the light of the full moon, he saw how pale she was beneath her black and silver veil.

How long will you be my lady? he wondered silently. *How long before our Houses feud once more, and I poison or behead you, or burn you at the stake?*

At this, she looked up at him, her eyes flinty. She didn't blink, didn't waver as he returned her gaze. Her eyes glowed a soft blue. The air between them thrummed with tension. He was delighted; this lady had a spine, by the God! He'd best look to his own person, or *she* would be the one to do *him* in.

He chuckled low in his throat, then turned his attention to his father.

As the two houses chanted in Latin and languages even more ancient, Laurent held his athame at the ready, preparing to cut open the wrists of the marrying couple. The hood of his dark crimson robe concealing his face, he towered like a dark statue before the altar. Isabeau's mother, Catherine, also wore black and silver; they were the colors of their House.

It was a glorious sight for those assembled, and power and passion flared and rose between the young couple as they were joined, soul to soul, until the end of days. Their wrists were cut and blood mingled together in flesh and into flesh, as Laurent and Catherine bound their children's left arms together with cords soaked in herbals and unguents designed to ensure fertility. Both Houses were strong and boasted many young ones, but those of the Coventry were scattered throughout the land, and there could never be enough witches and warlocks in France to please either family.

Once more, Isabeau began trembling, and lowered

her gaze. Jean was not fooled. The strong, cruel blood of Cahors ran through her veins. She was a skilled witch, and she had cast spells that could match many of his own in bloodless, single-minded purpose.

Indeed, he knew that she and her family believed they had arranged this match with their own magics, their aim being to tame the hot-blooded Deveraux. The two houses had never agreed on a single course of action to get what they wanted, which was complete control of their region of France, and in due time, the crown bestowed upon them by the Christian bishop at Reims. To win that, the Deveraux were active, direct, and violent. Enemies fell to curses or swords. Obstacles were cut down, burned, poisoned.

In contrast, the Cahors, while certainly no saints, preferred subterfuge and complicated diplomacy to further their own ends. Where a Deveraux would murder an inconvenient cardinal in his bed, the Cahors would entice him to their favor with jewels and maidens, or urge him to sin and then threaten blackmail. They pitted brother against brother, organizing whispering campaigns and planting false witnesses to such extent that no one with any modicum of power could trust another.

Thus the Cahors claimed to be more discreet and peace-loving. They argued that the Deveraux were too obvious and overt with their use of spells and magics, and the hidden things that only those allied with "un-Christian elements" would know. With their "impatience," the Deveraux provoked the common folk to grumble about witchcraft, and murmur about bringing down both families by appealing to the Pope.

The Deveraux, for their part, knew that the Cahors angered many of the other noble families and lines of France, to the point that several prominent castled names had refused to have anything to do with either Cahors or Deveraux. It was one thing to anger slaves; it was quite another to sever relations with slave owners.

Thus the Cahors, thinking themselves the cleverer of the two families, had decided to bind their heiress to the heir of Deveraux—they had no male issue in line for the castle—and Jean and Laurent had scoffed privately at their many spells and rituals designed to engender Jean's lust for Isabeau. What they did not realize was that for years the Deveraux coven masters had sacrificed untold virgins and propitiated the Lord of the Greenwood in all his many guises, in order to inspire the Cahors to the match in the first place. Laurent wanted Isabeau Cahors in his castle—whether as his son's wife or his own mistress, it made no difference. For if she lived in his castle, she was his hostage.

The Cahors loved their daughter and would let no harm come to her. It must be clear to them that she was more likely to live to an old age if she was the property of a Deveraux man, and the mother of Deveraux sons.

All this ran through Jean's mind during the ceremony, but at the instant that Isabeau's blood mingled with his own, he was enflamed with love for her. Uncanny surges of adoration made him reel; he had always wanted to bed her, of course—what red-blooded man would not, for she was an unparalleled beauty—but now he could barely stand for love of her.

I not only desire her, but I love her truly, he thought, reeling. *I love her in the manner in which* weak *men love women! I am unmanned! What have they done to me?*

At that moment, Isabeau inhaled sharply, and stared up at him, her eyes wide with wonder. *She feels it, too. Has someone enchanted us both?*

He glanced at his father, who was invoking the God to protect their union. His gaze slid from Laurent to his new mother-in-law, Catherine. She returned his scrutiny, and the merest hint of a smile whispered across her lips.

It was she, he thought fiercely. *How dare she? Before this night is over, I will strangle her in her bed.* Then a strange, new emotion washed over him. *That would cause Isabeau great grief. I cannot harm her lady mother . . .*

He took a step backward. *I have been poisoned. I am being manipulated.*

He said aloud, "This marriage—"

His father stopped chanting and stared at him. A hush descended over the assemblage.

He read in his father's eyes a warning: *I have toiled for years to achieve this match. Do not thwart me, lad. Don't forget, you have a younger brother. Should you prove to be a disappointment, he can easily take your place.*

Jean took a breath, and then he barely nodded, to show his father that he understood, and said, "This marriage joins two great houses. I am overcome with joy that my bride and I stand here tonight."

A cheer rose up—perhaps not a very enthusiastic one, for the Cahors were anxious about being surrounded by Deveraux, and many of the Deveraux opposed the match.

Isabeau said nothing, but her expression softened. A tear welled in her eye and ran down her cheek. Jean reached beneath her veil and caught the tear with his forefinger, then raised it to his mouth and slipped his fingertip between his lips. It was an intimate, loving gesture that was not lost on the onlookers, who murmured with approval and surprise. Jean was not known for his tenderness in matters relating to women.

The ceremony ended at last, and with trumpets and torches Jean led his bride into the great hall of Castle Deveraux for the bridal feast.

Echoing through the rooms of stone, a faint cry of agony caught Isabeau's attention. She looked up at her groom.

"Sacrifices," Jean told her. "We'll go a little later, to preside over the last few."

She dipped her head in assent. She still had not spoken, he noticed.

"Did they take your voice, so that you could not refuse this match?" he asked her, an edge in his tone.

The look she flashed at him was one of pure lust and adoration. "There is nothing I will refuse you, Jean de Deveraux."

His loins filled with fire and he smiled at her. She smiled back, and they led the way to the tables.

And they went to the dungeons later, and what he made her see, what they did together to living, breathing human beings . . . to sacrifices for the sake of their marriage, and their legacy . . .

Jer's eyes snapped open. His chest was heaving and he heard his own voice muttering, "No, no, no, no."

Eddie and Kialish were both crouched beside him,

Eddie with his hand on Jer's shoulder. He had been shaking him hard.

Jer was going to be sick. The atrocities he'd witnessed in his vision, the tortures . . . he was revolted. He shoved Eddie aside and ducked out of the lodge as fast as he could, staggered a few feet, and fell to his hands and knees. Bile churned in his stomach and he coughed it up, tears welling in his eyes as the acid seared his throat.

Then emptied physically but still not emotionally, he rose to his feet and lurched toward his car.

Eddie and Kialish caught up and walked abreast of him. Eddie said, "What's up, Jer?"

"I'm going home."

"What did you see?" Kialish wanted to know. "What happened, man?"

Jer shook his head. "Nothing I want to talk about."

His friends traded glances. "We can go to my dad," Kialish suggested. His father was a shaman. "I think you need him."

"Thanks." Jer didn't break his stride, but he flashed Kialish a grim smile of appreciation. "What I need is a new family."

He had told Eddie and Kialish a few things about his father and his brother, and over the months he figured they must have connected a few of the dots he'd left out.

Not all of them, but enough to at least be sympathetic. Kari knew less about his background, because he didn't trust her as much. She was power hungry and, truth be told, she was beginning to wear on him. Hey, great times together and all that, but she was pushy and nosy. He had to watch his back all the time around her.

As his friends looked on, he pulled his jeans over his loincloth and found his gray UW Seattle T-shirt among the clutter of books in the backseat. His hands were shaking. He leaned against the car to catch his breath, fished his keys out of his pocket, yanked open the driver's door, and slid in.

"I'm not sure you should drive," Kialish ventured. "You're too shook up."

"I'm fine." He jabbed the keys into the ignition. The engine roared and Kialish stepped back so Jer could shut the door.

With bare feet he peeled out, brakes squealing.

What's happening? he thought angrily. *My dad misses Lammas and I go on a vision quest to Hell.*

He wanted some answers. *Dad had damn well better have some. . . .*

Michael was furious. He kept it from his mistress as he spoke to her on the phone, but his wrath was such that he could have strangled her with pleasure, and dropped her dead body onto the floor.

"Of course Holly should live in San Francisco, if that's what she wants." His tone couldn't have been more casual. He picked up a pair of chopsticks from an empty bag of some take-out Chinese one of the boys had brought home and broke them in two.

On the other end of the line, Marie-Claire said, "She didn't know we existed. My brother Danny never told her about us."

Maybe Daniel Cathers knew Holly was the keeper of the family power, he thought, even angrier. *And now the little bitch wants to stay in California with a family friend.*

That's too bad . . . for the friend.

Just then, Jeraud slammed into the house. Michael gave him an inquiring look and raised a finger to indicate that Jer should give him a moment. His son crossed his arms and glared at him.

"So I'm going to stay here," Marie-Claire continued. "For the services. It's in the local papers," she added distractedly. "It's big news around here."

"And you're staying with this Barbara Davis. . . ." He trailed off, watching Jeraud's temper mounting.

"Chin," she finished. "Barbara Davis-Chin. It's a lovely house. There's a guest room. Holly's staying in it and I'm going to sleep in the living room. Nobody wants to be in Tina's room. That's the daughter."

"Give me your address," he ordered, then caught himself and said sweetly, "so I can check in on you. And to send flowers," he added in a moment of inspiration.

"Oh, Michael, that's so kind." She was obviously very touched. "I wish you could be here."

"Me, too." He paused. "I need to go."

"Someone's there," she guessed. "Will you call me later? At bedtime?" she added huskily.

"Yes. *Adieu.*" She loved it when he spoke French to her.

"*Adieu.*" The entire situation was high drama for her, and she was enjoying her part in it. Life as a Seattle housewife, no matter how wealthy, could be dull at times.

Michael hung up. "What's up?" he said to Jer.

"You said you didn't know very much about our family history. I think you know more than you've told me."

Michael assessed him. "I'm surprised at you. You've never seemed very interested in the old tree before. Did you find something interesting on the Net?"

"We were torturers," Jer said. "We killed hundreds of people." He stayed where he was, balling and unballing his fists.

We killed thousands, my boy, Michael thought, but aloud he said, "I doubt that very much. Who told you that? That girl you hang out with at the university? Sissy Spaced-out?" He made fun of Kari Hardwicke at every opportunity. If he could have managed it without raising suspicion, she'd be dead already.

"Is it true?" Jer demanded. He narrowed his eyes. "What else have you kept from me?"

Michael turned away, making a sudden decision. *Holly Cathers is coming here. This boy might be the one who has what it takes, not me or Eli. I could put her in thrall to him, make her the Lady to his Lord.*

And then I'll make sure he's always in thrall to me.

"I'm going to San Francisco," he informed his son. "I'll be gone for a few days."

"Don't you walk away from me! I want to know!" Jer shouted at his back. "Who are we? What are we?"

Michael chuckled to himself. "You know what we are, Jeraud. You've always known. We're warlocks, and we're allied with the Dark. We're what is commonly referred to as evil."

"You liar!" Jer roared.

A bolt of crackling green energy whipped past Michael and hit the wall, scorching the trailing ivy wallpaper. Michael was impressed that his son had harnessed such strong magical power. But he was also a lousy shot.

Slowly he pivoted around, gazing coolly at his child. He channeled force into his own facial features, his bones, even the cells of his hair. The transformation gave him added strength and an air of authority.

"Do not forget," he said in a low voice, "that I am your father."

Jer pursed his lips and swung out of the kitchen. Michael stayed where he was, listening to Jer's footfalls on the stairs, then down the hallway, and then into his room. His bedroom door slammed so hard, the kitchen windows rattled.

Michael walked calmly to the pantry and opened it. Its walls were brick, its shelves unfinished oak. On the right side of the third row of shelves, he pulled out a false brick that was nothing but a piece of facing. In the hollow space behind it, he pulled out a carved jade box.

In the box lay the preserved eye of an Ottoman Turk, a souvenir from the Crusades. The Deveraux House had sent many second and third sons in an effort to win even greater glory.

Michael spoke ancient Arabic over the eye, then held it up and stared into its shriveled brown iris. In its tissue, he saw a clear reflection of his son's movements upstairs in his room.

Jer was pacing and muttering. He stopped, lay down on his bed, punched the pillow, and sighed.

Michael watched him for about a minute longer. *He can be molded. I can use him to get exactly what I want: ultimate control of the Supreme Coven. Why didn't I see it before? Why did I think it had to be* me? *Or even my first-born, Eli?*

With a happy sigh, he put the eye back into the box, the box into the hollow, replaced the false brick, and crossed to the phone. He punched in the home office number of his travel agent, who had once been his mistress. He had broken it off with her "for her sake." She was only one of many whom he had dumped, who thought he had done it for the noble reason of not messing up her life.

"Hey, Pat, my love," he said easily, "yes, it's me. Listen, I need a ticket ASAP to San Francisco. Open-end return, okay?"

Upstairs in his bedroom, Jer touched his forehead. A sudden, brutal headache squeezed his temples. Breathing deeply, he intoned a spell to ward away pain. Nothing happened, and the pain got worse.

When in doubt, take Tylenol, he thought wearily,

rolling over. *And why do I even bother trying to talk to my father?*

He raised up on his elbows. Then he froze.

At the foot of the bed, magical green energy swirled in an oval shape about six feet high. It was about three feet across, and as it hovered in the air, a darker shape appeared in the center. Veins of deep ivy green crackled from it, and layers and shards of glowing forms tumbled around it in a circular motion, like the pieces of glass in a shifting kaleidoscope.

The shaper grew, and Jer could make out a head, shoulders, and limbs. It was a human figure.

The oval bobbled and began to close, and the figure cocked its head as if startled, observing the shrinking perimeter, then looked straight at Jer. The features were unclear. He felt, rather than saw, its gaze.

What Jer did next, he knew was not of his own choosing. He crawled on his hands and knees to the foot of his bed and held out his left hand. His mouth opened, and he spoke sounds he had never heard before.

From the oval, scarlet and green energy crackled, then darted forward to connect with his fingers.

Violently, Jer was thrown back against the bed, slamming his already aching head against the headboard. It felt as if his skull were being cracked open with a hammer, and for a moment he sprawled in a heap, unable to move. Finally, with a grunt, he sat back up, dizzy and sick to his stomach from the pain.

Once again the beams shot forward. The jolt was enough to knock him off the bed, and it spread over him like a pulsating blanket, pinning him to the floor. It shimmered over him from head to foot, sizzling, sending tendrils of aching, jittery sensation throughout his body. Shutting his eyes tightly, he braced himself for more pain, but this time none came. Something new was happening; it was as if something were trying to find a way inside him, poking and prodding the surface of his skin for an opening . . . or a weakness.

He spoke words of magic, very strong, very powerful, to kill the entity or the charge or whatever it was, or at least to render it inert. Though the sensation lessened, it didn't completely dissipate. He tried another spell. Nothing happened.

Hell with this, he thought, and opened his eyes.

At the foot of his bed, deep inside the oval, the human shape writhed in agony. The figure was completely engulfed in flames. It fell to its knees, arms flailing, trying to put itself out. Jer watched in horror as it rolled and jerked, its head arched backward, its mouth open in a scream Jer couldn't hear.

The oval constricted, telescoping in, and as Jer

reached toward it, the energy slid off his body like a net and returned to the pinpoint that was all that was left of the shape. He scrambled toward it again, but in the next instant, it winked out of existence. Every trace of it vanished.

The distinctive sound of crackling flames ricocheted through his mind, and then a man's distant voice, faint but filled with hatred:

Don't forget. She did this to me. Don't trust the witch. Show her no mercy or this will happen to you.

Then a loud wailing filled Jer's head; the resulting pain made him cry out and jerk into a fetal position, his arms protectively cradling his throbbing skull.

He had no idea how long he lay that way, but when he came to, it was morning, his head no longer hurt, and his father had left for San Francisco.

Part Two: Samhain
Lifting the Veil

☾

SAMHAIN
"When Death stalks the earth, witches come to play. For of all creatures they have nothing to fear, yea, only they."

"And I saw in that century a great darkness spreading across the land. It was a darkness born of strife and vengeance given birth centuries before. I saw the power wielded by two families and the destruction that they brought. It was as though all the demons of Hell had been brought forth to walk the earth and all manner of wickedness had been set loose so that good men trembled in their homes."

—Gregory the Wise, 1152

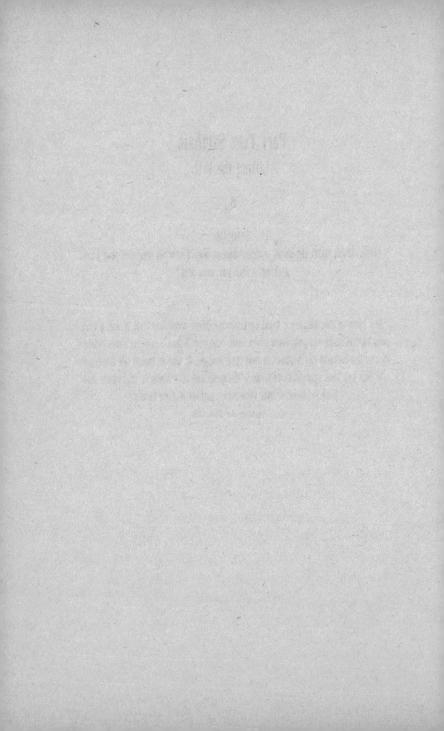

FOUR

SNOW MOON

☾

And now our dark purpose nearly done
We thank thee, Lord of Day, God of Sun
Deveraux answer your dread behest
We kill well on the Eve, on the Morrow, we feast

Our Lady guide us on this night
As we strive to finish well right
Cahorses' Purpose dark and strong
Help us House and Circle prolong

San Francisco, California

It had been Barbara's decision to hold two funeral services, one for her daughter on Wednesday, and one for Holly's parents the following day. As an E.R. doc, Barbara had knowledge of potent tranquilizers, and that was the only thing that got Holly through the ordeal of Tina's burial. Today would be a stronger test.

Now they stood on fresh grass beside her parents'

graves at Our Lady of Sorrows Memorial Park, Barbara in the same black long-sleeved wool dress she had worn to her daughter's funeral, Holly in the same black stretch skirt, boots, and black shirt. Most of the attendees wore black or navy. Elise's and Daniel's coworkers stood somberly behind the minister and the rows of chairs; their closer friends looked miserable on the gray folding chairs, eyes swollen with tears. There was her mom's yoga coach; there, her father's golf friends. Holly's classmates and her pack of stable brats had shown, but all she could do at the church service and now at the grave sites was register their presence with unblinking eyes.

Two matching mahogany caskets were poised above the opened rectangles, flowers heaped on them in equal amounts.

My parents' bodies are in there, she thought, trying to block out the images that formed. Most vivid was the nightmarish face of her father as she'd awakened in the hospital. She shuddered, feeling sick to her stomach, wishing the service was over and never wanting it to end. Wanting to be suspended here in time, so she wouldn't have to go on without them. Her mom. Her dad. *This is the part that's the nightmare. I'll wake up from this soon. I swear I will.*

A thin-faced, wrinkled, old minister Holly didn't

know going on about ashes and dust until she wanted to scream at him to shut up. Tears streamed down her face and she choked back a sob as Barbara gave her right hand a tight squeeze.

Her newfound aunt stood on her left, and a man who had arrived late at the service and had been introduced to her simply as Michael stood beside Marie-Claire with his arm around her waist. Holly assumed he was her aunt's husband, but no one had said so. He was very good-looking. His clothes were expensive. His loafers were like the ones her father had splurged on the last time they'd gone shopping in the city—over five hundred dollars a pair.

How can I even notice such things when I'm burying my parents?

The man craned his neck forward and looked at her. The heat rose to her face and she grew even more ashamed, as if he knew she'd been checking him out.

"It'll be over soon," Barbara murmured. She was weaving on her feet; Holly doubted she had slept or eaten since the plane had touched down at San Francisco International Airport two nights ago. Holly had heard footsteps each night, and since her aunt was bedded downstairs, it had to have been Barbara walking up and down the hallway, steadily, for hours.

The minister raised a hand and intoned, "'Yea,

though I walk through the valley of the shadow of death, I will fear no evil.'"

As if on cue, a cloud trailed over the sun, and the sky above Holly and the others darkened. Heads looked up.

It began to sprinkle.

Soft murmurs spread throughout the crowd and the minister looked up, temporarily losing his place. Umbrellas *fwapped* open and people moved in close, some sharing with others, and one of the attorneys from Daddy's office held his umbrella above the minister's head, who said, "Thank you," and pressed on.

The sky darkened as black, smoky clouds rose into thunderheads; lightning crackled inside them, and the sky rolled like a kettledrum.

It began to rain in earnest. A few people ducked bare heads apologetically at Holly and Barbara and began to leave. As Barbara accepted someone's proffered umbrella and opened it, she muttered, "I should have thought of tents."

It was Holly's turn to squeeze her hand. She didn't feel the rain; she didn't feel anything . . .

. . . except the man beside her aunt, watching her more closely now. He smiled faintly at her, and she shivered and looked away again.

The flowers on the caskets were being drenched,

the ink on the florist cards blurring. Holly felt a flash of unreasonable anger at Barbara. *This is San Francisco, for God's sake; why* didn't *you think of tents?*

Time passed, she didn't know how much of it, but the rain turned into a storm; Holly couldn't hear the words of the minister at all. Yet he droned on, completely ignoring everything else, oblivious that now most of the attendees were fleeing to their cars.

The clouds rumbled more intensely; then suddenly, without warning, a bolt of lightning shot down from the sky and hit an evergreen tree about a hundred yards away. To a chorus of surprised shouts, it burst into flame, which was quickly dampened by the oncoming torrents of rain. Nevertheless, Holly was jostled by the electric charge and felt the heat. Chaos broke out; there were screams as people ran in the opposite direction. Soon there was nothing but smoke to prove it had happened at all, and then a few burned limbs on an otherwise healthy tree. But the terror of the moment had ruined the service.

To the few stalwarts who remained, the thin, gray-faced funeral director in his black suit stepped forward with his hands extended.

"I'm very sorry," he announced, "but we really must leave. It's dangerous to be out here with the lightning." He gestured at the tree. "Especially with the metal tips and spines on these umbrellas."

He walked over to Holly and took her elbow. "I'm so very sorry." He looked like he meant it.

All she could think of to say was, "Barbara has a covered patio." She was thinking of the reception. She looked uncomfortably at the caskets.

"We'll lower them after it stops raining," he said.

Then she was being herded somewhere. It was the limo; and the person who was escorting her was the stranger, Michael. He put his hand gently on the crown of her head and said, "Duck down."

She did so. The door on the other side opened, and Barbara Davis-Chin got in, followed by Aunt Marie-Claire. Michael slid in next to Holly and shut the door.

Barbara gathered her up and held her tightly. She was crying. "This is horrible. This is so horrible." She brushed Holly's sopping wet hair away from her face with a shaking hand. "Oh, my God, what a disaster."

Marie-Claire nodded unhappily. She asked, "Do you think anyone will come to the reception?"

"Oh, God." Barbara shook her head. "I can't deal with that."

"We'll handle it," Michael announced comfortingly. "Marie-Claire and I."

Taking her cue from him, Holly's aunt nodded. "Yes. We will."

"Thank you. I think Holly and I will just go to my room and lie down." Barbara pulled Holly more closely against herself.

"I'll make you some tea," Aunt Marie-Claire soothed. "I'll keep the guests away from both of you."

They rode the rest of the distance in silence. Seated so closely beside Michael, Holly smelled the man's leather shoes and the faintest whiff of aftershave. The limo was redolent with wet wool and mud, and Holly knew that for the rest of her life, those odors would remind her of this hideous day.

"When we get home, I'll give you something to help you sleep," Barbara murmured to Holly.

"Modern magic," Michael said. He dug in his pocket and pulled out a tiny white stone box, opening the hinged lid. "This is an old family remedy." He held the box open for Barbara's inspection. "We boil it in water for tea. It's very effective."

Barbara merely said, "How nice," and took the box from him.

Holly closed her eyes, trying to breathe. It was tight in the limo and the man was sitting too close to her. Their bodies were touching and she was embarrassed, but it seemed ridiculous to be upset about that now. Of course, so much of today had been ridiculous.

My parents are dead. I didn't even get to say good-bye.

It seemed like forever until the limo driver rolled to a stop and opened his door. They were at Barbara's house in Pacific Heights, with its mansard roof and its elegant white urns flanking the doorway. She had always loved the Davis-Chin home, with its soothing elegance and the happiness it contained inside.

Michael got out first; then Holly. She waited beneath Michael's umbrella for Barbara to emerge, shivering with cold and terrified of having to face any questions from people waiting inside Barbara's house. There were cars parking and the front door opened; one of her father's colleagues glanced out awkwardly at her. He was holding a glass of wine.

"Ma'am?" the limo driver said to Barbara as he stood behind the passenger door.

Holly glanced up at the limo driver, who shrugged and bent down to peer into the limo's interior.

"Ma'am?" he said again, and then more urgently, *"Ma'am?"*

"What's wrong?" Holly cried, craning to see around him.

There was a silence. Holly's heart thundered.

"Call 9-1-1!" the driver shouted. *"Now."*

A bird burst from the car, grazing the tip of Holly's cheek with its wing. She recoiled with a yelp. Where the hell did that thing come from? She stared after the retreating bird as it flew high in the sky, turned, and then flew straight for the car, dive-bombing like a kamikaze pilot. It crashed into the closed passenger window on the side opposite the driver, splintering the fortified, tinted glass like a pane of candy.

With a horrible shriek, it collapsed onto the shard of glass, and was beheaded. Its body detached and thunked to the ground while the head must have rolled outside. Blood gouted from the creature's neck as its legs jerked and danced in a nervous paroxysm of death.

Holly doubled over and threw up, and Michael put his arm around her shoulders and whispered, "Let me get you inside."

Hours later, Holly managed to trudge from Barbara's hospital room at Marin County General to the beautifully appointed waiting room. The doctor on staff was new and hadn't known that Holly was "family." She made no protest. She could barely speak as it was.

As she stumbled across the threshold, Michael and Aunt Marie-Claire looked up in unison. They were seated on an elegant chocolate leather sofa, and the two of them were very striking side by side. They looked very much like a couple, and Holly wondered what was going on between them. Since Marie-Claire was married to someone else—Holly had figured that much out—she wasn't sure she wanted to know.

Marie-Claire cradled a Styrofoam cup between her hands; Michael had been reading the *San Francisco Chronicle*.

"How is she?" Holly's aunt asked.

Holly licked her lips and shook her head. Her stomach was churning. "They don't know what's wrong. She's not doing all that great."

She didn't mention all the machines hooked up to Barbara, monitoring her vitals, helping her breathe. Nor did she mention the scratches that covered Barbara's face and the fact that the doctors' couldn't positively link the bird attack to her condition. Or the pitying looks the nurses gave her as she sat helplessly by Barbara's side.

"Oh, dear." Her aunt reached out for a hug. Holly obliged. Her jewelry jangled in Holly's ear. "I'm here, Holly." She sighed and touched Holly's hair. "Unless there's someone else you'd like to call."

"No," Holly told her, although to be honest, the

list of someone-elses was long. She was too tired and upset to deal with it.

"Would you like something? Some tea?" Holly's aunt asked her, gesturing to the trio of vending machines against the back wall of the waiting room. "Don't try the coffee. It'll kill you . . . it's horrible."

Holly remembered Michael's little box filled with tea. Had they retrieved it from the limo?

The last thing she did was examine that stuff.

"Honey? Some tea?" Aunt Marie-Claire prodded.

"Sure. Thanks," Holly replied, more to give Aunt Marie-Claire something to do than anything else.

Her aunt got some change from Michael, then bustled over to the machines. Holly sat down on a leather chair at a right angle to the sofa. Michael folded the newspaper, stretching out his legs. His clothes and his loafers were wet from the storm, which still raged outside.

He was about to say something when a woman in a navy blue suit bustled into the room. She smiled too brightly and announced, "Hi, I'm Eve Oxford. I'm one of the social workers here." She perched on the very edge of a chair identical to Holly's on the other side of the coffee table. "Let's talk about Holly's living arrangements."

Wicked: Witch

★ ★ ★

At first, Holly refused to leave San Francisco. She insisted that she didn't want to abandon Barbara, who was still in the hospital, and then she couldn't bear to pack her clothes. But as the days slogged by, she realized that her aunt had a life back in Seattle, and she, Holly, was making her nervous by holding her up.

Michael Deveraux—that was his full name, and he was "a friend of the family"—had flown back to Seattle the day after the funeral.

And now, she and her aunt were on the same flight, a little over a week later.

Everything back in San Francisco had been handled by Holly's aunt. A friend of Holly's mother's was house-sitting, and Holly had gone to say good-bye to the horses at the stables. It was then that the owner, Janet Levesque, had told her that her parents had been making arrangements to purchase a horse for Holly as a high school graduation present.

Now, seated in first class with her aunt, Holly leaned her head against the window and thought of all the dreams denied. She had a trust fund and she was going to be "very well taken care of," as her parents' attorney had put it. Once she reached eighteen, she could buy herself five horses if she wanted.

"Holly, do you want some champagne?" her aunt

asked. In the time they'd been together, Holly had noticed that her aunt had a tendency to drink a little too much. Holly hoped it was because of the stress, and that she wouldn't keep drinking in Seattle.

Holly wanted to tell her she didn't drink, and that fussing over her was making her edgy. But when the flute of sparkling wine arrived, she accepted it with good grace, sipped it . . .

. . . and woke up as they were landing.

Startled, Holly jerked up her head. Over the roar of the descent, her aunt smiled and said, "Hey, sleepyhead. I was just wondering if I was going to have to carry you off the plane."

The plane touched down and the brakes were squealing, and her aunt had shifted her attention to her makeup. She looked perfect, as she always did, and Holly wondered if her cousins spent as much time worrying about their appearance as their mom did. Her aunt's carry-on luggage was bulky and heavy, containing lots of new makeup she had purchased at Nordstrom on Union Square. Holly found the woman's delight in cruising the makeup counters—and her binge buying—completely bizarre. As far as Holly could tell, she bought nothing in San Francisco that she couldn't get in Seattle—or, for that matter, online.

It's a compulsion, Holly thought. *She can't stop herself.*

As they deplaned and walked to baggage claim, her aunt sailed along, not giving Holly much opportunity to look around. She chatted lightly about inconsequential things—the nice day out, the guest room in her house, how much Amanda and Nicole were looking forward to meeting her. Her cell phone went off; it was Uncle Richard. He had just parked the Mercedes and would catch up with them.

Holly jerked as someone skittered their fingertips up her spine, then softly caressed the nape of her neck. Startled, she stopped walking and whirled around.

No one was there.

Holly frowned and touched the back of her head. She glanced left, then right, dodging an oncoming businessman who practically mowed her down.

"Honey?" Aunt Marie-Claire looked puzzled.

She couldn't have touched me, Holly realized. *She's too weighted down with her carry-on luggage, and she was walking ahead of me.*

Goose bumps broke out on her arms and chest. She murmured, "Sorry," and started walking again. "I thought I dropped something."

"Ah." Her aunt perked up and began chattering again.

They got their bags and she met Uncle Richard. She was surprised that her flashy, pretty aunt was married to a man like him. The only word she could come up with to describe him was "gray." He was dressed in gray, his hair was gray, and his demeanor was gray—not happy, not warm, not anything. He might as well have been the invisible person who had touched her.

No one touched me. I just imagined it, she told herself as the three slid into a black Mercedes. Still, as they pulled out of the parking lot and joined the traffic, she scanned the pedestrians and replayed the moment. *Maybe it was my mom or my dad,* she thought, tears welling. The nightmare face of her father rose up in her mind, and she exhaled sharply and sat back against the leather seat, exhausted.

And maybe I'm just having a nervous breakdown. It'd be nice to stop feeling for a while, check out mentally and just veg. Maybe I'll do that.

They wound down a highway lined with trees and through beautiful old neighborhoods that reminded her of home, with trees everywhere, so many, and then rain so heavy, she could see nothing. Then she dozed off again until her aunt said, "I hope you're not coming down with something, honey. We're . . . home."

Holly took a deep breath and climbed wearily out of the car. As she stepped onto the porch, her aunt bustled ahead and opened the door. "Girls! We're here!" she cried. "Your cousin's here!"

Aunt Marie-Claire led the way into a charming foyer of red Victorian flocked wallpaper, white wood wainscoting, and white marble floors. It looked a little like an ice-cream parlor, and Holly had to shut her mouth tightly to keep from voicing her observation; she wasn't sure her aunt would appreciate it.

Everything was thick with the odor of smoke, as if they had had a terrible fire.

"Nicole," Aunt Marie-Claire said. "Your cousin Holly's here."

"So I heard," the voice drawled.

Then the girl rose slowly from the couch and turned around. With a pang, Holly saw the family resemblance, seeing in her cousin's perfect oval face her father's coloring and his eyes. Nicole was incredibly beautiful, the kind of beauty that made people stare. Her black curls had been pulled into a thick bundle at the crown of her head, then tumbled down her shoulders and back. Her eyebrows were thick too, but nicely shaped. Like her mother, she had on a lot of makeup; her eyes were heavily lined and her lashes were so long, they looked fake. Her lips were a deep, dark red, her fingernails and toenails perfectly matched.

Barefoot, she wore black jeans and a red tank top with the word TROUBLE embroidered in silver and black threads. She appraised Holly coolly, taking in her jeans and peasant blouse, and said, "Hi. I'm Nicole."

"Hi," Holly replied, let down. She didn't know what she'd expected, but it wasn't such total indifference.

"We had a good flight," said Aunt Marie-Claire, as if Nicole had asked. "Bumpy near the end. Turbulence. Where's your sister?"

"Holly?" a new voice cried.

Holly looked beyond the living room to a sweeping stairway as footsteps thudded down it. In a few seconds, a second girl appeared. She didn't look at all like her glamorous twin. Her hair was short and mousy brown, and her features were pleasant but nothing more. She didn't have on any makeup at all, and there were freckles across her nose. She smiled brightly at Holly, dashing toward her. She had on a navy blue T-shirt and a pair of plaid pajama bottoms, and in her arms she carried a tiny white kitten.

"This is Amanda," Aunt Marie-Claire said.

"Hi." Amanda bounded over to Holly and put her right arm around Holly's shoulder. She hugged her. "I'm so glad you're here! How was the flight?"

"She slept most of the way here," Holly's aunt said, sounding amused. She turned to Nicole. "Sweetheart, any calls?"

Nicole nodded. "Yeah. I made a list by the phone in the kitchen."

Amanda gave the kitten a scratch on the head and held it out to Holly. "She's for you. To welcome you to Seattle. We all have one. All us girls, I mean. Nicole and me. It's a little girl."

Holly blinked and took the cat. The soft little creature weighed next to nothing, and she stared up at Holly with large blue eyes.

"Her name's Bast," Nicole said. "*I* named her."

"That's the Egyptian goddess of cats," Amanda filled her in. "You can tell her all your secrets."

Nicole snickered. "She's deaf, Mandy."

"She'll hear Holly anyway," Amanda said, smiling at Holly.

"Thank you." Holly was touched. She cuddled Bast under her chin, and the kitten began to purr and knead her chest.

"I'll show you the guest room." Amanda gestured for Holly to follow.

Nicole stayed behind.

They went down a long hall papered in gray and white. It was far more elegant than the ice-cream parlor entry. Holly's sandals clicked on the marble floor, and the cat purred as Amanda led the way. Then Holly's cousin turned to the right and headed up a flight of stairs of plain white wood.

"This used to be the servants' staircase," she said.

"Back in the old days. We don't have servants, unless you count me." She half-smiled. "Our house is supposed to be haunted. You'll have to let me know what you think."

"This is a big house," Holly said as they got to the landing and Amanda headed down the second-floor hallway.

"Mom added on. Have you ever heard of Michael Deveraux? He's a famous architect here. He did our house. We were in some magazines for it." She stopped at an oak door decorated with a carved, bas-relief rose and pushed open the brass knob. "This is your room, Holly."

It was done all in white—white lace curtains at the arched windows, white lace bedspread on a canopy bed, white wicker furniture. On the white floor was a white floor rug.

On the nightstand, a white porcelain vase held a single red rose, the only color in the room.

"I'm going to lose track of Bast in here," Holly said, and Amanda chuckled. She gave the cat another affectionate pat as they walked into the room.

"My dad will bring up your suitcases and stuff," Amanda told her, curling up in one of two wicker chairs. She picked up a throw pillow—also white—and settled it in her lap. "How long are you staying?"

"I don't know," Holly admitted. "I . . . I want to finish school back home. . . ." She trailed off. Her throat was closing up.

"I'm really sorry about your parents." Amanda shook her head. "It really bites, what happened to them. It was a big surprise to us. My mom hadn't heard from her brother in, like, forever. I had forgotten we even had an uncle."

Unable to speak, Holly only nodded.

Just then, the door pushed open. Aunt Marie-Claire stood on the threshold. "You're here. Good." She smiled at Amanda. "I knew I could count on my good girl. Listen, I have to take Nicole to drama class. I'll be back in a while, all right?"

Amanda dropped her gaze to the floor and took a breath. Then she picked at the pillow and said, "Sure, Mom."

"I'll probably go to the store while she's in class. Save a trip." Color rose on Marie-Claire's cheeks. "Do you want anything?"

"Nope." Amanda looked at Holly. "Do you?"

"Silly, she just got here." Marie-Claire's laugh rang false. She dabbed at the corner of her mouth as if to smooth out her lipstick, then said, "You'll be okay until I get back?"

"And even after you get back," Amanda shot back.

Holly wasn't sure if she was trying to make a joke, but Marie-Claire looked a little hurt.

"All right, then." Her gaze swept the room, then rested on the red rose. "How nice to put that there, Amanda. That was sweet of you." She shut the door behind her.

Amanda frowned after her. "Put what where? I don't know what she's talking about."

"Um, the rose?" Holly ventured. "On the night-stand?"

The other girl shrugged. "I didn't do that, Holly. Probably it was my dad." Her face softened. "He's like that. Very thoughtful."

A silence fell between them. Then Holly said, "So Nicole takes acting lessons?"

"Summer school. Drama club stuff." Amanda's voice was dismissive as she picked some more at the pillow, trying to sound casual. "My sister is an actress. My mom was into theater when she was our age. So . . ."

Holly took that in, understanding dawning. *Nicole is their mom's favorite, and Amanda knows it.* As an only child, Holly had never had to share her status with anyone. But when someone was nearly exactly like you, and yet she was the preferred child, that must hurt a lot.

She said tentatively, "It must be weird to be a twin."

Amanda gazed at her. She didn't blink as she replied, "It's weird to be Nicole Anderson's twin, that's for sure." She moved her shoulders and laid the pillow aside. "Do you want to do something, see the town? My dad would be glad to drive us."

Holly yawned. "To tell you the truth, I'd like to lie down for a little while. I'm really tired."

"You've been through a lot." Amanda rose out of the chair. "It's nice that you're here." Her voice was soft and wistful.

She's been lonely, Holly realized. *My guess is, Nicole doesn't hang out with her much.*

"I'll leave you alone to decompress. Get used to . . . everything." Amanda flashed her an uncertain smile and headed for the door.

Holly nuzzled Bast and added, "Thanks so much for the kitten. She's adorable." She laughed softly as the little creature tried to bat her nose. "She's so cuddly. It's like having a live stuffed animal."

Amanda smiled sweetly. "I'll tell my dad to leave your suitcases in the hall, so he doesn't wake you up." She turned to go, then turned back again. "I hope you like it here, Holly."

"I'm sure I will," Holly answered sincerely, though

she was pretty much wanting to go to her own home and crawl in her own bed. Then Holly asked, "Did you guys have a fire recently?"

Amanda looked puzzled. "You mean, in the fireplace?"

Holly shook her head. "I mean, did something catch on fire? It smells so smoky."

"I don't smell anything," Amanda observed, sniffing as if to prove her point. "We haven't had a fire. Well, except last night in the fireplace."

Holly shrugged. "Maybe I'm smelling something else. I've got some new perfume."

Amanda considered; then she brightened. "Dad made dinner last night. He's not very good at it. In fact, he usually sets off the smoke alarm." She chuckled. "I'll bet that's what it is."

"That makes sense," Holly agreed, not convinced. The smell was so strong, she couldn't believe Amanda didn't notice it. *Not that I think she's lying about it. It's just odd.*

"Mom's doing the honors tonight, because of you," Amanda continued. "She's really good. She studied at culinary school."

"Wow. Cool. You guys are talented," Holly said admiringly.

"No. Just my mom and my sister. My dad and I are

really boring." Her smile didn't reach her eyes. "We're the audience. They're the stars."

Holly was a bit shocked. She didn't know what to say. Without speaking further, Amanda left, closing the door behind her.

Holly took off her sandals and jeans and pulled back the white lace coverlet. The sheets were silky soft, caressing her as she lay down in her bra and panties. Bast mewed and crawled on top of her chest. Holly stared down her nose at the cat, who stared intently back.

"So, here I am," she whispered. "I'm . . ." Tears slid down her face. It was all too much. New cousins, new house. New bed. New everything. The kitten cocked her head, blinking large blue eyes at her filled with innocence and curiosity. "I want them back," Holly whispered. "I want everything to be the way it . . . it's *supposed* to be."

The little animal blinked, then lowered her head to Holly's collar bone. Bast kneaded her shoulder a few times and began to purr. She nuzzled her new mistress, settling in for a good catnap.

Will I ever stop crying? Will it ever stop hurting?

Suddenly the cat jerked up her head. She scampered off Holly's chest and dropped to the floor. Facing the closed door, she growled deep in her throat.

Her hackles rose; she arched her back. Her warning growl grew into a squall of anger; she put her ears back and hissed.

"Kitty?" Holly murmured. *It's probably my uncle in the hall. She must have heard his footsteps.*

Except she's deaf.

"Kitty?" she said, more urgently. "Is something wrong?"

The cat backed away, then turned tail and scooted under the bed.

Holly sat up. She stared at the door and the floor just in front of it. There was nothing there.

The cat kept growling, sounding very threatened. *She must feel the vibrations of someone walking.*

Then, without warning, the temperature in the room plummeted. It was freezing cold, so cold that when Holly exhaled with surprise, she saw her own breath. Freaked, she grabbed the bedclothes and twisted them around herself. The cat yowled again and leaped onto the bed, scrabbling up to Holly and pawing at the blankets. Holly grabbed her up and pulled her inside the blankets, where the cat mewed frantically and tried to burrow into Holly's stomach.

They must have a bad thermostat, she told herself firmly. *The cat's cold. That's all.*

And no one touched me at the airport.

"Amanda?" she called, but her throat was dry, and barely any sound came out at all. She cleared her throat and tried again, but her second try wasn't much better than her first.

Then she heard a footstep on the floor, near the doorway.

Inside her room.

Her scalp prickled; the hair on the nape of her neck rose straight up. The air in the room got even colder, if such a thing was even possible; she was shaking, she was so cold. Her teeth were chattering and the skin on her face seemed to tighten across her features.

The cat was going absolutely crazy, writhing beneath the blankets and squalling for all she was worth. Her sharp little kitten claws dug into Holly's thigh; she was dimly aware of it, but she was so cold—and now so scared—that it didn't hurt her at all.

She tried to speak, tried to move. She couldn't even blink her eyes. Couldn't swallow or breathe. She wasn't even sure her heart was still beating.

There was another footstep, very odd, like something that was almost *there* but not quite; it was like hearing a sound when one was deeply asleep but aware that one was dreaming. *Like in the hospital, when I saw Daddy so . . . so . . . dead. . . . Oh, no, don't let it be my father. . . .*

. . . No, let *it be my father. Oh, Daddy, I miss you so much. Please . . .*

The door swung open, and Holly opened her mouth to scream.

Uncle Richard smiled broadly and said, "Hi, honey. I've got your luggage."

The room was warm. The cat snuggled out of the covers and began to lick Holly's face, as if nothing had happened.

"Th-thank you," she managed.

"I'll just leave it in the hall for now. You're resting."

"No," she blurted. She didn't want to be left alone. But he had already shut the door.

She sat in the bed, afraid to move. She felt incredibly foolish but she kept staring at the empty spot where she had heard the footsteps. Her head began to pound with tension.

The steady ticking of a clock vied for her attention, but she couldn't stop staring at the spot, bracing herself in case something else happened.

I imagined it. I was asleep.

She didn't know how long she sat there, but eventually the room grew dimmer and a little chilly. She didn't want to sit there in the dark. Darting her gaze briefly away, she noticed a lamp on the wicker nightstand, beside the rose.

The rose, which was now out of the vase and lying draped across the stand. Droplets of water glistened on the white wicker.

Holly gasped and pulled her hand away, cradling it against her chest. Her heart pounded wildly.

The cat knocked the rose out of the vase, she told herself. *It had to be the cat. Or maybe Amanda, when she got up and left the room. By accident.*

Then a phone rang somewhere in the room, making her shout and jump out of the bed. The phone shrilled again. Holly saw it on the other nightstand, on the far side of the bed, and scrabbled across the mattress to grab it up. She knew she should let someone else get it—she was just a guest in this house—but she couldn't stand the ringing.

"Hello?" she breathed.

"Holly. It's Michael. Deveraux. Welcome to Seattle."

"Ah. Tha—thank you," she stammered.

"Are you enjoying your new home?"

It's not my new home. "It . . . it rains a lot." She was very uncomfortable talking to him.

"They put you in the guest room." She raised her eyebrows. "I suppose," he continued. "Since that's what it's for. I designed that space. Do you like it?"

"Yes. The floor . . . creaks."

"Mmm." He sounded displeased. "I told the carpenters to put extra nails in. So. Is your aunt available?"

Holly hesitated. "I'm not sure. She took Nicole to—"

"Never mind," he said, cutting her off. "I'll try later."

"Michael! I'm here! I'm sorry I took so long! Nicki needed a ride to drama," a feminine voice said clearly in the background. Holly recognized it at once. It was her aunt.

He was wondering where she was. That's why he called. They had a . . . a date.

Ashamed for Marie-Claire, Holly closed her eyes. "Okay," she croaked.

"I'll come by and check that floor soon."

"Thanks," she managed.

He disconnected. Holly did likewise and put the handset back in the charger. She sat for a moment, absorbing her shock.

Back under the bed, Bast growled again.

As quickly as she could, she slipped on her jeans and dashed across the room, avoiding the place that had upset the cat, and bolted out of there.

Breathless in the hall, she leaned against the door, taking in the sight of her pile of suitcases. She longed to carry them downstairs, call a cab, and go to the airport.

There was far too much weirdness here in Seattle.

As opposed to San Francisco, she thought miserably, *where Barbara Davis-Chin is lying in the hospital with an undiagnosed illness. And I apparently own a house that I'm too young to live in by myself. And I have been sent to live with relatives who didn't even know I was alive.*

And my aunt is having an affair.

A door farther down opened, and Holly let out a startled cry.

It was Amanda, who raised her eyebrows. She was wearing very small rectangular glasses and she held a book in her left hand. It was *The Mists of Avalon.*

Amanda said, "It's just me."

Holly ran a hand through her hair. "I'm sorry. I'm kind of jumpy."

"New house," Amanda said kindly.

She beckoned to Holly, and Holly trailed down the hall and into a beautiful bedroom furnished in warm woods, lavender, and cream. Amanda had a sleigh bed covered with a purple and green iris spread. Over an antique desk was a bulletin board with a few photographs and some notes stuck to it. Her closet was open, and a pile of shoes and a purple bathrobe was heaped on the floor. Most of the wall space was taken up with bookcases, and Holly noted lots and lots of fantasy novels.

"I like your room," Holly told her sincerely.

"Mom wants to redo it." Amanda shook her head. "I don't want her to touch it. Did you see the entry-way? Can you say Baskin-Robbins?"

Holly stifled a giggle. "I wouldn't change a thing in here." Holly hesitated and switched the subject from Amanda's mother. "Are you sure the kitten can't hear anything? It seems like she can."

"Yeah." Amanda made a moue of apology. "I'm sorry. We didn't realize it until after we picked her out for you."

"No, no, it's fine." Holly made a motion in the air that meant absolutely nothing, dropped her hand into her lap, and added, "It just seems like she can hear me. Maybe she's extra attentive to visual cues."

"We had her checked at the vet's. Mom wanted to get you a new cat, but Nicole said no. She said Bast was right for you."

Amanda squatted beside her bed and lifted up the coverlet. "I'll show you *my* cat. Frey-frey," she called. "Here, baby."

A chubby orange adult cat emerged, plopping itself down with great dignity and meowing up at Amanda. She bent down and scooped up the enor-mous feline.

"This is Freya," she told Holly. "She's mine."

"She's really enormous." Holly reached out a tentative hand to pet the cat. The cat accepted her attention like a duchess, preening and condescending, and Holly grinned despite herself. She knew a few horses like Miss Freya, proud and uppity but, in their hearts, craving affection and attention.

Amanda fondly stroked her pet. Holly joined in, then paused as the animal stared hard at her, accepting the lavish attention without blinking or moving its head. The intensity of Freya's gaze was eerie.

"I hope you like it here, Holly," Amanda said.

Holly swallowed. "I hope so too."

Freya meowed and settled into Amanda's lap.

FIVE

OAK MOON

(🌙)

Hands to Heaven, feet to Hell
The House of Deveraux casts its spell
Bring the sun out at night
To defeat the maiden's light

To Cahors faithful strong and true
Blessings old we beg anew
And Goddess hear us as we plead
This year kill the Green Man's seed

Seattle, mid-August

It rained in Seattle. Almost constantly.

Holly had heard that one got used to it—
eventually—as long as one packed a trusty umbrella or
threw on a rain poncho before heading out.

But on the fourth day of her stay with her relatives,
she holed up in the attic with a cup of hot tea, listening to the rain, and looking through a treasure chest of
her father's old mementos.

It was an old sea chest; on it were written the initials C.C. In the dusty, musty box were yearbooks, sports awards, and pictures. Lots of pictures. From the looks of them, Dad had grown up happy in Seattle with Marie-Claire and their parents, David and Marianne. He had appeared to be happy—there were lots of pictures of him smiling, doing things, being with his family . . . and then, abruptly, he left the University of Washington and went to UC Berkeley.

Where he met Mom, she thought wistfully.

And that was where his history stopped, at least in the collection of items Marie-Claire had preserved.

"Hey," her aunt said from behind her.

Holly started, feeling a little guilty. She hadn't asked for permission to come up here or to look through her aunt's possessions.

"What're you doing?" her aunt asked pleasantly. Then she cocked her head, studying the picture. "That was taken in his junior year. I was a freshman." She sounded very sad, and then she began to weep. "It's so hard to believe that he's gone." She added under her breath, "And that he didn't say good-bye."

"You . . . you hadn't spoken to him in a . . . a while," Holly managed.

Her aunt squatted on her haunches as she examined a sports trophy—Little League—and reverently placed it on the attic floor.

"No. I don't know what happened. He had a huge fight with our mother. I don't know what about. Then he left. He never contacted us again." She caught her breath as she lifted up a picture. It was Holly's father dressed all in black—jeans, sweater, jacket—and crossing his arm in front of a swimming pool. "I remember this day," she murmured. "That's the day he had the fight. The day he left. My big brother . . ."

She began to cry. She licked her lips and handed Holly the picture. "All this is yours now, honey."

"No, I—" Holly protested, then closed her mouth. Her aunt was right. It should be hers.

A few moments passed. Then her aunt played with the rings on her hands and said, "Things . . . some things are complicated." She reddened and wouldn't look at Holly.

She's talking about her affair, Holly thought with alarm. *No way do I want to go there.*

When Holly didn't respond, Marie-Claire said, "Well, I was looking for you to tell you that the girls want to take you out tonight."

It was Holly's turn to take a breath. *New kids. A new place. I'm going back to San Francisco for school . . . I'm not staying here.*

"I'd rather just stay around the house," Holly said. "I'm not up to . . . that."

"They want to take you. They insist," Marie-Claire said. She smiled fondly.

But at dinner, it was Amanda who insisted; Nicole had "some stuff" to do that included her being allowed to take her mother's car, and she promised her parents she would meet up with Holly and Amanda later.

Uncle Richard drove Amanda and Holly to The Half Caff, a funky-looking coffeehouse on a funky block of Hill Street. He kissed Amanda on the cheek and sweetly told Holly to have a good time, making sure the girls had lots of money.

He added softly, as if he hated saying it, "If you have any problem with your . . . ride home . . . call me."

Our ride home is Nicole, Holly translated. She was a little taken aback by the look father and daughter shared, a gentle, reassuring smile of recognition that there had been problems before, and that there was a distinct possibility that there would be more tonight.

They're the two outcasts, Holly thought, confirming Amanda's earlier description of their family dynamics. *Nicole gets away with her drama queen thing, and Marie-Claire . . . gets away with being unfaithful. And neither one of them cares if the others are hurt by it.*

"Okay, show time," Amanda said. "Put on your game face."

Holly swallowed. "Do I look okay?"

They were dressed nearly identically in T's and jeans, nothing too fancy, although Amanda had on a serious choker of garnets and a matching, very lacy bracelet. Holly wore her dad's old silver ID bracelet and a silver thumb ring and silver hoops, also an anklet of little bells that Tina had given her one Christmas.

The coffeehouse was large by San Francisco standards, and dominated by an enormous second-floor balcony that jutted over the main floor. It was decorated with a frieze of Greek warriors with spears, reminding Holly of the figures on the Palace of Fine Arts in San Francisco. All the tables were stone columns of varying dimensions topped with pieces of glass cut to fit. There were stone statues everywhere—busts of stern-lipped men, a sad-eyed Madonna, and tons of angels. Ivy trailed down the walls, which were painted to look like a vast countryside at twilight. The place was a cross between the ruins of a Greek villa and a Victorian graveyard.

"This is great," Holly enthused.

Amanda looked very pleased and said, "Yay, table," as she pointed to a two-seater near the frothing espresso machine. In her element, she led the way.

Holly glanced around at all the unfamiliar faces. There were the usual Goths but a lot of other groups, too. The café was raucous, noise bouncing off all the hard surfaces—the floor was cement painted to look like black and white marble. The atmosphere was like a school gym at the end of a pep rally, not the arty, study-heavy quiet she was used to.

The two cousins settled into their chairs and Holly picked up a hand-lettered menu. She glanced at the coffee selections, then began reading the extensive descriptions of the chai offerings.

"Hey, hi, Mani-*chan*," said a guy who was dragging a chair through the maze of tables and people. "About time you showed."

He was of medium build, with warm skin tones, crescent-shaped eyes, and hair that had been bleached and re-dyed light blond. It looked good on him, as did his earring and a Chinese character tattoo on his forearm.

"Tommy," Amanda said warmly. She dimpled at Holly. "This is my bestest best friend in the world, Tommy Nagai." She gestured to Holly. "My cousin."

"Hot," he said appreciatively.

"Leave her alone," Amanda ordered. "The rules of summer are almost over and this is her chance to score some social points. In a few weeks . . . back to

our correct hierarchy and she'll be with us by default."
To Holly, she explained, "I can't understand it. He's
nerdy, with nerdy pursuits, and yet not totally
scorned."

"That is true," he said, making a half-bow. "I am
nerdy in the extreme, and yet tolerated by the 'cool'"—
he made air quotes—"people. I suspect it's because I
display the proper deference, and always remember
my rank and station."

"And serial number," Amanda threw in, grinning.
"So, if you want to snag someone more upscale," she
said to Holly, "don't have too much to do with Tommy.
Because 'tolerated' is the operant word."

"What about *you*?" Tommy shot back, leaning back
on his chair and playfully plucking Holly's menu
from her hands. "She's living at your house, for God's
sake. Talk about social suicide. I'll have a chai latte
tonight."

"She can't help that," Amanda said reasonably.
"Besides, I have the Nicole advantage." Her smile was
laced with bitterness as she explained. "My mom won't
let Nicole go to any parties I'm not invited to. So"—she
gave an airy wave—"my semipopularity is purchased,
while Tommy comes by his more honestly."

"Plus, we both like *anime*," Tommy added.

Holly was intrigued by the difference in Amanda's

behavior, from her speech to the way she carried herself, and realized that her cousin was self-assured and relaxed around Tommy Nagai. *He doesn't threaten her because she doesn't think of him as boyfriend material,* she realized. *And yet, ironically, they'd make a great couple.*

"Anyway," Tommy said affably. "Let your cousin judge for herself. She may love what she sees." He flashed his white teeth at Holly and fluttered his lashes, but she could see that he liked Amanda beyond the "bestest best friend" role Amanda had given him. And Holly liked him at once for that.

"Um, I'm going back to San Francisco for my senior year," Holly told him. "I'm just here to visit for a while."

"Alas," Tommy said, and he sounded truly sorry. "Let's drown our sorrows in white chocolate-dipped biscotti." He handed her back her menu. "And I would like you to pay for me, Mani-chan, because the summer job is over and—"

Amanda cut him off, muttering, "Oh, no."

Holly followed Amanda's line of vision. From a table crammed with very stylish people, dressed-like-a-tart Nicole rose slowly like a rock star about to open her act. Neither Holly nor Amanda had realized she was in the house. Then two guys walked in through the front door, which was painted purple and black, like a bruise. Both of them were dressed all in black, with very dark hair, dark eyebrows, and sharply chiseled faces, but only one of them took Holly's breath away.

Tommy sighed as if he were used to this routine. In an absurdly polite tone of voice, he asked Holly, "Want something to go with your latte and biscotti? Like a friggin' barf bag?"

Holly flushed—he had caught her checking out another guy, which was rude when a guy was already in one's presence—and replied, "How much are the barf bags? Our coffeehouse back home doesn't carry them."

Tommy clearly appreciated her retort and said, "Doesn't matter. Only the best for out-of-towners. You're the guest."

"Just biscotti and the drinks," Amanda suggested. Holly nodded.

"Okay. But be careful—*she* likes to pick off all the white chocolate and then hand the disgusting remains back to you," Tommy said accusingly.

He frowned at Amanda, but her focus had also shifted elsewhere . . . back on the sexy guy, who was crossing the room and heading straight for their table.

He was looking directly at Holly, lion—no, sleek black jaguar—slinking toward his prey, every muscle tensed as if he were going to pounce on her.

"I'll decamp. Go put in our order, because in this section of the jungle, the waitress will never show," Tommy said lightly, but it was obvious he was not loving the moment.

"Hey," the guy said. He was looking right at Holly.

Holly glanced at Amanda, who tipped her chin and started picking at her fingernails, murmuring, "Hi, Jer." Her bravado and cheeriness had evaporated on the spot. She raised her head and cleared her throat. "Holly, this is Jeraud-Luc Deveraux. Holly's my cousin."

Holly looked back at Jer, taking in how dark his eyes were, then thinking, *No, they're green, with flecks of brown in them. They're so . . . extraordinary. . . .*

The room canted, as if all the tables and chairs and posters for local bands, and flyers for art exhibits tacked on bulletin boards, and the bubbling copper espresso machine and the baristas and the kids in black and the kids in letterman's jackets should all go sliding down to the corner farthest away from her and this one guy. Holly knew that she had met him before; she didn't know where, she didn't know when, but Jer Deveraux was no stranger to her.

"Bonsoir, ma dame," he said in French, the first word split into two deliberate words, turning the

phrase into an elegant greeting, *Good evening, my lady.*

Holly unhesitatingly answered back, not understanding why the words came so easily and naturally, *"Bonsoir, mon seigneur."*

"Yo, Jer." Tommy stood to one side of the table. He snapped at Holly and Amanda, "They're out of the biscotti. Maybe I can scare up some frog legs or snails, though, since it's French night at The Caff and I totally forgot my dictionary."

"Holly?" Amanda asked.

But Holly couldn't pull herself out of her daze. She couldn't stop staring at Jer.

Jeraud-Luc Deveraux.

That's not his name, she thought. *His name is . . .*
It's . . .

"Jean," Isabeau sobbed, reaching her arms out to her lady mother. The two were dressed in witches' regalia—heavy black gowns, hair entwined with veils and dead lilies and herbs. "Please, *ma mère,* spare him."

The room was furnished with two stools; the stone altar of the Goddess, dragged to the turret room by two serfs, who were then slain; and a brazier for warmth and light. The fire in the brass brazier was hot and full; shadows flickered on the grimy stone and on the fur of Diable, the dog Isabeau had left behind when she went to Castle Deveraux. The cur now lolled contentedly at her side as she knelt in the filthy rushes and clasped her mother around the knees, sobbing against the rich fabric of her gown.

"*S'il vous plaît, ma mère,*" she begged. "If you ever loved me, please, please spare him."

Her mother, the Queen Regnant of Le Circle des Cahors, sat stiff-lipped and cool, unmoved by her daughter's entreaties. With each new display of tenderness toward their traditional enemy, her upper lip curled, until she herself looked like a demoness. As she gestured to the dead lamb on the altar, the little creature sacrificed so that she could read Isabeau's fortunes in its entrails, she said harshly, "*They* will not spare *you.*"

They had secreted themselves in the highest turret room of Castle Cahors. The moon was fecund, her moisture sticky and warm and ripe for begetting spells and children and curses. Busy autumn air whistled through the round, stone enclosure, crackling with burnished leaves and the smell of apples. While Deveraux warlocks worshiped the God in dank dungeons, the witches of the Cahors sought out the tall places, where they could reach their arms toward the Blessed Lady Moon.

"They will spare me if I have a child."

Catherine's fingertips were bloody. She had

already inscribed a pentagram on Isabeau's forehead, and now she pressed her thumbprint into the center, where the Jews were said to believe the third eye, which belonged to God, gazed inwardly at one's sins.

She said steadily, and with all the certainty of a highborn witch, and one who knows her Art, "You will not bear a Deveraux devil."

"You must not force me to be barren any longer!" Isabeau shouted. She grabbed at her hair, tearing off her veil and throwing it to the floor. Then she crashed down to her elbows, covering her eyes with her hands, and wept. Her long, black hair streamed over her back and tumbled over the rushes.

"You knew our plan. You agreed to it." Her mother's voice was as cold as the stones beneath Isabeau's empty womb.

"But now I . . ." *love him,* she almost said, but her mother would sooner strangle her only daughter than hear her declare her love for a Deveraux. "Now I see qualities," she said feebly, and fell to silence at her mother's expression of contempt and outrage.

"You have failed," Catherine said. "You were sent to learn the secret of the Black Fire. But they will never share it with you," her mother stated, tapping her bloody fingertips on the sleeve of Isabeau's shift for emphasis.

"You must realize that we have been wordlessly

bartering with them, a son for the secret. They have refused. Now they plan to rid Jean of you so that he may sow sons in another's womb." She sneered at her daughter. "There is no place for warmth or softness in our dealings, girl. You should have learned that at my knee."

"It's been a trap from the beginning," Isabeau said bitterly. "You sent me there knowing full well everything that was going to happen. The moment Jean and I were bound together, wrist to wrist, was the moment I signed his death warrant."

"You knew that." Her mother sat up very tall, her back straight, her carriage regal. "You knew we planned to massacre them all if they didn't share the secret. You will return to us in a marriageable state, without Deveraux issue to bind you to them."

Isabeau sat up, and her mother smiled a little. "Ah, *Maman,* I did not mean to fall in love with him. . . . I am a Cahors, and always will be. But . . . but I . . . he is my husband now." She wiped her eyes and rubbed her hands on her shift. Then she got to her feet and walked to the brazier, warming her cold, cold hands over its natural, yellow flames.

"He has bewitched you," Catherine said, tapping her right forefinger against her left palm for emphasis. "Work your way back through the spell, child. He is a Deveraux, and he must die with all the rest."

Before Isabeau could protest, she went on. "Think, girl. We cannot let the blood heir of our greatest enemy survive the massacre of his entire family! He will curse us all, and his spirit will not rest until every Cahors, everywhere, is dead. He will hunt down our descendants and their descendants, and it will be on *your* head, yes, and mine, if we falter now."

Her mother reached down and picked up Isabeau's headpiece. She held it out to her daughter, who took it.

"Now, tell me about the entrances and exits on the castle grounds," her mother instructed her. "Leave nothing out. Do not think to trick me in order to spare him."

Isabeau wiped her nose. Her hands trembled. She said, "The—the north wall is less fortified than the others. Because it overlooks the sheerest drop." She swayed.

"Sit."

Catherine walked to the turret door and threw it open. Berenice, a lady in waiting from Toulouse, was caught listening at the door. She gasped and dropped into a deep curtsy.

"Wine," was all Catherine said. But after the chit went away, she turned to her daughter and said, "You would not want me to spare *her*, would you?"

Slowly Isabeau shook her head. Her gaze was steely. Recently a servant of the Cahors had denounced the family to the bishop, claiming they had sacrificed the newborn babe of the miller's wife to their Goddess. The traitor had been a young laundress who had been cast aside for another. Her father had insisted that the young nobleman who had kept company with her pay for having lowered her marriage value. But the bishop's thinking had run with that of the nobleman's family: the lower classes did not need to marry; it was a luxury for them, and if the girl had thrown away her chances, then it was the will of God.

But the damage of her spiteful gossip was done, and throughout the nearby city of Toulouse, the rumor spread that the Cahors were sacrificing babies.

After a time, the bishop had come to visit Catherine, and left with many boxes of gold coins to continue the Lord's work. He assured the nervous townsfolk that there were no witches, sorcerers, or warlocks to be found anywhere near such God-fearing Christian folk as they.

Still, the talk grew more heated, and both the Deveraux and the Cahors had reason to worry—the Cahors more so, because the foolish Deveraux conducted their magical lives with contempt for discretion and subtlety.

"Berenice shall be dead by morning," Catherine said.

Isabeau lifted the sacrificial knife from beside the slaughtered sheep. It had been forged in Roman times, and passed down from mother to daughter since then.

"I'll do it myself," Isabeau announced.

Her mother smiled and murmured a blessing on her daughter. Then she said, much more kindly, "You will survive this, Isabeau. It's difficult, I know. But when he's dead, his charms will lift, and you'll understand how basely he used you."

Isabeau sighed heavily. He had bewitched her, yes; but how could she tell her mother of the fierce magics they had created together, the unbelievable power that was theirs when husband and wife worked as one to bring forth the occult forces of darkness and shadow?

She had not known such power could exist. And now, to willfully put a stop to it? None lived who were as magically strong as she and Jean de Deveraux—not Jean, his father, nor even her lady mother, the great witch Catherine, whose name was already revered throughout Coventry. Witches made pilgrimages to their castle to meet the *grande dame*.

Until she had been bound to Jean Deveraux, Isabeau's only hope in life was to carry on her lineage with pride. She was not sure how to tell her mother that she, Isabeau, had already surpassed her. She was but sixteen, and her mother, almost thirty, and as the wife of Jean, she was the strongest witch in known Coventry.

As she bowed her head in obeisance to her mother, she thought, *I'll agree to all her plans, but in the end, I'll use our magic to save Jean. We'll run away together, and found a new coven, far away from these two warring families. We'll make a new House.*

Buoyed by that thought, she slid the knife into her leather pouch, kissed her mother's outstretched hand, and murmured, *"Bonsoir, ma mère."*

Her mother leaned forward and kissed Isabeau's forehead. She caressed the bloody dot on Isabeau's forehead, then kissed it as well.

"You're a wonderful daughter. I couldn't have hoped for better," she declared.

Her eyes shone with pride. Isabeau kept her own fear and shame out of her gaze, smiling back with ease. She was a Cahors, and a Cahors could swear passionate fealty with one hand while carving out one's vitals with another.

"We will set the massacre for Mead Moon," Catherine announced. "I will prepare those who need to know."

"They should be few," Isabeau cautioned. She touched her leather pouch for emphasis. "Else, it will be all over Toulouse."

"Agreed. Let us swear a blood oath to its success," her mother added, rising from her stool.

She swept toward the altar. Isabeau swallowed hard. It was said that to forswear a blood oath condemned one to walk the earth until it was made right; if she promised to kill her husband and then did not, she could become a restless spirit plagued to walk the earth until he was dead by her hand . . . in this world or the next.

Then I will so walk, she told herself. *Forever, if need be; for I shall never kill him.*

Together, mother and daughter laid their hands over the bloody, still heart of the lambkin. Catherine closed her eyes and uttered a sacred, solemn voice in Latin, Isabeau repeating it at the end of each line.

"Our pact is sealed," Catherine said at the end.

"Thanks be to the Goddess," Isabeau replied, near tears again.

They kissed again, cheek to cheek, and then Isabeau left the comfort of flame, sacrifice, moon, and mother to kill the overly curious Berenice.

"Jean," Holly murmured, as she came out of her daze or her vision or whatever it was.

Jer Deveraux was staring at her openmouthed. He blinked and whispered, *"Ma Isabeau?"*

And then it was as if the crowds swallowed his

brother and him up; they seemed to recede from view as Tommy came back to the table with a big tray filled with steaming cups and three enormous cinnamon rolls.

"You okay?" Amanda asked Holly, peering at her. "What was *that* all about?" She touched Holly's forehead. "Are you sick?"

"Those are Michael's sons," Holly said slowly. "Michael Deveraux."

"The wild bunch," Tommy said derisively. "The hell twins."

"Jer is nice," Amanda said. She looked at Holly again, and there was no missing the hurt in her expression. Jer Deveraux hadn't said two words to her.

"I . . . I'm not feeling well," she said to Amanda. "I'm sorry, but do you mind if we go home?"

Then she saw Nicole sail out the front door with Jer's brother, who was taller than he but less handsome. In fact, he looked kind of brutal and mean.

Amanda huffed and got her cell phone out of her purse. Then she caught herself and said, very kindly, "I'm not mad at you, Holly. It's just . . . she's not supposed to see him. And she was supposed to hook up with us. And, as usual, she does what she wants and nothing will happen to her."

But her eyes were brimming with tears as she completed the call.

Tommy frowned at Holly and said, "Did Jer put a hex on you or something? The Deveraux are warlocks, you know." He wagged his brows. "They're into sacrificing virgins. So, Nicole's safe."

"Don't be dumb, Tommy," Amanda snapped, wiping her face. Then her voice rose shrilly as she said into the phone, "Daddy? Ride? Holly's sick."

She closed the phone and said, "Drink some tea, Holly. You'll feel better."

Holly did as Amanda told her. She was dizzy and hot and sick to her stomach.

Maybe he *did* put a hex on me, she thought. *Because that was very, very, very weird.*

She scanned the room for Jer Deveraux, but he was nowhere to be found.

SIX

WOLF MOON

☾

Feed us now as hunger grows
Let us feast upon our foes
We shall dine upon their eyes
Hearts and brains, ribs and thighs

Our Lady listen to our cry
We throw our heads back to the sky
Bind our family heart and soul
Comfort us and make us whole

As usual, the Deveraux brothers were fighting. Eli had driven their Mustang convertible to The Half Caff, then disappeared with Nicole Cathers. Jer had had to find another way home.

Wish it had been with Nicole's cousin from San Francisco. Wow. What was that all about?

Coming down from his room, where he'd lain thinking about Holly Cathers, he'd discovered his brother alone in the living room. The fight had begun, and Jer was just warming up.

"You wipe," he snapped at Eli. "Why do you even bother with Nicole anyway? She's shallow."

"Shallow?" Eli cracked up. "Who are you, Emily Dickinson? She's *hot*." Eli was putting the finishing touches on a black-handled athame. He stopped, admiring his work, and laid the razor-sharp knife on the coffee table. He cracked his knuckles. "She wants to move in together after they graduate."

"You must have put a spell on her. That's the only way she'd want you," Jer said derisively.

Unruffled, Eli tested the blade on a piece of thick bark coated with mugwort, the witch's favorite herb.

"Hey, man, it's the Art or my six-pack abs. Some guys lift weights and some guys strangle pigeons. And some do both." He chuckled. "And I say, whatever keeps that hottie hoppin' is fine with me."

Lighting a candle, he held the blade over the flame, allowing the metal to be scorched. Then he flipped open a smaller version of their family Book of Shadows, looked down to recite the Spell of Dedication, then glanced back up at Jer.

"Anyway, thanks for entertaining the leftovers. Amanda's got the hots for you, you know. And you must've done something to that cousin. Haley or Kylie or whatever. Went catatonic on you, dude."

"Whatever." He didn't want to discuss Holly

Cathers with his smarmy brother.

"Of course, she didn't get to hang with *me* yet."

Jer examined his brother's blade. No matter what else Eli was, he was a careful craftsman who did awesome work. "Then there is a God."

"However, he doesn't happen to be the same God we worship." Eli snatched the knife back from his brother and swung it in a dramatic arc. The blade glowed with the magical green associated with their coven Tradition, which had reached its full bloom in medieval France. Looking pleased, he touched the tip with his finger and nodded approvingly as a dot of blood appeared. He sucked on it as he chuckled at Jer, apparently finding him very amusing.

Jer didn't react. His brother was a jerk, always had been, no doubt always would be.

"You want to help dedicate this?" Eli asked. "I'm just gonna do a quickie on it now. I'll do the whole deal later, with Dad and you in Ritual."

Jer shook his head with disgust. "You don't dedicate a new athame in your living room with the magical equivalent of Cliff's Notes. It totally lacks class."

"I say again, baby bro, whatever works." He held the knife in both hands and began mumbling rapid-fire medieval Latin at it.

Shaking his head, Jer walked away from the blasphemer and headed for the weight room. He flexed his arms and shoulders, warming them up in preparation for serious lifting. All the Deveraux men worked out; they stayed in good shape, ate well, and slept heavily. Michael had instilled lifelong habits in his sons; practicing the Art could drain a man's vitality, unless he was careful. Part of being a good warlock was tending to the vessel the God had given you.

He started to lie down on the bench, when he heard his father chanting in the dark, hidden chamber in the rotten heart of their house. By the rhythm of the litany, he knew that his father was summoning a spirit. That was a common enough occurrence in the Deveraux household.

Some guys watch football, we raise up the dead.

He scooted beneath the weight rack and gripped the bar.

His father's voice grew louder. The pitch grew higher, the rhythm staccato and punctuated with shouts. Intrigued, Jer half-listened.

Dad's arguing with someone.

Whoever it was answered back, also extremely pissed off. Jer cocked his head. He had never heard his father argue with a spirit before. That wasn't the way it worked. Mortals summoned spirits and the spirits did as they were bidden, more often than not without ever saying a word.

There was a lilt to the language he could almost place.

It's French, he realized. *Maybe it's a human man. Some guy who found out my father's been seeing his wife— that narrows it down to half of Seattle—and followed him down there. . . .*

The voices rose; the argument was growing heated. Jer closed his eyes and uttered a spell to increase the power of his hearing just as Eli swung into the weight room with his knife at his side. There was a fresh bandage over his wrist.

At least my brother had the respect to spill his blood to the God on his new blade, he thought.

"Hey, dork, what's going on?" Eli asked. "Who's Dad with?"

"I thought he was yelling at you," Jer replied evenly.

Eli snorted. "Yeah, right. Dad never yells at me."

"Then I don't know. Maybe he's giving some witch a bid on a new Bed of Aphrodite."

There was a witch in Nairobi who had hired their father to design a new villa for her, including a chamber designed to engender lust in her male companion. But something had gone wrong; the handsome, deep black sorcerer she had lived with for years had informed her that he had fallen in love with another . . . a man . . . and he never slept in her brand-new Bed of Aphrodite.

Shrugging, Jer picked up the barbell and raised it, straightening his elbows. He started pumping iron.

"Hell with you," Eli said reasonably, and left the weight room.

Jer's older brother went into the kitchen. That seemed like an odd place to go if Eli wanted to find out what their father was doing; it was located farther away from the Chamber of Spells than even the weight room.

Curious, Jer listened for a moment, but could hear nothing but normal kitchen noises—the clink of a plate, the hum of the microwave. The yelling downstairs had stopped. Quietly, he put the barbell down and rose from the bench. His chest sweaty beneath his T-shirt, he felt a sudden chill as he moved down the same hallway, also heading for the kitchen. With a deftness born of habit, he avoided all the creaking floorboards. He had long ago decided that his father, who was a perfectionist as well as an architect with connections in the building trade all over town, had intentionally left those boards loose so that he would be alerted to the comings and goings of his sons by the telltale sounds.

When he reached the threshold to the kitchen, he

stopped just outside the line of sight, then peered around the doorway in search of Eli. The pantry door was open, and Eli stood just inside it. His back was to Jer. He was muttering an incantation in Latin, a standard spell for invoking the power of seeing something at a distance.

He's got some kind of magic mirror and he's spying on Dad with it, Jer realized. *Clever guy.*

There was a scraping sound in the pantry—brick on brick—and then Eli started to come back out of the pantry. Jer dodged away from the threshold and continued down the hall toward the downstairs guest bathroom. He pushed against the door hinges to keep them from squealing, then went inside and pulled the door closed.

Eli moved on, tramping over the loose floorboards.

His brother checked the weight room for him, then began humming to himself and headed right. The door to the dark chamber was there; both the boys had been taught since infancy that they could never, ever go down there without express permission. They had had one chance each as tiny boys to learn that without an advance invitation, they would be in very, very big trouble. Eli hadn't listened, just plowed ahead and tried it more than once. Only their mother's intervention had saved him from a punishment so dire that it had proved the last straw for her: She'd left less than a week later.

"I refuse to live like this, nor to allow my children to live like this," she had said. Even though he'd been no older than three, Jer still remembered how she'd stood there with her arms around her sons.

But somewhere along her path to freedom from Jer's father, those arms had loosened. She had left in the night without warning, leaving both her boys behind. Jer remembered his father's rage, and all the lightning and thunder, and the rain. There had been so much rain. Buckets and torrents and floods; he remembered sitting in the dark black chamber with his father, whose voice was low, Michael murmuring, "Their God hated them so that He tried to wipe them out with a flood. Remember, my boys, that that is not our god. Our God looks after us always." And then he had added, so softly that Jer wasn't sure at first that he had heard it, "Unlike your mother."

Eli had hated her from then on. The next time Jer had mentioned her, Eli had beaten him to a bloody pulp; if their father hadn't stopped his older son, he might have killed his younger brother.

Jer liked to think that Eli's evilness had started then, out of the rage he felt at being abandoned. That would explain his cruelty.

And my own.

There were times when being a Deveraux was more than Jer could feel, or explain. There was something in the Deveraux blood, bone-deep and simmering, that if Jer didn't keep watch over it, bubbled up and boiled over. The need to hurt appalled him. The need to dominate made him break into a sweat and keep himself apart. He had only his close friends Eddie and Kialish, who, with their interest in shamanism, at least had some protection from him. Kari courted the danger in him; maybe that was why he was pulling away from her so hard these days.

In a crowd, Jer was a loner. And he was aware enough to know that that in itself made him attractive to girls. They liked a mystery. They liked to break the shell of a guy who had something to protect them from.

Amanda Cathers was a girl like that. Nicole might like to play the bad girl, dress sexy, and hang with his scary brother, but Amanda wanted to save Jer from himself. He didn't know which was sadder: that she imagined that she could, or that he knew that she couldn't.

We Deveraux are cursed. And how to explain that to some sweet, shy girl like Amanda, who would rather read about mystical priestesses and unicorns than see the truth?

Jer moved silently down the hall, bringing his mind back to the task at hand. He, his brother, and his father had all placed wards around the star chamber, magical spells that caused the minds of potential trespassers to wander, so that they forgot to investigate further the halls and stairs that led to places best left unexplored. Now those wards were acting against Jer himself as he drew closer to the shadowed realms of Deveraux conjuring and deathdealing.

He was sure that Eli and Michael had killed human beings in their quest for Dark Magics. He couldn't prove it, but he often asked himself why, if he believed such a thing, he stayed with them in the house in Lower Queen Anne.

Am I a coward, or am I waiting for a chance to strike, and stop them once and for all?

It was a question he had often asked himself. So far, he had no answer.

Until I can answer it, I have to stay here. And after . . . who knows?

Maybe I'll go somewhere completely unexpected.

Maybe I'll even find my mother.

Jer walked to the door that led to the chamber, or

rather to the staircase that led down to it. The door blended in perfectly with the hall, the only indication of its presence a subtle swirl in the wallpaper. He pressed it and the door fwoomed open like an airlock in a science fiction movie. He crept down two stairs in the pitch-black corridor, and listened.

He could hear murmuring, but only that. Two voices, one raised in anger. *Dad.* One answering. *Eli.*

Frustrated, he kept listening. If he moved one step more, the wards that protected the chamber would alert his family to his presence. Then he remembered his brother's incantation in the pantry.

He climbed the two steps backward, then pulled the door shut and walked back along the hallway.

I wonder if any other family spends their nights together like this, he thought bitterly. *Spying on one another, invoking demons, lifting weights. . . .*

He glided into the kitchen and from there, the pantry. Feeling along the walls, he whispered a Spell of Seeing, searching for the hidden artifact his brother had employed. There was no result. *He's used a ward to protect it,* Jer realized. He recalled a litany from one of the Books of Shadows his father had used to instruct them in the Art: *"Things that are Hidden are Things worth Discovering."*

He tried a different Spell of Seeing. When that

failed as well, he began to rap against the brickwork, looking for a hollow spot that could contain a cache place.

Finally his knuckles tapped against a brick on his right that didn't echo back in precisely the same way as the others. *Yes,* he thought, and gripped his fingertips around it. Gingerly he eased the loose brick out. It slid easily, which told him that it had been moved many times.

My brother's probably been spying on both *Dad and me.*

Cautiously transferring the bogus brick to his left hand, he bent down to see inside the rectangular space left bare by its absence. The light was not good, but he could detect a small, round object lying inside the area.

He was just about to take hold of it when footsteps and voices alerted him to the fact that his father and brother had left the chamber and were heading for the kitchen.

Moving fast, he replaced the brick. Then he smoothed back his hair and took a breath, grabbed a box of cereal, and started to come out of the pantry.

His brother said, "You think she's the one."

"I had a sense of it," Michael replied. "Meanwhile, we have Sir William to worry about."

Jer wrinkled his forehead as he listened carefully. Sir William Moore was the Master of the Supreme

Coven of the Art, the head coven to which the Deveraux Coven owed allegiance. It was headquartered in London, and Jer had no idea how many Dark Covens offered their loyalty to the Supreme Coven. He did know that Sir William was afraid of the power of the Deveraux, and had recently demanded that they prove their loyalty.

What Sir William didn't know was that in secret, Michael had pledged the sorcery of the Deveraux to Sir William's son, James. James had long plotted to overthrow his father. Michael regarded James as someone who could be more easily controlled than Sir William. Since Michael believed that the title of Master of the Supreme Coven belonged by right and tradition to the House of Deveraux, he had offered to back James if James tried to topple his father from the throne of the Master. Once the foolish young man was in power, Michael would stand behind that throne and arrange the situation to his own liking . . . no doubt by murdering James at the first opportunity, and raising either himself or Eli to the exalted position of Master.

Once a Deveraux led the Coven, the forces of light would be extinguished, one by one by one, until only the Black Arts tipped the scales of Fate, in this and other worlds.

Jeraud Deveraux was determined never to let that happen.

Even if I have to betray my own flesh and blood someday.

"We might have to kill her," his father was saying.

Jer started, furious at himself for losing his focus. *Who? Who are they talking about?*

Whoever she was, there was no way he would ever let his father and brother spill her blood. Even if it meant their own deaths, he would not knowingly permit them to kill an innocent.

What about the guilty, Jer? asked a little voice inside him. He knew it was his conscience, but it was cast in the voice of his Overlord, Sir William. *Proud warlock, you scorn your Tradition, yet still seek the privileges of your blood. If you discern good and evil, it is because they exist, and because you have the power to use them as you will.*

But once you choose to use evil—no matter the reason— you are Coven-bound . . . forever . . . and your soul belongs to us.

"We could always make it look like a car accident," his father drawled. "Like that other one we did."

"That was gross," Eli replied.

"But it did the job. He's dead, isn't it?"

Jer's heart literally skipped a beat. Rival Seattle architect Zane Thornwood had recently died in a car accident. Both he and Jer's father had bid on the same project in Pioneer Square. With his death, the contract had gone to Michael Deveraux.

His eyes welled and he felt sick down to the core of his base, warlock soul. He was afraid he might throw up.

So now I know it's true, he thought. *My brother, my father . . . they're murderers.*

The voice said, *You've known for years, you hypocrite. You just didn't want to do anything about it.*

Eli said, "True. But accidents like that are pretty easy to detect. We almost got caught last time."

"Ah, but we Deveraux learn from our mistakes. That's what separates the sheep from the wolves, Eli. I'm thinking we could take advantage of the wet streets. . . . It's so rainy in Seattle, and if you go too fast, you'll hydroplane. We could do that from a good distance."

"Maybe even from as far away as San Francisco," Eli said archly. "Where we kept a grieving lady company?"

"I can't keep anything from you." Michael sounded proud, also a little wary. "Keep an eye on her. We'll decide what to do by next moon."

Jer swayed, then realized he didn't have the luxury of reacting to the horror of what he had learned—confirmed—this night. Deeply ashamed of his former passivity, he sent out a silent message to his family's potential victim.

The time had come for him to take a stand against his own family.

Run, he ordered, *to me. By the power of the God, come into my influence and be bound to me. Find me. If my father wants you dead, you're dead already.*

And I'm the only one in Seattle who can protect you from him.

It was midnight. Holly and Amanda had gotten home hours ago. But Nicole was still out . . . with Eli Deveraux, Jer's brother.

Fuming at being dumped by her sister, Amanda talked about Eli as Holly lay on her bed, Freya curled up beside her. Bast was nowhere to be found.

"I wish he'd get put in jail for good or something."

Her face was getting red and she chewed on her left thumbnail before she apparently realized what she was doing and dropped her hand into her lap.

"Listen, she's not supposed to see him, but it's awkward, you know, with my parents being friends with his dad and all. He's done so much work on our house. His dad, I mean. He's an architect."

Amanda didn't know that Eli's father had been in San Francisco with her mother. Holly felt just sick for

Uncle Richard—and for the girls, if they should find out. More than one of her friends' families had been broken up by an affair. But she covered her reaction with a fake cough and said, "Okay."

"Eli will probably eventually come on to you, just to freak you out," Amanda continued. "Just totally ignore him. It's what I do." She joined Holly in petting Freya, and her features softened. "Jer's different. I swear, sometimes I think he was adopted." Her laugh was forced, and her face grew even redder. They spent a few awkward moments petting the cat. Holly was about to drop.

"I have to go to bed," Holly said. "I'm really tired, Amanda." She said, "I swear, I was delirious or something back at The Half Caff."

"I know. You're sick." She touched Holly's forehead, kind and honestly concerned. "Holly . . . ," she began, and Holly wondered if she was going to broach the subject of Jer Deveraux and spoken-for territory.

With a sigh, Amanda made some kind of decision. She said, "I'm glad you're here. Really glad." She gave her a pained smile. "It's fun to have someone to hang out with."

"I'm sorry I won't be staying much longer," Holly reminded her gently. *So you can still try to snag Jer,* she tried to tell her with her words. *I pose no permanent threat.*

"I'm sorry, too," Amanda said.

Freya the cat lifted her head and gazed steadily at Amanda. Then she swiveled her head at Holly, and put her head back down on Amanda's bedspread.

"Well . . . good night." Holly got off the bed and stood, yawning.

"Good night. Sleep tight," Amanda said in a slightly singsong way, as if she was determined not to let the Jer Affair get her down.

As Holly got ready for bed, she replayed the scene in the coffeehouse over and over again. She was fascinated. Embarrassed, yeah. *In fact, I could just about sink through the floor.* But it was so weird how mutual it was . . . the way they had both been drawn to each other . . . *But hey, hormones. He is a hottie.* And the French they had spoken to each other . . . *which I've studied, so no weird there. And he has a French name, so they probably speak a little in his family. So no weird there, either.*

But my vision . . . I saw him, and me, in another time. Only it wasn't us. . . .

Lack of sleep, she told herself. *So get some. You're all stressed out. You knew you weren't ready to face the world. So do some deep breathing, meditating, like Daddy showed you.*

With a pang at the memory of her father, she pictured a beautiful lake, and herself in a rowboat . . . and

Jer, taking up the oars while she sat in the bow. They were rowing somewhere . . . *to Avalon . . . like in Amanda's book she's reading . . . the mists . . . they're parting. . . .*

And we're doing magic, to save the world.

She drifted along, beginning to drowse. Settling in, she cuddled her cat and murmured, "He's amazing. If he liked me . . ." Too shy to complete the thought, she closed her eyes.

The cat's breath sighed against Holly's cheek. The tip of Bast's pink tongue scraped her face. Or the dream of a kiss.

Jeraud Deveraux . . .

The floor creaked; she was dimly aware of the sound. This house, this big, noisy house; it held secrets.

If he liked me . . .

Then he was in bed with her, beside her, and she smiled to herself. The dream caressed her like a tender lover, and she thought, *I've never really had a boyfriend. Not one I would . . . not someone special . . .*

Then hands, and lips . . .

And suddenly it was Michael Deveraux straddling her, his hands around her throat. His dark eyes glared at her with a killing look; his mouth was drawn back in a rictus of hatred, madness, and cruelty. His hair was tousled; his lips were swollen as if with kisses.

And he was choking the life out of her.

She could feel his hands around her neck; the weight of his body. She smelled wine on him, and perfume.

He's really here. Oh, my God, this is really happening! He's trying to kill me!

In a blind panic, Holly tried to claw him. Flailing with her arms, her legs, even her body, she couldn't breathe. She couldn't, and she couldn't; it was as if she were under the river drowning again, and then she sucked in air and expelled it forcefully, screaming.

In real time her cat howled, snarled, hissed. Holly's eyes flew open.

Bast jumped off the bed.

Holly was alone.

"Amanda!" she cried hoarsely, her throat raw from the dream strangle. Holly's dry mouth worked, but no more sound came out. With shaking hands, she checked her throat.

Against the window, a large black bird flapped its wings, as if it were hovering in the black night; and then it flew out of sight.

A dream, she told herself, taking in huge gasps of air. *It was just a weird dream, everything all mixed up in it because of Michael being with my aunt and what happened with Jer at The Half Caff. Just stress, finding a way out of me . . .*

She lay back down, not totally convinced. Her heart was thundering. Then Bast nestled against her side and purred. Holly pet the cat, her own eyes wide open, trying very hard to process what had just happened.

She became aware of a new smell in the room, something feral and dirty. There was a tang of blood in the dark air.

Muzzily, Holly flicked on the lamp, blinking in the yellow light.

Then a fresh cry tore out of her throat.

On the floor beside the bed lay a huge dead rat. It was a deep, shiny black; blood still trickled from a gash in its side.

"Oh, my God," she said, gasping.

Purring more loudly, Bast kneaded Holly's thigh and gazed up at her as if to say, *And I'd kill a thousand more for you.*

Just say the word.

SEVEN

STORM MOON

Winter storms fiercely blow
Bury in ice our every foe
Give Deveraux strength for the days ahead
Lean and strong and freshly bled

Goddess come and fill our dreams
In sleeping nothing is as seems
Show Witch the path you'd have us take
Grant us Sight for Cahorses' sake

Jer, Eddie, and Kialish took Kialish's Saturn to the woody inlet where his father lived alone. Kialish's mother had died when he was very little; perhaps that's what had created the bond between him and Jer, that they both had lost their mothers at a very early age. As always, Eddie accompanied Kialish; they had been lovers for three years.

They were the best friends Jer could have wished for.

Kialish's father was named Dan; he had grown up in

a time when the Native American tribes of the Pacific Northwest worked hard at "becoming Americans." Assimilation had been the name of their game, and to hell with cultural diversity. Not that anyone had known what cultural diversity was back then. There was being Caucasian, and then there was wanting to be Caucasian.

Dan lived in a beautiful wooden cabin he and other members of his clan—the Raven Clan—had built by hand. The small but clean two-bedroom house was warmed by a cast-iron wood-burning stove. He slept on a feather bed in a loft overlooking the living room, and built onto the back of the house, he had put in a redwood hot tub and an enclosed cedar box of a sweat lodge that reminded Jer of a sauna.

When the three guys got to Dan's, Jer presented Dan with a fat salmon he had caught and dressed himself, and received and gave the ritual blessing: *Good spirits infuse all you say and do and are.*

Wiccans would say, *Blessed be.*

Warlocks would say, *May the God aid your battles.*

Jer had been studying with Dan since he'd turned thirteen, which was when Dan had judged him old enough for the "Raven's Journey," as he called it. He told Jer that his own Deveraux totem was not Raven, but Falcon, and that that bird was important to Jer's family history.

"You are an old soul," Dan had also told him. "And your soul has unfinished business, in this world and the next."

Jer had listened hard to that soul, but in the passing years, he had not heard word one from it. Now, with the two visions, the name Isabeau, and the certainty that his father wanted someone—a woman—in Seattle dead, he decided that finally, his soul was speaking to him.

After Dan had put the salmon away, he drew ritual symbols in black body paint on his, Jer's, and the other guys' chests and foreheads. Kialish and he wore ravens. Eddie's totem was the salmon. Jer's chest was coated with a black falcon.

Then they had stripped down to loincloths and entered the sweat lodge, which was a room big enough to house at most five people. Dan had already laid and set the fire in a square metal brazier set into the wooden floor. Alderwood smoke wafted toward the wooden ceiling of the small, cube-shaped room.

After inhaling the ritual smoke, Dan passed a peace pipe to Jer, filled with pungent botanicals designed to send them more quickly and deeply into their spirit journeys.

Jer hesitated and looked at the others. Only he would take a journey; the others were there to witness it.

As usual, his friends were there for him.

Kialish held out his hand; they shook. Then Eddie did the same, before he settled against Kialish. Dan put his hands on both Jer's shoulders.

"You aren't sure about this," he said to Jer, "are you, my lodge son?"

Jer shook his head. Eddie and Kialish began to stoke the fire to encourage more smoke into the room. After a minute or two, their foreheads and backs rolled with sweat. Jer was sweating, too. Rivulets of perspiration trailed down his chest, smearing the large, taloned and beaked falcon Dan had drawn there.

"I need to know what my father and Eli are doing," he admitted, "but I don't want to know."

Dan nodded. "You want to remain uninvolved, passive, ignorant."

Though Dan spoke the words in a neutral tone, each one felt like a judgment that found Jer wanting.

Yes, he wanted to say. *I don't want to be a warlock. I don't want to have powers.*

But the truth is, I do. And I can't pretend that something isn't happening.

"I *have* to know," he told Dan. He turned to Eddie and Kialish. "Help me, my lodge brothers."

As always, the two gave him the signal that they were willing, a simple thumbs-up—a modern anachronism in the ritual-laden, old-fashioned world of Dan's sweat lodge.

I don't know why they like me so much, he thought honestly. Dan had spoken a lot about his air of authority, and the force of his powers, but Jer knew that that was not why Kialish and Eddie usually deferred to him as point man in their day-to-day lives. For some reason, they were drawn to him, found in him the qualities that they cherished in friends.

He inhaled the pipe smoke.

At once the botanicals hit him; he was reeling; careening, flying high above the air, circling and diving and screeching—

I am Fantasme, he thought. *I am the Falcon.*

As he flew into the arched stone window of the castle, he saw a man pacing. His back was to Fantasme, and he was dressed in a long robe of crimson with green moons and stars emblazoned on it; he wore a pointed hat, and his hands were clenched.

"I cannot do it," he muttered. "I cannot kill her. I haven't gotten a son in her, but that's the Cahorses' doing. I can surmount their spells. If I get her with child, my family will not touch her."

And then the door opened and another, older man stood in the doorway, glowering.

"You know it has to be done," he said sternly.

"They will not let her bear your child until you have given them the secret of the Black Fire. And that you— we—will never do. That secret is a Deveraux secret."

The younger man . . . *Jean, his name is Jean* . . . glared at *Laurent, his father* . . . and said, "Then why did we commit to this alliance? Why did you marry her to me?"

"It was a gamble," Laurent admitted. "We will not share the secret of the Black Fire with a Cahors. But we will, with the son of a Deveraux and a Cahors. But apparently, that is not good enough for them." He sniffed. "They want to have the secret now, not in a generation."

"And so, she must die," Jean said bitterly.

"If you don't do it, I will," Laurent concurred. "And you, having feelings for her, will be far more merciful than I." He huffed and balled his fists. "I was won over to the idea of this marriage by others of the Circle. The moment Isabeau was born, the idea of the alliance was born as well."

Jean was taken aback. "I . . . I didn't know that," he admitted. "I thought you were the primary strategist for my marriage to her."

"Not in the beginning. And I regret my weakness. They'll surely try to retaliate after she is dead."

Jean said, "Surely they suspect what we plan to do?"

"Surely," said Laurent. "And that is why the saying goes, 'He who hesitates is lost.'"

He pointed to the elaborately carved box on a wooden stand. In it lay Jean's athame, which Laurent had helped him to make. "Kill her swiftly, and do it soon."

He stood at the doorway, and Jean made a stiff, angry bow. Then he turned around and crossed to the box.

His face was . . .

. . . mine, Jer thought, reeling. *We could be twins. . . .*

And on the broad, strong wings of Fantasme, Jer flew out of the castle window, screeching and wheeling, crying out for Pandion, to warn her of her mistress's danger. . . .

Flying swiftly, flying swiftly . . .

"*Kill her swiftly . . . ,*" Jer said in a flat voice as the others listened. "*Kill her swiftly. . . .*"

He blinked, shaking hard as his spirit fell back into his body. Dan, Eddie, and Kialish had moved forward, listening hard, and Dan grabbed his wrist as Jer collapsed and fell forward, exhausted.

"Sleep now," he instructed. "Your lodge brothers and I will talk. When you wake up, we'll listen to your story."

Jer's head sank forward; he was aware that someone was extinguishing the smoke, and someone else was helping him lie on the wooden floor. Gentle hands put a pillow beneath his head and covered him with a blanket. A sprig of fresh rosemary was placed on his pillow, to help him remember his spirit journey.

He slept there all night.

Tomorrow was the first day of school in Seattle, and Holly would be there.

Her aunt had helped her register, brought her to the new student orientation, picked her up again. Holly had gone through the motions, walked in a daze behind the senior who had taken her and the other new kids on a tour of the school. She couldn't have told any of the Andersons a thing about it, because she honestly didn't remember a moment.

Amanda was beyond happy about Holly's staying. She finally had an ally in the house. And they could both complain about the lack of Jer to each other.

Neither of them had seen him since that night at The Half Caff. Nicole went out with Eli all the time, and she talked about seeing Jer, but Jer didn't say anything about their bizarre encounter, at least not that Nicole shared. Amanda told Holly it was a waste of time to ask her sister about Eli's brother; she was way defensive about seeing Eli and she never took questions about the Deveraux men with any sort of grace.

But Holly couldn't stop thinking about it; so much had already happened to her with Deveraux men, directly or indirectly. So on the night before school started, she dared to ask, "Was Jer there?"

Nicole snorted. "Are you two still clinging to hope? He *has* a girlfriend, you know. A grad student."

Amanda raised her brows and lifted her nose in the air, as if she were smelling something bad. "I'm surprised Eli doesn't burst into flames when he steps on the high school grounds. He hated it enough."

Nicole rotated her head, one of the many "acting exercises" she continually performed around the house. She would be in a special drama class this year, which was all she talked about anymore. Holly knew more about Nicole's schedule than her own.

"He has his high school equivalency."

"Jer *graduated*," Amanda told Holly. "He was in the honor society."

Nicole rolled her eyes.

"What about college?" Holly asked her, trying to

deflect the conversation further away from Jer. "Is Eli going?"

"He doesn't need it. He reads a lot." Nicole yawned. "I guess you don't know that the Deveraux are really rich." She moved her shoulders. "Really, really rich."

"Oh." Holly hadn't known.

"From their mom," Amanda said. "Their mom who *disappeared*."

"Oh, God, Amanda, don't start *that* up again," Nicole snapped. She gestured dismissively and said to Holly, "The whole thing was investigated. Sasha Deveraux walked out on their dad when Eli was five. It was this big thing all over town when we were little."

"She never contacted her own children," Amanda added. "She just went away."

Poor Jer, Holly thought, imagining herself abandoned as a child of three. Losing her parents when she was seventeen was bad enough. *And no wonder his brother's so out of control, with that father of theirs. She probably got tired of him cheating on her. . . .*

"That is so not true," Nicole insisted. "She checks in all the time. Eli told me."

Amanda shook her head but remained silent. There was an awkward moment; the tension grew, and both sisters looked at Holly. She had no idea what they expected from her, but she had understood for some time that they had put her in the middle of their rivalry. She had also understood that that had been a role she'd played at home, for her mom and dad. Had their marriage gotten rocky as she'd gotten older and spent less time with them? What would have happened if they'd survived until she'd gone away to college?

"Losers," Nicole said snottily. "Don't even think of hanging out with me at school tomorrow."

After she flounced away, the conversation died, and Holly wandered down the hall to the guest room.

She lay for hours, tears spilling onto her pillow. This was not how it was supposed to work out. Fresh grief broke through her first-day jitters like an open wound—*My parents are dead; Barbara is still sick, and I'm here. I'm not supposed to be here. It was going to be Tina and me, and the best senior year there ever was. . . .*

It rained that night. It rained almost every night.

It rains all the time in Seattle. How does anyone stand this?

The new school year was beginning, the university first, and then the high schools . . . and Jer, Eddie, and Kialish were sophomores now. Kari was still working on her PhD, so she would be there too.

Wicked: Witch

Everything in Jer's world began in the autumn, although it was the dying part of the God's year. In the magical calendar, harvest was upon them, for which the Goddess took credit; and then, in the winter, the Year King would die, swallowed up by the darkness of night.

As he stood on a hill overlooking the city, he saw glitter and sparkle—*faery magic*—so different from the darkness his father had taught him to worship.

The summer had come and gone, and he had kept his distance from Holly Cathers, too weirded out to approach her again . . . but unable to stop trying to connect, at least indirectly. He had tried a lot of ways to find out more about Holly, including looking her up on the Net. He knew a few things: She was an orphan from San Francisco, she was going to inherit some good money, and she liked horses. There were a few other thing on a Web site she had begun with a friend of hers named Tina Davis-Chin, who had died in the same rafting accident as Holly's parents. Her favorite color was green, and she was a July baby. *A Leo.*

But who she really was, who in the other world, he still had no clue. He had tried every way he knew how, short of asking his father, had tried every way he could to reconnect with the latest vision—the one about death—from sweating in Dan's lodge to casting runes to spilling his own blood to the God Mercury. None of it had done any good. It was as if someone had thrown up a magical barrier to prevent him from discovering anything.

Could it have been Holly Cathers herself? Is she a witch? Is she the "one" my dad was talking about killing? Because nothing has happened to her. So I'm thinking it's got to be someone else. He had been checking the obituaries in the paper, but no one whose name he recognized had died. That didn't mean much, but he took some comfort in it.

"Child of the Lady, come to me," he whispered to the glowing stone in his hand. "I will protect you."

As clouds scuttled the moon and dark birds cawed in the evergreens behind him on the cliff, the stone in his hand began to glitter and glow. A soft green light bathed the wound on his wrist, where he had implored Mercury to aid him.

"I shall be the Lord to your Lady, and save you from harm."

The stone's glow intensified, and Jer whispered encouragingly to it in ancient Hebrew. It was his preferred magical language, although as warlocks allied with the Supreme Coven, Hebrew was a less than welcome tongue, being too closely associated with the Christian Messiah, Jesus of Nazareth.

But Jer spoke to the stone gently, urging it forth

with words of heat and longing from the Bible's Song of Solomon. *If only the Christians knew the power in those words. . . .*

The stone bobbled in his palm, warming to his touch, the green glowing as brightly as a 100-watt bulb.

"Yes, yes, my Lady," he urged it like a lover.

In the glow of the stone, images formed very fuzzily at first, then gradually undulated into focus as the stone surged with power. Jer saw his father and brother in the chamber in their house. Filmy clouds of gray and black surrounded them, portents of evildoing to come. Jer couldn't hear them—his stone was not that strong—but his alarm rose as he watched his brother walk out of sight, then return holding aloft a hand of glory—a dead man's hand, the shriveled fingertips burning like the tapers on a candelabra. His father, robed and hooded in sorcerer's attire, raised his left hand high; in it he held his own athame, made by his own hand, and passed the blade through each flame.

They glided slowly to the altar where Jer himself had participated in the sacrificing of many small animals and birds. It was an ancient slab of carved stone featuring satyrs and centaurs and, in the center, a deep hollow for catching the blood of sacrifices. Other, smaller indentations were for burning incense, herbs, and sacred woods, the bowl shapes incised millennia before to align with the stars. The wonder was, that even though the altar had been moved hundreds of times in its existence, it still illustrated the annual starscape of the Seattle sky with uncanny precision.

At the top of the altar, presiding over all the dark deeds done in his name, sat an onyx figure of the Horned God. His head was that of a goat, twin curled horns spiraling to either side of crescent-shaped eyes set with rubies. Below the goat's fringed beard, the fanned hood of a cobra served as a neck. The torso belonged to a jaguar, and the front legs and paws to some unnamed beast of prey with talons fully half as long as its entire body. Its hind legs and tail were that of a crocodile.

This was the image of the profane Lord of the Deveraux Coven, upon whom all their magical influence rested. Even seeing his statue made Jer's blood chill. In their tradition, the Horned God was a real being, and he was not to be crossed, ever.

In a wooden cage fluttered four anxious hunting hawks. They were tonight's sacrifice, he knew. He took a breath, hoping that only the four birds were slated to be given up to the God. He would not be a witness to cruelty past that, and yet, he had vowed to stop the barbarism of his family if it came to killing a human being. He had to know what they were doing in the chamber without him.

Jer was practicing the ancient art of scrying. The bird's-eye view he had of his father and brother came courtesy of the ancient Middle Eastern conjuring stone he'd bought in one of the stalls at Pike's Fish Market earlier in the day. The fish market, a favorite tourist hangout, also sold souvenirs and unusual tchotchkes. The short, gray-haired woman in the Birkenstocks who'd sold the stone to Jer had presented it as an interesting bead to use in jewelry; she'd owned one of those hippie-dippy throwback stalls, not knowing she held potent magic in her hand when she slipped the stone into a paper bag for Jer.

A gentle wind flapped at the edge of his coat. The trees rustled and the lights below twinkled. Jer was becoming restive; all the objects his family had handled in their ritual thus far were standard to any Rite of Darkness. They must mean to commit no major mischief tonight.

Maybe I'll go see what Kari's up to, he thought.

And then what he saw made his gorge rise.

"No," he murmured aloud. "Don't do it."

He was so shocked that he looked away and took a deep breath. His hands began trembling so badly, he nearly dropped the stone, which would spell disaster.

Not only would it be damaged beyond repair, but his brother and father would be alerted to his presence, however remote.

Removing a white linen shroud with a flourish, Michael Deveraux presented to the Horned God a fresh corpse. In life, she had been a lovely young girl. She had been stolen from a morgue, her white-blue skin evidence that she had lain in an icy drawer for some time.

They meant to invoke a death curse, then. Tonight. Now.

Who is it? Who are you trying to kill?

Suddenly his father looked up, scowling. He waved a hand.

The scrying stone in Jer's hand went dark.

Numb, Jer stood on the cliff, eyes unfocused. The lights below, an illusion. What he had seen, the only terrible reality he knew.

My father sensed someone spying on him, he realized. *Does he know it was me?*

The stone, devoid of heat, sat lifeless in his palm. He spoke to it, whispering words of encouragement, of assurance, of love. But the scrying stone was dead. His father had taken its essence from it with the merest gesture, like someone batting a fly.

Above, the stars peered down, so many heartless

eyes gazing down on the follies of man, uncaring. All his life, Jer had been taught that no supernatural being interfered in the travails of humanity unless called to do so. The only way to interest the God or one of his many manifestations in one's situation was to make an offering. The Goddess was something else entirely. She did not walk with the warlocks of the Deveraux. She never had, and she never would. Any warlock of the Supreme Coven who dared to cross her would be struck by lightning, his ashes devoured by time.

Or so Dad said. And he's a lying murderer, Jer thought. *Can I turn to Her?*

He reeled, wishing he were down in the city of Seattle, walking among the blissfully ignorant, just a regular guy.

Down among the dead men, he thought ironically, quoting one of Sir William's favorite English folk songs. He thought back to when he had been thirteen and presented at the Court of the Supreme Coven. He remembered the enormous gargoyles, the blazing fire rings, the huge columns and vast expanses of black-and-white marble floors. His father's pride. Even Eli had been respectful.

He saw himself cloaked in the rich, black velvet robe, the circlet of hawthorn leaves rested on his head; in his right hand, the footed staff, in his left, the magic wand said to have come down from Merlin, Dark Lord of the Ancient High Days . . .

. . . *and maybe I could change things, move us a little closer to the light. I'd have the authority. If I got to the Throne, I'd have to have a lot of backing, warlocks who wanted to do things my way.* . . .

He felt ambition singing in his blood. His heart was pumping hard. His fingers were literally itching, eager to hold the symbols of the highest office in all Coventry.

Below him, the lights of the mundane world, the daily grind of simple men and women living lives of quiet desperation. Dying of boredom, wishing that fairy tales were true, gorging themselves on alcohol and food because their lives were, at the core, unendurable. . . .

Warlocks never lived like that. Theirs was a life of many worlds, untold dimensions, of seeking, grasping, taking. . . .

Jer's dark soul took flight at the possibilities open to him as a Deveraux and an adept.

The birds cawed more loudly now, their rasping song mocking his weakness. *I know that my father and brother are planning to kill a human being—and that they have done it before—but even now, I can't repudiate the Art. I can't walk away, pretend I'm not a Deveraux, become one of the mundanes.* . . .

He balled his fists in his coat, dropping the stone into his pocket, and stared at the dizzying depth below him. He could step off, end it. His soul was spoken for; at least he could take a shortcut, get there faster. . . .

Why was I born a Deveraux?

Why was I born?

But even then he was weak; he couldn't kill himself any more easily than he could have helped his family kill another person. Furious with himself, he turned on his heel and headed for the Mustang, parked a short distance away.

It was then that the birds flew higher, allowing other noises to creep into the night: the croaking of frogs, the scrape of crickets and tree branches . . .

. . . and the frantic honking of a horn, accompanied by the panther roar of an engine in overdrive, as a black Mercedes bulleted around a curve and flew straight for him.

"Oh, my God, oh, my God," Marie-Claire screamed as she came to.

She had fallen asleep on her way home from the motel, and now her car was out of control. As her headlights bounced off the trees and the road and the stars, careening around her in a dervish, she grabbed at the wheel and slammed her foot on the brake.

The squeal of her tires was earsplitting; the car spun into a 360. *I'm going to die,* she thought as she rode it out. Part of her mind was completely rational. *I'll look hideous. Closed coffin . . .*

From somewhere in the dim recesses of her memory, she remembered her driver's ed class. *Take your foot off the brake,* she ordered herself. But she was paralyzed with fear; she could do nothing but stare straight ahead as the car wheeled around like an overwound music box.

Then something, an unseen force, seemed to grab hold of her foot. Something compelled her to turn off the engine.

It's my guardian angel, she thought.

The car spun again, then lurched to a stop.

"God," she whispered, exhaling. She let go of the wheel with shaking hands and wiped her eyes. Tears clouded her vision, and as she tried to remember how to breathe, she clamped her right hand over her mouth to keep herself from becoming violently ill.

With her other hand she punched open the electric window. The whirring was covered by the sound of footfalls racing toward her. A shadowed figure was waving at her with both hands above its head.

It was Michael's son, Jer.

What's he doing out here in the middle of the night? she

thought. Shame flooded through her; she didn't want to speak to him, as if somehow he would be able to tell by looking at her that she had been with his father at a tawdry motel a few miles from the Deveraux house.

Before he could reach the car, she turned the key in the ignition, put the car in reverse, and skidded backward. Then she slammed it into drive, made a sharp left, and drove away as fast as she could, as if he might be able to catch up with her.

I don't think he saw me, she said, glancing fretfully into the rearview mirror. *I'm safe.*

EIGHT

CHASTE MOON

🌙

We take new charge of our fate
Take time to renew our hate
Before us every foe will flee
As we dance in ruthless glee

We dance beneath the moon's fair light
Laugh and careen far into night
Everything comes with ease
And Cahors take what they please

Kari Hardwicke's eyes were tired.

Seated in the tiny cubicle she called her on-campus office, she was working on her notes for Dr. Temar's Lit 204 class—Gothic Lit—or rather, on Dr. Temar's notes. She was his teaching assistant this semester and, so far, she did everything for him pretty much, except lecture. She composed his lectures and graded the students' papers.

Well, he did *manage to bring his own video in to show the class,* she thought. And she did mean "his own." Ken

Temar had written, directed, and starred in *The Truth about Frankenstein*. It had been broadcast on PBS, and it was part of the reason Dr. Temar had tenure at UW. She was beginning to wonder who had really done all the work on it. *They* were the ones who should have been given tenure.

But that's why God made grad students, she thought, sighing.

Her IM binged and she cheered up. It was Circle Lady, her mysterious e-mail correspondent. Circle Lady checked in about once a week. She knew an amazing amount about witchcraft, both stereotypical black magic stuff and the more authentic pagan forms of worship bundled together under the heading of Wicca. It was because of Circle Lady that Kari had developed such an intense interest in Jer. When he had walked into her class section during his freshman year, he had all the earmarks of someone who was practicing the Craft on the sly.

She'd pushed, and finally he'd opened up just a crack. Yes, his family practiced. No, she couldn't watch. Yes, they had a Tradition. No, she couldn't know its name. Yes, he would perform some rites and rituals with her.

How are you? Circle Lady queried.

Tired. Good, Kari replied.

Chaste Moon

Moon coming up. Samhain in a month.

Kari typed in, *Yes.* As a teenager, she had been fascinated to learn that there were all kinds of magical associations tied in with the more "American" holiday of Halloween. That had led to her studies in comparative religion, which had led to her graduate work in mythology.

How's Warlock?

Kari grinned at their code name for Jer. Of course, Circle Lady didn't know his real name. Kari was not stupid. For one thing, she wouldn't violate his privacy like that; for another, she was using a university computer for private e-mail. Last year, his being assigned to her study sessions would have been an issue. This year, the Administration could go hang, for all it mattered.

Warlock is great, she said.

Did he get all his classes?

You are such a mom, Circle Lady! :) Kari typed back.

My kids are gone. No one to fuss over.

She became aware that she was no longer alone. Someone was standing at the perimeter of her cubicle—no mean feat, since her cubicle had very little perimeter.

As she glanced over her shoulder, warmth suffused through her. It was Jer. His face was cast in shadow; in his black clothes, he could have been some demon lover from an English Gothic romance.

Speak of the devil, and he shows, she told Circle Lady. *Later, okay?*

Tell him hi. Bye.

Kari logged off. She said, "Hi."

Jer stepped into the harsh fluorescent light. He looked as if he had just witnessed a car crash—numb and confused and very, very upset.

"Hey," she blurted, jumping out of her office chair.

His only answer was to lower his head. As if he were drunk, she led him carefully to the chair and set him in it. He stared at his hands as if he had never seen them before. Then abruptly he rose.

"I shouldn't have come here." His voice was a harsh rasp. "It could be very dangerous for you."

Her laugh was startled, shrill. "Wha-at? Jer, are you on something?"

As he moved away from her, she caught his arm. He was sweating profusely. She said, "Take your coat off, Jer. You're boiling up."

Jer made no move to do so; he simply shook his head and muttered, "I'm fine."

He kept walking.

"Jer!" she cried. "What's wrong with you? Let me help you."

That must have been the right thing to say, because he froze.

"I want to," she prodded.

Slowly, he raised his head. His shoulders were hunched, his fists clenched. "You have no idea what . . ."

"I want to." She reached out a hand that he couldn't see, lowering it as he pivoted back to her and put his hands on her shoulders. He was much taller than she; she had to tip her head back to look into his eyes. She was afraid of the fear she saw in them.

"It's going to be dangerous." He searched her face. "All this stuff you think I'm into . . . you think it's so cool. So *interesting*." He was mocking her; once, he had teased her that *interesting* was her favorite word, and that she had overused it to the point that it didn't mean anything anymore.

Without another word, he grabbed her arm and escorted her out of her office and down the hall, hurrying her along. She stumbled against him and held on to his arm; he didn't even seem to notice.

Then he slammed open the exit door and took her outside. She smelled the evergreens and a hint of rain in the clouds as they stood together in the cool night. Stars shone; the moon was hidden.

"See that bush?" he asked, pointing at a shadowy clump across a narrow trail between the trees. He snapped his fingers. That was all he did.

And the bush burst into flame.

"We can do that to plants," he said, his voice deathly quiet. "And objects. And people."

She gasped, thrilled and terrified and shot through with a sense of dread so heavy, she felt rooted to the spot.

As the bush blazed into a ball of fire, she swallowed hard and said to Jer, "We?"

He turned to her and faced her full on. "My father and my brother," he said, "are trying to kill Marie-Claire Cathers-Anderson with magic."

Marie-Claire got home, and she was shaking.

I almost died.

She walked into the kitchen, and thought absurdly, *I hope the girls have a good day at school tomorrow. Senior year. Poor Holly, what a blow. She thought she would be home by now. So did I.*

I almost died.

She raised on tiptoe to the liquor cabinet and got herself the Scotch bottle. She unscrewed the cap and grabbed a shot glass. Two shots later, she was still shaking.

"Mom?" It was Nicole, standing in a pair of flannel pajama bottoms and a T-top. Her red hair was tousled, and she was yawning. "Mom, you okay?"

"I-I-" She took a deep breath, saw the bottle in her hand, and was ashamed. "Honey, I almost had a car accident. A very bad one."

"Oh God, Mom." Nicole's eyes widened. "Where? What happened?"

To Marie-Claire's surprise, Nicole poured her another shot of Scotch and handed it to her.

She socked it back. Then Nicole poured some for herself in another shot glass and tossed it back like a pro. She smirked at her mother as if to say, *Don't even start, Mom. Don't be naive.*

Oh, my God, I'm getting loaded with my own daughter.

"It was like . . . like I couldn't control the car," Marie-Claire blurted. Her words were already beginning to slur. "Almost like I . . . like someone wanted me to have an accident."

Nicole frowned. And then she gave her mother another surprise. She said, "Mom, Eli's been teaching me about . . . well, you know what everyone says those guys are into."

Marie-Claire stared at her daughter. Then she burst into laughter.

"C'mon, Mom, don't pretend you haven't noticed stuff around their house. And wondered." Nicole put her hand on her hip. "Look, I know you're sleeping with—"

"Oh, my God. Don't say it." Marie-Claire staggered backward. "Oh, my darling. I didn't realize that you know. I'm so sorry."

"No." She grinned at her mother, and Marie-Claire saw a different person there, not her bright, eager, aspiring actress, but a grown woman with her own life and her own secrets. "You're not. And I get why you do it, Mom. I really do. If I were married to a boring man—"

"Don't talk about your father that way!" Marie-Claire half-shouted.

"You were with him tonight," Nicole said calmly. "Don't deny it. Someone's probably jealous. Maybe it's Jer. He's so twisted."

"This isn't happening. We're not having this conversation."

Nicole took her mom's hand and led her into the living room. She said, "Let me show you a few things, Mom. Things I know how to do. If someone is after you in a magic way, I can help you protect yourself."

School was a waking nightmare.

As she wound her way through the maze of Hill High, the new faces blurred into the old ones Holly had expected to see on the very first day of her senior year. There was Grace Beck . . . no, that was someone else. There was Mallory Reaves . . . wrong again.

Not for one moment could she mistake Amanda for Tina.

Everything was too much, from the hand-painted posters announcing WE HAVE SCHOOL SPIRIT! to the admittedly nerdy friends of Amanda, who were trying way to too hard to be nice to her orphaned cousin. From the students already urging one another to sign petitions and join clubs and have LOTS OF SCHOOL FUN! to the new rooms and new teachers who loaded on the homework.

I would have some of these same reactions at home, Holly reminded herself. *New rooms, new teachers, lots of home-work.*

"We're almost done, we're almost through it," Amanda would say after each class period. Her aunt had arranged for them to have as many classes together as possible, while Amanda and Nicole had arranged to have as few opportunities to see each other at school as possible. They didn't even have the same lunch.

When it was time for Holly to go to her first class alone, which was chemistry, she was relieved to find Tommy Nagai there. Seated at a two-person lab table covered with glass beakers and a Bunsen burner, he waved at her as she hovered anxiously at the doorway.

"Lab partner!" he said, throwing wide his arms.

"Someone who will do all the work, yes? You're like that?"

He put his arm around her and walked her back into the room. "Here's where knowing me will pay off," he said. "Watch this."

He shepherded her up to the teacher, a gruff-looking middle-aged man with an atrocious haircut and retro glasses that made his eyes wrap halfway around his head, like an alien's.

"Mr. Boronski," Tommy said affably. "My lab partner, please? Transfer from San Francisco. Amanda Anderson's cousin. I want her."

Mr. Boronski tried not to smile, but he couldn't help himself. He wagged his head at Tommy and said, "You've got to play a little harder to get if you want the chicks to dig you. Right, Amanda's cousin?"

"Holly," she said, warming a little.

The teacher glanced down at a computer printout of student names. Like any self-respecting high school student, Holly was accomplished at reading upside down.

"Yes. There you are. Okay. Lab partners." He smiled at her. "Welcome, Holly. All I ask is that you keep him from talking all through class. For that alone, I'll give you an A."

"I yak," Tommy said joyfully. He took Holly's hand

and began leading her around the class, introducing her to the others. "Jason, Bob, Andrea, Brenda, Scott," he labeled a sea of faces. He pulled her along. "Other new person, hi, I'm Tommy and this is my lab partner, Holly. We will be ruining the bell curve for you."

The bell rang, and Mr. Boronski said, "Seats, please. Nagai, zip it."

Tommy trotted Holly back to their lab table. "In science class, we are all homeys," he told her. "Just watch me and you'll be the sweetheart of the periodic table."

"*Nagai.*"

"It means 'long' in Japanese," Tommy whispered to Holly, giving her a hey-hey-baby look.

She did something she had not expected to do that day.

She laughed.

Okay, school might not be a nightmare after all. . . .

With Kari wrapped around him, Jer stood on the hill for which Hill High was named, his coat flapping behind him like the wings of a great, black bird.

Kialish and Eddie stood to one side, holding hands, watching the parade of cars waiting at the curb for the students to emerge from classes. The school was very old and made of brick; Jer had loved it there.

It had been a refuge from his home life. And though he had never had many friends, he found Eddie and Kialish there.

"No black Mercedes," Kari finally said.

He had come to check on the Anderson women, Marie-Claire in particular. It did not bode well that her Mercedes was not there to pick up her girls.

If they killed her last night, found another way . . .

"Are you sure about this, bro?" Eddie asked him gently. "Maybe she really did have a car problem."

Jer closed his eyes and silently intoned a Finder's Spell. Seconds later, Kialish said, "She's in a different car."

Jer opened his eyes; sure enough, a black Jeep Explorer had pulled to the curb and Marie-Claire Cathers-Anderson was stepping from the driver's side. She hurried into the front entrance of the school just as the bell rang. Students began spilling from the wood-trimmed glass double doors.

Kari pulled her dark brown leather coat around herself and snuggled up to Jer. She said, "You don't really think your family would try to hurt someone, do you? And why her?"

You have no idea, he thought. He was conflicted, knowing that he needed help to work against his family, not sure that he should have gone to Kari. Even Eddie and Kialish were question marks. Shamanic magic was more about the journey of the psyche; his family's magic—Black Magic—was about getting what you wanted, no matter who it hurt.

"She looks okay, man."

Kari's arm tightened around Jer's waist. She snuggled up to him. She was loving all this; she had been an animal in bed last night, after he had set the bush on fire.

That's what's supposed to happen, he thought bitterly, *according to my brother. Magic and six-pack abs will get you the chicks.*

"I need to be alone," he said abruptly. "I need to prepare."

"Prepare," Kari said slowly.

He nodded and pulled away from her. She looked hurt. He didn't care; he really couldn't find it within himself. If *she* cared for anyone in this equation, it was she herself. It was all a game to her, something she wanted to learn about, be able to do herself. But help someone? Protect someone? She hadn't made that leap.

I shouldn't have gotten her involved in this, he thought. But he needed a male-female connection to make some of the magic he was planning to do.

He looked back down the hill, easily singling out Holly and Amanda—but not Nicole—as Marie-Claire escorted them back out of the school, moving her hands like a hummingbird's.

She looks so tired, Jer thought of Holly. *So sad.*

As she, her aunt, and Amanda made their way down Hill High's steps to the rental—her aunt's Mercedes was in the shop, awaiting a brake inspection—Holly heard the screech of a bird. Startled, she looked up, losing track of what her aunt was saying.

A black bird hovered about twenty feet above her, staring down at her. Even from this distance, she could see the sharp, curved beak, the taloned claws . . . and the eyes.

They seemed to stare at her . . . *glare* at her, Amanda, and Marie-Claire.

Unnoticed by her chattering cousin and her aunt, Holly took a step back. Her line of vision ticked downward.

Jer.

He stood on the hill across the street, a girl clinging to him, and two guys with him. The others were watching the bird.

Jer was watching her.

She went hot. She swallowed, looking away, wondering what he was doing there.

"Amanda," she said quietly, "Amanda, look."

" . . . with Tommy in chemistry!" Amanda said, laughing.

"Oh, my goodness," Aunt Marie-Claire replied, looking at Holly. "Mr. Boronski will have his hands full. Well, it's nice you both had a good day. Now where did I put the rental key?"

Above them, the bird cawed once, then flapped its large wings and flew away.

Holly glanced at her aunt and said, "I'm sorry, what?"

On the hill, Jer and the others turned and began to walk away. Holly tugged on Amanda's sleeve and gestured with her head.

Amanda looked up at the hill. She saw, glanced at Holly, and murmured, "That's Kari with him."

Marie-Claire had missed the whole thing. She smiled and said, "Here it is!" and showed them the key on a chain with a plastic badge that read, SEATTLE'S #1 BRAKE SHOP.

"And we're off, home again, safe and sound," she said.

Holly climbed into the car.

★ ★ ★

"That was a falcon," Kialish said as Jer and the others left the hill and headed for their cars. "Your totem."

Jer looked around the circle. They were an odd bunch to be starting a secret coven, weren't they? The few, the proud, the sweat lodgers. Would there be enough power here on which he could draw in his quest to protect Marie-Claire? He could only hope.

"I want you to learn," he finally answered. "Open your minds and your hearts, and help me." For a moment he found himself unable to meet their gazes. "My family's heritage is . . . more extreme than I've let any of you know. Eli and my dad, they're . . ." He looked down at the fire. Kari gave his hand a squeeze.

"They are so evil," he whispered finally. "I can't tell you very much. I'm . . . bound . . . but I will not be a part of their . . . *plans*" —he nearly spit the word out— "when they want to hurt people. What they do otherwise is not for me to decide, but I can't allow my father and my brothers to hurt anyone. I *won't*."

His friends looked at one another, but no one said anything for a long moment. "All right, bro," Eddie said finally.

Kialish cleared his throat. "We should go back to see my dad."

"I'm not sure," Jer said. He had been deliberating

about that. "This magic is very different from your father's. It's more ruthless and vicious. We've always known that. Always talked about it."

"Then he can help us find us new ways to fight it," Kialish insisted.

That was true. Jer inclined his head and said, "All right. You're right. Tonight we need to meet, to bind ourselves together, in blood. It's an old ritual and it will establish us as a Coven." He looked around the group. "Think about that. You are going to become a Coven of the Art. Once I initiate you, you're bound to loyalty to our Coven. And to me, as your master."

Eddie and Kialish nodded, both looking very sober. They knew this was an important moment.

"And then you'll teach us," Kari said, her eyes shining with excitement.

Jer's heart was very heavy. She still thought this was all a game. "Yes, I'll teach you."

He prayed that the lessons he had to teach were not painful.

Or fatal.

NINE

SEED MOON

☾

House of Deveraux arise
Take your vengeance to the skies
Let the world feel your ire
Paint the moon with black fire

Time to scheme and plant the seeds
Of distrust and dishonesty
Take the souls whom we have marked
Make them ours mind and heart

Things changed.

The dreams faded, and Holly slept better at night.
No Jer Deveraux showed up on her radar, but she
firmly consigned him to her "settling-in phase" and
wondered a little about Tommy Nagai . . . except the
guy was obviously set on snagging Amanda. And
Amanda had no clue, wouldn't even believe it when
Holly would try to tell her about it.

"We are oldest, bestest friends," Amanda told her.
"You're misinterpreting him."

Holly began to wonder if Amanda was afraid to like Tommy more intensely than she already did; if that would make him go away or stop liking her. She understood that kind of fear; she'd been there herself.

Holly began to feel at home in Seattle. She found things to like—one of them being that Seattle was a hip, sophisticated place like San Francisco. The kids were quick and smart; they shared the same kind of shorthand as back home. It was good to be well-read and ambitious. One got points for expanded horizons and broad cultural experiences.

It rained, but then, it had rained a lot in San Francisco. Holly learned to carry an umbrella with the same consistency that she carried a purse. So did Amanda, who "trained" her, reminding her constantly, "Don't forget your umbrella. Do you have your umbrella?"

Nicole, though, never wore a raincoat or carried an umbrella. She preferred the more theatrical style of running and screaming through the rain and tearing off her clothes the second she came home and heading straight for a hot shower. This abandon at times sent Amanda, Holly's former dour, Nicole-despising cousin, into spasms of good-natured revulsion— something that had developed over time, after Holly came to live there.

I've been here six weeks and they're both so different. So happy. It's like magic.

"What's wrong with you?" Amanda would demand, laughing. "You hedonistic, barbaric moron!"

Nicole would just wad up one of her ever-present midriff-baring tees and throw it at her. "You're just jealous you don't look as good as I do."

"Please."

Holly loved the changes in them both. They were more relaxed around each other. In fact, hanging with Amanda and Nicole had begun to prove sisterhood could be more than powerful, it could be liberating and fun. The terrible loneliness began to recede, although the ache of losing her parents was still as fresh as the day it had happened. But just being there, rain or no rain, faintly erased the fierce emptiness of facing the future. Her cousins could make her laugh when she really felt like an all-night cry session watching Jay Leno or David Letterman, switching back and forth until she made herself crazy. Bast and her cousins' cats were adorable too, always popping up when she needed their sweet, furry selves, sleek and ready to be played with.

Amanda was happy, Nicole was friendly, and Holly was beginning to believe that she had a place here.

Family.

Nicole kept urging her to tell Bast her secrets and to "help you get a guy." As they lay around in Nicole's room, where Holly was now more welcome and which was decorated in black with silver moons, a lot of theater posters and a signed picture of Winona Ryder, Nicole wrinkled up her nose, as if to take the sting out of what she said next.

"Just don't make it Eli. We're going to make a new life once we're released from prison."

"Eli. Ugh," Amanda said. "Let's don't go there. And on that note, I'm going to bed."

"I should too," Holly said.

As she slid off the bed, Bast trotted in. Hecate wriggled out of Nicole's arms, leaped off the bed, and joined her. They touched noses, then turned and sauntered out of the room together.

"They've probably gone off to plan your future," Nicole said to Holly. "Well, g'night." She smiled at her sister as well as her cousin.

"Don't make us late in the morning," Amanda warned Nicole as she, too, got up to leave. "And don't hog the bathroom."

"*Moi?*" Nicole fluttered her lashes.

Amanda gave her a look.

In the hallway, Amanda rolled her eyes. She said, "God, she drives me crazy. Just watch, she'll make us late." She shrugged and smiled, and Holly saw that the sting and hurt that had once haunted her cousins' relationship were still gone. "If you do pray to your cat tonight, beg her to make Nicole ready on time. If I get one more tardy in P.E., my grade's going to be lowered."

"How embarrassing," Holly empathized.

"How stupid. I won't get into a good school if my G.P.A. is down, and I won't have it happen over running around like a fool for forty-five minutes in thirty-degree weather." She made a face. "I should have caught on early, like Nicole. Taken modern dance."

Holly made a face. "I'm not big on pretending I'm a dancing tree."

Amanda laughed. "Well, it just gives her another reason to demand everybody's attention." She said it good-naturedly. "And on that happy note, *bonne nuit,* as we say around here."

Holly felt a pang. Her father used to wish her *bonne nuit*—good night—in French. Maybe it was a family tradition, from being French and everything. *There's so much I don't know about my parents. And maybe I'll never know. I should ask Aunt Marie-Claire to tell me some more about Daddy's childhood.*

"*Bonne nuit,*" she told her cousin, and went into her room.

Her deaf kitten scampered in after her. Holly took a deep breath and shut the door, leaning against it as she gazed around the room, watching to see if the cat freaked out. Weird things still happened in this room. The closet door liked to swing open in the night. The floorboards liked to creak. And the cat, who could not hear, didn't like any of it.

"So, my dear familiar," she teased the cat as the two of them walked toward the bed. "Here's my wish list: getting to school on time, a good night's sleep, and . . ." She trailed off, too shy to mention a foolish desire to see Jer soon, even to the cat. "That's all," she said.

The cat meowed and blinked her large blue eyes. She was such a petite little thing that her face was little more than her eyes and a tiny cupid-bow mouth and a dot of a nose.

Holly picked her up and whispered against her neck, "Oh God, I miss my mom and dad so much. I miss Tina. This was going to be our year."

The cat purred and extended her right forepaw in such a human-like gesture of comfort that Holly couldn't find it in herself to smile. The pit in her stomach became a tight knot. Her throat closed up with unspoken grief and she thought, *How long am I going to feel this bad? Am I going to miss them like this for the rest of my life?*

Tap, tap, Bast's forepaw touched on the back of her hand. She snuggled up and licked Holly's forearm, and Holly sank onto her bed.

She couldn't sleep; she tapped her fingers on her blanket to the steady drumbeat against the window. Just as she began to doze, she thought she heard a soft whispering outside her door. *Maybe it's one of my cousins. Maybe Amanda wants to talk about what happened in her room. Drama is obviously a touchy subject around here. . . .*

Holly yawned and opened her eyes.

She blinked.

Did I sleepwalk?

She was standing on the landing above the living room. She was in her nightgown, and she was looking down on Nicole and Marie-Claire, who were seated on the stonework in front of the large fireplace. Both of them were in their bathrobes. Nicole's was fire-engine red. Marie-Claire's was black.

Several bundles of sticks lay beside them. Nicole picked one of them up, kissed it, and handed it to her mother.

Marie-Claire passed it over the warm, crackling fire and said, "Oh, Goddess, grant to Amanda the wishes of her heart. May a good young man love her truly, and may she discover her own talents and gifts."

Holly was stunned. *What are they doing? Are they*

actually doing that Wicca stuff? My own aunt?

"Blessed be," Nicole said sweetly.

"Oh, Goddess, grant to Holly the wishes of her heart. Let her life with us be filled with ease and joy, and the feelings of a warm family."

Is that why they're getting along so well? Holly thought, shocked. *They've been . . . enchanting themselves?*

"And better clothes," Nicole added, giggling. Her mother gave her a stern look. Nicole cleared her throat and murmured, "Blessed be."

Marie-Claire put down the bundle and said, "Now you." She leaned over and gave Nicole a kiss on her forehead.

Nicole handed her another bundle.

"Oh, Goddess, grant to my beautiful Nicole the wishes of her heart. Fame on the stage, and love in her life."

"That's great, Mom," Nicole said. "You catch on quick."

"It's incredible," Marie-Claire gushed. "Who would ever have guessed?"

Holly was transfixed. Then, as mother and daughter carried the bundles of sticks to the fireplace, something brushed Holly's ankle. She caught her breath and turned to look.

The three cats, Freya, Hecate, and Bast, had

grouped around Holly's bare feet. Their yellow eyes gazed up at her. None of them moved; they sat still as if they wanted very much to speak to her. As if to say, *Blessed be.*

Then Bast opened her mouth and said in a perfectly human voice, "I shall serve thee, Holly Cathers. . . ."

Holly bolted upright, blinking at the sunlight streaming through the window of the Seattle guest room.

It was a dream, she thought. *The dreams are back.*

Bast sat at the foot of the bed, staring at her, and began to purr.

In the dark-hearted chamber of the Deveraux house, Eli and Michael made obeisance to the Horned God. Michael had butchered a dozen lady hawks, symbol of the House of Cahors, and a dozen ravens, symbol of the Deveraux. After a long Ritual of flame and fire, Michael conjured Laurent for his older son, who stared openmouthed at what he saw.

Their ancestor took his own sweet time, and as usual, the French warlock appeared as a moldering corpse. Tonight he was nearly transparent, and his flesh was a stomach-churning blue-gray.

"This is Eli, my son," Michael announced to the

half-formed cadaver. "Kneel," he said through clenched teeth to the boy.

Hastily, Eli knelt.

"One of two sons," Laurent said, through lips that did not move. "If he doesn't perform any better than your other child, he'd make a suitable sacrifice."

Eli paled, and Laurent laughed, the sound echoing off the grisly walls that had seen pain and death, and even worse. Michael bowed on one knee and said, "He is my firstborn."

"Firstborn sons are rare, and precious," Laurent observed. "So much the better when a father must part with his."

Michael remained silent, trying to gauge how serious Laurent was being. *Does he mean for me to kill Eli now? Is he testing me?*

Because I'll pass that test. . . .

He looked at his son with no other feeling in his heart except a mild regret. *Sasha was right; I can't love anyone. But she was wrong to leave me. There's such a thing as loyalty.*

Okay, I'm not big on loyalty, either. But she should have backed me up, not left me with two kids to take care of.

Laurent paced the marble floor, although his footfalls made no noise. Michael watched him calmly. Eli was glancing at their athames on the altar, maybe thinking about self-defense or patricide, Michael didn't know which.

"Your other son—Jeraud—has become possessed by the spirit of my child, Jean," Laurent announced. "That is why he has run away from you."

Michael's lips parted in surprise. Eli looked completely baffled, muttering, "Who's Jean?"

"Isabeau has succeeded in moving into the life of Holly Cathers," the Duke continued.

"The Lord and the Lady," Michael murmured, half to himself. He cocked his head as he regarded his patron. "You told me that it was only a legend, that Cahors magic mixed with Deveraux creates a far more powerful combination than the usual male and female magics I have attempted."

"Which you attempted with Marie-Claire, against my direct orders," Laurent added sternly.

"I was going to kill her," Michael protested.

"You should. She and her daughters contain power, as well. But above all, it is the little *cousine* who must be destroyed."

"Dad?" Eli whispered. "What's going on?"

"Shut up," Michael hissed at him. To Laurent, he held out his hands. "Give me the Black Fire, my lord, and I will burn them all."

At this, Laurent smiled bitterly. "First, the Cahors witches must be eliminated," Laurent said. "We cannot proceed with the Black Fire as long as they're alive. If Holly Cathers were to decipher the spell, learn how to conjure it . . . it's unthinkable."

Frustrated, but also hopeful, Michael crossed his arms over his chest and bowed. *"Oui, mon seigneur."*

"The anniversary of the betrayal is nigh. If Holly is not dead by Mead Moon, I will withdraw my patronage." He wagged a skeletal finger at Michael, the flesh hanging from it. In place of the fingernail gleamed a talon, long and curved as the crescent moon. "Don't forget, *mortal* man, that I have time and I can wait. If you and your sons disappoint, I will recruit other Deveraux warlocks to help me. You are not alone in this world."

Michael swallowed. It would be naive to assume they were the only descendants of the noble Deveraux Coven, but so far he had been unable to track down the others. *Someday . . .*

"Listen, um, my lord. Do we have to . . . should we kill all of the Cathers?" Eli asked Laurent. "Because one of them is my girlfri—"

The French nobleman stared down at him with utter disbelief. As Michael looked on, he advanced threateningly on Eli, raised his taloned hand, and sliced at him, narrowly missing the kid's cheek.

"Arrogant child! You will speak when spoken to!" he thundered. Furious, he turned to Michael. "In what manner have you raised your heir?"

To Michael's surprise, Eli raised his chin and said, in a strong, calm voice, "These are different times, Duke Laurent. And I'm not a child."

Laurent cocked his head. He looked at Eli long and hard, then said, as if to himself, "So it would appear."

It was a rainy Thursday night. In Nicole's room Holly cradled Bast, and the cat was purring like crazy. Nicole stretched out on her bed and Amanda sprawled on the floor. They'd emptied two bags of microwave popcorn and drunk enough Diet Dr. Pepper to float the entire city of Seattle as they'd watched the Claire Danes and Leo DiCaprio production of *Romeo + Juliet* for the umpteenth time.

The senior play had been announced. It was going to be *Romeo and Juliet.*

Nicole wanted the lead, of course. She was studying all the versions she could find, looking for her interpretation.

"I'm the only one who can do it right," she said, shaking her head at the TV.

"Uh-huh." Amanda yawned as her cat climbed onto her stomach.

"I mean it." Nicole stood up and stretched. Her towel-turbaned head reminded Holly of Erykah Badu. She struck a pose and her voice grew deeper than the sudden rumble of real thunder outside.

> *"Give me my Romeo: and, when he shall die,*
> *Take him, and cut him out in little stars,*
> *And he will make the face of heaven so fine,*
> *That all the world will be in love with night*
> *And pay no worship to the garish sun . . ."*

"You'll get the part, Nicole," Holly assured her beautiful cousin.

Nicole looked off into the distance, seeing maybe Romeo, or maybe footlights and hearing applause. "I am Juliet, you know. I'm better than Claire Danes. And besides . . ."

She stirred, as if remembering that she wasn't alone. "Anyway, it'll be mine. I'll make it mine."

Holly took that in.

Does she mean like with little bundles of sticks and blessings?

"Well, I hope you do," Holly said.

Nicole picked up Hecate. "I want the lead."

The cat swished her tail as if in reply.

★ ★ ★

A few more weeks passed.

Back in San Francisco, Barbara had been transferred to a long-term care unit in the hospital. She was still very ill, but no one knew why. She never got worse, but she never got better. The Cathers San Francisco home was being well taken care of; the horses at the stable were fine.

Nicole continued her campaign for Juliet, going so far as to learn the entire part before auditions were even held. Then, one rainy afternoon, Holly happened by the drama room to see when Nicole was going home. Nona Zeidel, the drama teacher, was seated at an oak desk next to a small stage draped with burgundy curtains. A distance away, two boys were painting a backdrop of a moonlit garden.

"I need it for my application to Cal Arts," Nicole wheedled as Ms. Zeidel nibbled on a bag of pretzels and flipped through an open script book on her green blotter. "Maria Gutierrez has no plans to be a professional actress. She wants to be a *math teacher*." She said it like it was a disease.

"Oh, my God, how boring," Ms. Zeidel groaned, rolling her eyes. She popped another pretzel in her mouth and cocked her head. Holly could see that she was considering it.

"And I can make all the practices." Nicole bent forward and tapped what looked to be an attendance logbook. "Check your records. I have never missed a rehearsal."

Then, as Holly watched, Nicole did something rather weird: She dipped her hand in the pocket of her black pants, and while the teacher was chuckling with her head lowered, she crumbled something in Ms. Zeidel's hair, then made a small circle with her forefinger.

Ms. Zeidel looked thoughtful as she glanced through her attendance book. She shrugged, smiling broadly, as if she had come to a decision. A favorable one, at that. "Well, you know the school policy. I have to hold open auditions. . . ."

"Thank you!" Nicole gushed. "I won't let you down."

Holly was astonished.

Footsteps sounded behind her; it was her aunt. She said, "Is Nicki in there?" At Holly's nod, she leaned into the room and gave a jaunty wave. "Hi."

"Mom! I got the part!" Nicole cried. She raced across the floor and flung herself into her mother's arms. "I'm Juliet!"

"And you're surprised?" Aunt Marie-Claire teased her, hugging her tightly. "My drama queen?"

"Oh, *you*." Nicole socked her mother playfully.

"Congratulations," Holly said, sounding a little stiff to herself.

"I wonder what my costume will look like?" Nicole burbled. "What do you think, Holly?"

Holly was still back at the hocus-pocus moment. "Something pretty," she replied.

Nicole twirled in a little circle. "But of course!"

Two weeks later, casting notices were posted in front of the classroom where Drama Club met every other Wednesday afternoon. Clusters of students jostled to read the posting. Various groans mixed with triumphant cheers greeted Nicole's, Amanda's, Tommy's, and Holly's arrival.

"I'm so happy!" Nicole clapped her hands together and did a victory dance inspiring more than a few wolf whistles from some passing jocks.

"The surprise! The joy!" Tommy joked.

"Congratulations, Nicole," Maria Gutierrez said, stopping to shake Nicole's hand. "You'll do great." She looked very, very disappointed.

Nicole flashed a smile at her, did the hug thing, the air-kiss thing.

"I know," she said, then laughed to show she was just kidding.

The four left school, heading for Tommy's father's Corolla. It was in the west parking lot, which was the place reserved for seniors.

"Let's go to The Half Caff," Nicole trilled. "I need to gloat!"

Holly looked over her shoulder at Maria Gutierrez, who was watching them go. Standing all alone, dejected.

My cousin cheated, Holly thought. *Even if that . . . that magic spell or whatever*—she could barely bring herself to think the words—*didn't work, she pretty much talked Ms. Zeidel into giving her the part. Not because she necessarily deserved it. Just because she wanted it.*

That wasn't fair. And it wasn't nice.

And if that's what . . . whatever she and my aunt think they're doing . . . then they should stop it.

Was she sleepwalking?

Holly was drifting down the hall of the house in Seattle; the floor was as warm and silky-soft as her kitten's fur, even though she knew it was really planked oak with a woolen floor runner down the center. And on the walls were containers made of the faces of beautiful young girls; their hair was trailing flowers and vines, swirling and bobbing as if they were water lilies. Above, more lilies hung down, swaying gently; centers of light glowed in each one.

They're the hall lights, Holly thought, and she nodded to herself. *Of course. The hall lights have always looked like that.*

She glided along, only slowly becoming aware that she was being led. The corridor was incredibly long, but if she concentrated very hard, she could make out the blue glowing figure who was walking far ahead of her, pausing now and then to give Holly a chance to keep up.

Yes, I'm coming, she told the figure. Then she realized the figure was on fire. It was walking sedately along, the blue flames rising to a point above its head like a torch. Smoke undulated back through the hall, hitting Holly's nostrils. *That's why it smells like smoke around here.*

The figure raised one of its burning arms and gestured at Holly, moving very slowly. Then it pointed to Holly's right.

As if she were made of wax, Holly swiveled her head to the right. The wall had melted away, and in its place a broad expanse of stonework filled her field of vision. The stones were not completely square, nor of precisely the same size: *handmade,* she realized. *Not from a machine.*

The smoke thickened, filling her lungs and making her choke and cough. She felt the heat; it was frighteningly intense. Lifting her feet from the lily-pod floor, she heard the crackling of the flames. The flowers beneath the soles of her leather shoes were disintegrating in the heat; they weren't lilies at all, but piles of straw. They were exploding into flame like bombs, and the sparks were catching Holly's woolen shift on fire.

Help! she shouted to the figure.

But the hallway had disappeared entirely. Panicking, she whirled in a circle and batted at her shift. Blisters rose on her hands as she put herself out. Her legs were seared.

She knew where she was now—in Jean's room, in Castle Deveraux—and she was searching everywhere for him. She was frantic; he should have been on his fur-covered bed, passed out as if from reveling. She had put enough fernroot in his nighttime drink to make him sleep for two nights; now she had the magic powder in her hand, ready to revive him.

Through the smoke and the flame, she screamed his name, passing Deveraux guards smothering in boiling oil and pillioned with poisoned arrows, courtesy of her own kinsmen. Through the brilliantly lit night and into the stables she flew, ignoring the frenzied shrieks of the horses and their grooms as she magically unlocked doors and didn't think to leave them unbolted for those behind her.

She ran down the halls into the kitchens, where the massive fireplaces, large enough to roast a bullock each, blazed out of control, dragon's tongues gouting forth from each of the cavernous stone maws. Of the cooks and their helpers she saw no sign, but a metallic tang was mixed with the smoke, and she saw a number of cookpots melted inside the fireplaces.

Quitting the kitchens, she dodged a figure all in flames, barreling down the passageway. She sobbed with frustration as the firestorm yielded up shrieks of agony from every quarter of the keep. Within and beyond these burning walls, her kinsmen were putting Castle Deveraux to the torch. With vicious abandon they were massacring the men of the Deveraux House. That had been agreed upon, and she had helped in every way that she could. No one knew of her private bargain with the Goddess, which was to spare her husband and allow them both to escape.

She clenched her fists as she burst into the bailey. The flames illuminated the scene as brightly as any summer day. A flock of geese, all burning, squonked and screamed as they died. Lambkins and their ewes had fallen on their sides, their wool smoking. None of this had been agreed to.

Then she saw her own kinsman, her Uncle Robert, rise up off Petite-Marie, daughter of a noble house in Paris, who had been sent to Castle Deveraux to learn the ways of a great lady. The poor child lay still as death, her skirts tattered, her legs uncovered. As she lay weeping, Isabeau's uncle pulled his sword from its sheath and held it with both arms above his head, preparing to drive it into the heart of the inert form.

"*Non!*" Isabeau screamed as loudly as she could. Robert glanced up at her, then gave his head a savage shake and slammed his sword into Petite-Marie's heart.

Blood gushed into the air; Isabeau ran to him and wildly pummeled him on the shoulders and chest, kicking at him, ignoring the spray of blood.

"This was not part of the bargain!" she shrieked at him. "Only the men! My mother said only the men!"

"You *slut!*" bellowed a voice behind the two Cahors.

It was Jean, alive; his face was white as the dead and tinged with gray, but he was on his feet and unhurt. With a cry of relief, Isabeau ran to him, her arms outstretched.

He cuffed her so hard, her head was thrown back; she toppled into the dirt. Her head hit first, and she was stunned into blindness for an instant. When she could see again, her husband stood over her, one leg on either side of her. Behind him, the walls of Castle Deveraux were a fiery backdrop to his rage.

"I have an escape route mapped out!" she said, looking up at him as she wiped her blood from the corner of her mouth. Her teeth were loose. "Friends, willing to hie us out of France! We'll create a new Coven, my love, based on light, not this terrible gray our families share—"

"Murderess!" he raged at her. "Traitor!"

He hit her again, so that what happened next was all a blur, a terrible nightmare that pierced her to her soul. As she tried to speak again, her attention was diverted to the movement on the crenellated roof towering above his head.

It was Laurent, his father, dressed in full warlock regalia. Beside him stood others of the inner coven, in their robes, their faces hooded, and they were all gesturing as one, arms outstretched, then raised higher . . . higher . . .

. . . and the Black Fire of the Deveraux erupted into being.

The Black Fire gleamed and roiled, shadow upon shadow of powdered heat, flashing and dancing like a desperate Nubian harem girl seeking the approval of a caliph, or else death would come to her . . . like a dragon stomping on the ashes of overheated bones. Like the disintegrating mass of a damned soul as demons capered through it.

The Black Fire, at last; what her House had schemed for, and the Deveraux had withheld. The Black Fire, which was said to consume every part of whatever lay in its path, so that the essence, too, was devoured, and something new, something evil allowed to grow in its stead.

The prize.

"To the end, a lying, murderous bitch," Jean flung at her. He pulled his sword and held it above his head, just as her uncle had done before putting Petite-Marie to death.

She caught a last breath and remembered the curse, that she would be doomed to walk the earth to pay for her crime against her husband and lord.

"There is a boat on the river," she murmured. "Run to it, Jean. My people are there. They have been well-paid."

Jean saw Isabeau's lips moving. He heard nothing. Perhaps the shout inside his head demanding that he spare her drowned out her words. Perhaps the fires and the screams around them were too loud.

He weakened, and he damned her and her mother for bewitching him.

We were too proud, he thought. *We imagined we could outwit the Cahors. I had charmed her and wooed her in her dreams, but when she came to me, and we were bound . . . I love no one else as I love her.*

I still love her more than my kinsmen, or my House, or . . . or my own very life. If only they would have permitted her to carry my child, we could have gone on, we could have made a new alliance between our Houses. . . .

We were always simple pawns, placed side by side to force the game. The Cahors moved first, and boldly, and they have checkmated us.

"Isabeau," he groaned wretchedly. "I curse you. I shall never forgive you."

Then he steeled himself to kill her. Drawing a deep breath in unison with her own, he raised his sword above her head.

She screamed—

—and the wall behind him collapsed. Jean half-turned, and saw the cataclysmic deluge of stone and Black Fire. Bodies tumbled toward him—his father, ablaze with ebony flames, and his inner circle, all flailing and shouting magical charms to extinguish the hellish destruction. Crushing animals, soldiers, a Cahors war wagon as it barreled into the yard; smashing into the Earth like the fists of giants, renting the ground into fissures. Smoke and heat and blaze—

In the last moments left to him, moments he could have taken to escape, Jean shouted a warning to

Isabeau. She lay unmoving, her arms held wide open. To him.

He flung himself on top of her in a protective gesture. He knew it was futile.

As the Black Fire washed over them, he murmured to her, "I love you as much as I hate you. I will hunt you, Isabeau of Cahors. And I—"

From behind her, someone tapped Holly on the shoulder. She jumped, startled, and turned her head.

The hall was gone again. She was still Holly, but she was standing somewhere else, a place redolent of smoke and heat.

Moonlight beamed down on her, and she raised her head and looked up at it.

A voice inside her head said, *Mead Moon. The Massacre of Deveraux Castle took place on Mead Moon.*

You have that long, before all is lost.

TEN

HARE MOON

☾

We seize for wives those we choose
Within their wombs our seed we lose
And after they have sons us borne
From limb to limb we'll have them torn

Welcome Goddess fill our lives
With your blinding, healing light
Our wombs are ripe as grapes from vines
Bring forth in us daughters divine

"Come on," Amanda said as they tried on costumes in Amanda's room. "Don't waffle on me, Hol. You said you'd go."

Rather than answer, Holly frowned at her reflection in the mirror. Relax? With everything that was going on? Sometimes she thought that she'd never be able to relax again. There was too much fear in her life now, too many nightmares and shadows.

But still . . . it *was* Halloween, and as much as the cheesy commercialism of it annoyed her sometimes,

Holly had to admit that she loved this time of year. It was, of course, quite a bit wetter in Seattle, but it wasn't like she had any control over her hair in this climate anyway. And if that was going to be the case, hell's bells—she might as well run with it.

She turned and faced Amanda. "How do you like my costume?"

Amanda, who had chosen a super-sleek all-in-black witch's look, studied her appreciatively. "Nice," she said with a nod. "And the hair is—*yeow*—definitely different. You're what, exactly?"

"Medusa. See?" Holly pointed to the silver ribbons that she'd wound around heavy strands of her hair. Nearly two dozen lengths of them bobbed every time she moved. "Tell me these don't look like snakes."

Amanda laughed. "It's a total *Monsters, Inc.* thing, Hol. And I like the silver makeup," she added as she stepped up next to her. "You're all Drew Barrymore in *Ever After.*"

Holly smiled. "Thanks. Liking that." She gave herself a final, critical glance as she smoothed a line along the long, toga-style gown—more silver and shiny but not really much beyond a silver cord belt and several lengths of tied-together fabric she'd spotted while on her hunt for a costume. Still, it all came together in a nice package.

"We'll be quite the pair," Amanda said. She looked dangerous and innocent at the same time, with her freckled skin and pale hazel eyes. Her light brown hair was pulled tight against her scalp and secured with a black satin rose. "Medusa and, um, how about . . . Elvira?"

Holly chuckled. "Maybe not quite the pair. Wanna borrow some socks to stuff in there?"

Amanda batted at her. "Let's go. Tommy's parties are fun, but he never buys enough food. We should get there early."

Tommy Nagai's house was the perfect setting for a Halloween party. It was a heavier, more gingerbread-style of Victorian house than the Catherses' Queen Anne. Old and imposing, it towered over the smaller houses from its spot on the corner of two cross streets in a well-seasoned neighborhood closer to the water. A painted lady in the most traditional sense, most of it was a brooding shade of teal-gray trimmed in muted purple. Darker gray wood surrounded the windows and doors, and the whole structure sat on a higher piece of ground landscaped along the front and sides with heavy, crisscrossed stones.

Staring up at it, feeling her footsteps lag a little behind Amanda, Holly thought that this must have been the mind-fodder for the classic haunted house and thunderstorm shots of a thousand black-and-white horror movies. Thank God it wasn't storming tonight—she just didn't need any clichés right now.

"You can't see it from here, but there's an addition on the back, a full greenhouse," Amanda said as Holly gawked. "Tommy's mother is one of those green-thumb types who can grow anything."

Holly squinted up at the windows, feeling the tension along her shoulders ease when she realized almost every window she could see was bright with welcoming light. "Three stories?"

"Four, if you count the attic," Amanda answered. "But I think they closed that off. On account of Tommy's secret insane wife." She pulled the collar of her black velvet jacket tighter and rubbed her arms. "Come on, let's go in already. I'm freezing out here."

Still reluctant without knowing why, Holly could only follow her cousin up the steps of the wooden porch and wait for someone to answer the doorbell. It was so dark and cold outside, windy—was there more rain on the way? It never seemed to stop raining in Seattle.

The front door jerked open, and light spilled onto the porch. "Yo, scary yet sexy American babes! Lab partner scary girl!" Tommy cried happily. He reached for Amanda and gave her a bear hug. "Come in—God, the temperature must have dropped twenty degrees in the last hour. In, in, in!"

Smiling, Holly obeyed, going with the flow as Tommy directed them toward a small sitting room off the spacious front foyer. They dropped their coats onto the growing pile on the couch, then followed him deeper into the house, and Holly found herself getting into the spirit of the party almost immediately.

The music was jammin' and everyone was laughing and talking—no frowny faces anywhere—and despite Amanda's warnings, there was enough food to feed an entire Army of Darkness.

Most of the faces were still new, but here and there she caught a flash of familiarity. Wait . . . was that Eli over there, with Nicole stuck to his side like a dark-haired imp? They started to turn in her direction and she back-stepped quickly, putting at least a half dozen of the party-goers between her and the couple. Had they seen her?

Amanda said something in her ear, but someone had turned up the volume and Holly missed it. "What?"

"I said I'm going to get something to drink," Amanda practically shouted at her. "Do you want something?"

"A beer," Holly said automatically, though she wasn't sure how much she felt like drinking. "Something light."

Amanda nodded and slipped into the crowd, presumably toward the kitchen. Holly had lost sight of Eli and Nicole. More and more people were arriving and the excitement level was rising—Holly could feel it in the air, like a layer of electricity sparking just above the heads of everyone. Now and then she caught a flash from the corner of her eye at ceiling level, as though the chaos and laughter and *humanity* in here was actually overfeeding something, making it explode into being for a brief, hot second before it fizzled away.

Not to be overdramatic or anything, she told herself.

She tried to stay in one place so Amanda could find her again, but she found herself inadvertently circling and moving out of the way of people as they tried to push past, turning this way and that to get a better look at the costumes. There was the usual array of Frankensteins and Vampirellas and, to her, a less-than-appealing array of rubber masks with plenty of painted-on blood and gore. But now and then Holly came across something original, like the cute guy with the red hair who was walking around in a hat and a long, London Fog trench coat. He looked so normal, like some kind of businessman . . . until he whipped open his coat to reveal pant legs that only went up to his knees and nothing else but a construction-paper fig leaf between him and the rest of the world.

Grinning to herself, Holly pulled her gaze away from what little there was of his costume and tried to figure out where she should be. But the crowd was so dense, and she hadn't been paying enough attention— now she wasn't even sure she'd managed to stay in the same room. The foyer was in the center of the house and it had three wide doorways in addition to the one leading to the small sitting room. Each doorway opened into a room that opened into another room, almost like a labyrinth. The same heavily polished woodwork covered every edge and corner; the same rich walnut wainscoting split all the walls.

Had she and Amanda started in the dining room, or the living room? The only feature unique and large enough to pick out was the massive, curving staircase in the front foyer, and she made her way to the bottom of it. Where was Amanda? Her cousin had probably gotten sidetracked, run into some friends or whatever. Maybe Holly would be better off just searching for her—she felt like a fool just standing here at the foot of the stairs, looking for all the world like the date who'd been stood up and didn't know what to do with herself. She scanned the crowd, feeling more and more anxious but not knowing exactly why. Maybe she should—

Across the room, her gaze locked, and she could admit to herself that she had been looking for him.

Jer.

He wasn't wearing a costume. He was dressed in his customary black; with his dark hair, eyes, and brows, he reminded Holly of the Devil. That girl was with him, and two other guys, and they were very ill at ease.

She inhaled and everything in the room went sharp, then abruptly faded away in a strange, lightly swirling gray fog as he started walking toward her. *Am I supposed to breathe now? Or stand still?* Was her heart even still beating? She felt like a mouse, helpless and paralyzed when it realizes the killing gaze of the hunting hawk has found it.

It should have taken him a little while to navigate the crowd, but oddly enough, it didn't—she blinked and he was right in front of her, standing so close that she could see the candle flame reflected in his eyes, the hint of a day's growth of beard on his chin. His scent was clean and earthy and warm, and having him so close—only an inch or two away—sent little pulses of excitement rippling along her bare arms.

Standing there, Jer tilted his head in an almost

quizzical movement, as if for the barest of instances he didn't understand what was happening to him, to *them*. But that flash of confusion was forgotten in the next second, when someone from the party—no more than a shadow in Holly's peripheral vision—bumped him from behind and pushed him straight into her arms.

He reached out reflexively, and the instant his flesh touched hers, they were lost.

Jer's hands slid down her arms, and their fingers entwined. Holly felt as if she'd been deliciously scorched, soaked through with flammable sensation. Her face filled with heat; her arms and hands burned; her chest tightened with unexpected desire so that she could barely breathe.

When they turned together and moved up the staircase, she couldn't have said where they were going and why . . . only that they needed to get there together and they needed to do so *now*. The laughter from the party, the music and the sounds of conversation, it was all gone; now there was only her, and Jer, and the mist, which had shifted into a soft silver-green that enveloped the two of them and separated them from the rest of the world.

Holly felt the stairs beneath her feet only in the vaguest sense—there wasn't any solid wood beneath her shoes, more a sense of pressure as she climbed, the two of them walking on their own personal carpet of cloud. They reached the top of the stairs and he paused, looking around as if trying to decide which way to go. Holly glanced behind her, knowing in her mind that somewhere down there was a mass of people, but she couldn't see or hear anything at all. For one quick moment she tried to snap out of it. As if he sensed her effort, Jer squeezed her hand, then slid his thumb across her skin where their hands were clasped. The sensation was unaccountably erotic, and Holly nearly gasped aloud.

He moved down a hallway swirling with mist and Holly followed, pausing with him twice as he pressed his ear to a door and listened. The third time he tried, he finally seemed satisfied that no one was inside and he pushed open the door. The graceful plumes of fog stayed at the threshold as if unwilling to cross; without letting go of her hand, Jer pushed the door shut with the toe of his shoe and turned to face her.

There was no small talk, no question about will or whim or why on earth they were in this room like this. Holly stepped in front of him and tilted her head, and when his lips came down on hers, everything else in her world, in her *universe,* simply stopped. There was only her, and Jeraud Deveraux, and this small, private slice of space and time that they could share.

It was so very strange—Holly felt as if she had known him for years, or at least for a lifetime. The feel of his hands sliding down her arms and around her waist, the way the muscles of his chest quivered beneath her fingertips, the rhythm of their hearts beating in utterly perfect unison—it was all so familiar, so *right*. Her hand came up, and she relished the softness of his hair as it ran through her fingers, arched her back to press her breast more firmly against the palm of his hand when he pulled apart the ribbon that held the side of her costume together.

When he lowered her to the surface of the bed, nothing else mattered but Jer and being with him, getting as close to him as she could. He rolled on top of her and she pulled at his sweater, wanting to feel his bare skin against hers—the weight of him was driving her crazy with desire as every part of her screamed to join with him, to be with him as one, body and soul. They were so close—

"Holly?"

Holly blinked. Had she heard something? Someone calling her name? No, of course not—the swirling mist was back, but she and Jeraud were the only people in this room—

"Holly, *stop!*" Amanda shouted from the doorway.

Jeraud's expression, one moment suffused in passion as he kissed her, suddenly twisted and he whipped his face to the side, his eyes flashing with rage. "Go away!" he snarled.

Startled, Holly sucked in air and felt a spike of discomfort shoot across her temples.

"Amanda? Is that you?"

Wind swept across her face and her eyes widened as she saw her cousin standing at the side of the bed. Everything behind her was glowing, as if she were backlit by the moon, and she looked furious.

Amanda reached forward and grabbed her by the hand.

A sound exploded inside Holly's ears, like a crack of lightning inside a huge metal can. Pain razored through her palm as she suddenly felt like she was holding a live coal. Light, hot and yellow, boiled out of nowhere and surrounded them, and when she tried to cover her face with her hands, Amanda's hand came with hers, swinging wildly. At the apex of the movement, Holly felt the comforter below her fall away as she was lifted up and off the bed. She lost her grip on Amanda's hand and sailed across the room like a thrown rag doll.

When she opened her eyes again, all that was left

was the anxious face of her cousin and the agony in her left arm.

"How are you doing?"

Perching on the edge of the hospital bed, Holly looked up to see Amanda cautiously peeking around the curtain of her area in the emergency room. The other girl looked even paler than normal, and thin inside her black gown.

"Better," Holly said with a shrug. She regretted the move immediately when it set off a dull ache along the arm now immobilized against her chest in a nylon-and-canvas sling. They'd iced it to the point of freezing it off before the doctor had given it an excruciating double tug to set it properly, and now all she was waiting for was the last of the paperwork and a prescription for pain pills.

She desperately wanted to get out of here and go home—it was bad enough that she'd broken her arm, but did she have to endure sitting here in silver body powder and a costume and being stared at by everyone who passed? It was humiliating. Add to that the nauseating smells of overused antiseptic, bleach, and latex, plus the seemingly never-ending squawk of the intercom system, and Holly could have screamed . . . continuously. "I just can't wait to get out of here."

Amanda nodded sympathetically. "I hate hospitals, too." She didn't say anything for a long moment, and Holly shifted uncomfortably on the table. Had that been her earlier in the bedroom of Tommy's house, had she really almost fallen into bed with a guy she barely knew? The whole episode seemed weird, like it had happened to someone else . . . but of course, she had the proof of her own behavior right here, in the form of a nice, nasty jab up her arm that hit her at about every third pulse.

But what threw me across the room like that? Amanda? No way could the slender girl have done something that required such strength. *And what about—*

"I burned my hand," Amanda said abruptly. She held out her left hand and, grimacing, unfolded her fingers. "See?"

Holly stared down at it, feeling her heartbeat quicken. After a moment, she used her right arm to hold the sling out enough so that Amanda could see the burn on her own left palm. "Look," she said softly. "I have a nearly identical burn on mine."

Amanda's mouth fell open. "What? Let me see." She peered at Holly's hand, then finally twisted hers until she could get it side by side with Holly's immobilized one. "Wow—that looks like some kind of pattern, a flower of some sort."

"Yeah," Holly agreed. She had to practically press her chin against her chest to see it. "What do you think it means?"

Holly glanced at her cousin and found the other girl staring at her. Amanda said, "No clue."

Holly said slowly, "One clue."

Kari sulked all the way back to her apartment, where Jer was living, now that he had broken with his family.

"What were you doing to her?" she demanded. "You said we had to go there to warn them, and then I find you . . ." She clamped her mouth shut and stared out the window. "*Kissing . . .*"

Jer wanted to say, "I'm sorry." But he wasn't.

Holly.

Her name danced on his lips, in his veins. Touching her, feeling her move beneath him, knowing that she wanted him . . .

But it's not just about us. It's something to do with what is going on with my father and my brother.

They are witches. I felt it. I knew it. And those visions that I've had . . . their family and mine are linked. I've seen enough, I know enough. . . .

We share a legacy. We were to become the new dynasty, but our parents betrayed us . . . then Isabeau betrayed Jean . . .

. . . and now she walks, until she kills him again. . . .
But why? For what reason?

Kialish and Eddie remained silent in the backseat of Kari's VW Beetle, respecting the artificial bubble that was created by lovers who quarrel in public. They had left Kialish's car at Kari's apartment.

When they arrived there, they quietly said good night and left. Kari was still yelling at Jer.

And the only reason he let her do it was so that he wouldn't have to interact with her. His mind was on Holly Cathers.

My mind, and my spirit, and my body . . .

Holly lay in bed, drifting on painkillers, remembering each touch, each kiss with Jer.

My mind, and my spirit, and my body . . .

What happened? Why did he come to me, do all those things to me?

Bast touched her forehead, then her cheek, and then she settled beside Holly's face and stared long and hard at her mistress. Holly stared back, and then she fell . . .

. . . into the arms of Jean of the Deveraux, who was carrying her to their marriage bed, murmuring, "Je t'aime, je t'adore, Isabeau. You witch, you have bewitched me."

He laid her down ever so gently and murmured to her,

245

"Let me get a boy on you. Let me unite the House."

She opened her arms to him, her fierce, dangerous, damned husband, heir to all that was Deveraux.

I am lost, she thought with glorious abandon. *I am his. . . .*

Holly jerked awake. Bast licked her paw with sedate tranquility, then flopped onto her side and stared at Holly.

"I am his," she said aloud. She felt as if she were floating above the bed, rushing headlong down a stream.

"I am his."

Then she looked down at the bandage covering her burn. When she tried to exactly replay what had happened, she couldn't.

Was it . . . was it something supernatural?

Bast stared at her.

Was it . . . could it have been . . . magic?

The cat began to purr.

The next day dawned drizzly and wet. The wild night of Halloween was over. Decorations and pumpkins sagged in the rain of All Hallows' Day. Back in San Francisco, Holly knew a lot of people would be celebrating the Day of the Dead. It would seem that such was not the case in Seattle, at least not among the people in Upper Queen Anne.

There was no word from Jer, no sign of him, to follow up from what had happened the night before. Holly was devastated.

After school, Aunt Marie-Claire and Holly had to go to an attorney's office to sign guardianship papers. Both were somber. It was a closure.

Marie-Claire had dressed carefully for the occasion in a dark suit and heels, and her trademark heavy makeup and jewelry. She looked like a TV evangelist's wife.

Holly didn't want to go. She didn't want a guardian. She wanted her parents to be alive again.

While her aunt made a few calls, she went looking for Amanda, who was in her room reading a book. She looked pale, and very tired.

Holly came in, her arm aching, and Amanda put down the book and watched Holly intently.

"So," she said nervously. "You're going to the lawyers to become an Anderson."

"No. I'll still be a Cathers."

"I think . . . I think I'm a Cathers too," Amanda said faintly.

Without another word, Holly unwrapped the

bandage on her hand and held it out to show her cousin.

Amanda pressed her burn mark against Holly's.

They looked at each other.

"I have to tell you some things," Holly said in a rush. "I've had these dreams, and these . . . these weird things have happened. And my father . . . I think my father stayed away from Seattle for a reason."

"We all have reasons," Amanda said slowly, but it was clear she wanted to hear whatever Holly had to say.

Quickly, before she had to go, Holly had told Amanda all about the sleepwalking and the visions . . . and about Jer.

And about Nicole and her mother, in the living room.

"It sounds so crazy, when we talk about it like this," Holly concluded.

Amanda slowly nodded. "Crazy."

Her aunt called, "Holly?"

"Let's talk when you get back," Amanda said.

Holly nodded.

She went downstairs. She was wearing her black pants and a black wool sweater of Amanda's. With November the weather had changed overnight from vaguely cold, like San Francisco, to truly cold.

She walked toward the front door and put her

hand on the doorknob of the ice-cream parlor foyer.

A chill skittered up her spine. *Say no,* a little voice told her. *Don't go outside.*

Her aunt joined her, smiling at Holly as she waited for Holly to open the door.

Don't.

Not knowing what else to do, Holly opened the door and went out onto the porch.

They began to walk down the stairs together.

She thought about people who had premonitions about getting on airplanes that crashed; or staying away from buildings that started on fire; or refusing to answer a door when a serial rapist lurked on the other side. Then she roused herself; this was her aunt—what was she going to do: tell her she suddenly had a funny feeling about accepting her as her guardian?

"Nicole probably had a rehearsal," her aunt said. "She's going to make a wonderful tragic heroine." Her eyes sparkled. "I was in so many plays when I was in high school."

"It must have been fun," Holly said weakly.

"It was. I'm not going to let Nicole make the same mistake I did. I didn't really believe I had any talent, and it seemed kind of pointless. . . ."

The Mercedes was in the driveway. Her aunt clicked the security remote and let her in, trilling on and on about the fabulous theater. She got in too, and began to buckle her seat belt.

" . . . so many opportunities these days, with cable movies and so much regional theater . . . ," Marie-Claire was saying as she started up the car. . . .

GET OUT! screamed every nerve ending in Holly's body.

Without her effort, the door on her side opened. Someone yanked her out, and she fell hard onto the driveway.

"Aunt Marie-Claire!" she shouted as an invisible hand yanked Holly, dragging her along. Her palms and knees stung.

"Holly?" her aunt cried, leaning across the passenger side to stare in amazement at her niece.

And then, with Aunt Marie-Claire still in the car, the car burst into flames.

Observed and released to her uncle in the waiting room, Holly joined the anxious crowd waiting to hear about Aunt Marie-Claire. Eli Deveraux was with Nicole, who turned to him at one point and whispered, "Is my eye makeup smeared?"

Holly was losing it, reliving the deaths of her parents and Tina. The hospital volunteer kept telling her over and over that her aunt was all right except for a few burns, and that it was a lucky thing Eli and Nicole had driven up at just that moment. It was due to his heroic rescue efforts that she and Aunt Marie-Claire had been saved.

He stood there preening, accepting Nicole's fervent thanks and a strong, grateful handshake from Uncle Richard.

Then Michael Deveraux showed, all preoccupied successful architect with his expensive loafers and his cell phone. Holly saw the expression of pain cross her uncle's face at the sight of him. Michael turned away as the man acknowledged him, then said to his older son, "Eli, thanks for calling." Uncle Richard bobbed his head once. He remained silent, but his jaw was set hard and a muscle jumped in his cheek.

He knows about Aunt Marie-Claire and Michael. Her heart broke for him, and she felt horribly complicit. She had seen them together in San Francisco. They had been together at the funeral. But what could she do, arrive at this man's house and say, *By the way . . . ?*

Michael's dark, deep-set eyes narrowed and he pursed his lips into an angry line, studying her as if he could read her thoughts. In a self-defensive gesture, she started to look away, then returned his expression with one of steely fearlessness.

I'm not afraid of you, she lied.

His answer was a smile of utter contempt.

Then the E.R. doors hummed open and a woman in scrubs pushed Holly's aunt toward them. Hunched in her wheelchair, Aunt Marie-Claire looked old. Seeing her that way was a shock to Holly, and she felt oddly guilty for seeing her that way, knowing how important beauty and youth were to Marie-Claire. Her aunt's cheeks and arms were bandaged, and there were liver-colored bruises around her eyes.

Her aunt's first look was for Michael; her second, for her husband. And it was while she was looking at Uncle Richard that her facade fell, and she was a very frightened middle-aged woman whose last remnants of beauty may have been taken from her.

"I . . . I guess it's a good thing I didn't spring for that face-lift yet," she murmured as her husband's arms came around her and held her close.

Eli moved to his father. They spoke in low voices. Then they both stared at Holly. Her cheeks burned, and this time, she turned away.

"You're beautiful, honey," Uncle Richard told his wife.

"No," she whispered. "No, Richard."

"Let's go home," Uncle Richard said hoarsely. "All of us."

Nicole opened her mouth, then closed it. She

cocked her head at Eli and grimaced apologetically as if to say, *Sorry, but I'm one of 'us.'*

Eli looked pissed, and Nicole moved her shoulders and held open her hands as if to calm him down.

Holly was stunned. *She was going to leave with him. Her mother nearly burned to death and she was going to flounce off with her slimy boyfriend.*

Outraged, she took Nicole's arm and said, "Yes, *all* of us."

As the Cathers family trooped behind Marie-Claire in her wheelchair, Holly completely ignored the two Deveraux men. The vibes coming off them were unnerving. She wanted to ask them where Jer was, but she didn't say a word.

Nevertheless, their gazes followed her as she passed them. Her back stiffened. Her lip trembled and she bit it, hard. Lines were being drawn between them and her; she could feel it, although she didn't quite understand it. The Deveraux were taking a stand . . . against her.

This is a turning point, she thought. *Everything that's been happening . . . it's coming to a head. How I know that, I have no idea.*

But I do *know it.*

ELEVEN

DYAD MOON

☾

Passion burns and fire grows
We triumph now over all our woes
We cast our foes upon the pyre
Burn them now with Hell's own fire

And now we plant in maiden's heart
Indecent thought for it to start
Tempt the lords of castles great
That from your passion may grow hate

School was a rush and a crush the next morning, and a refuge from everything that was happening. The Deveraux had nothing to do with her school—neither brother went there—and she felt a little safer here than at home.

After she'd gone to bed, her heart about to burst from her chest, she managed to calm down and convince herself that everything that had happened could be explained in a natural way. People's cars did have mechanical problems, after all. And this was Seattle, not Amityville.

And I have the broken arm to prove it, she thought sarcastically as she and Amanda moved through the halls of the high school.

Time to admit it: Magic is real, and it is taking over our lives.

"Hey," Amanda blurted, shocked to a standstill. She slid a glance toward Holly, and the two girls moved more closely together.

Jer walked toward them on the path to the gym bordered by tall privet hedges. He was dressed from head to toe in black and carrying a long black leather coat.

Oh, my God. She was terrified, and exhilarated. Her body was electrified. *He used magic on me. He . . . he's a warlock.*

Just like everyone says.

"How's your mother?" he asked Amanda, staring at Holly's arm.

"Okay. Well, no." Amanda shifted her weight. Then she glanced from Holly to Jer and back again.

There were circles under his eyes, and his beard growth was longer than usual. He said, "I'm . . . I'm not going to let anything happen to you."

She stared up at him. "Something has already happened," she said slowly.

They regarded each other. He reached out a hand . . . she began to take it . . .

I'm drowning in his eyes.

His chest rose and fell and he licked his lower lip, almost as if he were a vampire about to sink his fangs into her neck.

The bell blared, startling Holly out of her reverie.

Amanda said, "Come on, Holly," and took her arm.

Jer looked as if he were about to say something. Then he nodded silently, and walked away.

Holly was terrified.

"Holly," Amanda said, swallowing hard. "Um, I used to have this friend," she said tentatively. "Her aunt was into voodoo."

"Is that what you think this is?" Holly asked.

They stopped walking. "I don't care if we're late," Amanda said. "We're not saying the word we need to say." She took a deep breath. *"Magic."*

Holly took an equally deep breath. "Warlocks."

Then Amanda raised her brows. "Witches?"

Holly studied Amanda's arm, and then her own. She felt so numb, so frightened, as if someone had just told her she had one more hour to live. She looked back up at her cousin and said, "Maybe we should call your friend. Did you pack your cell?" Pagers and phones were not allowed on campus.

"Of course not," Amanda said bitterly. "I'm the good one. Nicole's the one who breaks all the rules and gets away with murde . . . everything." Amanda turned white. "Oh, my God. *Nicole.*"

Holly stared at her. "Amanda, you don't think Nicole set your mom's car on fire . . . ?" She swallowed. "When I saw her and your mom, with all the sticks . . . they were doing *good* stuff. Making wishes for happiness and love for us."

"We have our cats for that," Amanda said sarcastically. She bit her thumbnail. "How long have they been doing stuff like that, with the sticks and all. They had a whole secret society going. What else have they been doing?"

"Amanda, I know it hurts that they didn't include you, but they were doing things for *good*. Why would your own sister try to set your mom's car on fire?"

Amanda burst into tears. "Because Nicole and I know about her and Michael Deveraux. They're sleeping together! Oh, God, Holly. My poor father. He knows, too, and it's killing him. So he goes to work and makes more money so she can buy all her makeup and her stupid jewelry . . . I hate her sometimes. I just want to kill her. . . ."

"I know, I know," Holly soothed. She felt herself on the rapids again, trying not to drown. "But you wouldn't really kill her, Amanda. You don't have it in you. And neither does Nicole."

Amanda sank down on a stone bench and started sobbing. Holly put her arm around her shoulders and they sat together for a while. While Amanda cried, Holly tried to make sense of it all. Her attraction to Jer, all the weirdness . . . was Jer trying to hurt them?

But he just said he won't let anything happen to us.

"Let's get out of here," she said. "Ditch school and . . . I don't know, go to the mall."

"And call my friend," Amanda murmured.

"Yes, we'll call your friend."

They found a pay phone, but Amanda realized that she didn't have the number with her, and the directory couldn't find a listing for Cecile Beaufrere in New Orleans. They agreed to look in her phone book as soon as they got home, but they couldn't go there yet—school was still in session, and Amanda's mother would realize that they had ditched.

"If Mom's even home," Amanda had muttered hotly. She started to cry again.

Holly tried to distract her. Bargains were to be had at drugstores, so they went to the Rite Aid at the mall first. It was such a mundane, everyday place—kind of like one's own garage—that Holly figured they would be safe there.

In the basket dangling from her right hand was a bottle of nail polish and two pairs of tights, and for the moment her mind had blocked out the dark problems of Michael Deveraux and magic and death; when she turned down the housewares aisle on her way to the pharmacy area, the only thing she was thinking about was vitamin C and should she buy regular or buffered?

Something whacked her hard on the back of the head.

Shocked, Holly whirled as a blue plastic Tupperware container clattered to the floor.

"Hey!" she said sharply. "Who threw that? Not funny!" She waited but there was no answer, of course—kids, probably. Sometimes they found the oddest things funny. Once when she'd been twelve she had ripped all the labels off the cans in her mom's pantry; at the time, she'd thought it was hilarious, but now she could understand why she'd spent a week grounded in her room.

She sent a final glare over her shoulder toward the other end of the empty aisle, then shook her head and put the Tupperware back in its spot on the shelf.

There was a stinging along the back of her right

arm and she jerked as a glass—real *glass*—bounced off her elbow and shattered at her feet. Another one zinged off the shelf, catching her high on the forehead.

Everything on the shelves around her began to tremble.

She turned in a slow circle as drinking glasses shook and a large display of kitchen knives rattled ominously. Inching backward, turning, turning, turning . . . she had maybe fifteen feet to go when the rattling changed to chattering and a sort of charge built up around her.

"Amanda?" she cried.

At the same time, a young woman turned into the aisle. She was pushing a baby carriage.

"No! Go back!" Holly yelled.

Startled, the woman yanked the carriage to a halt and stared at her. Around Holly, the merchandise on display suddenly quieted. Was it over? She said to the woman, "I'm sorry. You must think I'm on dru—"

Everything seemed to fly at her at once.

Holly screamed and dove for the floor, landing painfully on the arm still bound by the sling. Her basket thumped in front of her and she grabbed for it and yanked it over her head as everything from plastic tumblers to kitchen spoons pelted her. Knives, measuring cups, eggbeaters—in a cartoon it would have been funny; girl as a crippled, three-legged crab trying to scuttle away from a rock storm. The only thing that was the least bit in her favor was that everything whipping off the shelves appeared to have been sent to where her head had been, without regard for her change in elevation.

She screamed again as something large and sharp landed point-down on top of the basket; she felt it scrape across her scalp. There was more screaming going on—the woman down at the other end, other customers and employees who'd come running to see what all the noise was about and then freaked out. All Holly could do was desperately clutch her way across the debris-strewn floor toward the end of the aisle. She'd made it to within a few feet of the aisle's end when everything went suddenly, blessedly quiet.

Too terrified to stop, Holly propelled herself the last of the distance and spun on the floor, peering from beneath the protective covering of the basket. The shelves were empty, or nearly so. As she and the others stared, one lone item, a heavy wooden rolling pin, rolled to the edge of the next to the bottom shelf and paused, as if it were seeking its target but couldn't find it. Finally it swung back and forth a few times, then simply fell over the edge and was still.

Heart pounding, Holly cautiously lifted the hand-basket off her head and looked at it. A chill ran up her arms when she realized what had made it feel so heavy on one side—there were almost a dozen knives stick-ing point-first out of the top, as if they had found the space above her head and just *dropped*.

Holly threw the basket away from herself as a couple of people reached out to help her to her feet. She ached in too many places to count, and she was probably going to be bruised all over by tomorrow morning. Before she could finish getting her bearings, someone was leaning into her face, his angry words filling her nose with a cinnamon-scented breath mint.

"Look at my store," the man shouted. "The cops are on their way, and you'd better have an explana-tion!"

Holly scowled at the man, a short guy whose face was flushed with anger. His *store*? She'd very nearly been killed here, and all this jerky drugstore manager could think about was his *store*?

"What kind of a place is this, anyway?" she demanded in a loud voice. "You stock your shelves so that a truck goes by outside and everything falls on the customers? It's not even safe in here—why, I ought to *sue* you!"

The manager gaped at her, his face going from anger-induced pink to the color of unflavored yogurt. "W-what?"

Holly leaned down and swept up the knife-studded basket, then brandished it at him. The blades vibrated menacingly, and the growing crowd of people around them gave a collective, *"Oooooh!"*

"I come in here for a pair of tights and *this* happens? Is this some kind of *joke*? Yeah, let's have the police hear about this, all right—in fact, I can't wait for them to see this!" She looked around. "Where's my cousin?"

"Excuse me, please."

Holly turned to see an older man, more distinguished-looking and with a close-cropped, thinning head of hair making his way through the crowd. "Julian," he said with a deceptively cool smile toward the shorter man, "go in the back, please. I'll handle this."

Julian—whose name tag Holly now noticed said ASSISTANT MANAGER—seemed to shrink a little, and he nodded. "It was vandalism," he muttered.

The new arrival eyed Holly critically. "Are you all right, miss? Shall I call an ambulance?"

"Holly?" Amanda ran over. "Oh, my God."

"Get me out of here," Holly whispered.

Amanda reached down and clasped Holly's hand.

Energy jolted through Holly. Amanda felt it too.

Once they got outside, Amanda said, "Some kind of barrier kept me from getting to you. I couldn't move. I'm so sorry."

Holly's legs wobbled. "Don't feel bad. What could you have done?"

"Taken your hand," Amanda said.

The two looked at each other, each revealing the burn mark that showed their strange bond.

"Do you think . . . think it might have made a difference?"

Amanda nodded. "Let's go home and call my friend."

After everything that had happened, Cecile Beaufrere was not home. Amanda left a message on her voice mail, to the effect that she "really, really, really needed to talk to her about, um, stuff like in New Orleans. And hi, Silvana," she added.

Nicole, who of course didn't know what had happened, started wheedling to go to The Half Caff after dinner. A local band was playing, and apparently that was the signal to the local kids to show. She reminded Holly of the cats, batting and mewing for something they wanted.

"But, Daddy," Nicole whined, stomping around

the living room, "everyone's going to be there!"

"I sure hope not," Amanda murmured to Holly.

"Do you think she's in danger too?" Holly asked. They had been trying to decide what to say to Nicole, wondering if she would believe them. She believed in enough to cast spells with Aunt Marie-Claire. But that was . . . gentle magic. Like wishing before one blew out the candles on a birthday cake.

"Sweetheart, we've just had a lot of accidents around here," her father said reasonably. He gestured to Holly. "You need to be home, with your cousin. She's not going to want to stay with us if this keeps up," he added wanly.

"I'll pay you back later if you get me a ticket to San Francisco," Amanda said to Holly through clenched teeth.

"Daddy, honestly," Nicole fumed.

She droned on and on, and on . . . and on . . .

With the warmth in the room and her tiredness—and her need to withdraw, be alone, think things over—Holly started to doze. The warm flames danced. They danced. . . .

It was in this room. Michael drugged Marie-Claire on this couch and tried to create the Black Fire, because no one remembers it no one remembers it no one remembers that we are . . . we are the . . .

. . . witches . . . he promised to kill us . . . he wants to kill . . . we were a noble House and a Coven. . . . We used to be the Cahors and . . . we forgot . . . we are the Cahors witches. . . .

Nicole brushed her elbow as she swept past, startling Holly from her reverie.

"Hey," Amanda said, smiling gently, "welcome back to the land of the living."

"I was . . . was I dreaming?" Holly asked aloud. Muzzy, she touched her forehead and looked around. She couldn't remember what her dream was about. She knew it had something to do with . . . with . . .

She shook her head. *My mind is a complete blank.*

"I think snoring may qualify as dreaming in some people's dictionaries," Amanda replied with a chuckle. "But you missed an earthshaking event while you were out."

Holly braced herself. "*Now* what?"

Amanda waited a beat, then whispered, "Nicole did *not* get her way."

"Go, Uncle Richard," she murmured to Amanda. Her uncle didn't hear her—which had been her intention—and he innocently exchanged the section of paper he had been reading for another section, unaware of the conversation across the room.

Amanda and Holly sat quietly on the couch, eyeing the fire. Then Nicole appeared above them on the stairwell and said, "Dad, Mom said she *wants* me to go."

"Surprise, surprise," Amanda grumbled.

"I don't think it's a good idea," Uncle Richard said, looking up from the paper. But on his face was a look of total resignation.

Holly kept drowsing on the couch. Uncle Richard announced he was going up to bed, and suggested the two girls do the same.

"Who knows when your sister will be home," he grumbled, then took the stairs without another word.

Amanda rose, stretching. She said, "I'm going to my room, but I'm going to try to stay awake until Nicole comes back." She smiled at Holly. "Want to join me? We could zap some popcorn and watch *Charmed*."

"Ha-ha, very funny." Holly smiled wanly, grateful that she wouldn't have to sleep in the guest bedroom tonight.

They trailed after Uncle Richard on the stairs, parting in the hall to get on their pajamas.

Bast was on her bed; she lifted her head when Holly came into the room and dropped down to the floor. As Holly changed, the cat sidled against her affectionately and began to purr.

"We're going to hang out in Amanda's room," Holly informed her.

Bast trotted toward the door, and Holly followed her.

"I swear, not only can you hear, but you speak English, too," Holly said a little uncomfortably.

The cat meowed, and Holly opened the door.

But she couldn't keep her eyes open. She was exhausted, and Amanda's bed was very soft. As Amanda nibbled at the popcorn, Holly scooted down and got comfortable. Bast curled up beside her.

"Dude, you need to watch this part," Amanda said. "It's about warlocks. Maybe we'll learn something useful."

I can't believe what happened in the Rite Aid, Holly mused, drifting. *That was so terrifying. Someone was attacking me with magic. Someone was trying to kill me.*

They've tried twice.

I'm so tired . . . I don't want this. I want to go home. I want everything to be the way it was supposed to be. . . .

Oh, Bast, fix it for me, little goddess kitty. . . .

"Yee-ha!" Tina yelled, flashing her a wide smile.

"Yee-ha!" came the answering cries from Holly's mom and dad as the raft lifted into the air.

She was on the river again. The sun was shining

brightly, warming her skin even as the spray from the river rapids splashed her. Her parents were smiling—laughing, even—as everyone on the raft got caught up in the exhilaration of the white-water run. Holly grinned and drove her paddle in deeper. Now *this* was what a vacation adventure should be.

She laughed with sheer delight as the raft continued its roller-coaster journey down the river. Just ahead loomed the huge stone outcropping, its raw, rough lines pushing majestically into the clear sky. The current swept them around a slick black granite boulder. Then, without warning, the raft dropped over a short precipice, and Holly's stomach dropped with it. Now she remembered that with the adrenaline rush came risk.

When they landed, water roiled over the sides, and they rode deeper in the river. Holly dug her paddle in furiously, but the raft barely responded. Thick, black clouds swiftly flooded the sky, blocking the sunlight, and a lone raven briefly circled them before flapping away with one shrill cry. A long, deep grumble of thunder was the only warning they had before the heavens opened up, and immediately they were both blinded by the driving rain and soaked to the skin. The raft picked up speed, but refused to respond to their desperate paddling. All five of them tried to steer, even as the river pushed them onward, seemingly determined to grind them between the huge monolith ahead and the giant boulders in the middle of the rapids.

No. Not again.

Holly tried to cry out to Ryan, to Tina, to her parents—tried to warn them of the grave danger they all faced—but she couldn't form the words.

Suddenly, she was in the water again, feeling it rush over her, dragging her down.

Once more she fought, unsuccessfully, to unbuckle her safety straps. Once more the cold swept through her body as the waters closed over her. She tried to fight her way to the surface. Once more, she ran out of air, and once more, the brackish water began to fill her lungs.

Even as she began to panic, thrashing about in a futile attempt to reach air, part of her remained detached, quietly observing and remembering.

The blue glow will come next.

There it was, right on cue. It glowed, it shimmered, it slowly coalesced. . . .

River algae streamed from its head in a grotesque parody of hair. Rotting strips of flesh hung from a caricature of a human face, with shiny bits of bone peeking through. The monstrosity reached out, its thin, grasping arms of rotting, fetid tree branches held wide to embrace her. Its mouth opened.

"Time to die now, Holly."

The corpse was right, of course. She should have died on the river with her parents the first time they made this trip.

I'm dreaming. This is just a really bad dream. The whole thing is a dream. I'm back home, in San Francisco. . . .

And in her dream, she was back on the riverbank, the only survivor. As she huddled, cold and frightened, the corpse rose from the river, drenched, water sluicing down its legs and arms.

It lurched closer. She shrank from it, but in the way of dreams, she couldn't move, couldn't get away.

Closer still.

"I am Duc Laurent de Deveraux, and I am your enemy. I avenge my House with your death, little witch." The stench of decay from its breath hit her like a blow to the chin.

She shuddered. Why wasn't she waking up?

In dreams, you're supposed to wake up before the monster gets you.

She could smell its breath now, even worse than its body odor, a revolting combination of rotting fish and decomposing leaves, hot and musty. Another step forward and it could grab her, and she knew if it grabbed her, she would die. *But I know I'm dreaming. This is a lucid dream. People who have them can direct them.*

You can create anything you need, anything you want.

She wanted to destroy the monster, and she wanted to live.

Anything you want.

Her parents, arm in arm, appeared before her on the bank. The sun was shining, and the river birds were trilling. For a moment, the dead man became unimportant. Her parents looked happy and in love.

Then the phantom loomed over her father's shoulder.

"Daddy!"

Her eyes flew open. Her parents were gone. All that surrounded her now was the darkness and the sound of Bast's snores. She sucked in air, gut-punched by the sudden loss . . . again.

"Well, that was pointless," Eli drawled.

Michael sighed and shook his head as he covered the dreamstone. "Nothing that gives you information about your enemy is pointless, son. You should have learned that by now."

"Information? I thought you were going to kill her." Eli pushed away from the table, stood, and began to pace across the room in front of Michael.

"Knowledge is power, Eli; don't ever forget that. If you know your enemy, you have power over him . . . or her." He chuckled at Eli's skeptical look. "I'm hardly a one-trick pony, after all. Just wait."

Eli gazed levelly at his father. "Is that what you're going to tell Laurent to do? Because my guess is, he's tired of waiting."

Michael crossed his arms and tilted his head. "Are you *threatening* me?" he asked in a pleasant, singsong voice that was loaded with malice.

"No way, Dad," Eli replied, just as pleasantly.

"She'll be dead before Yule," he promised. Then he caught himself, because he didn't have to prove himself to his own child. So he said, "And mind your own business."

"Deveraux Coven business *is* my business, *mon père.*" Eli lifted his chin. "Don't forget, you're not the only Deveraux in this house. I have a stake in how well you do."

Michael kept smiling. "That's right, son." Gave him a wink.

Left the room.

Thought about killing him.

Thanksgiving.

Holly was dispirited. Alone, she walked along the seashore in a black pea coat, mittened hands in her pockets. Her right hand clutched the strange collection of objects she had discovered in her locker a few days after Halloween. Dried salmon skin had been wrapped around a piece of ivory upon which a stylized bird had been carved. Four eagle feathers had been attached to the skin with—of all things—what looked to be the thin strap of a woman's T-shirt. A sprig of ivory had been wound around that.

There was a note, which read, *This is a ward. Soak it in salt water, then point it to the north, south, east, and west. We are with you. Jer.*

"Throw it out," Amanda had insisted, and Holly might have done just that . . . except that that afternoon, after Holly had done as Jer had written, Michael Deveraux called her aunt and said that he was very sorry, but he and his sons would not be able to come for Thanksgiving dinner after all.

And there were no more attacks.

She sensed, however, that the quiet was just a lull before the storm. She didn't understand why Michael Deveraux wanted to harm her family, but she was firmly convinced that he was behind the attacks.

She had planned to go back to San Francisco to see Barbara Davis-Chin, who was still in the hospital. But Amanda's friend Silvana Beaufrere and her Tante Cecile were coming to Seattle for Thanksgiving vacation. Tante Cecile had been concerned enough about the situation Amanda described that she had decided to investigate on the scene. They were due in some-time today, and she and Amanda were going to go over to their hotel to visit them after Thanksgiving dinner.

Despite the discovery of the ward inside her locker, Holly hadn't heard from Jer since. He was nowhere to be seen, and she had heard at The Half Caff that when anybody asked his father where he was, he told them some lame story about going to visit a sick friend in Portland. Tommy, in his role as liaison to the land of cool people, heard that Eli had gotten drunk at a party and told everybody he and his father were going to kill his brother when they found him. Of course no one took his threat seriously . . . except Holly and Amanda.

The seacoast before her was stony. Gulls hopped along the shore, pecking for fish or hermit crabs. Salt lined Holly's lips and she sniffled, her nose running from the chill. Seattle smelled of clean ocean water and pine trees, fresher than San Francisco. When she was in Girl Scouts, she had written her pen pal that San Francisco "smells like Chinese food." It had become a family joke.

Staring out to sea, she had no idea if she was look-ing toward Alaska or Japan or California, but she knew that part of her was beginning to think of this place as her home and the Andersons as her family. Oh, not in the way she felt about her parents—and she wasn't sure she would ever feel close to Uncle Richard—but she had been living here for almost four months. Granted, life here was incredibly strange, but what surprised her was that as time went on, all the bizarre things that had happened here began to feel normal to her.

"Warlocks and witches and wards, oh my," she whispered to herself. But her joking fell flat. Tears slid down her cheeks. She had never expected to have a life like this. She had never even known one *could* have a life like this.

She wished she could make sense of it. *Tonight,* she thought, *Amanda's friend's aunt will stick pins in something and alakazam! everything will be revealed. The pathetic thing is, I half-expect it will really be that way.*

Suddenly the gulls began to screech. Like a blanket lifted by invisible hands at four corners, they rose into the air, whirling in a spiral. Cawing, wings flapping, they flew to the open sea en masse, wheeling into the distance.

Wow, Holly thought nervously. Though she studied the spot where they had been, she saw nothing. The gray waves of Elliott Bay still crashed against the stones. The evergreens growing at the water's edge still whipped in the wind.

Abruptly the gulls screamed back toward the shore, some of them making a near-perfect 180. A flapping, cawing blanket of feathers and movement, they careened toward the water, swarming and jittering. Holly cried out, darting out of their way, stumbling and falling on her butt.

They hunkered into a clump, skittering and jostling, then took off again, as quickly as they had the first time.

Only this time, they left something behind:

Holly caught her breath, then pushed up from her stinging palms and stumbled toward the object. It was a book, or a fragment of one, the pages both scorched and sodden, the majority of them reduced to soaking-wet ash that clumped off and splashed into the breakers as she lifted it into her hand.

She was no scholar, but she knew Gothic script when she saw it.

And she also recognized the one word that jumped out at her: ISABEAU.

Thanksgiving dinner was delicious, but there was no warm heart in the Anderson mansion. Aunt Marie-Claire drank too much, and Uncle Richard was quiet.

Nicole was impatient to be finished so she could go visit "friends." Amanda and Holly exchanged glances, still unsure what to do or say to her.

They bided their time and, finally, managed to snag use of Uncle Richard's Toyota before Nicole could ask for it. The Mercedes had been totaled in the fire, and the new "family car" was a Volvo station wagon. Problem was, the family never went anywhere together, and to Holly, the wagon's purchase represented some kind of dysfunctional fantasy that they did. Nicole was left to drive it, which was not as fun as the Toyota.

She and Amanda tore out of the house, wild to be gone, in a hurry to get some answers. Holly had shown Amanda the book, and Amanda had been just as freaked out by Holly's description of the seagulls as Holly had been during the experience.

They drove to the Capitol Hill section of Seattle and found the bed-and-breakfast, a charming little wooden inn with five bedrooms.

"Bonjour," Amanda sang out happily as she and Holly rapped on the door to the bedroom nearest the stairway, having been shown up by the proprietress of the inn. The lady had provided her guests with a picture-perfect Thanksgiving dinner, the evidence of which was still on the dining room table.

"Bonjour," replied a warm, honey voice as the door opened.

A smiling, dark-skinned woman stood on the other side. She was dressed in a dark gray dress and black leather clogs. Her black hair was smoothed back into a simple ponytail. She was carrying a pink box labeled CAFÉ DU MONDE.

"Amanda," she greeted, holding open her arms. "Hello, sweetie."

Amanda embraced her, then turned to Holly. "Tante Cecile, this is my cousin."

The woman appraised Holly for a couple of seconds, then extended her hand. She kept her gaze fastened on Holly as Holly held out her hand in return.

Their palms touched. Holly felt something very warm, as if Silvana's aunt were holding a heated object that she was pressing against Holly.

"You brought me beignets, didn't you?" Amanda cried happily as she pointed at the box. "Oh, thank you, thank you, thank you!"

Then a young girl who was a younger version of Tante Cecile danced into the room, shutting a door behind her.

"Girl, you're so skinny!" she cried as she raced into Amanda's arms. "Haven't you been skipping P.E. like we used to?"

Amanda's face lost some of its mirth. She said, "Things have been awfully tense around here." She gestured to Holly. "Show them the book."

Holly took the soggy book out of the plastic bag she'd stored it in for the trip over. She explained how she had found it. Then she told Tante Cecile about the ward; when she pulled it from her pocket, the woman's brows rose.

"Someone who knows a lot about shamanism made that for you," she observed. She looked at Silvana. "I think we ought to get to work right away, honey. We'll have to socialize later, all right?"

Chills danced up Holly's spine as Tante Cecile gestured to a small table opposite the king-sized bed, where five candles formed a pentagram and in the center of the circle sat a Ouija board.

Holly blinked. She had seen a Ouija board once at a slumber party when she was ten. One of the girls had brought it and in the middle of the night they had all gathered around it, giggling nervously, laughing to cover their fear. Nothing had happened, not really. One girl had claimed the pointer had moved, but everyone thought she was faking it, maybe to get attention, maybe to scare them all more. *Maybe she hadn't been faking,* the thought rose unbidden, tickling her mind with memories of fears past.

Swallowing the lump in her throat while trying to push aside her skepticism, Holly slid into her chair. It was silly—after all, she couldn't be both cynical and frightened, could she? But yet she was.

Slowly she lifted her eyes to meet those of the lady who had flown all the way from New Orleans to help her and Amanda. Tante Cecile sat, grim, staring at her in a way that creeped Holly out.

Tante Cecile released her gaze, and Holly sagged slightly in relief as the other woman gazed first at Silvana and then at Amanda. The silence stretched taut between them as the candles flickered. Finally she nodded and the four clasped hands, Holly very carefully because of her arm. Amanda raised her own up to connect with Holly's; Holly's palms tingled slightly where they touched Silvana's and Amanda's palms.

Then in a low, commanding voice, the older woman began. "We are gathered here to seek knowledge. We call upon the spirits of the past to clarify the present, to show us what has gone before that we might understand what is to come."

There was silence for a moment and Holly could feel her imagination beginning to run wild. Were the candle flames higher than they had been a moment before? When had the shadow appeared across the Ouija board?

"All place hands on the guide."

Holly allowed her cousin to pull her fingers forward until all of their hands rested on the Ouija's marker, the thing that could move from letter to letter.

"Show us that we might see, show us that we might know, show us things of the past and what is yet to be," Silvana and Tante Cecile chanted together.

"Show me," Holly whispered.

Suddenly the marker shot out from beneath their hands and flew across the room, crashing into a mirror and shattering it. Holly didn't see it happen, though. Holly couldn't see anything, and all she could feel was the blinding pain. She struggled to breathe, but her lungs felt as if they had been flattened. She couldn't move, and then as suddenly as it had come, the pain was gone. Everything was gone. No sight, no sound, no feeling, nothing and, finally, not even her thoughts.

Silvana and Amanda stared at the broken mirror until a strangled gasp from Tante Cecile pulled their attention back to the table. Something wasn't right, they could both feel it, and as one they turned toward Holly.

Only Holly wasn't there.

A pale, shimmering woman sat in her place. Her clothes were centuries old and her hair fell in waves all the way to her waist. Her cheekbones were high and hollow and her eyes shone an unearthly blue. She looked at each of them slowly, as though moving her head was a great effort. She began to move her lips, but no sound came out.

"Wh-where is Holly?" Amanda demanded, unable to keep the panic out of her voice.

Tante Cecile quickly put her hand over Amanda's. "Don't be scared, Mandy. She and this woman are sharing the same space and time."

"She's . . . possessed Holly?" Amanda asked. She glanced at Silvana, who looked as scared as she felt.

"Yes, and at the same time, no. This is something far greater than that. She's almost a part of Holly."

Tante Cecile turned to the woman and spoke to her in French. Then, as if the woman were speaking underwater, a strange, disembodied voice answered in English.

"I . . . my name . . . Isabeau." The pale woman's whisper was low and her words vibrated in the air in a way no human's could have. "I am one who has gone before."

"Who are you?"

"I was born a Cahors, one of you, and I married a Deveraux, one of them."

"When?" Tante Cecile asked.

"Six hundred years past. At Beltane, it will be exactly six hundred years ago."

"May Day," Silvana whispered to Amanda. "May first."

"Why have you come?" Tante Cecile asked.

"Have you read the book? The one from the beach?"

"No," Tante Cecile admitted.

"Ah." The woman sighed. "I loved him so. He could have been a good man, had I time enough—"

"Isabeau," Tante Cecile interrupted. "Stay focused."

"You must stop it from happening again." The ghostly figure sighed. "It happens every night, in my time. I am tortured by it. Again and again." She began to weep.

"Stay with me, Isabeau," Tante Cecile said firmly.

"It will happen at Beltane in your time. It is the six hundredth year, which is the same alignment of the stars as when it occurred. It will come into your world, and it will happen again. You must stop it." Her sigh ricocheted around the room.

"Stop what?" Tante Cecile asked.

The woman sobbed. "Massacre. Oh, Jean, *mon amour, mon homme . . .*"

"Where is Holly?" Silvana asked. "May we speak to her?"

The figure sighed again, tears streaming down her

cheeks. "She is in me, her eyes will soon see what my eyes have seen, all these centuries, so much death. She will know, and she must stop it. Already she has seen my death and my betrayal of my husband, my love, Jean."

"And what is she seeing now?" Tante Cecile asked.

"She is seeing the darkness, the intertwining of Deveraux and Cahors, a great secret and a terrible destiny. Through time, it has been a war and a vendetta. Destruction is the child of my womb, and all I wanted . . . it was not for me to want him, to want his love . . . but I did. . . ."

Paris, 1562

"*Tell me about the Black Fire!*" *the Queen, Catherine de' Medici, demanded.*

"*There is no Fire, there hasn't been for nearly two centuries,*" *Luc Deveraux spat, blood spraying from his lips. Coughs racked his body, and more blood bubbled up on his lips.*

The queen placed a finger under his chin and lifted his head so that his eyes met hers. Even on his knees he was nearly as tall as the petite Catherine. Her eyes bore into him with a cold hatred.

"*I think you're lying to me.*"

"*Why would I lie?*"

"Why would you tell the truth? Your family is not known for it. After all, despite your pledges of loyalty, support, the kind sympathy your father showed me when all France hated me, 'the Italian woman,' you and your family have always been plotting against me. For the first ten years of my marriage you were the ones who cursed my womb, made it impossible for me to bear a child. Well, I foiled you at last."

The tortured man looked up at her. "Yes, and how many of your children will you live to see on that throne? The bearing of them does not signify that you can keep them alive long enough to produce heirs of their own."

She looked as though she would strike him, but she was a queen and she had servants to do that. She nodded almost imperceptibly, and one of them began lashing his back with the whip again. Luc Deveraux bit his tongue, refusing to let her hear him scream. How many dozens of his kinsmen had already been under this lash in the last fortnight? How many had she tortured? How many had she broken? He did not know, but she would not break him. He could not tell her what he did not know, and he refused to tell her that which he did. He would die first.

At last the man with the whip ceased his efforts and Luc drew a ragged breath. He stared in hatred at the woman pacing in front of him.

"Tell me what I want and this will all stop. Tell me about the Black Fire. Tell me what your family is plotting with the

Huguenots. They will not tear France apart. There can only be one king, one people, one religion," she stated.

Weakly he whispered, "There is no plan."

"I wish that I could believe you," she said coldly. "I don't like torturing you, and I fear that you will never tell me what I need to know, that you will die first."

He said nothing, wondering what she was thinking, what she intended to do. A flick of her wrist sent the man with the whip outside, closing the door behind him. For the thousandth time Luc tested the strength of the chains anchoring his wrists to the ceiling. Even if he could pull the restraints from the stone he doubted that he would have the strength to stand.

The door opened and his torturer reappeared, pushing a woman with long, black hair before him. Her hands were bound behind her and he handled her roughly, finally bringing her to stand before Luc and the queen. Marie stared at him with her pale eyes out of a face streaked with dirt and tears. Catherine nodded and her man yanked back Marie's head and held a knife to her throat.

"Luc, you know that I do not make idle threats. Either you tell me what I want to know, or he will slit your wife's throat."

Luc spat a mixture of blood and saliva onto the stones. "Kill the whore. May she burn forever for betraying me."

An amused smile twisted Catherine's face. "I take it you do not love your wife."

"I hate her," he answered, rage rushing through his body.

"And yet I think you love her, as well," the queen replied. "I know something of loving and hating one person and I can see that you do, your eyes betray you."

"I have nothing to tell you, believe me or not, but kill the witch and save me the trouble."

"Interesting choice of words, Luc. I think I'll leave you two alone for a while. I have some things I have to attend to." The queen headed to the door. She turned before leaving. "My daughter is marrying tonight, the groom is the Huguenot leader, Henry of Navarre. Little does he know that his wedding bed is likely to be his deathbed as well. Now, I have to see to arrangements for our guests." She spat the last word, then forced a smile and swept from the room, her servant trailing after her.

Seattle, the present

Now Isabeau spoke directly to the four women of the séance:

"During the Religious Wars, Catherine de' Medici tortured dozens of the Deveraux family, seeking the source of the Black Fire, but none could tell her. I watched her through the eyes of Marie, a Cahors married to Luc Deveraux. Before he bled to death from the many lashes he had received, Luc killed Marie with a knife she had secreted in her dress in the hopes of saving him. I saw and I could not stop it. That night Catherine's daughter married the leader of the Huguenots. The next day Catherine had all the Protestant Huguenot wedding guests slaughtered. Instead of being a union of peace, it was a trap. On St. Bartholomew's Day, the massacre occurred.

"Following this, several of the survivors of the Deveraux family, the few who had escaped the queen, fled to the New World. Here they have flourished, nourishing their power and their hatred for centuries. Jeraud is a descendant of these Deveraux as you and Holly are descended from my family, the Cahors, the name changed slightly in the New World to provide protection and allow a new identity to spring forth, if only for public life.

"The cycle is starting again and in a few weeks it will be the six hundredth anniversary of my shame, my failure."

Stunned, Amanda stared at Isabeau, trying to take in all that she had revealed. Suddenly the pale figure shuddered and her eyes rolled back for a moment. She seemed to fade slightly and then she returned, stronger, her eyes blazing. "My time draws short, we cannot long occupy this space. As I grow stronger,

Holly fades. But this is not my time, it is hers, and I can only pray to the Goddess that she does not make the mistakes that I did."

Before their eyes, Isabeau drifted away, her features slowly shifting and solidifying into Holly's. At last the blue eyes closed and the body shuddered.

A moment later the eyelids fluttered open and Holly's dark eyes stared out at them. Her eyes bulged from her head and her face looked frozen in a strange, strained mask. Suddenly, the muscles all went slack and as her body slumped in the chair, Holly gave a great gasp and gulped air into her lungs.

"I saw, I saw," she gasped, unable to continue.

"We know," Amanda answered gently, reaching out to touch her hand. "We heard."

Holly said, "They don't know the secret of the Black Fire. But they want it, very badly."

"Enough to kill for it."

Part Three: Beltane
The Awakening

☾

BELTANE

"I had a vision last night and it frightened me greatly. I saw the head of a great family take for wife a mortal enemy. Their passion was great and their power unearthly. And their mating destroyed all within their path."

—Duke Kensington to his scribe, Joshua, May 1, 1612

TWELVE

MEAD MOON

☾

Disguise our evil with faces kind
A goodly exterior, a darker mind
And turn the gentle to my power
And poison the most innocent flower

Transform us and make us new
Give us strength through and through
Lady hide our hearts and fates
Grant us the gift of masquerade

Thanksgiving was over, thank God, and they were on the verge of Christmas. But Marie-Claire Anderson was heartsick.

He knows, she thought miserably. *My poor, sweet, boring husband knows I cheated on him.*

That evening, Richard had tiptoed into their bedroom to check on her, and she had lain with her back to the door, pretending to be asleep. He had whispered, "Oh God, baby," and started to cry. She could hear him weeping in the hall like an abandoned child, and it nearly killed her.

He went back down the hallway, and she decided to follow him, try to explain that she was almost middle-aged, and she needed—needed badly—to feel young and desirable. That he plunked away day and night at his computer, never noticing her new clothes, her haircuts. And so she tried harder, bought more makeup, more clothes. Worked out.

He never said anything.

I was starving, she wanted to tell him. *Michael . . . he fed me.*

Her minor burns were gone, but she had stared long and hard at her face and seen the wrinkles and creases. She had been terrified. *Who wants an old woman? Richard doesn't want anybody. And Michael . . . Michael has abandoned me. It was just an affair. I should have known that. But I've been so lonely . . . and so afraid.*

Sitting up, she pushed herself out of bed, fumbling for the light switch. She was drained; it was all too much, the fire and the E.R. and now this, her marital crisis. *Will we get divorced? Can we make up?*

Her mind spun.

The bedroom door was ajar; she timidly eased it open and walked into the hall, calling her husband's name. There was no answer.

She continued down the hall, spotting a flash of white. *One of the cats.* She smiled sadly at the sweetness of kittens and little girls, her own innocence lost.

I will win him back. Nicole and I will make him come back, she thought. *We have our little tricks, she and I. . . .*

And then she remembered that Richard had brought her something to drink earlier in the evening. *Some tea.* She was ashamed; that tea had been a gift from Michael, who claimed it enhanced physical youth and beauty. She'd laughed . . . and started drinking it religiously, every night. Her legs wobbled like rubber and she held out a hand as the wall slid toward her. She moved on down the hall, looking for her lost love.

The guest room door was open, and someone was sitting on the bed. Her contacts were out, and she hadn't put on her glasses. She couldn't make out the figure.

But it gestured toward her, and who else could it be but Richard? The girls were at a party . . . *so many parties when you're that young . . . and free, and you have your whole life. . . .*

"Honey?" she slurred.

The figure beckoned her.

She staggered toward it.

Your whole life . . .

★ ★ ★

Michael Deveraux smiled as he and Eli stared into the Turk's eye.

"I'll kill her now," he said to his son. "It's a perfect time."

In the Chamber of Spells, Eli nodded eagerly. He wasn't used to killing living human beings, but he had definitely acquired a taste for it.

Michael whispered to the darkness,

"Dark is dark, light is light,
Know now that which is not right.
The time has come, the time is near,
Live the love and live in fear.
When it came, the soul will cry
Tonight, her innocence shall die.
Fight the world and look within,
Hesitation shall not win."

And the door to the guest room in the Anderson house opened and Richard Anderson said to his wife, "What are you doing in here?"

She looked down at the bedspread. Finally she said, "There are these big veins in the backs of my hands, Richard. I look at my hands and I can't figure out why they're mine. They're so old and ugly."

"They're the hands that held the girls when they were babies." The boring husband took the tired fingers in his and closed his large, pale, flabby hands around Marie-Claire's. He brought them to his lips and said, "Let's go to sleep, honey. You're very tired."

Nicole woke up.

She looked around, realized she had fallen asleep on the couch in Eli's house, and frowned in confusion. Where was he? Why hadn't he awakened her and driven her home?

She tried to stand up, and realized she couldn't. She was off-balance and out of focus.

I didn't have anything to drink, she thought. I didn't do anything tonight. We were here to . . . she tried to remember. *. . . He told me we were going to watch a movie.*

The space in front of her swirled with colors. Then all at once, a shape snapped into focus; it was a figure made of silver light, and it was holding a mirror. The face of the mirror was black, but as Nicole peered into it, she saw:

Eli making me something to drink in the kitchen; Eli putting something in it; Eli laughing with his father as they watch me sleep; I am a Cahors witch and Holly is my Coven Mother; Holly is the strongest one; they are trying to kill us so they can get the Black Fire; Jer is Jean and he loves Isabeau, loves Holly; Eli is going to kill me tonight and I must—

Nicole woke up running down the street.

What am I doing here? she wondered, stopping and stumbling around in a sweater. *Did I have a bad dream? Did he drug me? What the hell was that all about?*

She wore a short black dress and clunky heels, and a sweater. Her coat was back at the Deveraux house, but she couldn't go back. She was shivering because it was snowing, but she was outta there—

What am I doing?

—Help me!—

And Holly said to Silvana, Tante Cecile, and Amanda as they stayed in the circle, "Nicole has joined our side. And if we don't go get her right now, she's going to die."

They found her wandering the streets in Lower Queen Anne. She was half-frozen, delirious, and staggering like a drunk.

She was hysterical, trying to make sense of everything.

"I was, like, asleep on his couch. Or I thought I was . . . and then I dreamed that I was going to die, that he was going to kill me. I woke up running down the street. Oh, my God, am I having some kind of drug experience?"

Amanda cleared her throat, indicating that Holly should do the talking.

Where to begin?

"You know those spells you do? Those little things you ask to make come true?"

Nicole looked uneasy. "How do you know about that?" She raised her hands to smooth her hair.

Then Holly looked down at her palm. Her eyes widened. "When did you get that burn mark?"

Nicole shrugged. "I don't know. Halloween."

"What burn mark?" Amanda asked from behind the wheel.

She pulled the car over.

"Sleep well, fair lady hawk." Michael's grin was pure evil as he crossed his arms. He peered at the black wall in front of himself and, without giving it a second thought, began humming a tune under his breath. The song was as old as his magic; his magic, as old as song. It was another timeless pairing that would not soon depart.

Within moments, a portion of the wall directly across from Michael's eyeline began to blur. It swirled around until an elliptical glow appeared. At first purple, then blue, the glow finally settled on silver. Still humming, Michael stared into the glow as it subsided into a shiny texture. Instead of seeing his own reflection in the makeshift mirror, he spied the back of a young girl's head, her dark, curly hair shining in the otherwise dim and shadowed house.

Michael's watch beeped once, announcing midnight's arrival. The time was at hand.

The figure walked toward a staircase and was about to flick on the light when Michael calmly blinked once. He stopped humming, ending on a note as low as he was. The girl gasped, her arm still outstretched, never to quite reach the light switch. She crumpled to the floor, the other hand pressed to her heart.

Michael furrowed his brow. He didn't order one heart attack to go. The spell was intended to make her fall down the staircase and make everything look like a simple household accent. But instead, what was this? A heart attack? That wasn't as likely. People would question a healthy eighteen-year-old girl suddenly having some sort of attack.

Then she turned over, and he saw that he had not murdered Holly Cathers tonight, as he had intended. Her eyes were opened, forever wondering.

The youthful-looking Marie-Claire had died tonight, instead of Holly.

Ah well, he thought, *she was on the list.*

★ ★ ★

Marie-Claire Cathers-Anderson was dead.

And the weird thing about grief is that nothing stops for it. Tante Cecile went to close up their home in New Orleans in order to move back to Seattle full time. It took her longer than expected, and Silvana went to live with friends in nearby Port Angelus.

Christmas came and went. Uncle Richard was barely present; as he had during the troubled times of his marriage, he worked too much, taking himself away from his children and his troubles. Holly could only watch, thinking that maybe someday when all this was over, she would look for a magical poultice to ease the man's aching heart.

He took no joy in anything, not in the fact that soon his twin daughters and his niece would graduate high school. Nor that Nicole's debut as Juliet was due to take place in a couple weeks. He got up, was pleasant, disappeared for hours, returned, was pleasant, and disappeared into the room he had once shared with his wife.

It was clear to Holly why Nicole wanted to have nothing more to do with magic, even though Amanda tried repeatedly to explain that magic had killed their mother, and that Michael Deveraux had tried numerous times to hurt them all.

Holly took Nicole to The Half Caff, just the two

of them, and tried to talk about it.

"Look, Holly, all of this started happening when you came to Seattle, okay?" Nicole flung at her. "So why don't you just go back to San Francisco?"

"Because it won't end," Holly said, leaning forward on the glass table to be heard over the din. "He knows now. We've learned about the history of the Cahors and the Deveraux. We have to assume that the Deveraux know about it too. We're part of a blood feud that goes back centuries. And according to Isabeau, they're going to attack us full force on May first."

Nicole crossed her arms over her chest and said, "All I want is to be in my play and be left alone."

"You can't. None of us three can," Holly said.

Nicole sighed . . . and shook her head.

"I can. I'm not going there, Holly, and you can't force me."

If the three girls in Richard's care had tried to tell him about what was going on, he probably wouldn't have been able to help them anyway. So they remained silent, and kept him out of it—hoping that his ignorance would keep him alive.

"Baby?" Kari asked as she swung into her apartment. "How was your day?"

Jer looked up from the brand-new athame he had

completed; he was also compiling a new Book of Spells—his old one was back at his house.

He wondered if he should tell her that when he had left the house this morning to go running, a large black bird had been circling overhead, screeching and diving, obviously searching for something. Jer figured he had been that something.

Or if he should tell her that every night, after she was asleep and he began to drowse, he thought first of Holly, and silently invoked a Spell of Protection over her and her family; and then the nightmare began. It was the same, night after night—himself, hung upside down in his father's dark chamber, while an enormous falcon plucked out his eyes. In the corner, a moldering corpse watched, enjoying his torment, speaking in medieval French to the falcon, whose name was Fantasme.

If my father can get to me, he'll kill me.

With the participation of his Coven of three, and the advice and guidance of Kialish's father, Dan, he had set wards all over Kari's house. It was probably even more protected than the Deveraux house in Lower Queen Anne. But nothing kept Michael Deveraux from his goal, at least, not for very long.

So he lay low, and got news of Holly and her cousins from Kialish and Eddie, who were freer to go about their business because Michael had never known of their existence.

I wonder if the girls are working magic? he thought as Kari took the athame out of his hand and sat in his lap. *I hope Holly has been hearing the messages I send to her . . .*

. . . in dreams. . . .

At night, Jer Deveraux flew to Holly's side, and they soared into the star-filled skies. He came to her, and kissed her, and ran his hands along her body. And they flew like birds on the wings of dark passions, he the falcon of the Deveraux, and she the lady hawk of the Cahors.

"I have whispered spells to protect you. I have done dark magic to keep you well. Don't pull away; I am a dark creature. I am a warlock. I am no Wicca, no sweet pagan. My family worships the Black Arts.

But if we can make this grow, this love between us, this bond, maybe I can free myself," he told her in her dreams. "If the Goddess will accept my service, maybe we will finally lay our ancestors to rest, and create the new Coven that Isabeau still dreams of. . . ."

January, February, and March saw no more attacks from Michael Deveraux. Holly silently thanked Jer for his help. She and Amanda took the respite to learn all they could about magic, reading night and day, practicing, learning just what they were capable of. They set up protective wards around their house, and around each member of their family.

Nicole refused to participate, but the two cousins persisted in their own training.

This is a new world, Holly thought. Despite the danger they faced, she was enthralled. *We can do so much . . . if I had known all this a year ago, I could have saved my parents, and Tina. . . .*

She worked on spells to heal Barbara, and spells of defense and counterattack. She worked on deciphering Isabeau's book, absorbing their heritage . . . claiming her birthright.

And then, in April, two cats showed up on the porch of the Anderson home.

Amanda, home alone, had eyed the two strange cats. One was a Siamese, a pretty, petite thing with silken fur and big, beguiling blue eyes; the other was an attractive calico, a chubby female whose face was half black, half spotted around pale green eyes.

Amanda loved cats and had grown used to them hanging around—cats were drawn to people who practiced magic—but she'd never seen these two before. They looked much too well-groomed and fed to be strays, but neither wore a collar or binding charm.

She approached the steps warily, but the felines

seemed harmless enough. When they realized she was coming up, both stood and stretched, then made little mewling noises of welcome, as if they'd been waiting for her. She couldn't help but soften a little—they looked so pretty and sweet-faced. It wasn't until she was lifting her foot to the top step that both suddenly hissed and attacked her ankles.

There'd been no declawing of these two, and Amanda cried out as the cats' teeth and nails streaked across the thin skin above her shoes. She tottered dangerously on the top step, then twisted and found a handhold on the porch post as the calico released its bite and tried again. For its trouble, Amanda gave it a face-full of her shoe; it screeched and toppled down the stairs, where it squatted and hissed nastily, preparing itself to attack a second time. The Siamese's yowling added to the noise—Amanda heard herself cursing the cats soundly—and its claws raked across her shin, leaving a fiery trail as it swung around and tried again. Amanda stumbled backward on the porch, away from the stairs but losing her balance. If she fell and these animals got to her face, or her eyes—

Something large whizzed past her eyes and landed squarely on the Siamese's backside. It screamed, loud and sharp, then bolted; righting herself, Amanda saw Nicole swing the end of the windshield squeegee again, taking it to the air like it was a baseball bat.

"Get the hell out of here!" One of the herb pots on the railing shattered as the end of the broom caught it, then Nicole hefted the broom and shook it at the now-fleeing cats.

"Nicole, that's enough," Amanda said. "They're gone already."

Her sister grimaced as she slipped an arm around Amanda's waist and helped her limp inside. From the station wagon, Holly came hurrying into the house as Amanda fell gratefully on the couch.

She took a wad of tissues out of the box Nicole offered, then winced as she swabbed at a score of bleeding scratches across her ankles and lower shins. "They went after my feet, but I really think they were going for the full-body takedown. I think if they'd have gotten to my eyes, I'd have been a goner."

"Bastards," Nicole repeated. "We should take you to a doctor. You'll need a tetanus shot, at least."

"Later," Amanda said. "Right now we have to worry about Michael. He's renewed his attacks."

Nicole took a breath. "Okay," she said to her sister and her cousin. "I'm in."

"Jesus, doesn't the man ever *stop*?"

Holly didn't expect an answer to her angry

question, and she didn't get one—right now, the three of them were much too occupied. It had seemed like such an innocuous, easy thing to do—they would run by Tommy's under the cover of early dusk and pick him up because he'd complained to Amanda about strange noises outside his house all day. Then they would bring him back to their place, where they could all help protect one another. Staying together would minimize their risk and centralize their power—if a spell was needed, it would be that much more powerful with all of them chanting it. A great, grand scheme, and it had all gone to proverbial hell when they'd arrived at Tommy's and discovered the roof was covered in undulating black shadows.

"What *are* those things?" Holly whispered.

"Okay, according to a book I just read, some people call them spirit suckers," Nicole answered in a low voice. "Very bad, black magic—three of them can kill a person in only a few minutes, and there must be dozens on top of that house. I just don't know why Deveraux would set them on Tommy."

"I do," Amanda said. Her voice was frigid as she pushed her hair back from her face. "To get to us via that old trickle-down method—if something happens to Tommy, it'll hurt me to the core, and that, in turn, will weaken the three of us."

"True." Holly studied the roof, watching the shades of darkness glide over one another, seeing where they would creep over an edge and tentatively touch a window, then withdraw. It was almost like they were *tasting* the glass, seeing if there was something finer to be found just beyond its fragile protection. That something was Tommy, and the thought made Holly nauseated and almost afraid to ask her next question. "Why don't they . . . just go inside? Slide through the cracks or whatever?"

"They can't," Nicole said. "Apparently, they're creatures conjured for a specific purpose and person, but they have a history much like the legend of the vampire—no entry without permission. They can, however, be *carried* inside on the back of another being—they'll go for the first moving thing they see within their range. Tommy's just lucky he hasn't had any visitors since they materialized. Oh, and they can also attack if the object of their attention inside comes *out*." Holly saw her cousin's eyes narrow as she spoke. "Right now, he's trapped."

"Damn," Amanda muttered without taking her gaze away from the front of the old Victorian.

Nicole chewed thoughtfully on the end of a fingertip. "We'll have to draw them off," she said finally. "But we *can't* let them attach themselves to us—if we do, they'll just ride us until they can get in contact with Tommy. The only way you'll ever be free of them is if you—or he—dies."

Holly gasped. *"Die?"*

Amanda was more concerned with the problem at hand. "Draw them off with *what*?" she demanded.

Nicole's pretty face split into a cunning grin. "With a little something of our own."

Holly's eyebrows raised. "Oh?"

Nicole smiled even wider, until her teeth gleamed in the soft glow of the streetlights shining through the car's windows. "Learned a little something myself," she said huskily as she dug through her purse, finally pulling out a small bag twisted shut with twine and a thin black ribbon.

"By example, from Tante Cecile. Okay, I'm going out. Don't make *any* noise." She eased the door open and slid outside, watching the roof carefully. Holly and Amanda followed, taking extra care not to close the doors behind them, afraid even the slightest click would draw the attention of the spirit suckers.

Standing outside, Holly felt absurdly exposed, suddenly afraid that the black-on-black creatures thirty yards away could somehow see them, sense them, maybe even *smell* them. There was something hideous and terrifying about those things, much more so than flying knives in the open daylight of a drugstore—at least then she'd been able to *see* what was coming at her, to understand what it could do to her. But these . . . she couldn't help but shudder.

Nicole's fingers delicately undid the knot holding the top of the small bag closed. When she spoke, it was barely more than a whisper on the breeze.

> *"Dark are the shadows in Dyad's light,*
> *Heed as we beckon the evil one's bite.*
> *Turn them to the creatures that we raise this night,*
> *Sink them back to the earth before morning's light."*

As the last word passed her lips, Nicole swept the bag in an arc from left to right in front of the three of them. Black powder fluttered out and sparkled momentarily on the air, like finely ground obsidian. When it had settled soundlessly to the ground, Nicole took their elbows and pushed them back toward the car. "Inside," she directed. "Quickly!"

"What did you do?" Amanda asked. "What was that?"

Nicole gave them another of her stealthy grins and pointed out the windshield. "Look!"

Following the direction of her finger, Holly and Amanda stared out the window. At first they saw nothing in the low light, then the ground itself began jerking. Not too much, and not everywhere—just a spot over here, a circle beneath the bushes over there, a vague spot next to the walkway. All in all, about a dozen areas of quivering soil.

"What's going on?" Holly asked. "What—"

"Oh, gross," Amanda said suddenly. "Nicole, this is *disgusting.*"

"But useful," Nicole responded without missing a beat.

Closest to the car, at the edge of the street where they'd parked rather than pulled into the driveway, a half-decomposed rabbit was dragging itself out of a widening hole in the ground at the base of a tree. As they watched, more and more little animals, sad and dead, struggled up from their graves—a sparrow with a maimed wing, a rotting frog, a tiny, baby squirrel that hadn't survived its adolescence. And within seconds the noxious black shadows were flowing down the side of the house and covering the reanimated animal corpses.

"Nowhere is it written that spirit suckers have to use a human as a carrier," Nicole said blandly. "Or even that a carrier has to be alive. They just go for the first moving thing. They can't control their carrier, and once they attach themselves, they're stuck, either until their carrier dies or they find their target." She shrugged, but it was clear she was pleased with herself.

"These little wild things aren't likely to go marching into Tommy's house—even dead, their instincts'll tell them to run and hide. And the spell will send them back to their graves at dawn."

"Wow," Holly said, suitably impressed. "That's excellent."

"Thanks," Nicole said. "Come on—let's go get our boy."

They climbed out of the car, instinct insisting they still remain cautious and quiet. Tiny figures shrouded in cloaks of deeper black were dragging themselves off into the night, and the roof of Tommy's house looked clear in the wan moonlight shining intermittently through the clouds.

But only a few feet away from the porch, Amanda froze. "Oh, my God," she muttered. "Nicole, *look.*"

Nicole jerked around and peered at the yard, trying to see what had spooked her sister so badly. "What? What's wrong?"

"It's Sailor Bunny." Amanda's voice was filled with horror. "Oh Nicole, what are we going to do?"

"Sailor Bunny?" Holly lifted up on her toes, searching the darkness, but she didn't see anyone. "Who's Sailor Bunny?"

Nicole grabbed her wrist and yanked on it, hard. "Come on—we've got to get Tommy to open the door and let us in before Sailor Bunny gets to the porch. Before Tommy sees him!"

Holly's head jerked as she was hauled up on the porch after her cousins. "But who—"

"Not who, *what*," Amanda said grimly. She raised a fist and began hammering on the front door. "Tommy, it's me, Amanda. Let us in, quickly! Tommy, come on!"

The panic in Amanda's tone made the hair raise on the back of Holly's neck. "What do you mean 'what'?"

"Sailor Bunny was Tommy's cat," Nicole told her in a tight voice. "He died a couple of months ago. I never thought about it, but I guess Tommy buried him in the wildflower patch at the side of the house."

"Tommy, come *on!*" Amanda was practically screaming now. "Open the damned door!"

Something scraped dully along the concrete where the bottom step of the porch met the walkway. Amanda's throat convulsed, and she strained to see in the darkness below, even though she didn't want to. "So that means—"

"Sailor Bunny will want to come home," Nicole said flatly.

Light suddenly flooded the porch, filling their

vision and temporarily blinding them. "Boy, am I glad to see you guys!" Tension leaked from Tommy's words. "Sorry I took so long—"

They didn't let him finish. Amanda shoved him back inside and Nicole and Holly were right behind her, twisting and slamming the door shut just as something heavy thumped against it.

Tommy staggered, then righted himself, bewildered. On the other side of the door, a steady scratching began, punctuated every few seconds by a faint, cracked sound that was half hiss, half mewl. "Wait—what *is* that? That sounds like . . . like . . ."

Amanda sighed and sent her sister a hard look. "Tommy, we have a whole bunch of things to tell you all at once. But . . . um, do you have a shovel?"

In Kari's apartment, Jer's coven was floating.

Glowing, too, shot through with light as was every other item—from the couch, to the lamps set here and there, to the smallest knickknack or picture frame on a side table. Each item in the room seemed to have a shifting, inner fire inside it. Even the ivy plants radiated golden-green where the vines twisted around their climbing poles.

Jer had never imagined such power, had never felt

strength like this, had had no inkling of what was to come when he and his friends had gathered and each of them had knelt on a corner of the deep velvet throw on which he'd drawn his pentagram. Now an earthy-smelling incense wafted along the air, and candles, two black, one white, and two red, tipped each point, but their flames were more like powerful torches than candlelight. His left hand clasped Kari's and his right was encased in Eddie's. Between Eddie and Kari knelt Kialish, and Jer could see him from below his own half-closed lids. Kialish's eyes were closed and his face, like that of his partner's, was utterly serene.

Perhaps that was where this surge of power, this incredible *energy* had come from—the two young men were inseparable, like two pieces of a puzzle made only for each other. Different from the traditional man-woman duo, perhaps it was this very uniqueness that brought with it a strange new force—

—like the unseen energy that was literally lifting them all off the floor. Jer smiled slightly and concen-trated on the flames, trying to make them shrink, then grow again. To his delight, they obeyed, shriveling to almost nothing, then climbing high and strong at his mental command. Yes, this was a learning experience for all of them. And they would learn, all right, the four of them, explore not only the challenges of newly discovered power that they could feed to each other, but other things, too. With that willingness to learn would no doubt come new power, and other things, too.

Like the ability to defeat his father . . .

THIRTEEN

WORT MOON

☾

Act your will on those we've cursed

The Deveraux name will grow and spread

As we dance upon the Cahors dead

And poison the most innocent flower

Poisons to destroy, poisons to maim

Poisons to control, poisons to chain

Upon their knees our enemies fall

In defeat or death they obey our call

Tante Cecile had a vision.

She called and told Holly to go down into the basement of the Andersons' mansion. There she should find more history of the family, in the form of a journal much like the one Isabeau had deposited for Holly on the beach.

Yecch. Spiders.

Holly shuddered and brushed away yet another cobweb dangling down from the low ceiling over the stairs as she made her way into the basement.

She stopped at the bottom of the stairs and looked around in some dismay. The basement was crammed to the rafters with an assortment of boxes, trunks, old suitcases, and bags. She sighed deeply. It was going to be a long and messy search.

It was too bad her cousins had gone out, Nicole to rehearsal and Amanda to the library to see if she could find some more books about witchcraft.

Where to start?

One would think the stack nearest the stairs would be the newest stuff, but judging from the thick layer of dust and the omnipresent cobwebs, it wasn't. It'd obviously been a long time since anyone had been down here; an empty glass stood on the windowsill, a grimy layer of dust floating in it. She'd have to remember to bring that upstairs when she left.

Intent on her task, she didn't hear the soft scrambling in the walls.

An hour later, she found what she had been sent for: a potential treasure trove of information about the feud between the Cahors and the Deveraux. The large book was old and bound with some kind of skin— *again with the yecch*—and her high school French wasn't quite up to the task of translating the archaic version of the language in the faded manuscript before her, but she caught enough words here and there to guess at the meaning. The two surnames were there, no doubt about that . . . *foeu—that should be the ancient version of feu, or fire . . . yes, there was ignire in the same sentence, and taken together, that had to mean ignite. . . .*

A strange sound echoing in the quiet, a sort of clambering, as if someone were climbing up a gravel hill, broke her concentration. She looked around and cocked her head, listening intently. There it was again. It seemed to be coming from inside the walls. *Ewwww. Mice.*

Maybe the cats should sleep down here for a few nights, and decrease the surplus population. She shrugged and returned to the ancient manuscript, trying to puzzle out a few more words. Then, with a sigh of frustration, she set it aside. Maybe they could find someone to translate it for them later, but she was at the limit of her linguistic ability.

She dove into the trunk again, this time pulling out a rectangular piece of black silk cloth. Carefully, she unfolded it to reveal a border of delicate lilies embroidered in silver, with a silver hawk in the center—the Cahors family emblems. She caught her breath. This was definitely another of the family heirlooms.

Wow. Something's riled up the mice, for sure.

She peered at the walls, looking for mouse holes, but there was too much junk piled up against them for her to see much of anything. She shrugged, and set the shawl aside on top of the manuscript.

They came when she was bent over the trunk, delving into its contents once more. Not mice, but rats. Large, brown, long-tailed rats. Dozens of them. Without warning, they poured out of the walls from behind the trunks, their claws clicking on the cement floor like a hundred miniature castanets.

Startled by the noise, Holly started up and banged her head on the trunk lid, dazing herself for a moment. In that short time, the rats had seemingly multiplied a hundred times—there were rats everywhere, and all of them were headed straight for *her*.

The path from the trunk to the stairs was already covered in wall-to-wall rats, chittering and snapping at one another; there was no easy out there. Any doubt that she was the target of the rats' interest vanished when the first ones reached her and sunk their teeth into her boots. She hurriedly shook them off, but more surged forward.

Better think of something quick, Holly.

The only protection spells she had learned required materials she didn't have. Her ward was upstairs; here, there was nothing around she could use as a weapon . . . or was there? She grabbed the book and started swinging.

THWACK! A rat went flying across the basement,

landing with a satisfying thud against the wall. Her cousins *would* be out of the house, today. THWACK! Two more rats temporarily out of commission.

Bast! Call the cat!

"Bast, help! *Aides-moi!*" she screamed as loud as she could.

THWACK! THWACK! The rats were moving in fast now, and she couldn't keep up with them. Her arms were getting tired. She expected to feel their teeth in her legs at any minute, and once they drew blood, she knew it would be all but over.

She caught a glimpse of a ginger streak coming down the stairs, followed by two other blurs, one black, one white, before the three Cathers cats launched themselves into the fray. They knew just what to do, and they were merciless.

The pile of dead and seriously injured rats grew quickly, and it didn't take long before the rest of the pack decided to withdraw. Within minutes, it all was over, with only the blood and bodies of dead rats to prove it had happened at all.

"Thank you, Freya. Thank you, Hecate. And thank *you*, Bast." She picked Bast up and kissed the top of her head before gently setting her back on the floor.

Bast meowed in reply, and Holly got the hell out of there.

★ ★ ★

The book was a history of the Cahors and Deveraux, but had no author and no hint as to when it was written. Tante Cecile could only say that Isabeau had come to her in a dream and told her where to find it.

It told them this: that the six hundredth anniversary of the Massacre of Deveraux Castle was on the next full moon, which was Mead Moon. And it said one thing that Holly, Amanda, and Nicole kept pondering:

The ones whom I trusted most were my betrayers.

And the weird thing was, senior year kept happening. As if someone was checking off all the events that should matter most to them, the cousins did Senior Ditch Day; and went to the prom with Tommy Nagai as their escort; and then it was the last part of April, and time for the school play. . . .

. . . and Jer Deveraux, leader of the Rebel Coven, couldn't believe that Nicole and her cousins were proceeding with everything as if their lives were normal.

Maybe I'm the one who had to forfeit the normal life, he thought, *because my life has never been normal.*

Meanwhile, Kari finally confessed and told him about Circle Lady on the Web, and the cyberpagan's interest in "Warlock," and he dared to hope:

Jer: Yo, Circle Lady, Warlock here.
Circle Lady: Hello. I've heard so much about you.
Jer: I think you know me very well.

But she wouldn't come right out and admit that she was his mother. He burned to ask her directly, but the times were blistering with danger. She had already risked so much contacting Kari, and she avoided his prying like a mouse dodging a cat. So he took the risks, telling her everything he knew, and finally, the one thing she did tell him was this:

Circle Lady: The girls you speak of are in great danger, and may die on the next full moon.

So he worked with that, taking the knowledge to his coven, discussing it with Dan.

Under his guidance, sweating in the lodge alone, Jer had seen part of his family's history that his father had kept to himself, and Jer reeled.

★ ★ ★

Wort Moon

Castle Deveraux crouched, magnificent and terrifying, dark as a raven and soulless as a demon. It sprawled low along the ground, its very belly within the earth, and only its hunched shoulders punched toward the sky. To the fearful villagers it was the embodiment of evil, the dwelling of the devil himself. Still, these were not things that were whispered, not even between husband and wife as they crouched at their hearth on cold nights and listened to the wind crying outside. And at noon if strange shadows danced over the top of the castle, they just crossed themselves and hurried about their business, lips pressed tightly shut in fear.

Whether the castle had been polluted by the people living in it or the people by the evil lurking in the walls of the castle, none knew. The origins of both the Deveraux family and their castle were unknown, going back many generations and lost in the mists of time. The oldest living man in the village, the old blacksmith, could only vaguely remember stories he had heard from his earliest childhood, seventy summers past. Now blind and idle he lived inside his mind, waiting for his body to die and trying to remember the things that had been whispered to him about the castle. They were whispers he had heard from his older brother.

The next dawn had found the older boy dead, torn to pieces by wolves who had dragged him from his bed while he slept and left his body at the edge of the forest. Two different stories the old man had heard on that night so long ago. One was that the devil had created the castle from dirt and his own blood, set it upon the great hill and placed his chosen ones in it. The other story had frightened the old man even more, but now he couldn't even remember it if he wanted to.

The walls were strong, built of dark stone that reflected none of the sun's light but only swallowed it in darkness. Still, it could be seen from a great distance, hideous in its appearance. At a monastery far distant it had once been visible through a window in the chapel. Many a priest both young and old had found himself shivering while staring at the distant castle instead of the statue of the Virgin whom he was praying to.

The Deveraux were wealthy with connections far above those of the humble priests. Still, it was hard to ignore the evil they felt spilling from the place and to close their ears to the strange sounds sometimes heard late at night when no godly person should be awake. Eventually something had to be said, and it was. The Bishop was sympathetic, reassuring, and had a solution. Within a fortnight a beautiful stained-glass window graced the humble chapel. A barrier between the good priests and the evil of the Deveraux Castle. And though puzzled, the good priests were slightly reassured and more than a little grateful. After all, they had no idea that the money to pay for the window had come from the very castle whose sight it was meant to obscure.

Life continued on for the priests who felt much safer because of the window. Its bright reds and greens comforted them and protected them. The colors shielded them from the outside world, keeping them and all their knowledge, all their faith, safely locked up in the monastery. And one dark autumn night while they held a midnight mass the window and its bright colors kept them from seeing the flames that were engulfing the Deveraux Castle.

But they knew it was burning. Deveraux women, children, and men at arms . . . the priests knew they would die that night, by Cahors hands.

They prayed fervently for success. They prayed that the Deveraux would be completely wiped out.

And then, the Blessed Virgin willing, the church would turn on the Cahors, and make them taste the flames as well— the fires of the stake, and an eternity in Hell for their witchcraft.

Within the castle all were asleep, or were meant to be. Inside the stables a horse squealed, frightened by a demon that he alone could see. A tired keeper rose from his bed to quiet the animal. His son, a boy of five, looked up at him with sleepy eyes. The child was curled against a horse's stomach for warmth, the beast's shoulder pillowing his tiny head. The horse lifted his head as well, ears swiveling uneasily.

"Go back to sleep," Pierre instructed boy and beast. Both dropped their heads back down and closed their eyes.

The keeper had worked in the stables since he was his son's age. He had been the head stableman for the past ten *years. Nothing the animals did surprised him anymore. For that matter, nothing his masters did surprised him either. He had seen and heard many things over the years that would have made a lesser man run and hide. He prided himself on his courage, though, and his loyalty. His was a good job, one that he could keep along with his life if he just kept his mouth shut. Loose lips were what had gotten him this position, the loose lips of the previous stablemaster. The man had talked too much and when they had found him dead, trampled to death by the horses, Pierre had vowed that he would not make the same mistake.*

He walked slowly down the line of stalls, gently enough not to waken the sleeping horses and loudly enough not to startle the ones who were yet awake. He stopped outside of Thunder's stall. The big stallion was always jumpy, and Pierre believed it was he who had been making all the noise. The horse was fast asleep, though, on his side and snoring gently.

The squeal came again, from the last stall, and Pierre felt the hair on the back of his neck stand up as he moved toward the dark head of the gelding, Philippe. The horse's eyes were wild and he tossed his head when Pierre tried to lay his hand on his muzzle. Philippe was the gentlest horse in the stable, the steadiest, the calmest, and the one that Pierre had always sworn could see things that people could not.

Instead of being comforted by his presence, Philippe grew

more agitated, kicking at the stall and beginning to foam a little at the mouth in anxiety. Pierre felt the bile rising in the back of his throat as the horse's fear communicated itself to him. Something was dreadfully wrong. He heard something behind him that was not yet a sound, but more of a feeling, a thought that tickled his mind.

He turned and tried to draw breath for one strangled scream.

And as he gurgled and died in the straw, the Cahors wife of young Jean, the Lady Isabeau, looked down on him with pity. Then she beckoned a young man in silver and black chain mail forward and said to the Cahors assassin, "Go with the protection of the Goddess," and the Massacre had begun.

"Black Fire," Jer gasped to his Coven. "They did it because we would not share the Black Fire . . . everyone thought it was lost with the death of Jean . . . my death . . . but I did not die . . . I went to Normandy . . . I found others like me . . . we were persecuted . . . the Italian woman nearly wiped us out . . . to England . . . and there, we found Cahors descendents, and we followed them . . . Quebec, New York, Pennsylvania. . . ."

"Yes, yes," Laurent whispered, seeing into a heavily warded place where Michael and Eli could not go. *"Yes, I see it. I see what my son saw. I know."*

The decaying corpse of the nobleman regarded his two acolytes, Deveraux father and son, and said, *"I will share the secret at last. The secret of the Black Fire. And we will use it on Mead Moon to destroy the House of Cahors forever."*

Michael said, "What of my other son?"

Laurent regarded the man. *"Have you perhaps thought to strengthen his magical abilities by pitting him against yourself?"*

Eli gaped at his father, who laughed and said, "It worked, didn't it? In his eagerness to protect those three little witches, he has learned the secret of the Black Fire, hasn't he?"

"If he can be brought back into the fold, he might live," Laurent pondered.

"We'll all live," Michael said airily. "I know now that you need us, Duc Laurent. We have form and shape in this world, and you don't. So . . ."

The ghostly Deveraux chuckled and said, *"We'll see. Mead Moon will tell the tale."*

The three cousins talked about leaving town for Mead Moon. Then Tommy showed up at their house, breathless and freaked out, and said, "I found this on my bed when I got home from school today."

It was the beak of a bird wrapped in ivy, with a note

that read: *Give this to Holly if you want her to live.*

On the other side of the note was written:

Greetings to the Leader of the Cahors Coven from the Leader of the Rebel Coven: Play it out. We'll show, and we'll help you.

—J. D.

"Is it Jer or is it Jean who wrote the note?" Amanda asked.

"And can we trust him?" Nicole wondered aloud. "Isabeau betrayed him, and he swore vengeance. He's followed her through time and space, and I'm not so sure what he will do if he finds her again. Especially on Mead Moon."

Nicole said, "It's Jer now, not Jean."

And he loves me, Holly thought. *Or does he?*

The three glanced uncertainly at one another, then at her. Tommy said, "You're the big cheese, Holly. Whatever you say, we'll do."

"We?" she asked, looking at him with raised brows.

"Hey, I was your lab partner. It doesn't get any scarier than that. I figure this . . . pfft, no biggie."

"Thanks, Tommy," Holly said warmly. "We need all the help we can get."

★ ★ ★

And so, to play it out. The show would go on.

On Mead Moon, Holly and Amanda sat with Uncle Richard in the heavily warded auditorium watching Nicole's debut as Juliet. Nerves were frayed, senses alert.

Tante Cecile had phoned three days ago to say that she was on her way in from the airport, and she would be there soon.

She had not been heard from since.

"... *cutting foreign throats, Of breaches, ambuscadoes, Spanish blades, Of heaths five fathom deep; and then anon drums in his ear, at which he starts and wakes—*"

Holly sat bolt upright, heart pounding in fear. Amanda had nudged her.

"Trance?" Amanda whispered, and Holly was very afraid.

"Dunno," she mouthed.

"... *and, being thus frighted, swears a prayer or two, And sleeps again.*"

The actor playing Mercutio was really hamming it up.

"*This is that very Mab that plats the manes of horses in the night.*"

Horses. She remembered a stable filled with horses and people. *Not San Francisco. Somewhere else.*

Castle Deveraux.

Her heart pounded. She was perspiring with fear.

"My mind misgives some consequence, yet hanging in the stars, shall bitterly begin his fearful date with this night's revels," Romeo intoned gravely.

"Not if I can help it," she whispered.

Amanda nodded slowly and turned her eyes back to the stage, where Nicole was about to make another appearance as Juliet. On the other side of Amanda, Richard sat quietly, but Holly could see the tears streaming down her uncle's face. Tommy was back-stage working as "propmaster." Nobody was fooled by his sudden interest in theater, but they assumed he was crushing on Nicole and had taken the job to be near her—an assumption magically encouraged by Holly.

Nicole was stunning as Juliet. She carried herself with grace, and the passion that burned from her eyes made her entire face radiant.

"My only love sprung from my only hate! Too early seen unknown, and known too late! Prodigious birth of love it is to me, That I must love a loathed enemy," Nicole intoned on stage.

"This is weirdly appropriate," Amanda whispered. "It's really freaking me out."

"I know the feeling," Holly whispered back. "And I—"

* * *

Then she fell into a black place and she was—

Isabeau let the other assassins in, then retired to her rooms. Soon her kinsmen would come and set her world upside down. She had devised a plan, though. It was a betrayal of her family, her mother, perhaps even herself, but she was forsworn to it. It was a true oath, not the lie she had spoken while she touched the dead lambkin's heart beside her mother. No matter what the cost, Jean must live.

She had servants waiting at the river ready to spirit them away as soon as it was time. Patience, she schooled herself. Soon they could start a new life together, create a new coven, and defeat the violence and hatred of their kin. Their love was strong and it would shine like a beacon and attract others. Together they would forge a legacy that would not be soon forgotten.

A step in the hall made her start. She strained her ears, listening, was it time so soon? No, it was a servant, late to finish his chores and now hurrying off to bed, to sleep. The Lady willing, he might even wake again whereas his masters would not.

Her hands shook and she clenched them in her lap, willing herself to be calm. She would have but one chance, one hope. Everything must go exactly as she had planned. To move too soon would spell disaster, to move an instant too late would bring certain death to her beloved Jean. So, she waited, ready, anxious, and watchful.

The sense of urgency began to press more and more heavily upon Holly. She found herself squirming in her chair, only half aware of her cousin's lament about the slowness of time while waiting for word of her love. Holly felt like two people, one who belonged right where she was in a high school auditorium watching her cousin in *Romeo and Juliet*. The other was . . .

Isabeau leaped to her feet, her straining ears hearing the frightened shouts of men. She snatched the tiny bottle of magic powder in her hand. It was time! She fought the urge to run and see the battle; soon enough the battle would be upon her and it would consume both her and Jean if she wasn't very fast and very clever.

As she took to the stairs she reminded herself that her kinsmen were equally cunning. If they were just now being discovered they would have been here already for a couple of hours. The thought lent her feet wings as she raced into Jean's chambers. She muttered an oath under her breath as she turned this way and that. She had drugged him so that he would sleep until she came to revive him. She knew she had put enough

*fernroot in his evening drink to make him sleep for two nights,
so where was he? Suddenly a burning arrow whistled past her
ear and landed on the fur-covered bed. The fire spread quickly
until the smoke began filling her lungs.*

Holly began to cough and she heard a few others
follow suit. Her nose began to itch. Someone must
be smoking. She looked around in irritation, wondering who it was. She saw no one, but the smell was
definitely getting stronger. Now other people were
looking around for the source. Suddenly someone
shouted—

"Fire!"

*Isabeau could hear a dozen voices take up the cry below.
Jean's was not one of them. She would have known his voice
out of a crowd of hundreds. She took one last frantic look
around the room before the smoke forced her to the door. As she
turned to go, a finger of flame reached out and touched the hem
of her garment. She smothered it quickly, backing out the door,
before it could engulf her entire dress. She ran to each of the
other rooms, quickly scanning each only to turn to the next. At
some point she began shouting his name, desperately hoping he
would hear her and answer.*

*At last she found her way back to the stables, where flames
were already engulfing both man and beast. A few words sent*

the doors flinging open before her only to slam shut again after her passage. Any pursuers could not follow; unfortunately, neither could those seeking safety.

After the stables she was in the courtyard racing back toward the main hall. Everywhere around her men fell, victims of arrows or boiling oil. The stench of burning hair and flesh was worse than the smoke, and Isabeau was forced to slow her steps as she began to gag. Still, she pushed on as quickly as she could while her chest and body heaved in revolt.

She made it back to the great hall and tried once more to shout for Jean. The acrid smoke was burning her lungs, though, so her words came out as little more than a whisper. Time was running out and she fought the panic that rose inside her. She would find him, she must.

She turned and stumbled toward the kitchens. There, the massive fireplaces, large enough to roast a bullock each, blazed out of control, dragon's tongues gouting forth from each of the cavernous stone maws. Of the cooks and their helpers she saw no sign and could only hope that they were far away and safe. There was a metallic tang in the air mixed with the smoke from cookpots melted inside the fireplaces.

Quitting the kitchens, she dodged a figure all in flames, barreling down the passageway. She sobbed with frustration as the firestorm yielded up shrieks of agony from every quarter of the keep. Within and beyond these burning walls, her kinsmen were putting Castle Deveraux to the torch. With vicious abandon they were massacring the men of the Deveraux House. That had been agreed upon, and she had helped in every way that she could. No one knew of her private bargain with the Goddess, which was to spare her husband and allow them both to escape.

She clenched her fists as she burst into the bailey. The flames illuminated the scene as brightly as any summer day. A flock of geese, all burning, squonked and screamed as they died. Lambkins and their ewes had fallen on their sides, their wool smoking. None of this had been agreed to. Then she saw her own kinsman, her Uncle Robert, rise up off Petite-Marie, daughter of a noble house in Paris, who had been sent to Castle Deveraux to learn the ways of a great lady. The poor child lay still as death, her skirts tattered, her legs uncovered. As she lay weeping, Isabeau's uncle pulled his sword from its sheath and held it with both arms above his head, preparing to drive it into the heart of the inert form.

"Non!" Isabeau screamed as loudly as she could. Robert glanced up at her, then gave his head a savage shake and slammed his sword into Petite-Marie's heart. Blood gushed into the air as Isabeau ran to him and wildly pummeled him on the shoulders and chest, kicking at him, ignoring the spray of blood.

"This was not part of the bargain!" she shrieked at him. "Only the men! My mother said only the men!"

"You slut!" bellowed a voice Isabeau knew well.

★ ★ ★

"The doors are locked!" came the hysterical cry from the first person to reach an exit. Holly jumped to her feet, grabbing Amanda's arm and Uncle Richard's hand as she moved toward the stage, fighting the mass of people suddenly intent on escaping the auditorium.

"Why aren't the sprinklers going on?" Holly shouted.

"Magic much?" Amanda yelled back.

"Girls, you're going the wrong way!" Uncle Richard shouted.

"We have to get to Nicole!" Holly cried to Amanda. "There are magics at work here, I can feel them!" She didn't know if Amanda had actually heard her, but she came along willingly at least.

Holly's uncle was another story; he started pulling the two of them toward the closest exit and saying, "Keep behind me."

With an aggressiveness she hadn't known he possessed, he began pushing people out of his way as he continually checked on her and Amanda over his shoulder. He was like a lion protecting his cubs.

Holly said to Amanda, "We have to do something!"

"Don't panic," Richard assured them. "I'll get you out of here."

The two looked at each other; then they clasped hands and Holly whispered a Spell of Glamour in ancient Latin. Then she added, "Uncle Richard, go outside. We are safely with you."

She wriggled her other hand free. Amanda did the same, and Richard barrelled along, apparently unaware that they were no longer with him.

Halfway to the stage they found Nicole, struggling against the crowd. Her beautiful gown was torn in several places and she was out of breath.

"Did I just see you bite someone?" Holly asked her cousin.

Amanda had a more pressing question. "Where's Tommy?"

The three raced backstage.

An unearthly shriek rose as a pillar of fire erupted where they had just been standing. The heat from it washed over Holly, blistering her skin. She threw herself blindly forward, trying to put as much distance between herself and the hungry flames as possible. Even as her heart began slamming around in her chest like a frightened bird, she clenched her fists and felt power rising inside her.

Amanda made it to the stage a heartbeat ahead of them. She pulled herself onto it and had disappeared from sight before Holly could stop her. Nicole bounded onto the stage and Holly began to follow her. She stopped in her tracks, though, when she heard Nicole chanting.

It sounded like a protection spell of some sort. They were going to need a lot of protection, but not half as much as Jer was or the people still milling about trying to find an exit. A memory flashed back to Holly. She remembered her vision of Isabeau running through the burning barn, doors locking behind her, trapping everyone inside.

She stared again at the people. Five minutes before, they had been watching their friends and children and grandchildren in a play. None of them had asked for this. None of them could have expected this. They were just going about their lives when they were struck down.

Jer had done this. He had told them to stay, play it out. . . .

As she stood staring, Amanda reappeared with Tommy in tow. He was ashen and coughing, but otherwise seemed fine. Holly gestured to one man who was on fire. He was running crazily around in circles while three men tried to pull him to the floor to help put out the flames. Blinded by his pain, he fought them off, never realizing that they were trying to help. He would never know how close he had come to being saved as the flames engulfed his body forcing the others to scatter.

"It's all happening again!" Holly shouted. "The massacre! These people, they're ours to *protect*. We can't let them die. We have to stop it."

The three girls joined hands as the blanket of smoke grew thicker. Holly said, "Open the eyes of those who do not see and open the doors and set them all free."

Holly felt the magic flowing through her, tingling where her hands clasped with her cousins'. Suddenly, all the doors to the auditorium burst open and the haze lightened enough for people to begin to see well enough to stumble outside. In the distance, sirens wailed. The fire engines were on the way.

"Tommy, help them. Make sure they get out, and more importantly, make sure you do," Amanda instructed him.

He stared from one to another before nodding his head in reluctant agreement. Without another word he jumped off the stage and disappeared in the throng of people.

A shudder rippled up Holly's spine. Acting on instinct she leaped to the side, pulling her cousins with her. Flames emerged once more where they had been standing.

Nicole calmly reached up and extinguished her burning hair. "Well, girls, let's stay on the move."

"Great, but are we looking inside or out?" Amanda asked.

A whisper brushed through Holly's mind. It was faint and she strained to hear it; ignoring the discussion her cousins were having, she tried to block everything out but the whisper. It came again.

"Inside."

But was it a trap, or was it good advice?

She was unaware that she had spoken until Amanda said, "Okay."

"Backstage," Holly added. She took off and the others fell in behind her. She didn't know where she was going, but she didn't have to. The voice was in her head, clearer now, and it told her where to turn. They quickly reached the scenery workshop and stepped inside the large room. Catwalks soared more than twenty feet in the air up amidst the fly galleries where unused backdrops were stored, held in place by chains that could also be used to lower them when they were once again wanted.

The three girls moved to the door at the far end, but a voice behind them froze them in their tracks.

"Well, well, what do we have here? Three Cahors bitches. Nice to see you again, ladies."

Holly whipped around to see Michael Deveraux standing just inside the door.

"Thanks, but we prefer to be called witches," Nicole retorted as she centered herself and then lashed out with a wave of energy pulled from deep within.

Michael lifted a hand casually and sent the wave of energy hurtling back at Nicole with twice the energy she had sent it. It hit her in the chest and knocked her flat.

"You see, Eli. Magic isn't just about spells and potions, it's also about physics. You throw something at a wall, it comes back at you with twice the force."

Holly turned to see Eli lounging in the far doorway. "Nicely done."

"That only works if you're a wall," Holly said, as a bolt of lightning left her fingers and flew toward him. The other two girls stared at her. "Clasp hands," she ordered them.

Michael caught the electricity easily and it crackled at the tips of his fingers. He proceeded to pass it back and forth between his hands, occasionally letting it arc between them.

He stared with an amused grin at the girls. "Oh, I'm sorry, did you want this back?" he offered, moving his hand as though he were about to throw a ball. "Or maybe I should give it to your cousin?" he suggested before throwing it at the weakened Nicole.

"No!" Amanda shouted before diving in front of the ball. When it hit her, it lit up her entire frame for a moment, until her head appeared almost as a skeleton's. Holly watched in horror as Amanda fell unconscious to the ground.

"Isabeau, help us," she murmured.

Michael and Eli were closing now, slow and cat-like. Pillars of flame danced behind them, giving them the appearance of demons fresh from Hell.

"I'm afraid you can't stop me," Michael informed her, unable to contain his delight.

"But I can," a voice called from on high.

Jer stood dimly silhouetted on the catwalk above. The sword in his hand reflected the light. Holly thrilled and cringed at the site of him. He was magnificent, angry, and dangerous.

"I had hoped you would join us, Jeraud. Needless to say, I'm very disappointed," Michael called upward.

"Actually, you'll find that it was *you* who should have joined *us.*"

Moving from the shadows, Eddie, Kialish, and Kari also stood on catwalks. Kari swiftly clambored down to join Holly by her fallen cousins as Eddie and Kialish locked hands and began to chant. As easily as though they were candles, the flames behind Michael and Eli were extinguished. Michael's eyes widened in surprise.

Holly could feel the flames dying all through the building. She tried to throw her will, too, into the magics being used even though she did not know the words spoken by the shaman's son and his lover.

Kari crouched briefly over Amanda and Nicole and when she stood again, she nearly fell. Holly caught her and noticed the paleness of her face. Before she could ask Kari what was wrong, Nicole and Amanda rose as well. They were weak-looking but they managed to stay on their feet.

"I gave them some of my energy," Kari explained. "We need them."

Holly nodded briefly and then the four girls clasped hands.

Michael and Eli began to chant; a chant half-remembered from Holly's vision.

They were calling the Black Fire.

"No!" Holly shouted.

No, Jer echoed.

Murmuring a Spell of Protection, he leaped off the catwalk. He felt the rush of incredible speed and then a bone-jarring impact as he landed on his father, who was chanting the profane words with Eli. Father and son both went crashing to the ground, while Eli moved out of the way. Jer was the first to gain his feet, amazingly unharmed.

He rammed his fist into Michael's left cheek; the warlock caught Jer's hand and twisted it, sweeping out with his right leg to throw Jer off balance. Then he conjured a fireball in his hand and sent it directly into his son's face.

The pain was horrible, but Jer instantly negated the spell with one that Dan had taught him. Then he prepared to launch a full assault, springing at Michael and slamming him to the ground. He heard his brother chanting to create a fireball of his own, and knew himself to be dead in seconds. . . .

"Get him!" Eddie shouted as he rushed Eli.

Jer stayed focused on his father. He had no idea if his lodge brother—now his Circle acolyte—could take on Eli successfully, but he couldn't risk looking away from his father.

But as he launched himself at Michael, he realized that the older warlock had set up a barrier between them. Soft green glowed in a wall, separating the two. Jer ran at it with both fists, arcing them over his head and then slamming them down on the glowing mist, but it was like hitting Plexiglas. Next, Jer conjured a spell to break it.

Michael only smiled. Then he closed his eyes and resumed the chant to bring the Black Fire to life.

"No!" he bellowed. "Stop!"

Without breaking rhythm, Michael smiled triumpantly.

"Jer!" Holly screamed.

The Black Fire exploded into existence in the middle of the room. Midnight tendrils of savage heat and destruction lashed out from the molten center. The legs of the nearby catwalks caught fire; wood went up in an insant, like hair.

Everyone scrambled; Kari dove underneath a table set with refreshments for the cast and flipped it on its side. Nicole grabbed Amanda and fell with her to the ground, each huddling against the other. Holly joined them.

The three clasped hands.

"We need a spell. We need to fight this," Holly said. "We're all going to die."

Eli was too close to the fire. It reared over his head like a wave at the beach; panicking, Eli fell to his knees and held up his arms.

Jer watched as his brother's skin turned black within a moment. And then . . .

Eli threw open his arms and screamed words into the fiery holocaust. From the center of the blaze, huge wings flapped; the cry of a falcon shot through the roar of the Black Fire. . . .

And a bird materialized, its beak massive, its talons enormous; it was blue-black and magnificent; it was a ghost and yet it had form, and shape, and substance. It grabbed up the burning warlock with its talons, screeched three times, and disappeared.

Stunned by the sight, Jer forgot for a moment about his father. Michael dissolved the barrier and a powerful blow to his jaw snapped his head backward and he fell to the ground, momentarily stunned. Michael straddled him, leering, and lifted Jer's sword above him.

"You preening little peacock!" Michael shouted. "I should have let Sasha take you!"

Jer waited for the blow, trying desperately to recover his strength and wondering if he could block it. But at that moment, the fire doubled in size. Michael's eyes went wide. He dropped the sword and began to back slowly away before turning to run.

Then Holly moved into action, summoning up her strength. She kept hold of her cousins' hands, her palm burning with magical energy.

We have to stand our ground, make this our moment, stand our ground, break the curse. Stand our ground . . .

. . . it's so hot; I'm so scared . . .

We can't stop it, Jer thought. *It's too much.*

Jer chanted a spell and then scrambled to his feet. Tongues of black flame reared through the roof of the theater; waves of ebony heat rippled and gleamed over every surface the fire could touch.

"Get out of here!" he shouted to anyone who would listen. He shoved at Eddie and Kialish to make them leave. He conjured magic in Kari's direction to send her toward the exit.

But the Black Fire pulled to him, called to him . . .

He, too, would go, after one last look at the fire. . . .

The roaring, burning heat shot toward Holly, who was standing with her cousins. It yanked her, and only her, into its maw. As her cousins watched in horror, her body writhed in the blackness.

"Holly!"

Jer dove toward the conflagration . . .

. . . but it was Jean who stopped mere inches from it, and watched in rage and satisfaction as the flames began to consume her.

"Let it be so again. Let her burn," Jean whispered.

But she was his to love or hate. His to protect or kill. She was his and nothing would take her from him this time. He stepped into the fire and pressed his palms to hers.

"What are you doing? The fire will kill you!" she shouted.

"*'I have more care to stay than will to go. —Come, death, and welcome! My love wills it so.'*"

Holly's eyes dropped to their clasped hands and a strangled sob escaped her. When she lifted her head it was Isabeau who looked up at him with her haunting eyes. "I loved you. I am sorry," she whispered, at last able to tell him.

Jean nodded. "I know."

And in the keep of Castle Deveraux, in the bonfire of hatred, ruin, and evil, Jean and Isabeau did not burn. They lay, he above her, she below; and they did not burn.

It wasn't until one of Jean's bodyguards spotted them, and pulled him from the blaze . . .

. . . that Isabeau ignited in a horrible, agonizing moment; she writhed as she died, screaming his name.

Jean! Jean!

"Die, Cahors witch!" Jean's bodyguard had shrieked.

And in that moment, her family symbol was branded into

*her palm, so that all who saw her spirit would know she was
of the traitor Coven. . . .*

Jer could feel the flames licking at them, hungry,
passionate, angry. But the flames without were nothing
to the flames within. He felt such power welling up
inside him, surrounding him, binding him to her until
their love, their magic together kept them safe. They
could stay in the flames forever and so long as they
were together they would come to no harm.

Jer threw back his head and shouted in French.

Without warning, the roof overhead began to
crack. Huge pieces fell like bombs, the structure disintegrating. The smoke of the Black Fire sailed up, up,
threatening to blot out the very sky, the Black Fire
smoke taking the shape of a skull, laughing down at the
tableau like a hideous, appreciative audience.

Suddenly Holly was jerked backward, her hands
pulled from his. Her eyes widened in horror.

"No!" she shouted. "Let me go! He'll die if you
don't let me go!"

And Jer stepped forward to follow, but searing
pain rooted him to the spot. His flesh was on fire.
Every nerve in his body screamed with the unimagin-
able agony. His hands, his face . . . everything was
going up like dry paper. He could feel his skin melt-

ing from his body, and his legs slowly collapsed.

She abandoned me to the flames, and now I'll die.
Isabeau will have her revenge.

This was the end, then.

Come death and welcome. Holly wills it so. . . .

Screaming, Holly tried to break free of Amanda's
and Nicole's hands, but she could not.

"He's bewitched you! You'll die in there with
him!" Amanda shouted.

"No! It's the way to save him!" she cried, fighting,
struggling . . . forgetting to use her magic.

Horrified, she watched as Jer's skin turned black
and his body collapsed. The smell of burnt flesh permeated her nostrils until it was the only smell she
could ever remember.

And then she remembered her magic.

In a sudden burst of inspiration, she screamed at
her cousins, "It always rains here! It always friggin'
rains here!"

Yes!" Amanda yelled. "Of course."

Hot tears streamed down her face as they pressed
their palms together. "Help me, ancestress," Holly
whispered.

The glowing blue form of Isabeau shimmered
into being, covering Holly with her spirit, yet not

allowing a total merge, as she had before.

If he dies, I will rest, Isabeau reminded her.

"You won't. You'll hate yourself," Holly insisted. "And I will hate you!"

How long it took Isabeau to decide, Holly had no idea. But then she guided Holly's mouth, and words tumbled out. Her cousins held fast, though the lily brand on their three palms had started to smoke and burn through their flesh.

Elaborate French of another time and place rang through the coursing Black Fire, around the bonfire of it, the writhing figure in the middle. Hurry, *vite, vite,* Holly begged her ancestress. *The man we love is in there. Je vous en prie, ma mère, je vous en prie . . . oh, please, oh, please, save him.*

The fire began to die.

Seconds later the rest of the building began to collapse, and someone had their arms around her, dragging her away. She was screaming for Jer, shouting for . . .

"Jean!" she shrieked hysterically. "Jean!"

It was too late.

All that was left was ashes.

EPILOGUE

☾

It was over.

Jer was dead. His father had evidently escaped, and his brother . . . who knew where Eli had gone, in the grasp of that enormous bird?

Now the members of Jer's circle, together with Holly's, had come to empty ashes into Eliott Bay.

They had no idea if they were his ashes; the entire theater had been destroyed. A town scandal had erupted because the sprinklers never went off, and innocent heads would no doubt roll, but Holly could do nothing about that.

Holly wept. The gulls sobbed and wheeled, and the others—including the members of Jer's Rebel Coven—kept a respectful distance.

I am still bound to him, she thought. *As Isabeau was to Jean. She was doomed to walk the earth until she killed him, and I'm doomed to grieve my whole life. . . .*

She broke down, completely losing it, until strong arms grabbed her shoulders.

It was Tante Cecile.

"Cry, and then carry on," the woman said. "Magics are still at work. I was prevented from getting here in time to help by magic. And I can feel magic everywhere. Your Coven may have no time to rest, Holly." She gestured to Jer's group. "You'll need to persuade them to join you. You're going to need them."

Holly went into the older woman's arms and buried her head against her shoulders. "I'm not . . . I can't . . ."

"Yes, you can," Tante Cecile said firmly. She nodded, and Amanda and Nicole joined them, putting their arms around her and Holly.

Slowly, Kialish walked toward the circle. Eddie, Kari, and Dan trailed after.

Kialish held out his hand and Holly, sobbing, took

it. He pulled her against his chest, where she buried her head. He began to cry, too. Eddie joined them, arms around them both. Dan joined them.

He said to Holly, "Those of the Black Arts rule by cruelty and fear. He was learning that there was another way. If he could have brought all that power to the light . . ."

It was no comfort. Not then. Nothing could comfort her. Her soul was ripped and bleeding, and she had no idea if such a wound could ever heal.

For a time, Kari held herself stiffly away from Holly. When Holly looked over at her, the woman gazed at her steadily and said, "You as much as killed him, you know. If he hadn't had you to worry about . . ."

"Leave her alone, Kari," Kialish said harshly. "She's going through enough."

"What about me?" Kari demanded.

She turned on her heel and stalked away.

London, Headquarters of the Supreme Coven

Sir William regarded Michael Deveraux with skepticism. "And so, you want me to save your son," he drawled.

He was seated on the throne of skulls, his own son, James, standing beside him with his arms crossed over his chest. James's face was a neutral blank, but he was speaking volumes to Michael with his eyes. After all, Michael was the secret ringleader of his bid to depose his father and seize the throne for himself.

"Yes. He knows the secret of the Black Fire."

That was not entirely true. After the fire in the school theater, Michael had learned, to his horror, that he and Eli alone could not call up the fire. Not alone. It had been Jer's presence combined with theirs that had allowed it to materialize.

He needed both his sons alive. Eli, through his own quick thinking, had called up the spirit of the family falcon, Fantasme, and saved himself. He was waiting even now in their quarters, his face still burned but on the mend.

"And you will pledge your own allegiance, and that of both your sons, if I make . . . that . . . something that stays alive."

Dispassionately, Michael regarded his younger boy, Jeraud. Lying on a hospital gurney, Jer was less a living human being and more a writhing mass of melted flesh. If he lived, he would be a monster.

Suitable punishment for turning against his own flesh and blood, Michael thought derisively.

"Yes," he said to the Coven Master.

"Very well. And you will swear a blood oath to

that." He gestured for a black-robed acolyte to come forward. The young warlock carried a splendidly jeweled athame on a black pillow and presented it to Michael, who sliced open his wrist and dripped it on the burned flesh of his son.

He'll die eventually, Michael thought, and though he meant Sir William, he realized it was also true of Jer. *But by then, I'll have what I want.*

Sir William chuckled and dipped his head forward, receiving the oath with great formality. Michael smiled to himself, pleased with his own cleverness.

"Very well, Michael, leader of the Deveraux Coven. You have sworn allegiance to me," he said in a muffled voice.

Then his hands moved forward to throw back his hood, and Sir William raised his head.

Michael caught his breath and fell to his knees.

Before him sat not Sir William Moore, but the Horned God himself. The King of Hell, the Lord of the Flies, the Devil. . . .

"Your family is mine now," the demon said, chuckling. "For *ever.*"

And from the piteous ruin of his aching body, Jer Deveraux wailed, *"No."*

★ ★ ★

In her room in the Anderson home, Holly dreamed.

I am Isabeau, and I am Holly, and he . . .

He is alive, with my parents, and we are on the river. Tina is laughing.

See how the sun dances on her hair.

See how the sun dances in Jer's eyes. The ghosts are at rest.

At rest. At rest . . . oh, my God, Kari's right.

I killed him.

Tears slid down her cheeks. On cat's paws, Bast crept respectfully toward her and breathed on her cheek.

What do you want? she blinked with her large cat eyes.

"Bring him back," Holly wailed.

And then she opened her own eyes, fully awake.

Clenching her fists, she said to Bast, "I will bring him back. If I have to work at it my whole life. . . ."

The cat meowed, whether in agreement or in protest, Holly couldn't tell.

Holly sat up, weary to her bones, numb with grief . . .

. . . and ready to begin.

At her window, a gray hawk hovered. A lady hawk.

"Spirit of Pandion," she whispered, "will you help me?"

Epilogue

The bird screeched once, cocked its head at her, and did not fly away.

In her room in the Anderson home, Holly dreamed.

wicked

Curse

To my daughter, Belle, who is magical.

—Nancy Holder

To my husband, Scott, and the magic of true love.

—Debbie Viguié

ACKNOWLEDGMENTS

Thanks to my wonderful coauthor, Debbie, and her husband, Scott, for being friends I can count on. Thanks to our Simon & Schuster family, Lisa Clancy, Micol Ostow, and Lisa Gribbin. To my agent and his assistant, Howard Morhaim and Neeraja Viswanathan, my gratitude always.

—N. H.

Thanks to my coauthor and mentor, Nancy, for being such an inspiring writer and a dear friend. Thank you also to all the people without whom this would not be possible, most especially Termineditor Lisa. Thank you to all those who have offered me encouragement and shared the joy and pain of creativity: Chris Harrington, Marissa Smeyne, Teresa Snook, Amanda Goodsell, and Lorin Heller. Thank you also to George and Greta Viguié, the parents of my beloved husband. Without you he would not be the man he is.

—D. V.

Part One
Waxing

🌙

"When the moon in the sky begins to swell, all the world grows with her, planning, scheming, waiting. It is at this time that the womb grows ripe and all dark purposes are set in motion."

—Marcus the Great, 410

ONE

SINGING MOON

☾

We shout our defiance to the skies
To the sun shining in our eyes
The House of Deveraux has power
And it grows with every passing hour

Attend, anon, each Cahors Witch
For words alone can make us rich
The Crone bids us listen each hour
For words bring knowledge and knowledge power

Holly and Amanda: Seattle, the first moon after Lammas

In Autumn of the Coventry year, one reaps exactly what one sows, multiplied sevenfold. It is as true of the souls of the dead as it is of sheaves of grain and clusters of grapes.

A full year had passed since Holly Cathers's parents had drowned, and her best friend, Tina Davis-Chin, with them, whitewater rafting on the Colorado River. Death had invaded the Anderson home in

Seattle, taking Marie-Claire, the sister of Holly's father. Marie-Claire Cathers-Anderson lay rotting in one of the two plots she and her husband, Richard, had purchased together once upon a romantic dream of eternity. The reality of her adultery made it very hard for Uncle Richard to hope for another, better place where she waited for him—a fact that he told Holly often, now that he had taken to drinking late at night.

Tina's mother, Barbara Davis-Chin, lay sick in Marin County General back in San Francisco. She had once been an ER doc there with Holly's mom. Now that Holly had learned of the witchery world and taken her place at the head of her own coven, she knew Barbara's condition had been no accident.

Barbara's illness was Michael's first attack on us because he wanted me here in Seattle. I had planned to live with Barbara, but he needed me here . . . because he wanted to kill me.

Bolts of lightning sizzled overhead amid cascades of icy cold rain. Supercharged volts fanned out like search parties as their many-armed, air-splitting zig-zags slammed in to the earth. Holly felt very vulnerable in the family station wagon, a slow-moving duck wading through the puddles. Three blocks from Kari Hardwicke's place, she got out of the station wagon and ran the rest of the way.

Heavily warded, Holly wore a cloak of invisibility

that Tante Cecile, a voodoo practitioner, and Dan Carter, a northwest Native American shaman, had worked together to create. She had taken to wearing it whenever she had to go out. The cloak was by no means perfect, often losing its power to conceal her, but Holly had worn it faithfully ever since they had gifted her with it less than a week after the battle of the Black Fire last Beltane.

The coven was waiting for her at Kari's grad student apartment, which was located in a funky reconverted Queen Anne mansion near the University of Washington at Seattle. Kari was the one who had demanded the coven convene for a Circle. Last night at three A.M.—the Dark Hour of the Soul—she had suddenly awakened from a terrible nightmare that she could not remember. Drawn to the window, she had watched in horror as monsters dove past her turret room—huge, jet-black creatures that she was almost certain were oversized falcons.

Falcons were the totem of the Deveraux family.

If Michael Deveraux had returned to Seattle, and if on top of that, he had found a way to rescue his evil son, Eli, the Cathers/Anderson Coven was in deep and possibly fatal trouble. Michael Deveraux longed to conclude the blood feud begun by the Cathers and Deveraux ancestors so many centuries ago. That vendetta demanded no less than the death of every Cathers witch alive—namely Holly and her cousins, Amanda and Nicole.

As leader of the Cathers/Anderson Coven, it fell to Holly to protect them all and to save herself.

She had very little in the way of weaponry. She had known she was a witch for less than a year, while the Deveraux had never forgotten that their ancient lineage ranked them among the most hated and feared warlocks of all time. While her last name was Cathers, her ancestors had been of the noble witch house of Cahors, of medieval France. Over time their identity had been lost along with their real name. Holly believed that her father had known about the witch blood that ran in his veins, but she wasn't certain of that. She did know he had broken with the Seattle branch of the family, and it was only upon his death that Holly had learned he'd had a sister, and that she, Holly, had cousins.

Holly wondered what he would think if he knew she had reluctantly embraced her witch blood, and that she now led a full coven. Never mind that that coven was a ragtag mélange of traditions and powers, consisting of Amanda; Amanda's friend Tommy Nagai; Cecile Beaufrere, voodoo practitioner, and her daughter, Silvana; and the remnants of Jer's Rebel

Coven—Eddie Hinook and his lover, Kialish Carter, and Jer's former lover, Kari Hardwicke. Kialish's father was the shaman who had helped with her cloak, but he had not formally joined the Circle.

The Cathers/Anderson Coven was like a tiny paper boat in an ocean, when compared to the forces of evil massed against it.

Lightning arced directly overhead, interrupting her worrying. It seemed these days she was always worried.

Along the street, faces glanced anxiously through rain-blurred windows as Holly ran past them. The inhabitants no doubt enjoyed a measure of comfort in the knowledge that lightning rods protected their houses. But Holly knew that if Michael Deveraux sent the lightning, no conventional protection would save a building from being burned to the ground.

"Goddess, breathe blessings on me," she murmured as she kept to the shadows and moved her fingers firmly shrouded in the cloak. "Protect my Circle. Protect me."

It had become her mantra . . . and sometimes, the only thing that kept her from panicking completely.

Every night, I go to sleep wondering if Michael Deveraux has returned to Seattle . . .

. . . and if I'll wake up the next morning.

7

Wicked: Curse

★ ★ ★

In her anxiety over Holly's arrival, Amanda Anderson placed her face and hands against the cold window pane in the turret room of Kari Hardwicke's apartment. The scar crossing her right palm would give her away as a Cathers witch to any knowing set of eyes, be they bird or warlock; remembering that, she plucked her hands quickly from the glass and cradled them both against her chest.

Behind her, Tante—"Aunt," in French—Cecile Beaufrere and her daughter, Silvana, bustled around the apartment checking on the wards they and Dan Carter had helped Holly and Amanda install. The two had closed up their New Orleans house and moved back to Seattle to help Holly's coven fight the Deveraux. For their own personal protection, mother and daughter had woven amulets of silver and glass beads into the cornrows of their soft black hair, and they looked like Nubian warriors preparing for a great hunt.

"It would be better if Nicole were here," Silvana murmured. "The three Cathers witches united make stronger magic than just Holly and Amanda." Proof of that lay in the fact that each of the three bore a segment of the Cahors symbol, the lily, burned into her palm. Placed together, the cousins were stronger magically than they were separately.

But the three were only two in the current incarnation of the Circle. They had been reduced to two immediately after the Battle of the Black Fire. The reality of what they were doing had hit Amanda's sister, Nicole, too hard. She had run away, leaving Seattle behind, and the two remaining Cathers witches had no idea where she was.

While it was difficult for Amanda to blame her sister, it left everyone else weak and vulnerable to any potential attacks by the Deveraux. Holly had convinced the coven to spend the summer training, growing in the Art, and trying to work with Jer's followers. And all during that summer, they saw no trace of Michael Deveraux, head of the Deveraux Coven and Jer's father, whom Jer himself had repudiated. Nor had they seen Michael's older son, Eli, who had been carried off, burning with Black Fire, by an enormous magical falcon.

No one had seen a Deveraux since.

The screech of a bird echoed through the thunder. Holly glanced up, squinting through the rain. A flock of black birds soared and cartwheeled, tempest-tossed, their eyes flashing, their blue-black wings beating back the storm.

They were falcons.

Holly hurried on, reaching the apartment without alerting the birds—or so it appeared, and so she prayed—and Amanda opened the door before Holly could knock. Like Holly, Amanda had matured, her face thinner, her mousy hair streaked through with summer highlights. She was no longer the "boring" twin to Nicole's vibrant drama. She was steady and wise—in magical terms, a priestess. Holly was grateful to her core for Amanda's presence.

"Were you . . . did you get here okay?" Amanda asked, taking in Holly's sopping wet appearance.

"The car was too much of a target," Holly said. "I came on foot."

"Don't you own a broom yet?" That was Kari, who was terrified. Holly forgave her her snide comment, but she was tired of all the snipes Kari had shot her way over the past months.

She hates me, Holly thought. *She blames me for Jer's death.*

She's right. I killed him.

Holly cleared her throat as the others assembled, all facing her. They looked at her expectantly, as if she would know what to do now. The truth was, she had no idea.

"We need to form a circle. Who will be our Long Arm of the Law tonight?" she asked, gazing at the three men in their midst. As was common in many Wiccan traditions, in Holly's coven the women performed the magic while the men kept the circle safe from harm. She who conducted the rite was the coven's designated High Priestess. Her male counterpart was called the Long Arm of the Law. In the Cathers/Anderson Coven, he cut all harm with a very splendid old sword, which Tante Cecile had located in an antique shop and the coven had infused with magic.

"I'll serve," Tommy said, inclining his head.

"Then kneel," Holly instructed him, "and receive my blessing."

He got down on his knees. Amanda came forward with a beautifully carved bone dipper of oil in which floated Holly's favorite magical herb, rosemary. The herb was associated with remembrance; it boggled Holly that her family had carried Cahors witch blood in their veins for centuries, and yet the memory had been lost.

Holly moved her hands over the oil, silently invoking the Goddess, while Silvana presented the sword to the circle and placed it between Tommy's clasped hands. It was made of bronze, and extremely heavy. Runes and sigils had been carved into the hilt and etched in acid on the blade, but no one in the coven—not even Kari, who, as a graduate student, was steeped in the knowledge of various magic traditions and folkways—had been able to translate or decipher any of them.

Tommy breathed deeply, becoming one with the sword and with Holly's own rhythmic breaths. The rest took their places around Holly and Tommy in the circle, forming a living, single magical being.

We're one, Holly thought. *We have a power the Deveraux do not. Through love, we are trying to break down our barriers and work fully together. Their system is based on power, wresting it away from others and holding on to it at all costs. And I have to believe that love is stronger than that.*

"I bless your brow, for wisdom's sake," she said, making a pentagram with oil on his forehead.

"I bless your eyes, for good vision and sharp sight." She dotted each closed eyelid with more oil.

"I bless your sense of smell, for detection of hellish sulfur." She ran a line of oil down his nose.

She blessed his mouth, that he might call out a warning in case of attack. She blessed his heart, for courage, and his arms, for the strength to wield his sword well against trespassers.

Then she deliberately placed her thumb on the sharp edge of the sword, wincing as she cut herself. Drops of blood ran down the blade, feeding it.

Love might be the coin of the realm, but blood still fed the circle. The Cahors had not been a gentle house; in their day they had been just as ruthless as the Deveraux. What Holly hoped for was evolution, a chance to reinvent her family's path. Since so much had been lost in the intervening centuries, she was trying to find the balance between new magical forms and the traditions her coven must observe in order for the magic to work. It was slow going, a process of trial and error . . . but if Michael was back to threaten them, she would have to do whatever it took to keep her people safe, no matter how "unevolved" it was.

But this was not the time for such ruminations; she quickly finished Tommy's anointing.

"I bless you from crown to heel, Tommy. Rise, my Long Arm of the Law, and embrace your priestess."

Tommy stood tall as Holly handed the dipper back to Amanda. Then she put her arms around him, careful not to touch the sword with her body, and kissed him gently on the lips.

She took a step backward, and Tommy said, "I will sever any snares our enemies have set."

"Blessed be," the circle murmured.

Amanda and Kari let go of each other's hands, allowing Tommy to pass.

"I will smite our enemies' imps and familiars, be they invisible or disguised," he continued.

"Blessed be," the circle said again.

With great effort, he raised the sword toward the ceiling.

"And I—"

A terrible scream shattered the moment. Something flashed, glowing green. Wind whipped through the room, frigid and solid like ice. The stench of sulfur invaded the space.

Tommy staggered backward. "Look!" Kari screamed, pointing.

Grunting, Tommy jabbed the sword tip toward the ceiling. The glow was pierced; a phosphorescent, semiliquid stream of green tumbled around the sword tip and dripped onto the floor. Kari jumped away from it, and the rest of the circle struggled to keep their hands clasped.

The glow vibrated, then faded.

"Oh, my God," Kari gasped.

Skewered on the tip of the sword was the likeness of a falcon jerking in its death throes. It was not a real bird, but a magical representation; the green glow thickened and became blood, steaming and fresh. Tommy's hands were coated with it, and it was dripping onto the floor.

As Holly stared in dread fascination, the bird's mouth dropped open. A disembodied voice echoed throughout the room:

"You Cahors whores, you'll be dead by midsummer."

With one last shudder, the bird stopped moving. Its eyes stared dully out at the circle.

There was a silence.

Then Amanda said, "He's back. Michael Deveraux is back."

Holly closed her eyes; dread and stark fear washed over her.

Here we go, she thought. *The battle lines have just been drawn. How can we possibly fight him?*

More to the point . . . how can we hope to beat him?

Nicole: Cologne, Germany, September

Nicole threw a terrified glance over her shoulder as she raced down the corridors of the train station. A train rumbled away; her footsteps echoed like staccato points to the bass line of its leave-taking. The pink and gold streaks of dawn chased the shadows, and she was terribly grateful; the night had held sway far too long, and she was exhausted.

I should have stayed in Seattle, she thought. *I thought I'd be safer if I ran away . . . but there's that old saying about dividing and conquering . . . except that I don't know what it is. . . .*

Ever since she'd been in London three months ago, something had been following her. It was not a person, not in the traditional sense; it was something that could glide along the walls of buildings and perch on gabled rooftops—something that could trail after her with a rush of wings and a lone cry. She had not been able to see it; but in her mind, it was a falcon, and it was Michael Deveraux's eyes and ears, harrying her like the little mouse she was.

She wasn't certain that it had ever actually located her. Perhaps it was blindly lurking, waiting for her to use magic to reveal herself. That idea gave her hope that she might survive long enough to figure out what to do. *I'm terrified to contact Holly and Amanda. . . . What if that reveals my presence to whatever this thing is? Like answering "Polo" when the blindfolded guy who's saying "Marco" is six inches away from you?*

She was on her way to holy ground; she had covered much of Europe from London to France to Germany by leapfrogging from church to graveyard to chapel to cathedral. She didn't know if her gut instinct to seek safe harbor in mosques, synagogues, and Christian churches was correct. All she knew was that she felt better within walls built by people who adhered to some sort of faith tradition . . . as if their faith protected her from evil.

She listened to that instinct and to the urge to keep moving. The shadow was following her, and she had the feeling that if she kept moving, it might never land on her—might not carry her off, the way that huge falcon had carried off Eli.

Did he die?

What about Holly and Amanda? I abandoned them. I'm so ashamed. I was so scared. . . .

She had ridden a train all night. Her destination this dawn was the famous Dom of Cologne, an ancient medieval cathedral said to house relics of the Three Kings. She had read about it in a guidebook; she had bought and memorized more guidebooks about religious buildings in Europe than could be carried in a fully stocked travel store. She had taken an enormous number of trains. She had spent tons of money.

Problem is, I'm almost out of money. . . . What am I going to do when I can't run anymore?

Up the steps, she stopped. A hundred feet away, rising at the edge of a square, the tall Gothic structure loomed like a monolith. Its spire stretched toward the heavens; the rosettes and statues that cluttered the entry were dark gray, welcoming.

Gray magic is what the Cathers are all about, she thought. *Our ancestors, the Cahors, were not very good people. They were just . . . less evil than the Deveraux.*

We aren't necessarily the good guys.

Still, heaven seems happy to shelter us.

Taking a deep breath, Nicole raced across the square and pushed open the doors of the church.

It was cool inside; a row of men in brown robes tied with black sashes stood with their backs to her and sang in Latin. A priest in a collar raised his eyes inquiringly; she knew he saw a young woman in jeans and a peasant top, carrying a backpack. Her dark hair was coiled on top of her head and she wore no makeup. She was sunburned and there were circles under her eyes.

In three months Nicole had had an unbroken night of sleep exactly twice.

I'm so tired and scared.

Scowling at her, the priest waved his finger in her face. *"Hier darf man nicht schlafen, verstehen Sie?"* he asked her sternly. *Do you understand that you may not sleep in here?*

"Ja," she said breathlessly. Her eyes welled with tears, and the man immediately softened.

He walked a few steps backward, gesturing to the pews. There were no other people there except for the row of monks singing an early-morning Mass.

Nicole inclined her head and said, *"Danke schön."* "Thank you" was one of the "Useful Words and Phrases" she had memorized from one of her guidebooks.

She slid into the nearest pew and sat back, staring up at the celestial heights of the arched ceiling high above her. As she let the atmosphere of the church permeate her being, she could visualize the sun piercing the darkness above the spire.

And then, in her mind's eye, a dark shadow flitted between her and the sun.

She gasped aloud. The traveling shadow was the silhouette of a bird. And she sat inside this deceptive trap like a doomed, helpless mouse.

Then the church bells ran pealing out the message, *All is well, all is well.*

And that was a damn lie.

Jer: The Island of Avalon, October

The lie was that this was being alive.

Each instant that he lived was an eternity of torment. Each breath he took was a bellows in his chest, stoking the Black Fire flames as they roasted his heart and his lungs.

If he had been capable of coherent thought, Jer Deveraux would have begged the God to let him die. And beneath that supplication would have fluttered the terrible fear that he was dead already . . . and in Hell.

Echoing through his throbbing skull, words he

could not comprehend told the tale of the rest of his unbearable existence: "If you have not killed Holly Cathers by midsummer, Michael, I will kill your son and feed his soul to my servants."

And Michael Deveraux had answered, "I am yours to command in this and all things."

From her perch in the shimmering blue mist that was the magic of the Cahors, the lady hawk, Pandion, ruffled her feathers and cocked her head. She heard a plaintive cry, as that from a mate, and prepared to take flight in search of it.

And from the green-glowing ether that was his rookery, Fantasme, the falcon familiar of the Deveraux, sharpened his talons on the skull of a long-dead foe.

Holly and Amanda: Seattle, October

We are all still alive. It's been almost a month since the apparition of the falcon in our Circle, and we have managed to keep Michael Deveraux at bay.

Holly stared out at the ocean, allowing its vastness to sweep over her, engulf her until she felt small once more. She drew strength from her solitary walks along the shore; sometimes she wondered if Isabeau's ghost walked with her, supporting her as she struggled to keep the coven together and to keep them safe from

Michael Deveraux. There was power in the heartbeat of the waves, the ebb and flow of the great waters. The ocean was in its turn mother, lover, and enemy. The gentle, rhythmic lap of the waves was like the soothing beating of a mother's heart as she cradled her baby.

Holly closed her eyes and let herself listen to the sound. She breathed in the fresh salty air, and for a moment she might have been anywhere—in San Francisco, her old home even, instead of her new one in Seattle.

Tears squeezed out from beneath her closed eyelids and rolled slowly down her cheeks. It had not been a good day. Any day you had to start with a phone call to your lawyer was not a good day.

Holly was only nineteen, yet dealing with her parents' attorney had become a part of her life. Between talking to him and the financial planner who helped oversee her inheritance, she thought she might scream. There were always questions to answer and more papers to sign. They wanted to discuss her finances and her options for the future.

What if I have no future? What if I die tomorrow? she thought, a wave of bitterness choking her. *I'm fighting for my life, for the lives of my family and friends, and nobody gets it. I don't have time to worry about what I'm going to do five years from now. I probably won't even be here.*

Still, she knew that she should be grateful. If it weren't for her parents' careful planning, she wouldn't have time to practice spells and learn all the practical things that could help extend her life. She would be too busy trying to work to keep herself fed. It was especially important now that Uncle Richard had given up all pretext of going to work. Good thing Aunt Marie-Claire had money, or Amanda would be in serious trouble.

In a way she envied Kari. The older girl still at least got to pretend that she had a life, something other than magic and spells. She was still going to grad school. Tommy and Amanda were trying to go to college as well. Holly knew that Amanda in particular, though, was struggling. Holly figured college was just one of those dreams she herself had to give up the day that she learned she was a witch. *And that other people want to kill me.*

She sighed heavily. The day had only gone from bad to worse when she had called the hospital to check on Barbara. Most weeks the news was the same: no change in status. This week, though, she could sense something, an uneasiness in the doctor's voice that hadn't been there seven days before. Something was wrong; she could feel it. She was sure that Barbara was somehow doing worse. *And the doctors won't admit it.*

She felt herself begin to tremble. Barbara was her last tie to her own home, her parents, her childhood. Half a dozen times she had wanted to go to see her, to reassure herself that Barbara was truly still alive. But there were always more spells to learn, more protection rituals to perform. And there was the deep, dark fear in the back of her mind that if she got close to her, Barbara would die. *Everything I love withers.*

So she had come to the ocean to lose herself in its vastness, to seek its solace. The sea had comforted her before, and she prayed that it would again.

The waves reached up gently and tickled her toes, their caress soft and persuasive. The water called to her to come, explore, be one with it and its power. A tempting offer from a tempestuous lover. But Holly knew that the ocean could whisper words of soft promise one moment and then turn on you the next. It could change in seconds and kill so easily.

Never turn your back on it. Her father had told her that when she was five. She had been splashing in the waves for an hour when her mother called her to go put on more sunscreen. She had turned and tried to run out of the water. A huge wave had come out of nowhere and knocked her down. The undertow had sucked at her body, threatening to pull her out farther with it. She remembered trying to struggle, but the current had been too strong for her and she couldn't stand up or get her head out of the water.

Daddy had swooped in and picked her up, carrying her carefully from the water and stepping backward the entire time. He had deposited her, frightened and crying, into her mother's protective arms. She would never forget the look in his eyes as he bent down.

Never turn your back on the ocean, Holly. It may be beautiful, but it is also very dangerous.

She shivered now as an icy wind whipped around her and a wave slapped at her ankles. She took an involuntary step backward. Another wave slapped at her and she hopped back another step. The sound of the ocean was changing; instead of a gentle lapping sound, a dull roar jangled in her ears.

Startled, she had no time to react before a fresh wave crashed into her, soaking her in an instant in icy water waist-high and grasping at her with invisible hands.

The undertow pulled at her and she nearly lost her footing as she stumbled backward, shock quickly changing to fear. *You are not five!* her mind shouted at her as she fought to make it up onto the sand when another wave crashed around her chest. It knocked her off her feet and swept her several yards out.

I'll be swept out to sea! Oh, my God, is this happening?

Her long skirt wound around her legs, binding them like a mermaid's tail. Her arms were dead weights inside her heavy jacket. She could barely move, much less swim.

The fresh burst of panic focused her attention. *I have to get out of these clothes.*

"Goddess, grant me strength in battle and from death," she murmured in a Spell of Protection. Whether it worked or she was buoyed by the thought that she was never truly alone, she managed to snake first one arm and then the other out of her heavy jacket. It bobbed in the waves like a bloated jellyfish.

She worked on her skirt next, but her hands fumbled at the drawstring. She couldn't manage it; still terribly bogged down, she turned and tried to start swimming back to shore using only her arms. Within seconds, she was exhausted. Then a wave crashed over her and she coughed violently as her lungs dispelled the water she had just sucked in.

No sooner had she managed that, though, than another wave crested over her head. And another. Her brain began to numb and it locked on to the horrible images of the rafting trip that had claimed the lives of her parents and best friend. *It's been a year and now the water has come for me,* she thought fuzzily.

I'm not the same helpless girl I was then, though. I'm a

*witch, and a powerful one. I should be able to do something to
save myself.*

She turned to look out to sea, her legs wearily
treading water. What was it bodysurfers did? They
rode the waves.

I can do that, too.

A huge wave began rolling in; Holly took a quick
breath. "I can do this!" she cried as the wave reached her.

Her body was tossed up into the air, and then she
was on top of the water, slightly in front of the crest of
the wave.

She flew with dizzying speed toward the shore.
Almost upon the beach, the wave broke behind her
and threw her up onto the sand. Her mouth and eyes
filled with the stinging granules as she clawed her way
wildly up away from the water.

At last the strength in her limbs gave out and she
collapsed, barely managing to roll onto her back as she
coughed weakly. Her eyes stung and her face was raw,
as though sand had been forcefully shoved into every
pore and crevice. Her eyes began to tear fiercely and
she let herself cry—to flush out her eyes, and to flush
out her terror.

I nearly died. As I should have a year ago.

*Don't be ridiculous. I was not "supposed" to die. I was
meant to live. I have a coven to run, followers to protect.*

At last the tears stopped flowing; she blinked rapidly trying to clear her vision. Slowly the sky shifted into focus . . . and it was low and dark and menacing.

The air was heavy; it almost seemed to crackle. She glanced quickly around. Nothing seemed familiar. Had the wave washed her up farther down the beach?

Electricity crackled down her spine as she slowly straightened. There was magic here and it felt very, very old. Feeling strangely compelled, she turned around so that her back was to the ocean.

Oh, my . . .

TWO

FALLING LEAF MOON

We grow stronger with each death
Reborn with each foe's last breath
With each sacrifice we renew
Our oaths to the Lord, loyalty true

We spin the wheel of the year
And know there is no cause to fear
For truth it is, that what has died
Strengthens us and dwells inside

The castle was ancient but beautiful. It called to her in a high tenor chant like a medieval troubadour telling the stories of King Arthur and his court. She felt as though she were floating as she moved toward it, her footsteps silent. The vast heap of stones was alive; she could feel it.

"Something wonderful happened here," she whispered.

A shadow crossed her mind. "And also something horrible."

Somehow she had covered the ground between her and the great walls without noticing. She reached out her hand to touch the weathered stone and her fingers tingled where they made contact. Power surged through the wall. It reached up her arm and wrapped itself around her, as though to bind her to itself for all eternity.

From within, something called to her, though she could not have told how or who. She placed her whole hand against the stone and leaned against it. Slowly, her flesh melted into the wall, merged with it, passed through it. As her hand went, the rest of her followed.

For a moment everything was dark and damp; fear rose again in her mind, and she thought, *I'm drowning in the ocean; it's a trick!*

The panicky moment passed, though, just as she passed through the wall. She turned to stare at the wall for a moment, to marvel in amazement.

Something still called her, compelled her to follow. . . .

She passed through wall after wall. The last wall proved a challenge, resisting her pushing at first, but finally giving way to her efforts. She found herself in a room luxuriant with light and warmth from a fire blazing in a great hearth. When at last she stepped completely through, she realized that she was not alone in the room.

Seated before the fire was a man with his head on his fists. She walked up slowly behind him, without even a whisper of sound to give herself away. *Who is he? Why does he sit with shoulders slumped in despair?*

He must have felt something, for he looked up quickly, dropping his hands down toward his sides with a heavy clink.

She understood: Shackles bound the man's wrists and ankles. Holly reached out to touch the band about his left wrist but was painfully repulsed. The man was a captive, both physically and magically.

What could be his crime?

"Living," he answered.

She jumped backward, startled. She had not spoken out loud; how had he heard her?

"I can feel you, even though I can't see you." His voice was hoarse, yet hauntingly familiar. "It *is* you, isn't it, Holly?"

He turned his face directly toward her, and for one brief moment she thought he saw her. She shrank backward, but his eyes passed over her and continued on, sweeping the area around her.

And now she could see his face clearly, or rather, what was left of it.

"Jer!" she gasped.

"I'm not so sure of that anymore," he answered

grimly, fixing in on the location of the sound and staring unnervingly at her left earlobe.

He held up his left hand, and in the flickering light from the fire Holly could see that it was horribly scarred.

"A souvenir. A reminder of how close I came to death and how much I've lost by being alive."

She didn't understand his words, but she tucked them away in her mind. There would be time later to decipher his meaning.

"Where are we?" she asked.

He shrugged. "The island of Avalon."

She gasped. "Then this must be . . ."

"Yes. There is powerful magic in these walls. The Supreme Coven has owned this land ever since the death of the dark warlock Merlin. He worked his spells within these walls."

"Merlin? Supreme Coven? But where is it? Where is Avalon?" she asked, growing desperate. Something was pulling at her; she was slipping away.

Then he reached out to her, hands stretched and shaking with the effort from the weight and magic of them.

"Holly," he said hoarsely, "don't come. I couldn't help myself, couldn't stop myself from sending my soul out. You are my other half, and I am yours. But don't come. Exist without me, forever if you have to. Even though you won't be complete."

He gazed at her with longing, with love, with despair. "Don't look for me," he said.

"I—" Before she could promise him—*No, I won't promise; I will find you!*—she was ripped away. Back she sailed through all the walls, faster and faster, an undertow pulling at her, the pain accumulating, the hurt to her lungs profound—the hurt to her heart even more so.

She slammed against the last wall, and it groaned for a moment beneath her weight before giving way.

Pain surged through her right ankle.

Then she was back on the shore, in pitch darkness, running as fast as she could toward the water. Unseen hands hastened her along, and when she reached the ocean, they pushed her in.

The undertow caught her and dragged her so far out to sea that she could no longer see the shore.

Oh, my God, no. I was safe. Don't do this to me. Don't pull me out. I was safe!

Angry and frightened, she tried to fight the waves, to struggle back toward the unseen land.

A wave washed over her head and she closed her eyes tight against it. When at last she reopened them, it was once again daylight. The sun was yellow, tired, and wan, but it was shining.

There, not more than fifteen yards away, was the Seattle beach where she had been standing right before getting pulled into the water.

Holly gasped and swallowed sea water. She began coughing desperately. She was going through it all again, exactly as she had moments—*minutes? hours?* before. Remembering the huge wave, she turned and looked for it. There it was! She took a breath, offered up the same words, and felt the surge of power as the wave picked her up and carried her to the beach.

It took just as long to cry the sand out of her eyes, but when she opened them this time, Amanda was staring down at her.

Nicole: Spain, October

Cologne had frightened Nicole out of Germany.

Now in Spain, she moved like a hunted creature. Banners were up in the store windows to celebrate Halloween, presented as an American holiday; now it was late, the stores were closed, and no one walked the cobblestone streets. Silence hung thick like a blanket in this place whose look, whose feel, whose very smell was foreign to her. Nicole wrinkled up her nose. Coming to Madrid had seemed like a good idea at the time; there were hundreds of chapels, a cathedral, churches by the score.

But suddenly she wasn't so sure she should be there.

It feels very wrong.

A noise behind her caused her to twist. She forced herself to relax as the stumbling drunk waved at her before veering off on his way home, perhaps to an expected chastening from his long-suffering wife.

She folded her arms tight across her chest and forced herself to walk. The youth hostel she had checked in to was not that far, and at the moment she wanted nothing more than to be tucked into her little bed, safe and asleep.

I wish I were back home in Seattle. As it had a hundred times before, the thought came unbidden to her mind and she waved a hand in the air, as if she could push away the thoughts and feelings bombarding her: grief, relief, fear, homesickness.

She and her mom had started practicing magic because she had learned a few tricks from Eli. It had been fun, a secret game the two of them had played. Corn dollies and sympathetic magic.

The stakes have risen considerably, she thought wryly.

Nicole shivered. She had seen too much in the past year. Too much death, too much horror. *Too much magic.* The power that she had felt when she linked with Holly and Amanda had been terrifying. She couldn't deal with it. *And so here I am, in the middle of Spain trying to forget who and what I am.*

Another sound, a soft step perhaps, reached Nicole's ears. This time the hair on the back of her neck stood on end. Someone was behind her, she could feel it. She increased her speed, desperately fighting the urge to glance behind and see who or what was there.

Don't let it be a bird; don't let it be a bird; please, especially, don't let it be a falcon.

Suddenly she heard it, the crackle of electricity. She threw herself to the side just as a bolt of lightning ripped through the place where she had been standing. She landed hard on her side and twisted quickly to see where the attack had come from. Pain knifed through her. A cloaked figure stood ten feet away, laughing crazily.

"This is my home, witch. You have no business being here," a hissing female voice informed her.

"I'm not . . . not a witch," Nicole stammered.

"You lie! I can feel it. And since you have trespassed you shall be punished."

The figure raised its arms and began chanting in a strange tongue.

Nicole half-stumbled to her feet, every protection spell she had ever known fleeing her mind. She was helpless. She turned to run, opened her mouth to cry out, and fell against another hooded figure.

She screamed as she stared up to where the face should have been. All she could see was darkness. From the darkness a voice began to speak in a low, commanding tone. Nicole pushed herself away and took a half-step in the direction of the witch. What she saw brought her up short.

Four other cloaked figures had materialized as if from air. One of them extended an arm and the witch collapsed to the ground, clawing at her throat.

"Philippe, what have you done?" the figure behind her shouted in English.

"I only took her speech until such time as she is able to speak civilly to a stranger." That voice was very French.

Nicole whirled back to face the figure she had fallen against. Slowly, long, pale hands reached up to pull back the hood. A shock of dark curly hair framed a handsome face with piercing eyes. A wry smile twisted his lips as he looked down at Nicole.

"Welcome to Madrid, little *bruja*. I am José Luís, warlock and servant of the White Magic. And these," he added, gesturing to the others as they also removed their hoods, "are my friends."

* * *

On the beach, Holly stared up at Amanda.

"What happened?" she asked slowly.

"I was going to ask you that," Amanda retorted. "God, Hol, did you fall in?"

"I . . . I don't know." She grimaced at her wet clothes. "I . . . I dreamed or something." She looked back up at her cousin. "How did you find me?"

"I've been looking for you everywhere," Amanda said.

"What's wrong?" Holly demanded.

Amanda shook her head grimly. "I'll explain in the car. Let's go."

She reached down and, clasping Holly's hand, helped her to stand. Holly leaned gratefully on her cousin as they hurried toward the car.

"I'm soaking wet," Holly protested as Amanda opened the passenger door of Richard's car.

Amanda gave her a gentle shove. "Get in. We've got bigger things to worry about than upholstery."

Holly acquiesced and sat down, grimacing at the squishing sounds her clothes made as they encountered the seat. She didn't even have time to put on her seat belt before Amanda started the car, put it in gear, and floored it.

Holly scrambled to buckle herself in. As they flew around a corner, Holly smacked her head painfully against the window. She could feel more sea water dripping out of her ears as her head tilted.

"Ouch! Slow down, Amanda!"

"No time," Amanda muttered between clenched teeth.

Amanda cast a quick glance her way before putting the car into another sliding turn, tires screaming in outrage.

Another corner and Holly's stomach lurched even more. When the car straightened out, she looked at Amanda. The other girl's jaw was set and her face was pale—too pale. A faint trickle of blood crept down the side of her forehead and started tracing a path down her cheek.

Shocked, Holly saw a lump on the side of Amanda's head and noted that her hair was clumped and bloody around it.

"Michael's pumping up the volume," Amanda explained. "I was attacked at the house by some kind of invisible force. So I called Kari's house. No answer. Silvana and Tante Cecile's. Nothing. No Tommy, either. I worked my way down the list, and no one's picking up. So I figured: headquarters. Which for the time being is Kari's apartment. But I didn't want to go there without you."

Another corner forced Holly to turn her attention

back to the road, and she wished she knew a spell that could keep her from heaving.

Holly said weakly, "That sounds bad. Punch the turbo."

They arrived at Kari's apartment complex about a minute too late for Holly's stomach. She staggered from the car, collapsed onto her knees, and thought she might be sick—again. Amanda bounded from the driver's seat and headed for Kari's door at a dead run.

Amanda shouted from inside the apartment, and Holly pulled herself back up to her feet and stumbled toward the door. Inside, an overwhelming stench of gas caused her to fall to her knees and retch again.

In the corner Amanda was frantically working over four inert forms. She looked up and shouted, "Holly, turn the gas off!"

Unable to stand, Holly crawled to the kitchen, coughing and gagging the entire way. She made it to the oven and checked it. Everything was off.

"The pipes must have burst!" Holly forced herself to shout.

"Then come help me!" Amanda yelled.

Holly dragged herself out of the kitchen and over to Amanda. Her head was starting to spin and she felt herself losing focus. Suddenly Amanda clasped her palm and Holly felt the now-familiar surge of power that pulsated around them and through them. Her head cleared and she stared Amanda in the eyes.

Together they began to chant over their four friends.

Slowly Tommy stirred and looked up at them. "Something is binding us," he slurred.

Together Amanda and Holly passed their hands through the air over Tommy's body until they could feel something break free. He sat up abruptly and turned to help the other three.

Kialish, Eddie, and then Kari woke and were freed. At last the six of them stumbled to the door and made it outside just as the gas inside sparked.

They fell to the ground as a ball of fire washed over the top of them. In unison they began chanting. The skies opened up and rain poured down, dousing the flames. The thick waters quickly snuffed out the fire inside the apartment.

"Cool!" an onlooker cried appreciatively.

Holly turned to see one of the other grad students at the college standing and staring.

"Talk about your synchronicity. Fire, then rain."

"Amazing," Holly said weakly.

Then she got sick again.

Wicked: Curse

Michael: Seattle

I almost had them this time, Michael thought as he paced in front of the altar in his Seattle home. *It went wrong somewhere.* He turned and raised his hands in angry fists. He would have his revenge. The witches would still pay.

Laurent, his ancestor, would know what to do. The phantom knew more than Michael wished . . . including the fact that, just as in 1666, the Deveraux Coven had recently been censured by the leader of the Supreme Coven, the most powerful ruling body on the warlock side of Coventry.

"Laurent! My lord and master, prithee, come to me," Michael petitioned, in perfect medieval French.

Nothing.

"Laurent," Michael called, respectfully. *"Je vous en prie.* A moment?"

"I think you'd rather talk to me," a voice behind him chortled.

Michael whirled around and found himself staring at a tiny creature. It was black and misshapen, its face broad and flat like a frog's, its nose more of a demonic snout, and fangs curled over the narrow lips. Its eyes were reptilian, green, and virtually spinning with madness.

"Where is my ancestor?" Michael asked carefully. He had no idea what this thing was doing here; for all he knew, it was here to kill him.

"I have a ssssecret," the creature informed him in a sing-song voice.

It's an imp, Michael thought. *I've heard of them; never seen one. . . . Laurent may have sent one instead of answering my call himself.*

"A ssssecret," the imp reiterated.

Michael stared at it. The thing rubbed its hands, one over the other, each finger ending in a slice of cartilage that was more than a fingernail, less than a bone. It was hunched and very, very ugly.

The imp wagged its brow above elongated, hate-filled eyes. "I know about the curse," it bragged.

"Curse? What curse?" Michael demanded in his most authoritative tone of voice.

The imp chittered like a squirrel. It bobbed and swayed as if it were completely mad.

"The curse against your sworn enemies."

A cautious smile tugged at Michael's lips. "Cahors?" he asked carefully. Then, in case his usage of the ancient name confused the creature, he added, "Cathers?"

"Yessss." The imp nodded, leaning forward as if to share something very, very interesting. "They don't like water much."

"And why is that?" Michael asked, enjoying for the moment a bit of fencing.

The imp pulled back its lips, exposing its teeth as it

grinned wildly at him. It said in a low, dramatic voice, "They tend to drown. That is the curse your ancestors laid on them. Drowning."

Michael was disappointed. The crazed, repulsive thing didn't know what it was talking about. If that was true, then Holly would have drowned in the ocean three days ago when he had tried to suck her in, or a year before, in the river with her parents.

"You're talking of dunking witches," he said dismissively. "If they float, they're guilty. If they drown, they're inno—"

The imp shook its head impatiently. "No, no, they *tend* to drown, true," the imp said. It pointed a single, scaly finger skyward. "But their loved ones *always* do. That is the curse laid upon the Cahors witches. By one of your own ancestors, may I hasten to add." It smiled again, as if it were about to fling itself at Michael and chew his face off his skull.

"Indeed," Michael said slowly.

"Indeed," the imp assured him.

A smile—*ah, the possibilities!*—spread across Michael Deveraux's face.

France, 13th century

"Your daughter, *madame,*" the emissary from the Deveraux announced with a flourish. Bowing over his leg, he gestured to the liveried servant who had accompanied him. The other man, a mere villein dressed up like a peacock in Deveraux red and green, smirked as he opened a small ebony box and tipped it over.

Ashes and small pieces of bone spilled onto the carpet that ran the length of the Great Hall of Castle Cahors. Like motes in the dying afternoon twilight, all that was left of Catherine's only child drifted down; sparkles of blue—the remnants of her witch blood's essence—caught the light like tiny sapphires, or the very tears of the Goddess herself.

Seated on her carved wooden throne, wearing a formal gown of mourning black, her hair pulled back and covered with a veil, Catherine, High Priestess of the Cahors Coven, remained stiff-lipped, but her heart caught in her throat. Though she knew that Isabeau had burned to death in the fire, the evidence still shook her. But she was a queen, and the daughter of kings and queens; she had lost kinsmen in the Crusades, in other battles, assassinations, and duels. Death was no stranger to her family, nor was the concept of sacrificing one of their own to further the ambitions of the family.

On the walls of her Great Hall, swords, shields, spears, lances, and battle axes hung crossed, in rows, and in circles. There was no room on the walls of the

Romanesque room for art, only the stark realities of her existence. Each moment, each day that the Cahors house continued could be counted a victory. Without her vigilance, the Deveraux would have surely found a way to grind the bones of all the Cahors to dust and ash, and to parade their triumph before stricken Coventry, now faced with the prospect of an unchecked and savage family of warlocks—the Deveraux.

Beyond her casement window, smoke still roiled from the ruins of Deveraux castle, the result of her carefully orchestrated scheme to burn the warlocks in their beds. Her daughter, Isabeau, had been instrumental in that, betraying Jean, heir of the Deveraux Coven, to whom she had been wed mere months before.

All would have been well if they had shared the secret of the Black Fire with us, she thought angrily as the last of Isabeau's ashes filtered to the carpet. *They forced my hand, and they know it.*

Retaliation is inevitable, and it will be brutal. Of that I have no doubt.

"What makes you think that you can mock my grief in this manner and then leave my castle alive?" she asked the Deveraux emissary.

"Honor," he said simply.

She regarded him. "Whose?"

"I carried a flag of truce," he reminded her, "when my horse cantered into your bailey. Your husband, Duc Robert, gave me safe passage so that I might bring your loved one home to you."

"I see." Her tone was almost conversational as she rose from her throne, descended the three steps from the dais, and crossed to the vast array of weaponry at her disposal. "And as a Deveraux, you assumed that his word carried more weight than mine, though I am the High Priestess of our coven?"

For the first time, the man looked uncertain.

"He guaranteed my safety," he stated flatly.

Without another word, she plucked a battle-axe off the wall, whirled around, took quick aim, and flung it directly at his head.

It chopped his face in two; then the top of his head lobbed backward, much as the hinged lid of the box containing her daughter's ashes had done, and he collapsed in a gory heap on her beautiful black-and-silver carpet.

"*Madame la reine,*" gasped the liveried villein who had smirked at her daughter's remains.

For him, she conjured a fireball and flung it at him. It landed in his hair. He shrieked for more minutes than she had care to listen.

So she swept from the Great Hall like the queen she was.

"And so, it falls to you," she said to the prostrate girl before her.

Three days had passed since Isabeau's death. It was in this very turret room that Isabeau had begged her to spare Jean de Deveraux, her new husband. Her huge, dark eyes had filled with tears, ignoring the warnings implicit in the entrails of the lambkin Catherine had sacrificed, begging for mercy for a man who would not grant her the same in return.

Because Isabeau was not yet with child, the Deveraux were planning to murder her in her marriage bed, thus to sever the alliance with the Cahors. The heads of both families had made an unspoken bargain: Isabeau would unite the houses by giving birth to a son if and when the Deveraux shared the secret of the Black Fire with the Cahors. Neither had been willing to go first; the stalemate had made Catherine impatient and Isabeau vulnerable. And so Catherine had laid siege to their castle and forced their hand.

"I knew it was a risk," she murmured, coming back to the present, and to the girl in front of her. "I knew that in all probability I would lose my daughter.

"And so, it falls to you," she repeated.

The girl was named Jeannette, which Catherine found propitious. Perhaps if Isabeau and the Deveraux prince had made a girl, they would have named her thus. This Jeannette was one of the bastard children of Catherine's first husband, Louis. He had many of them, but Jeannette carried within her blood the strongest magic of the male line. Long ago it was a witch who had brought strong blood to the Cahors line, and magical power was more pronounced in Cahors daughters than in sons, just as Deveraux sons carried their family's powers from generation to generation.

Jeannette had Louis's golden hair and quicksilver eyes; she was lithe and petite, a darling child of fourteen, and as she lay trembling before the great queen, she whispered, *"Je vous en prie, madame.* I am not worthy."

"You're afraid, and right to be," Catherine mused. "You're not well armed in the ways of the moon, and I have little time to prepare you for your role." *I should have had one waiting to step forward,* she thought. *That was an oversight, an incredible pride on my part.*

I assumed I would be able to protect Isabeau. I was so terribly, terribly wrong.

And now she is but dust. She is dead, and Jean is dead, and the two houses must both start over.

Catherine swept her skirts to her private altar.

Candles burned, and herbs; small doves huddled inside their cages, cowering as if they realized their fate. A golden statue of the Moon Lady, young, vibrant, and beautiful, stretched forth her arms to hold the libations Catherine had provided: ripe grain, wine, and the heart of a fine buck.

Seated atop the statue's head, preening and watchful, the lady hawk Pandion observed the proceedings. She cocked her head, her bells jingling, and fluttered her wings. Then she hunkered down to watch her mistress make magic.

Catherine grabbed one of the doves and stabbed it with the athame she held in her left hand. The warm blood gushed over her hand and onto the head of Jeannette, who gasped but said nothing.

Two more times Catherine anointed her with blood, then blessed the wine and gave it to Jeannette to drink. It was redolent with herbs designed to strengthen the girl's powers, and when Jeannette's head rolled back and her eyes lolled, unseeing, Catherine whispered spells over her for hours, hoping against hope that this young, untried girl would become a suitable heiress for her own mantle as High Priestess of the Cahors Coven.

And so began her work on Jeannette.

The young witchling was never allowed to leave the turret room. She wasn't yet strong enough to fight the magical influences of the Deveraux, who were surely plotting revenge. Catherine's spies had told her that Jean's place had been taken by one Paul, and that he was mighty and bold . . . but no Jean de Deveraux.

Moons passed, nearly six of them. Jeannette was practically half-mad from being locked up in the turret, and began to speak of visions she was having of the dead Isabeau, whose spirit would not rest.

Catherine was delighted to hear that her child had not yet departed for higher realms; that Isabeau was earthbound made her wonder if she could revive her, perhaps pour her soul into this little vessel. Never mind that such an act would no doubt cause the death of Jeannette's own soul. She was a bastard, and so far she had done nothing to fan any flames of warmth in her new mistress's heart.

The queen of the castle spent long hours casting spells and runes in order to contact her dead daughter. She made untold sacrifices. She raged, she pleaded with the Goddess . . . and she went unheard.

Finally she went to Jeannette, humiliated that such a chit could manage what she could not.

"My daughter. What stops her rest?" Catherine demanded of her.

"I . . . I don't know," Jeannette said miserably. "I

only see her in my mind, and know that she's not happy."

"Not *happy*?" Happiness was a foreign concept to Catherine. What on earth did happiness have to do with anything of import? Happiness was a sop to those who had no power, no fortune. There was no such thing, but rulers and bishops said so to keep the serfs and villeins in their traces.

"She is not happy," Jeannette repeated. And then she murmured, "And neither am I. Oh, stepmother, please let me leave this room!"

"You're not ready," Catherine insisted.

"I am! Oh, I beg of you, I am!" Jeannette threw herself on her knees and clasped Catherine around the legs. "I am going mad!"

Catherine touched the crown of Jeannette's hair, then moved firmly away. "Patience, girl. Soon. Soon you will have the wings you need to fly with Pandion." She smiled at the bird, who screeched at her in return.

But alas, Jeannette could not wait. Four moons later, Catherine learned that she had bribed one of the male servants to unlock the turret room, slipped out, and run to the forest to commune with the spirits. She had danced for hours, skyclad, then snuck back, put on her clothes, and pretended that nothing had happened.

This happened each moon for the next three moons.

Catherine's fury was matched only by her anxiety when the bishop arrived from Toulouse, as he did upon occasion, and with great unease, asked to speak to Catherine "of divers unsavory accusations against your ward."

Cahors was on the route from the wine valley to Toulouse; it seemed that travelers overnighting in the forest had witnessed Jeannette's pavane to the Goddess, and reported it to their priest. More rumors flew; soon the town was mumbling against the Cahors, calling them witches as they had done in the past.

There were prelates who knew the truth about the Cahors and the Deveraux, and others who did not. Each generation of French Coventry went about handling the Church as efficiently as possible. It had fallen to Catherine to be saddled with a virtuous Christian man who agreed wholeheartedly with the burnings that had been raging all over the continent.

"Of course you can understand my concern, *madame*," the bishop said to Catherine, as they walked in Catherine's beautiful rose garden. Isabeau's ashes had been buried there, and now a beautiful lily— symbol of the House of Cahors—drew nutrients from her mortal remains. "If such an abomination has found lodging in your family, that is to say, in your own bosom." He colored. "To turn a phrase."

"To turn a phrase," she said, "my husband's bastard is my concern, not yours."

The old man held up a finger. "All the souls in Christendom are the Church's concern, my daughter."

In the end, Catherine angrily capitulated and gave the prelate what he wanted. She herself denounced Jeannette, claiming to have seen her flying on a broomstick, and the bishop's guards dragged her screaming from the turret room, which had been stripped bare of all witchly trappings far in advance of their entry. A crucifix hung on the wall with a statue of the Madonna. Gone was Catherine's altar, and the bloodstains of the many sacrifices, and the arcana of witchly pursuit.

And gone was Pandion . . . until Jeannette was tied to the stake in the Cathedral yard in Toulouse. And then the lady hawk of the Cahors wheeled above her head, capering in the currents of hot air as Catherine's hopes, once more, burned to ash.

THREE

DEAD MOON

☾

In the night we dance and laugh
As our foes taste our wrath
Death we are and death we bring
Delivered on a falcon's wing

We dance upon each dead man's corpse
Laugh and shout till we grow hoarse
We treasure all our enemies' moans
As lady hawk talons crush their bones

Jer: The Island of Avalon

"You're going to live after all, *mon frère sorcier*," a voice said.

Jer couldn't tell where it was coming from. He tried to open his eyes; they were bandaged shut.

He couldn't move—or rather, he had no idea if he was able to move, or moving his body already. Agony permeated his being; he had no sense of a self beyond the pain that wracked him.

His father used to debate the notion of eternal torment with a warlock friend. Michael had held with the common belief that after a time, the victim would stop feeling the torture; that any sort of sensation, be it ecstatic bliss or the burning, scorching sensations that plagued Jer now, would become meaningless. The body would simply stop responding to them.

That was so wrong.

Pain begins in the mind, Jer thought, *and even my mind was burned. I am completely, utterly destroyed.*

Holly, he called out in his desperation, *save me. You can make it stop. You have the power.*

In a strange delirium he had dreamed of her; he had sat imprisoned in a room, shackled as a lure for her. He had begged her to stay away from him, as well he should do now. His family was covenanted to kill her.

She has a better chance if Eli died from his burns. Fantasme's spirit materialized and rescued him, but I pray to the God that the Black Fire killed him . . . more quickly than I seem to be dying.

He is evil, true, but he is my brother.

I can't wish this kind of pain on anyone.

Then a voice—the same voice—whispered in his ear again, "You're going to live."

He knew that voice; it was a part of him, an undying piece of his own soul. It was the voice of Jean de

Deveraux, the son of the House of Deveraux when the Cahors perpetrated the massacre upon Castle Deveraux.

"I did not die, either," Jean assured him. "They all believed that I died in the fire, but I survived. I told no one. I escaped with a small band of followers, and I stayed out of sight.

"I survived, and carried my warlock bloodline through my heirs in France to England and Montreal, and then to the Wild West.

"And you're going to survive, too, and kill my love," Jean continued, whispering in Jer's mind. "You shall kill Isabeau. And then she shall rest, and I will rest as well, because I will have my revenge at last."

Then another voice said, "You're going to live," and this one came from outside Jer's mind. "You will live, and you will join your father in his scheme to overthrow mine."

It's James, Jer realized. *The heir to the Moore Coven and son of Sir William, who is the leader of the Supreme Coven. Our family has secretly allied with James.*

That had been their original stance. But after Jer had been burned, Michael had pledged Jer to the service of Sir William in return for Jer's life. Upon sealing the bargain, Sir William had transformed into a hideous demon. *Is he a devil? Did my father make a deal with Satan himself so that I could survive?*

Suddenly the pain lessened, and Jer gasped with relief.

"It hurts, the Black Fire, doesn't it?" James murmured. "That's why we want the secret. The Supreme Coven wants this weapon so we can finally wipe out those idiot witches in the Mother Coven."

Jer was confused. Surely his father had already shared the secret. No way would Sir William let him hold a trump card like that.

"I can practically read your mind," James drawled. "Something has gone wrong, Jer. Your father can't conjure the Black Fire anymore. We have no idea why he continues to fail."

Jer was taken aback.

"I think it's because he needs you and Eli both, that there must be three Deveraux present to make the fire burn. With you out of commission and away from him, it isn't working. My father thinks I'm wrong. He thinks that bitch Holly is blocking it. So my father sent him home to kill her.

"What about you, Jer? Would you kill her if I ordered you to? You're with me, or you're against me. You're going to get well, and you, your father, and your brother, are going to conjure the Black Fire for me."

Eli must be alive, Jer thought, and he was both dismayed and relieved at the thought. *I still care about him.*

Blood is thicker than water after all . . . warlock blood, that is. . . .

"Sit up," James commanded him.

Magic thrummed through Jer Deveraux, binding up seared flesh; reopening veins that had melted shut; clearing the scars from his lungs and his heart. His breathing came more freely; he sucked in both air and magic, and the glow pulsated and spread throughout his body, expelling with his exhalations. He was dizzy, almost high, and then the pain was almost gone. *Almost, but not quite.*

Then Jer found himself seated in a wheelchair on a cliff, facing out to sea. Magical energy swirled and undulated around him, motes of green phosphorescence danced over his skin.

His skin, which was black and shriveled and repulsive.

He stared in horror at his hands, dangling loosely in his lap. They were charred stumps, bones poking through the lumps of cindered flesh. A witch at the stake would have looked no worse.

I'm a monster, like Sir William. Maybe he was burned by the Black Fire too. Maybe my father conjured it before, years ago, and Sir William bears the scars.

Tears rolled down his face. His body shook with grief and rage and deep, abject humiliation.

I can never let Holly see me like this. She'd pull away,

probably throw up. I couldn't take that.

"You begin to understand what the Cahors are capable of," said Jean de Deveraux's voice inside Jer's head. "*Eh, bien,* that's what I looked like too, after my wife betrayed me. And why I both love and loathe my Isabeau. And why you must kill the reigning Cahors witch, who is known as Holly Cathers. My Isabeau can possess her and she has betrayed us both now. So they must die, the one with the other."

"No," Jer croaked. He had no idea how long it had been since he had spoken a word. "Holly did not betray me."

"But she did," Jean insisted. "*La femme* Holly, she knew that bound together, Deveraux and Cahors— *pardon, on dit* 'Cathers'—could stay untouched within the flame of the Black Fire that your family conjured last Beltane. By holding on to each other, you both could have stood inside the flames for an entire moon, had you so desired.

"But she moved away from you in the fire, did she not? *Mon ami,* she abandoned you to the flames, as Isabeau swore to do to me, knowing full well that you would suffer like this."

"Her cousins dragged her away!" Jer rasped. "She had no choice."

"How pathetic, that you lie so poorly to yourself,"

Jean said contemptuously. "She's the strongest witch in the Cahors line since Catherine, Isabeau's mother. If she had really wanted to save you, she could have."

"No," Jer whispered, but he had no rebuttal; deep in his sizzling, superheated Deveraux soul, he believed what Jean was saying.

Then he had another vision: He was standing on the shoreline in Seattle, with Holly; the waves flung themselves against their ankles, and then their calves, and their knees. But his arms were around Holly, and she was kissing him deeply, her entire body pressed against his. She was hungry for him, and so eager. . . .

. . . and the waves crashed around them, and crashed; Holly held him tightly and kept her mouth over his. The chill waters yanked at them and tugged hard.

They tumbled out to sea, caught up in the cresting waves and the chasms between them. Jer fought, trying to keep his head above the rollercoaster of water, but Holly clung to him and pulled him down, down; her mouth was over his and he couldn't draw a breath. She had effectively cut off all his oxygen. In his panic and frustration, he tried to break free, but he couldn't. She was drowning him.

"She will be the death of you, if you don't kill her first," Jean whispered. "Isabeau is bound to take my life, through you if she must. She cannot rest until I am obliterated."

And then James spoke, as if he were part of this vision, as if he lived both outside and inside Jer's mind:

"Remember who your friends are, Deveraux," James added.

Jean continued. "And never, ever forget your enemies. In the lives of witch and warlock, blood feuds go on for centuries. *Mademoiselle* Holly may want to love you, may even be able to convince herself that she does; but she is the living embodiment of all that is Cahors, and she is your mortal enemy."

Holly and Amanda: Seattle, October

It was a very dark and stormy night, nearly Samhain, and Uncle Richard was drunk.

Holly and Amanda had just gotten home from Circle, both taking off their cloaks of invisibility to find him sitting in the living room in the dark, compulsively eating the miniature chocolate bars purchased for trick-or-treaters, straight out of the bag. He didn't even pretend anymore; he was drinking Scotch straight out of the bottle. In the early days after Aunt Marie-Claire's death, he had mixed drinks for himself, making them progressively stronger; then he had taken to drinking out of a shot glass. That was before he had

had proof that Marie-Claire had been having an affair with Michael Deveraux.

Poor Uncle Richard had discovered the truth in a horribly prosaic way: Marie-Claire had kept a diary, and Richard found it. She had written of her nights with Michael in unstinting detail and Richard had read every word.

"Daddy?" Amanda asked gently as she knelt by his chair.

He sighed and ticked his gaze to her, his eyes rheumy and bloodshot. There was a week's growth of beard on his face. He smelled.

She and Holly had not been able to talk Richard into moving away. He was determined to fall apart in his own home. Since he didn't work anymore, letting his business die day by day, week by week, it had proven to be a challenge to ward and protect the house while he was around. But the coven had managed it. He was relatively safe . . . or to be completely frank, in as much danger as the others.

"Uncle Richard?" Holly queried. She moved her hand and blessed him. He didn't seem to notice the furtive hand gesture, and it didn't seem to make him any better.

"I'll make you some coffee." Amanda brushed past Holly and went into the kitchen.

Holly took up the vigil next to Uncle Richard's chair. She put her hand on his and said, "I'm so sorry."

He turned his head and stared at her; and in the dim light of the moon, she saw that his eyes had rolled up in his head. Startled, she drew away.

But he caught her hand and held it tightly, nearly crushing the bones. His voice eked out, weird and disembodied, as he said, in Michael Deveraux's voice, *"Die soon, Holly Cathers.*

"Die horribly."

Nicole: Spain, October

As they crept down the streets of Madrid, Philippe kept close to Nicole, obviously eager to be near her, perhaps more intent on keeping her safe. He was a rock, and she was grateful for his strength and his interest in keeping close by; for the first time in a long while she felt safe. He was not as dramatically handsome as José Luís, who had wild Gypsy blood in his veins. He was more like her Amanda: pleasing to look at, but not startling. The extremes of looks and emotions were left to others of their covens: in Amanda's case, Nicole tended to steal the show; in Philippe's, it was José Luís.

Philippe did stand out from his coven, though, in that he wasn't Spanish. He was from Agen, a small town in France.

Now he spoke to their leader, saying, "José Luís, we need to leave the streets. It's not safe tonight, not even for us."

"Tienes razón," José Luís agreed. He raised his voice so that the others could clearly hear him, "Come, we go."

They had been together for several days, keeping on the run, finding safe houses that José Luís and his lieutenant, Philippe, had set up long ago. They were warriors in the cause of White Magic, and they had many enemies. Philippe told her that something had been tracking them before she had arrived, but she had the feeling that her presence was like a homing beacon, pointing the way to their coven.

Alicia, the witch Philippe had silenced, had left the coven, jealous of Nicole and irritated that she had been charmed when she'd spoken against her.

José Luís was the tallest of the group, and the best dressed. He was wearing black leather pants and a black-washed silk shirt. His curly hair fell past his shoulders, and he had casually pulled it back and secured it in a ponytail with an elastic band he took from his pocket. From his features she would have guessed his age to be about thirty, but his eyes looked older, *much* older.

Philippe, who appeared a few years younger, had

swarthy skin and bright green eyes, a startling combination in contrasts. He wore jeans and sweaters against the cold of the Madrid autumn, expensively tooled cowboy boots, and, on occasion, a cowboy hat. His chestnut hair was cut short, very stylish, and on the one occasion that she had touched it, she was startled by how silky it felt to her touch.

Though he was usually jovial, now he was all business.

He feels it too, she thought.

José Luís had introduced the oldest member of his coven as "Señor Alonzo, our benefactor, our father figure."

Alonzo had snorted in derision, but extended his hand to Nicole. She had clasped it, and in one smooth movement he twisted her hand so that he could kiss the top of it. He released it easily and stepped back. Everything about the man bespoke grace and elegance.

Armand was their "conscience," José Luís had told her. His dark eyes crackled and his mouth was set in a hard line. There was something dark and dangerous about him, as if he were a villain from some old-time movie.

Pablo was José Luís's younger brother. He looked younger than Nicole herself, perhaps fourteen, and he was very shy.

At the time she had met them all, she had thought, *What a motley assortment!*

And Pablo had replied quietly, in heavily accented English, "But we get the job done."

Startled, Nicole had stared at him. Philippe chuckled. "Pablo is gifted in ways that are beyond the rest of us." The boy just blushed harder and continued to stare down at his shoes.

"And who are you?" José Luís had asked at last.

It was her turn to blush. "My name is Nicole Anderson. I'm just . . . I'm . . . visiting Spain."

"You're a long way from your home," Jose observed, scrutinizing her. "And you are of the witch blood. I sincerely doubt, *mi hermosa,* that you are . . . *visiting* Spain."

She nodded, tears stinging her eyes.

"I'm . . . I'm in trouble," she managed. "Big trouble."

"Warlock trouble," Pablo filled in.

Nicole nodded. She had no idea if she should tell them what was going on; she worried that she might endanger them. "I . . . I'm so scared."

José Luís smoothed over the moment. "*Está bien. No te precupes, bruja.* You will be safe with us. You can be part of our coven."

"But I don't want to be part of a coven," she heard herself protesting.

José Luís had laughed. "It's a little late for that."

And that had been when Philippe stepped forward and said, "I will watch out for you, Nicole."

And he had, ever since. It was he who conjured wards around her to deflect magical seeking spells; and he who made sure she had enough to eat when they stopped for meals; and he who watched her in the night as she bedded down, studying the air around her, making sure she never slept close to a window.

He, who had obviously begun to care for her . . .

. . . and she for him.

Now, on the dusty streets of Madrid, the sense of being hunted grew stronger with the darkness. Tonight, Nicole's senses were screaming that someone—or something—was gaining on them, fast.

"Philippe is right. I think we should leave," Pablo announced. "It's become too dangerous here. We can go to the French border. We have friends there."

The others began to murmur, quietly assenting.

Nicole shook her head and stepped back, pulling her hand from Philippe's grasp. "I can't go with you. I'll . . . I just want to go home. I shouldn't have left in the first place." In a tiny voice she added, "It was very cowardly of me."

He nodded sympathetically. "I understand, but that is not possible at the moment. When it is safe, we will do what we can to see you home."

"All the way to Seattle?" she croaked.

His grin broadened. "Yes, even all the way to Seattle." He clapped his hands. *"Bueno, andale,"* he said to the rest of the coven. *"La noche esta demasiado peligroso." The night is too dangerous.*

Several of the covenate made the sign of the cross. Nicole was startled and about to ask about it when the band began to move.

As if of a single mind, they slunk through the center of Madrid, turning down side streets as one, never speaking, never hesitating. As though in a dream, Nicole allowed herself to be swept along with the five cloaked figures. Philippe once again had her by the hand, and she found herself half trotting to keep up with his long strides.

An hour passed before they finally stopped in an alley beside a small car. Nicole hesitated as the others climbed in. Philippe smiled at her.

"We are safe. For the moment."

Nicole nodded slowly, staring from him to the car. His smile began to fade, and he glanced at the shadows whence they had come.

"I sense that there is not much time," he said. "We must go now if we are to escape. Do you feel it?"

She nodded. "Yes," she said unhappily. "I do."

It felt as if someone were staring down at them from a great height—like a huge, winged creature preparing to take flight, flap its enormous wings, and pluck all of them up with its razor-sharp talons. She could almost hear an eerie, echoic screech.

The falcon, she thought. *He's coming.*

Philippe urged Nicole into the car. "This is an old Deux Chevaux," he told her. "A French car. We call them 'two horses' because that's all the horsepower they have." He grinned. "But even a Deux Chevaux beats something made in Spain."

"Tiene cuidado, macho," José Luís said with mock menace.

"Tais-toi!" Philippe shot back. He gave Nicole a quick wink and a smile. "You see? Even in danger, we can joke and insult one another. We are a strong band, Nicole. We will be all right."

She tried to smile back, but her anxiety was rising with each heartbeat. She found herself in the front seat wedged between José Luís and Philippe.

"Um, seat belt," she murmured, fumbling for the straps.

"It is okay. I am a good driver," Philippe informed her with a crooked smile.

She nodded grimly.

"We cannot go back for our belongings," Philippe told her. "Do you have your passport? Your money and things like that?"

She patted her pockets and nodded. "Yes." She had brought very few things with her, but she was sorry to give them up. She felt so . . . naked with nothing to change into. *And no shampoo. No toothbrush.*

Pablo leaned forward and said something to Philippe, who murmured, "Ah, *sí,*" and turned to Nicole. "We'll buy new things," he said kindly. "Once we are safe."

Three hours later they pulled up to a villa just as dawn broke behind it, the light dancing on the white walls of the low, sprawling country house. Flowers edged a cobbled path to the front door.

The sight took Nicole's breath away.

It's too beautiful to be dangerous, she thought, knowing in her heart that that didn't make any sense.

José Luís stepped out of the car and Nicole moved to follow him, but Philippe laid a hand on her arm, stopping her. "Best to let him go alone. He needs to, how do you say, make a check?"

Nicole peered out the window and watched as a tall man left the villa and approached José Luís. The two men strode toward each other purposefully, each swaggering slightly. When they got within fifteen feet of each other they began shouting. She couldn't understand the words, but they didn't sound friendly.

The men stopped when they stood nearly toe-to-toe. They were gesturing wildly and seemed to be arguing even more heatedly. At last José Luís threw back his head and laughed. The other man did as well, and then they embraced.

At last they broke apart and José Luís returned to the car, a smile stretching his sharp features. He gestured for everyone to join him, and as Nicole stepped from the car she shook her head in bewilderment.

"What was that all about?" she asked him.

"Just a little family reunion," José Luís answered with a sparkle in his eye.

Nicole flipped her hair back over her shoulders and decided not to question him further. *At least not about that,* she thought. She fell into step with Philippe as José Luís led the group around the house.

About half a mile behind the villa there was a small cottage, which was, apparently, their safe house. When they reached it, José Luís confidently opened the door and ushered them all inside. The place was small but clean; several cots lined the walls.

Nicole's eyelids felt heavy and the crisp white sheets looked cool and inviting.

I am so tired, she thought. *Tired of running. Tired of worrying.*

Wearily she sat down on a chair and slipped off her heavy-soled shoes. Her jeans were dusty. Philippe had given her a sweatshirt that read UNI DE MADRID, and that was dirty too. Her mouth was gritty; when José Luís went to a small cabinet, opened it, and brought out a bottle of wine, she accepted a swig along with the others and used it to rinse out the bad taste. Then someone volunteered that there was soap and shampoo in the bathroom.

"Mujer," Philippe said to her, "go and have a, how do you say, a soak?"

The wine had gone to her head; she felt a little fuzzy as she blurted excitedly, "There's a bathtub? Really? Are you . . . it's okay?"

He gestured to the cottage. "It's heavily protected. This may be the only chance you have for some while." He grinned at her and added, "A beautiful woman such as you should have some pleasures."

She blinked; warmth coiled in her lower belly and spread, and she felt the heat rising in her cheeks. He took her hand and raised it to his lips.

He's thinking about me in the tub, she thought.

As he pulled off his boots, Pablo glanced up at her, reddened, and looked away.

So is he.

Not for the first time, she became very aware that she was now the only female in the coven. The other witch, Alicia, had not been very welcomed to begin with, and no one had been sorry to see her go. And yet these men were not precisely warlocks, not in the same violent, harsh way as Eli and his father. They were male witches.

It's more like Eddie, Kialish, and Kialish's father, she thought. *It's a different thing. I wonder what Holly and Amanda would think about that. Maybe Jer's a male witch too. Maybe that's why he always had so much trouble fitting in as a Deveraux.*

It was strange. She knew that once, not long before, she would have made the most of the opportunity and basked in the attention of five men. She felt herself blushing and stole a glance at Philippe. All that seemed a long time past. There was only one man she really wanted attention from now.

Rummaging in the cabinets, Armand, the quiet, serious one, said something to José Luís, who in turn cocked his head questioningly at Nicole.

"Armand asks, are you Catholic?"

"No." She frowned at him, gazing past him at Armand. "Are you?"

"We're Spanish." He chuckled. "*Bueno,* Philippe is

French, but *sí*, we are all Catholic. In fact, we call Armand our 'conscience' because he was once a student of the priesthood. He wishes to conduct a Mass for us." José Luís smiled reassuringly as her lips parted in astonishment. "A white Mass, not a black one."

"But . . ." She hesitated. "We pray to the Goddess."

José Luís shrugged. "It's all the same, Nicolita. But what I am thinking is, it would be better if you took your soak. We who are of the faith will say our Mass."

"All . . . all right."

Señor Alonzo held up a finger, saying something to José Luís. He looked puzzled.

Then Philippe said, "Towels," and the others nodded. To Nicole, he explained, "They were trying to remember the word in English." He smiled at her. "They want you to know there are fresh towels in the bath."

"Thank you. *Gracias,*" she attempted. Smiles broke out all around.

Self-consciously she made her way into the bathroom. She found a light switch to her left and flicked it on.

A beautiful claw-foot tub sat to her right, and there was a small partition for the toilet and sink basin. She found the dark purple towels in a cupboard above the toilet, a bottle of what seemed to be shampoo, and a thick, fragrant bar of Maja soap wrapped in paper embossed with a picture of a flamenco dancer.

Breathing in the delicious perfume, she carried everything to the tub and turned on the double spigots. The tub was clean; she guessed that the man who had greeted José Luís so oddly kept the safe house clean in the event that it was needed. She was grateful for that. She was doubly grateful for Philippe's kindness in suggesting she take a bath.

Kindness? She smirked at herself. *Face it, Nicki. There's something there and you both feel it.*

There was a rubber stopper in the bottom of the tub; she plugged the drain and let the water run. Her head bobbed as she waited, and she thought, *I'll have to be careful. I could fall asleep in here.*

From the other room, a single male voice sang out in a rising, falling chant. The others echoed it. Then the first voice sang again, and the others responded.

They're chanting.

From deep inside her, ancient blood called to the rhythm, the mournful, gentle melodies. Part of her knew these words, these notes; it was in her blood, in her spirit, and in her soul.

The Cahors lived in a Catholic country. Does my spirit stretch back that far, like Holly's does?

Pondering, she peeled off her dirty clothes and

stepped cautiously into the bath. Easing her sore body down into the warm water, she moaned under her breath as aching muscles uncoiled. She couldn't remember the last time she had actually relaxed.

She lay back and closed her eyes, listening to the chanting. Her mind began to drift. . . . She thought of happier days, when Mom was alive, the two of them having just discovered magic. They had started blessing the family every evening, and Nicole had hoped that her mom would stop sleeping with Michael; that she, Nicole, could light a spark between her parents and they would love each other.

And that I could make Eli good. . . .

I loved him.

Tears slid down her face as she finally let go and allowed herself to feel some of her grief. Her mother was dead.

I miss Amanda. And Holly. And my cat. Oh, how I miss Hecate.

And then she was drifting along . . . drifting and bobbing . . . on water . . . *down a river; she was the Lady of the Island, and she dare not see the imprisoned one; if she looked on him she would go mad because he was so hideous. . . .*

"Nicki . . . ," came a voice. "Nicki, where are you? My father is sending the falcon to find you. Let me find you first."

"Eli?" she slurred. Her body was so heavy; her

head weighed a ton. She was aware that she was slipping lower into the water, the beautiful river that wound past the island . . . where . . . Jer . . .

"Nicki?"

She sank slowly, like Ophelia, with holly and lilies twined in her hair. Down, deeply down, the water caressing her chin; then down again, to her lower lip . . .

Drifting along as men sang holy words, and Eli whispered at her . . .

. . . and the waters met over her upper lip. Through her eyelids, in a magical way, she became aware that someone was standing beside the tub, and saying to her in a language she didn't speak, but in the ways of dreams and enchantments, she could understand, "Wake up, Nicole. Wake up, or you will die."

But Nicole couldn't move. A strange lassitude had overtaken her. She let herself slide deeper into the water. . . . It was so warm, so inviting . . . and she was so very, very tired . . .

. . . of living. . . .

The woman's soft voice said fearfully, in the same lilting foreign language—*it's Old French,* Nicki realized—"The curse is water. . . ."

FOUR

SNOW MOON

(

Prepare now, House of Deveraux
To wreak vengeance on all our foes
Careful now as we plan the worst
Think and scheme, pray and curse

We huddle together beneath the skies
Their darkness reflected in our eyes
Rest and plot the overthrow
Of the House of Deveraux

Holly and Amanda: Seattle, October

Holly and Amanda took turns watching over Uncle Richard as he collapsed into a drunken stupor and began to snore. They had no idea what to do with him, and they called Tante Cecile on her cell phone for help. She had come over immediately, with Silvana in tow.

The voodoo priestess had called upon the *loa*, the gods, who could also possess people, and they advised her to keep him locked in his bedroom until a full exorcism could be conducted. As Richard had no witch blood in his veins, Tante Cecile assumed that Michael had been able to possess him because he had been weakened by drink. It was a known fact in occult circles that people in altered states of consciousness were easier to invade than those who kept their wits about them. Those of the old traditions—the Druids, the pagans, shaman, Orphic Mystery cultists, and even ancient Christians—willingly relinquished themselves for the use of their spirits and gods through potent herbs, fasting, and even pain.

But Richard was another matter.

"Michael could try to force him to hurt you," Tante Cecile told them as she sat with her daughter, Amanda, and Holly in the living room.

Amanda nodded dully. Holly's heart went out to her. She'd been through so much.

Then her cousin muttered, "He's already hurt us. He stood by while Mom . . . She needed someone stronger."

Holly traded shocked looks with Silvana. "Amanda, you're not blaming your dad for your mom's . . . that she went to Michael Deveraux." She couldn't bring herself to say the word "affair."

Silvana chimed in. "For heaven's sake, Amanda, Michael Deveraux bewitched your mother!"

Amanda balled her fists. "He didn't need to bewitch her. She would've . . ." She took a deep breath. "Daddy doesn't know this, but Michael wasn't the first."

"Oh, Mandy, no," Holly said softly.

"Yes. *Yes.*" She touched her fingertips to her forehead. "I found her other diaries right after the funeral. I read them, and then I burned them. But Daddy got to her most recent one before I could. That was the one about Michael."

The others were speechless. Holly thought back to her parents and how unhappy they'd been together. *Did either one of them cheat?*

She couldn't bear the thought.

Suddenly a trio of stricken yowls pierced the silence. It was the cats, howling in terror, the three flashing down the stairs and racing into the living room, where Bast deposited a dead bird at Holly's feet. It was about two feet long, far too large for a cat Bast's size to bring down, very black and shiny. A trickle of blood dribbled onto the carpet from its breast. As it lay on its side, one lifeless eye glared up at Holly.

As Amanda and Silvana jumped to their feet, Tante Cecile bent over the cat's gory trophy and murmured an incantation. From her jeans pocket she pulled a chicken claw and gestured at the air above the body, then around it. Silvana joined her; they were speaking a language Holly didn't know, but she took Amanda's hand and said, "Within, without, our wards hold. The circle cannot fall."

Amanda joined in. "Witchly sisters are we, strong of spirit, stout of heart; we demand protection from the Goddess; we are her moon children."

There was a sudden flurry in the chimney, as if of birds trying to fly out; Bast leaped into Holly's lap, raised up on her back legs, and put her paws on Holly's chest. Her yellow eyes stared into Holly's. Holly stared back. Hecate mewed plaintively, over and over and over again.

A chill crept through the room; Holly almost felt a hand on her shoulder and jumped slightly. Tante Cecile eyed her carefully and said, "She is with us."

"She?" Holly asked.

Tante Cecile stared at Amanda, who glanced around the room and cried out, "Mom?"

"No, Amanda," Tante Cecile said sadly. "Isabeau."

Holly swallowed. Amanda nodded, disappointed but focused on the task at hand, and took a deep breath. She murmured, "Blessed be."

"Blessed be," Holly added.

Tante Cecile said, "Ignore the bird, girls. Make a circle with me."

The trio moved away from the sofa and closer to the fireplace. As Tante Cecile bent down and placed logs on the andiron, she turned to Holly and said, "Make a fire, honey. It's cold."

Holly nodded. She found a place inside herself and filled it with the heat and color of fire, imagining it, seeing orange, yellow, and red flames, smelling the smoke. She said in Latin, *"Succendo aduro!"* and the fire ignited.

No one was surprised. Holly had been able to start fires for months. Black Fire was another story.

I don't know what one has to be or do to be able to conjure that, she thought, *and I'm not sure I want to know.*

Though the others brightened at the sight of the fire, Holly felt no warmth from it. She was getting colder, and the chill was seeping into her bones.

Amanda said to her, "Holly, there's a blue glow around your head."

The others nodded. "I see it too," Silvana said.

She looked down at her hands; they were not glowing. Then all of a sudden it was as if someone had drilled a little hole in the center of her skull and poured chilled pudding into it. The sensation seeped through her head, giving her a cold headache and half-freezing her face in place. She felt slowed down—her breathing, her heartbeat, her thoughts. She became aware that the other three had grouped around her and someone pushed her gently into a chair. Then they placed their hands on her head and Tante Cecile began to speak in French.

Holly felt herself answering, also in French.

"Je suis . . . Isabeau."

Then Holly lost track of what was going on; she was vaguely aware of the outer world, but her attention was being forced on an image she saw with her mind's eye: a beautiful woman—her ancestress, Isabeau—locked in a passionate embrace with Jer . . . no, not Jer Deveraux, but his ancestor, Jean, husband to Isabeau . . . *they're in their marriage bed. . . . The hangings are red and green, the colors of the Deveraux; mistletoe and oak and ivy twine everywhere; it's like a forest; there are herbs burning in the fireplace for fertility. The moon is full; her heart is full, and so is his. They have enchanted each other; passion has ignited; they are in desperate love . . . not expected . . . not welcomed . . .*

". . . *though we couple*," Isabeau thought inside Holly's head, "*we are mortal enemies, fully prepared to murder one another in this very bed; if he does not . . .*"

And then the image blurred, as if someone had changed a channel.

Now Holly was standing in a strange bathroom,

calmly looking down at Nicole, whose head had just sunk beneath the water. Bubbles sputtered on the surface.

"Aidez . . . la Nicole," Isabeau said inside her mind. "I tried to wake her, but she cannot hear me. She will be able to hear you, Holly. Wake her up!"

More bubbles trickled upward to the surface.

"Nicole!" she shouted aloud. "Nicole, wake up!"

Nicole's head shot up from the water; she looked around, startled.

The cold sensation immediately dissipated, and Holly became aware of the other three women, whose faces were filled with concern.

"What about her? What's wrong?" Amanda cried. "Where's my sister?"

"Isabeau," Tante Cecile commanded, "speak to us."

There was no reply. The room was warm to her, and she felt alone and very dizzy.

Isabeau had left.

Holly said, "It's just me now." She took a deep breath and told them what she had seen.

Amanda grabbed Holly's shoulders. Her face was contorted with fear, her features constricted while her eyes were huge.

"Nicole woke up, right? She's okay?"

"As far as I could tell," Holly said honestly.

"No clues about where she was?" Tante Cecile queried.

Holly shook her head. "I'm sorry. It was just a bathroom."

"Don't be sorry," Silvana put in. Her silver beads flashed in the firelight as she shook her head. "You probably saved Nicole's life."

Holly nodded. "I feel that. I'm certain that I did." She gestured at the dead bird, pointed at it, and murmured a quick spell of levitation. As if by invisible hands, the inert bird lifted into the air and floated to the fireplace. Then it was flung with contempt into the fire.

It burst into flame and was instantly consumed.

Then one by one, the cats walked to them, joining their circle: Holly's cat, Bast; Amanda's beloved Freya; and Nicole's Hecate. All three named for goddesses, all three more than cats.

"Blessings on you, Bast," Holly said. "You caught an enemy."

The cat blinked up at her and began to purr. The other two sat on their haunches beside Bast, and stared up expectantly at Holly.

"Your familiars," Tante Cecile told her, "are waiting for you to tell them what to do."

Holly and Amanda looked first at each other and

then at the cats. Amanda said, "Patrol the house. Kill any enemies that you find."

Holly said to her cousin, "That's a good idea. And we should also—"

A sharp contraction rippled through her. Her eyes rolled back in her head, and she collapsed.

She began to jerk uncontrollably, arms and legs flailing. She heard Amanda shouting her name, heard Silvana and her aunt crying out in French.

Then she was struggling under rip-current waters rushing everywhere, tumbling her over. She was back in the Grand Canyon, reliving the accident, clutching at the straps that held her in the raft. She knew in her soul that nearby, her father was already dead, her mother had but seconds to live, and Tina was going to last longest of all, nearly an entire minute longer than Ryan, their river guide, who was losing consciousness at this moment. And she was drowning.

Then the blue glow materialized, as before, and took form as Isabeau, who floated toward her, her fingers nimbly working the buckles . . .

. . . and her voice filled Holly's mind once more: *It is the curse of the Cahors,* ma chere *Holly. Those who love us die not in flame, but by water. They die by water.*

It was the Deveraux who put that curse on us. They have hounded us through time, attempting to kill us off.

You must survive. We must end this vendetta . . . forever.

On the floor, Holly gasped for air, sucking it in hungrily, starved for it, and began to cough.

Tante Cecile patted her hard on the back; water spewed out of her mouth, and the other two girls cried out.

Amanda was beside her in an instant. She took Holly's hands in hers and said, "Your fingers are wet."

Holly blurted, "Amanda, there's a curse on us. People we love, they drown. It's the curse of the Cahors."

She buried her face in her hands. "I killed my parents with my witch blood. I killed them because I'm cursed!"

"Hush, now," Tante Cecile ordered her. "You didn't kill them."

"But it's real," Holly insisted, pulling her hands from her face and lifting her head. "Isabeau told me." She clutched at Amanda. "What do we do?"

"We use that knowledge, and we work with it," Tante Cecile cut in. Her face was filled with grim purpose. "Silvana, get a big bowl of water from their kitchen. If that's how they play, that's how we play. We are going to drown whatever is possessing Richard Anderson."

* * *

It was wild work, and it went by in a blur of nerves and exhaustion.

The four gathered in the bedroom, where they had bound an unconscious Uncle Richard to the bed. As Silvana lit candles and sounded a small gong, Tante Cecile chanted and talked to the *loa*. The cats joined in, howling. Then something dark floated out of him, and at Tante Cecile's instruction, Holly grabbed it with both hands and plunged it into the bowl of water.

It struggled in her hands and then went limp. She pulled her hands away, and it was a strange, tiny creature that reminded Holly of a cross between a frog and an elf.

"It's an imp," Tante Cecile said with satisfaction. "You killed it."

Holly nodded, near collapse. On Tante Cecile's instruction, she dragged herself off to bed.

Sleep came quickly to Holly, but the oblivion of rest was short-lived. Soon she was dreaming, and she was standing once more in the room with Jer. She tried to speak with him, but no words would come, and he lay, hunched over on his side, asleep. For a minute she watched the rise and fall of his chest, willing him to wake and to see her.

It was no use.

Suddenly a hand brushed against the back of her

neck. She jumped and turned around, heart racing, and prepared to fight.

A woman in a long white gown stood there. Red hair fell in waves all the way down to her knees. Her face was unearthly beautiful but with sad, haunting eyes that pierced Holly's soul.

She shook her head slowly as if to silence Holly's unspoken questions. Then she raised her hand and beckoned Holly to follow. Holly passed with her through the wall of the cell and then followed her for what seemed ages through twisting corridors lit only by sporadic torches.

Neither the woman's nor Holly's feet made any sound against the stone floors, and the silence unnerved her. At last Holly strained, trying to clear her throat, to make some sound to shatter the silence that overwhelmed her. Her throat felt constricted and she felt the fear growing in her. She had to speak, to say something. . . .

The woman turned and laid a pale finger against her ruby lips. Again she shook her head and slowly pointed toward a dark alcove in the wall. Holly could see nothing in the blackness and finally shook her head in frustration. The woman glided back toward her and gestured for Holly to close her eyes. When she did, the woman's fingers pressed gently on her eyelids.

When her touch was gone, Holly opened her eyes. Her vision was sharper, clearer, and within the alcove she saw two huge beasts staring with unblinking eyes right at her. She jerked backward, but the woman's hand was on her arm, steadying her. She pointed to the animals, then to her own eyes, and shook her head no.

Somehow the beasts couldn't see them, but what Holly saw of them terrified her. Both were as big as lions, though they had the general shape of dogs. Their eyes glowed red and their brown-black fur stood up all over their bodies coarse and unyielding as spines. Their fangs were three inches long and saliva dripped in a steady flow from their open mouths. *Hellhounds,* Holly thought as she shuddered. *They can't see me, but they might be able to hear me.*

The woman turned and began to move on, and Holly hurried to follow behind. At long last they passed into a room where the woman stopped. She turned slowly to Holly and moved her arm, as if displaying the room to her. Holly gazed about her, her newfound sight seeing everything in excruciating detail.

Bottles of strange-looking liquids lined musty shelves. Still more bottles and flasks littered each of six huge work tables. Ancient manuscripts written in half a dozen different languages lay open everywhere. In the middle of one table a tall pointed hat with stars on it sat in a prominent place.

She felt a smile break out on her face. It looked just like the hat Mickey wore as the Sorcerer's Apprentice. She strode forward to touch the hat, trying to hold in her laughter. Her fingers were an inch from it when the woman clasped her wrist hard.

Holly bit back a startled exclamation of pain as she looked at the other woman. A warning shone in her eyes as she shook her head fiercely. Puzzled, Holly turned back to look at the hat. The stars on it were suddenly alive, glowing and twisting about on the hat in a crazy kaleidoscope. Heat was pouring from its surface and Holly pulled her hand back quickly.

She stared in wonder as the hat slowly returned to the inanimate object it had been before. *What would have happened if I had actually touched it?* She could feel the power emanating from it now; she had been too amused by it earlier to notice. The woman half smiled at her before extending her hand toward one of the walls.

Holly followed her gaze to a weathered and water-stained hanging. It looked to be ancient parchment, or maybe it was leather, stippled with faded gray shapes and letters.

It's a map.

Excitement rippled through her.

She's trying to tell me where Jer is!

She scanned it; all the words were in Latin, and she didn't recognize the lay of the land at all. Frantic, she scrutinized the shapes and cursed her geography teacher for being so boring that Holly had slept through every class.

There!

There was a small island with an *X* over the top of it. She tapped it with her finger and glanced questioningly at the other woman as she glided over.

The apparition dipped her head in acknowledgment. Holly turned back to the map, searching desperately for something that she recognized. Another island, much larger, seemed to be close by; the shape of it tickled something in Holly's memory.

England! It has to be.

Triumphant, she turned back to the other woman, only to find her staring toward the wall opposite with a look of fear on her face.

Someone's coming. I can sense it too.

On the table, the hat began to glow. . . .

Her fear palpable, the woman waved her hand above her head, and everything turned black. Then someone burst into the room, bellowing, "Sasha!"

Holly screamed and bolted upright.

Amanda burst into her room, eyes wild, hair

sticking out in all directions. She grabbed Holly by the shoulders and shook her.

"Holly, are you all right?"

Holly managed to nod, composing herself, wiping tears from her eyes, swallowing around the tightness in her throat. Unable to speak, she motioned for a glass of water, and Amanda ran out of the room. Amanda was back in seconds with a Dixie cup from the bathroom. Holly downed the water gratefully, her throat finally loosening.

Finished with the water, Holly looked up at Amanda to tell her about her dream and strangled back a gasp. Amanda's face seemed huge to her. She could see every blemish in her cousin's skin, could clearly distinguish every strand of hair. She blinked fiercely, willing the enhanced sight away.

It remained. She groaned and sank back onto her pillow, squeezing her eyes shut.

"What is it?" Amanda asked, quieter now.

"I had a dream. There was a woman. Someone . . . a relative, I think."

Amanda sounded concerned. "Isabeau?"

Holly shook her head. "No. I don't know who she was. She took me to this room where there was an old map. I found this island on it and it was close to England."

Holly risked opening her eyes a bit. Amanda's expression was one of puzzlement.

"Wait right here," she murmured getting up again.

"Gladly," Holly answered, closing her eyes again. She felt sick and queasy, so disoriented that it was as if the bed were rocking. Almost unconsciously she reached for Bast, who rose from her haunches at the foot of the bed and sauntered toward her mistress.

Amanda was gone for several minutes. Holly began to drift. Bast slipped herself under Holly's arm and began to purr.

Holly felt a little better, and she murmured, "Thank you, sweet kitty."

Bast nuzzled her and pressed her nose to Holly's cheek.

"Sorry," Amanda apologized as she returned and eased back down on the bed.

"Where are Tante Cecile and Silvana?" Holly asked.

"They went back to their place," Amanda said. "Tante Cecile wanted to check their wards."

"Your dad?"

"Still sleeping," Amanda told her. "Or passed out. I don't know what the difference is when you're drunk." She sounded sad and bitter. Then she brightened. "Meanwhile. Geography. I found an old atlas I got in junior high. Who'd have guessed I'd ever use it?"

"Tell me about it," Holly replied, warily opening one eye.

She could see the texture of the paper as Amanda shoved the atlas under her nose. She groaned and tried to focus on the pictures. There was England.

"Do you see it? The island you saw?"

"No," Holly confessed, knowing she couldn't blame it on the image being too small. "It was right there, though," she said, pointing to where she remembered.

Amanda closed the book. "Holly, it was just a dream."

"No, it wasn't."

"Okay, suppose it wasn't. You said it was an old map. Maybe the island's not there anymore."

Holly frowned, bemused. "Are you saying it sunk or something? Like Atlantis?"

Amanda shrugged. "Could be. If it's magical."

Holly opened the book back up, her eyes barely slit open. She found the page again and stared hard at it.

"Maybe no one can see it," she said slowly. "Maybe it's simply been forgotten." She trained her acute visual strength on it, willing any hidden lands to be revealed to her.

"But . . . that makes it disappear off a map? That's unlikely."

"'Occult' means 'hidden,'" Holly reminded her.

Bast kneaded her arm, and Holly yawned as her eyelids drifted closed. She could feel sleep tugging at her; she didn't have the strength to resist any longer.

As she fell asleep, she wasn't even aware of Amanda leaving.

Morning.

And no more dreams.

Bast had wandered off, and Holly had gotten up. Now, standing in front of the bathroom mirror, squinting to avoid staring at her own pores, Holly knew what she had to do. She pulled her hair back and fastened it in place with a silver Celtic barrette and left the bathroom. She walked downstairs, rehearsing what she was going to say to Amanda.

Downstairs she found her cousin hunched over a bowl of Rice Krispies. Amanda glanced up at her.

"You slept a long time," Amanda said. "I warded my dad and checked all the house's wards." Her gaze traveled to the spot where, upstairs, her father's bedroom was located.

Holly grabbed a bowl and joined her at the table.

"I have this weird eyesight thing going," she told Amanda. "Like I'm seeing everything super close up. It's not fun."

"We'll work a spell," Amanda ventured.

"After I eat something," Holly replied. "I feel pretty nauseated."

"Have any more dreams last night?"

"No," Holly admitted. She poured in milk, stared at the bowl, and pushed it away. She knew she wouldn't be able to keep down a thing. "But I've been thinking about the one I did have."

Something in her tone must have alerted Amanda, because the other girl stopped and stared at her suspiciously. "Why do I think that I'm not going to like this?"

Holly folded her hands on the table. "Amanda, I'm going to go find Jer."

Amanda picked up her glass of orange juice and drank it down slowly. When she had drained the glass she put it down with a solid thud on the table. She locked eyes with Holly, who squinted to avoid seeing the blood vessels in her cousin's eyes.

Amanda spoke in a calm, firm voice. "Absolutely not."

"What?"

"Michael could attack again at any moment and we have to be prepared, which means we can't scatter to the four winds."

Holly took a deep breath. "I have to find him. He's

alive somewhere and I have to go to him."

Amanda did not relent. "Is that you talking or Isabeau?"

"It's me," Holly said, her temper beginning to flare. "Jer helped save us from his father before and he can help us again."

"So, this is an altruistic gesture," Amanda said sarcastically. "Nicole's already missing, and you're going to go save Michael Deveraux's son, for the good of the coven, the fight against evil."

"Absolutely." Holly nodded.

"Liar."

The word hung in the air between them. Holly felt her cheeks flame even hotter. She didn't know which made her angrier, the accusation or the fact that it was true. She stood up slowly, feeling her fingertips begin to tingle with electricity.

"I am going and I don't need your permission." She turned to go.

Amanda leaped to her feet.

"Holly, have you ever stopped to think that Michael might be deliberately doing this to divide us? We're weak without Nicole. If you go, you'll make us weaker. For all we know Jer is dead. How could he have survived the Black Fire? We both saw it burning him."

Holly slammed her fist down on the table, her desperation getting the best of her. "And whose fault is that? We were fine until you pulled me away from him!"

"Are you insane?" Amanda asked, starting to shout. "The building was falling around us; the fire was devouring everything. What was I supposed to do, leave you behind?"

Tears slid down Holly's cheeks. "We would have been fine together, the magic we share—"

"It's the magic that Isabeau and Jean share," Amanda cut her off. "It has nothing to do with the two of you. You're just the unwitting hosts. You were that night, and that's what they want again. To use you, both of you, in their own little weird twisted dance."

Holly's hand flexed and tiny sparks danced along her fingertips. "Jer and I have our own magic that has nothing to do with them."

"Really," Amanda flung at her. "Or is it just that you've got the hots for a Deveraux?"

"But I dreamed—"

"Sometimes dreams are just dreams!" Amanda yelled. "Not every dream you have means something! It's just because you freakin' want him, Holly! Get a clue!"

"Oh, yeah, then how come I have Superman's vision now?"

There was a bewildered pause from Amanda. Reluctantly she said, "Okay. That I don't know."

Holly took a deep breath. "In my dream, the woman touched my eyes and I could see everything sharper, clearer. It's like I can see everything. And I can 'see' that I'm supposed to go find him." She picked up the cereal box and thrust it into Amanda's arms. "Go over there," she ordered her cousin.

Amanda studied her for a moment. Then she strode across the kitchen. She held the box up toward Holly. "Read the ingredients for me."

Holly focused in on the box and began to read off the ingredients. "Rice, sugar, salt, high fructose corn syrup, malt flavoring."

Slowly Amanda walked back to the table and set the box of cereal back down. She looked at Holly's eyes; Holly tried hard not to squint. Then she sighed and sat back down at the table. "What the hell is malt flavoring?"

Holly shrugged. "How should I know? At least you can see I'm not lying."

Amanda clearly wanted to avoid that statement. "Regardless, Holly, I don't want you going off after Jer right now. Be patient. We'll work something out together."

"I can't be patient. Jer might not have that long," Holly said quietly.

She turned and left the room. There was no more sense in arguing.

Both had made up their minds.

"You can't leave me alone here!" Amanda yelled at her. "He'll kill us, Holly! He's just using you!"

Stricken, Holly hurried to her room, slammed the door, picked up a vase on her nightstand, and hurled it across the room.

Tommy.

Amanda grabbed her purse and stomped out the front door, answering Holly's slam and her crash—*bitch probably broke that vase. That's okay; it was ugly anyway*—and had swung her leg into the station wagon when she realized that her father was still upstairs in his stupor or whatever.

Holly can deal with him, she decided.

She had demon-dialed Tommy's number as she backed out of the driveway; it was ringing, and she flooded with relief when he picked up.

"Hello?"

"It's me," she said, "and it's all so crazy." She started to cry. "Tommy, I'm so scared and I hate this and she's talking about splitting on us and—"

"Half Caffe," he cut in. "I'd suggest you come here, but the 'rents are having some kind of Democratic fundraiser and there's no privacy. Rich knee-jerk liberals are laying their fur coats on my bed and telling me to vote for the Clean Water Bill."

Despite her mood, she smiled. Tommy Nagai had been her best friend all her life. Through thickest and thinnest, he had watched her back. She felt bad that they had started to drift a bit, now that magic took up so much of their lives.

"I know it's dicey to show in public," he continued, "but we've warded the Half Caffe pretty well, don't you think? And since Eli and Jer are both out of the picture, I'm thinking it's pretty safe. Michael's too old to know about it, unless the guys mentioned it. And my take on that family is they didn't sit around the dinner table saying, 'Would you like to hear about my exciting and fun-packed day?'"

It felt good, normal even, to listen to his banter and know that once again he was going to be a prince for her.

"I'll be there," she told him.

"Can't wait, Amanda," he replied.

Amanda.

Tommy gave his hair a brush in the men's room of the Half Caffe. He looked okay . . . for him, and if you liked Asian Americans, he was way ahead. He had excused himself from his parents' party by pointing out a window and observing to a clump of guests that since it had begun raining, there was plenty of clean water, at least for today, and his work there was done. The guests had chuckled appreciatively.

Tommy knew how to work a room.

And I think this room's clean, he thought, as he meandered back into the din that was the main hangout of Seattle's young crowd. It was a coffeehouse, decorated with oversized marble statues, murals of forests, and a balcony from which he and Amanda had spied on many of their high school friends and enemies. Their first year of college was pretty much blown, thanks to Michael Deveraux; only Tommy had managed to keep his grades going, and that had been because it was easier to do that than to deal with the parental pressure that would have resulted if they had fallen off.

He climbed the stairs to the balcony and found a table *a deux*—a section of a plaster column topped by a glass circle. The rain had made the interior gloomy, so the staff had set votive candles in little pumpkins on each table. Nearly everyone in the place had on some little bit of Halloween gear—skeleton earrings, splatter T-shirts—and Tommy felt a pang for the old days, when he and Amanda were social outcasts, Nicole was an insufferable snob, and he had wanted to shake Amanda and say to her, "I want you to be my honey, Amanda, not my best bud."

Ah, youth.

His waiter, costumed as Count Dracula, stalked him until he ordered stuff he knew Amanda would like: chai tea latte and a cinnamon roll. Then the waiter was happy, plopped down a couple of waters, and left Tommy to wait for Amanda.

And there she is.

She rushed in, looking nervous, closing up her umbrella as she shook an errant raindrop or two from her curly, light brown hair. She hadn't been cutting it as much—no time, when warlocks are trying to kill you—and he liked the softness around her face.

She saw him, waved, and came up the stairs. They hugged, because they always did, but this time Tommy held her for a few beats longer.

She started sniffling against his shoulder. Alarmed, he drew away, then realized she wanted him to stay put; he put his arms around her, soothed her, saying, "Shh, shh, I bought you a roll."

She giggled softly and went to her chair.

He was sorry about that, but he took his own and raised his brows, ready to listen.

"She wants to split. She had this dream. Jer's on an

island and she wants to go to him," Amanda said in a rush.

"An island," he repeated.

She rolled her eyes. "In England, or somewhere near England."

"Ah." He folded his arms. "Because there are so few there. Just the Orkneys, and, oh, tiny Britain itself, and—"

"And we've got warlocks trying to kill us and all she can think about is her one true love, who is also a warlock."

"Movies these days," he said smoothly, as the waiter brought over the tea chai latte's and the roll.

"Yeah," she replied, getting it.

They waited while their things were placed on the table. Then Amanda sat back in her chair and sighed heavily.

"This dream," he ventured.

"He's locked up. Or something. I don't know. She can't leave us here by ourselves. We'll be massacred."

He agreed, but he didn't say anything. He just let her talk.

"It's not fair, it's not right, and I think we should tell her she can't go. She's our High Priestess, for god's sake!"

"In the same movie," he continued, as the waiter

came by again to refill their water glasses.

To his surprise, Amanda guffawed. She pounced on his left hand, which was lying innocently on the table, and said, "Oh, Tommy, I just love you!"

His heart skipped a beat. *Oh, if only you did,* he told her silently. *Amanda, a truer heart has never pumped oxygenated blood cells. . . .*

He picked up his cup and said, "We should hold a circle. Talk to her. You're right; she can't act as if she's not part of a greater whole. We're already all pissed off at Nicole."

She released his hand and he was very sorry about that. But her eyes had a new shiny quality to them, as if she were looking at him a little differently, and he dared hope . . .

. . . as he had been hoping for over ten years . . .

"You're right. We should hold a circle. Oh, Tommy, what would I do without you?" she chirruped.

He smiled gently at her. "Let's don't find out."

Her lips bowed upward; her cheeks got rosy, and yes, there was definitely something new in her eyes.

"Let's don't," she agreed.

Michael: Seattle, October

It was Samhain—Halloween—and upstairs the doorbell kept ringing. Michael knew the trick-or-treaters were confused and disappointed; the Deveraux house was usually one of the best places to go. Intent upon maintaining good ties with the community, his treats were always very lavish.

This year, he had better things to do on the night of one of Coventry's major sabbats.

Now in the black heart of his home—the chamber of spells—he had donned his special Samhain robe, decorated with red leering pumpkins, green leaves, and blood droplets and brought out special ritual arcane: green-black candles in which swirled human blood; a ritual bowl cut from the skull of a witch hanged at Salem; even a special athame, presented to him by his father the first time he had raised one of the dead.

Observing the preparations, the imp sat and stared, as imps will—impishly—at Michael. Michael took a deep breath, forcing himself to be calm and centered before the ritual. Excitement was rippling through him though. Through throwing the runes and reading the entrails of several small sacrifices, he had verified the truth of the curse of the Cahors. Their loved ones usually died by drowning.

He had a wonderful new way to strike out at the Cahors.

Chanting in Latin, he reached into a tank of water and pulled a baby shark out by the tail. He held the gasping creature above the altar and raised his knife in his other hand. "Oh, horned god, accept this my sacrifice. Raise up all the demons and creatures of the sea that they might aid me in destroying the Cahors family."

He stabbed the squirming shark and let its blood drip onto some dried coriander and bitter root on the altar. When the creature at last stopped squirming he dropped the body upon the altar as well. He picked up a candle and set the herbs on fire; in moments the body of the shark ignited and began to burn.

Michael leaned forward to breathe in the smoke. The stench was terrible, but the feeling of power was almost overwhelming. He closed his eyes. "Let the creatures of the sea hear my voice and obey me. Kill the witches. Kill every last Cahors.

"Let all the demons harken to my cry. Today the Cahors witches must die. *Emergo, volito, perficio meum nutum!*"

In the smoke above the altar, images slowly appeared, snapping into clarity . . . and into reality. Off the coast, sharks cast back and forth as though catching a scent of blood in the water. They worked themselves into a frenzy as they moved closer and closer toward the shore.

Farther out to sea the ocean began to boil. Dead

fish bobbed and floated to the surface, cooked completely through in an instant. The waters roiled, and slowly from the depths of the ocean something stirred, awakening.

It groped its way from its watery grave, hungry, searching. Blind from having lived so long in the blackness at the bottom of the ocean, it could still sense movement near it. Every living thing fled before it in terror. It opened its mouth to expose hideous teeth, jagged and each nearly a foot long.

Spiny scales covered its eel-like head as it cast this way and that searching for its prey. Slowly its serpent body unfurled itself and its powerful legs began to thrash. Long toes with wicked nails slashed through the water as it made its way to the surface, killing everything in its path.

Only the water sprites who sailed through the water like silent ghosts did not run from it. Instead they laughed soundlessly and spiraled around it.

"On this Halloween night, a killer whale has tipped over a small fishing boat. Witnesses who were on a nearby vessel saw the beast ram into the boat hard enough to flip it. The two men inside the boat disappeared and it is not known whether they drowned or were killed. In other news . . ."

Holly turned off the car radio.

She pulled up to the cliff from where she liked to stare out at the ocean and stopped the car. She got out, still squinting. Driving had been a trick with the enhanced vision, but she thought it was maybe starting to fade.

That would be a distinct relief.

She sighed as she strode to the edge of the cliff and looked out at the waves. Something wasn't right. There was a dark spot not that far from shore; she frowned and strained her superpower eyes, trying to see what it was. A fin broke the surface of the water on the edge of the spot; then another and another until she saw ten of them: sharks.

They were diving in and out of the spot; with a shudder Holly realized that it must be blood. They had killed something, and from the looks of it, it was large. She watched the ocean predators circling and diving, and though she felt afraid and somewhat repulsed, she couldn't force herself to look away.

At last the activity began to die down and the sharks turned in a pack and begin swimming up the coast. The spot remained behind, not breaking up on the water, like a shadow.

Her cell phone rang and she jumped. Her hand was shaking slightly as she pulled the phone from her purse.

"Yeah?"

It was Amanda. Holly half-listened to her cousin as she watched the fins slowly disappear in the distance. The coven was meeting to discuss her desire to rescue Jer.

"All right," she said coolly. She felt defensive. *They have no right to keep me from going if that's what I have to do.*

"We're going to meet on the Port Townsend ferry," Amanda continued. Port Townsend was a beautiful enclave of old Victorian homes on an island across the bay.

"Ferry?" Holly asked, the word piercing through the thoughts in her head. "But, Amanda . . ."

"Tante Cecile has said protection spells. She also says it's the only place we can discuss this privately. *He* has spies everywhere."

"But—"

"Just do it, Holly," Amanda snapped.

Amanda hung up.

"It's not safe," Holly murmured to the dial tone. "I know it's not safe."

As Holly turned and walked back to her car, Michael stared into his scrying stone and smiled.

Seated beside him in Michael's chamber of spells, the imp's grin broadened. He opened his mouth and spoke in a perfect imitation of Amanda's voice, "'Just do it, Holly.'"

Michael laughed. "Now do Tante Cecile."

"'You'll be safest on the ferry, Amanda,'" he mimicked.

"That's great. That's perfect." He patted the creature on its back.

Part Two
Full

☾

"When the moon in the sky is round and bright
Evil comes out to play that night
Witches cavort and mad men rave
And creatures reach out from beyond the grave."

—Druid Prophecy

FIVE

QUIET MOON

☾

Green man hear us as we plead
Grant us the power that we need
In the darkness we crouch and wait
Help us as we hone our hate

Goddess help us in our quest
Keep our enemies from rest
In the stillness let them hear
Their own hearts pound loud in fear

The Cathers/Anderson Coven: Seattle, October

Kari frowned as she glanced at her watch. She was leaving her apartment, joining the throngs of Halloween celebrants as she walked toward the secured parking lot where she kept her car.

She was running late to catch the ferry for the Circle meeting. She and Circle Lady had been engrossed in an e-mail conversation that she had been loathe to break. The two had spent less time contacting each other as

Kari became more involved with the coven. It was safer that way, but she missed the conversations with the other woman, so it had been a nice surprise when Circle Lady had IMed her about an hour ago and said, "How are you?"

At least, I think she's a woman. Problem with the Internet is you never can tell.

Kari had spent time pouring out her frustrations about Jer and Holly to Circle Lady—boy-girl stuff, like how come "Warlock" had basically dumped her and what could she do about it? Of course she hadn't mentioned anything about magic, battles, blood feuds, possession, or Black Fire. In fact, she'd managed to leave magic out of the conversation almost entirely.

Circle Lady had asked a few questions about Warlock—how he was, etcetera—and Kari had shot back, "Who knows?"

Which was true.

She was at the lot; the attendant, dressed in devil red, a pair of short horns sticking out of his dark hair, grinned at her as he unlocked the gate.

"You goin' to a party?" he asked conversationally.

"Yes," she replied, distracted. "A party. Uh-huh."

"No costume," he chided.

"I'm going as a witch."

He shook his head. "You need a broom. Pointy hat."

She glanced uneasily at the sky, looking for falcons, glancing around for burning bushes, not loving any of this. She remembered the conversations she had used to have with Jer back when she was stupid and naive, had done everything she could to get him interested in her so he would show some magic to her. She had begged him to let her help him with his rituals. It had all been so exciting back then, dark and a little dangerous.

Well, now it's a lot dangerous, and I'm not sure how long I can take this. Nicole had the right idea bailing like she did. If it wasn't for school I'd be out of here in a minute.

That wasn't entirely true.

Okay, and if I knew Jer was safe, the dork. Even if he's hot on Holly, I still care about him.

She drove to the ferry landing, parked, figured out which ferry to take, and noticed with a mixture of relief and apprehension that it hadn't left yet.

I wouldn't mind missing this meeting. Sparks are gonna fly, if I know Holly. And I am not loving meeting on a ferry in the middle of Elliott Bay. We might as well hold signs over our heads for Michael to read: DEAD MEAT.

She hesitated for only a moment before climbing out of her car. After all, there was safety in numbers, and the way things had been lately, she could use a little safety.

★ ★ ★

The ferries of Washington State were sleek and modern vessels replete with nice lounges and snack bars. As the costumed crowd swarmed onto the Port Townsend ferry, Holly got herself a Diet Coke and found a large table that would accommodate the entire coven, if they squished in. She wondered if Kialish's father would show. He was a friend of the coven but not a member. Maybe he would feel that he had no right to interfere.

She sipped her soda, waiting nervously, distractedly admiring some of the costumes—lots of fairies, lots of guys with pretend axes in their chests—wondering what was going to happen. She pressed her fingers to her temples; she'd have to ask Amanda for some aspirin when she showed up. The last of the supervision seemed to have gone, but it had left a nasty headache. It didn't help that she couldn't figure out why on earth Tante Cecile had insisted they meet on water.

Last call was sounded and the ferry began to cast off from the dock. It was after dark, and the glittering lights of the Emerald City played out in the side windows; ahead, the water was dark and deep.

There was still no sign of anyone else, and she began to worry.

Did something happen to them?

She wasn't certain whether she should go in search of them or stay put; she decided to stay where she was.

The engines picked up speed and the ferry moved into the waters, leaving behind the city.

Still she waited. Half an hour dragged by.

Then she finally saw Eddie, who turned and gestured to someone behind him. Kari and Amanda caught up to him, Kari glaring at her; the three trooped toward her, and Kari demanded, "Where have you been?"

"What do you mean?" Holly frowned. "I've been here. Isn't this where we planned to meet?" It seemed the logical location.

"You weren't here," Amanda chimed in, also looking peeved.

"I was too." Holly felt her temper rise. "You must have missed me." Then she looked past the three of them. "Where's everyone else?"

"We don't know," Eddie said, looking unhappy. "We figured they were with you."

"Something's up," Holly said. "Meeting out here is crazy."

"Tante Cecile said it was the best place," Amanda said. "She called me and said so."

"Well, where is she?" Holly asked.

"Look," Eddie cut in. "Whatever's going on, I

don't like it. And I for sure don't like the idea of you splitting on us to go on your big quest to 'save' Jeraud Deveraux. You're our leader. You can't abandon us the way Nicole did."

Holly took a deep breath. "I thought about that."

Eddie visibly relaxed, his sharp features softening. "Oh?"

Kari, however, frowned and said, "Holly, if you sense that he's alive and you don't do something about it—"

"I'm going to do something about it," she cut in, her voice rising. "I'm handing leadership of the coven over to Amanda."

"Fine," Amanda bit off. "I'm leader." She glared at Holly. "You can't go."

"You have to be leader." Eddie balled his fists in anger. "You were chosen to be the leader. You carry the power."

It was Holly's turn to raise her voice. "Don't tell me what to do, Eddie. Your coven couldn't protect him. What makes you think ours can? The vision got sent to *me*. By my ancestor. To save him."

"Because she's in love with Jean!" Amanda exploded. "She doesn't give a rat's ass about what's happening to us with Michael. She's obsessed with her dead lover, and they can be together through Jer and you. She was as ruthless in her day as any Deveraux, and she doesn't care who dies trying to save her little channeling partner."

"I . . . I . . ." Holly faltered. *I love him. But Amanda has a point. Is that any reason to abandon these guys?*

"I forbid you to go," Amanda announced, drawing herself up imperiously. "And I will do everything in my power, magically and otherwise, to keep you from going."

As if on cue, the floor began to shake. The walls rattled; some guys at the next table over frowned and said to Holly's group, "Wow, tough takeoff. We're from Montana. Do they always do that?"

"No," Holly said, glancing at Amanda. "And they don't take off, exactly."

The vessel shuddered again. Voices began to rise. A man got to his feet and said over his shoulder, "I'm going to go see what's going on."

"Something's wrong," Holly said. She stood.

The others followed.

As they made their way out of the snack area and past the rows of theater-style chairs, the enormous report of an explosion rocked Holly and sent her sprawling. Parts of the ceiling fell loose; a window buckled; the boat began to list.

Claxons blared an alarm. A man's voice interrupted the elevator music that had been playing and said,

"Ladies and gentlemen, please stay calm. Please proceed to a designated life jacket area, where you will receive a life jacket from one of our easily identifiable crew members. Please stay completely calm. There is no reason for panic."

"Bite me!" Eddie shouted. "There's plenty of reason!"

Scrambling out of the middle of the walkway toward the wall, then thinking better of it because of the exploding windows, Holly closed her eyes and invoked protection; Amanda joined in, and then Kari and Eddie. They ran, joining hands; as one, without discussion, they went outside.

"Are there life jackets out here?" an anxious woman wearing a cheery Halloween sweater yelled in Holly's face. When Holly didn't respond quickly enough, the woman darted past her to another passenger, glomming on to him and shouting, "I need a life jacket!"

The ferry was lurching forward awkwardly like a giant child's pull toy on a string. It was also listing heavily to the right. Passengers were fleeing out the doors, jostling the four; screams rose in the night as the shriek of grinding metal rose higher and higher.

Then a strange, alien wailing filled the air, joining with the claxons in a terrible cacophony. The wailing was coming off the side of the ship; Holly burst through the massing throngs and fought her way to the railing.

"Oh, my God," she breathed, looking down into the water.

Shrouded in darkness, occasionally illuminated by the lights of the ferry, it was a nightmare, a creature composed of huge taloned claws, tentacles, a clawed beak, and eyes that glared balefully up at her. In its eyes—each as large as a car tire, each a bloodshot circle of blackness—gleamed not precisely intelligence, but an evil intention, a hunger, a glee. It blinked when it saw Holly.

It knows me.

Birds wheeled overhead, shrieking and screaming as they dive-bombed at Holly. She saw that they were falcons, blue-black and aggressive, several times nearly hitting her as she ducked.

Then creatures emerged from the dark water on either side of the monster; they were of vaguely human shape, but covered with scales, their fingers hooked. As Holly watched, they hammered their hooks into the side of the ferry and climbed their way up the hull, very fast, very close.

The ship listed again, harder.

Eddie came up beside her and grabbed her arm. "I

think it's going to sink," he shouted.

She pointed. "Look."

As its minions hoisted themselves nearly to the top of the rail, the monster rose from the waters, hefting itself up on some giant stalk or pair of legs—God knew what—and its tentacles whipped in Holly and Eddie's direction.

Eddie grabbed her, throwing his arms around her and pulling her away from the side.

The ferry canted again. Passengers lost their footing and slid toward the wheelhouse containing the snack bar and the rows of chairs. Holly and Eddie were swept up by the momentum, and together they slammed hard against the bulkhead.

Amanda was on the ground with a huge gash in her forehead. Kari was bending over her, shouting to Holly, "Do something!"

"Amanda, are you okay?" Holly cried. She put her hand on her cousin's head and murmured, "Heal her, my Goddess."

Amanda looked up at her, blood gushing from the wound. "The Goddess isn't the one who put it there, Holly."

"Michael Deveraux!" Kari shouted to the falcons swarming above them. "I'm going to kill you myself!"

I knew this meeting was wrong. I knew it! Holly

thought, fury mingling with fear. *I should have said something, should have refused to come.*

Water rushed through the doors of the snack bar, swirling up to their ankles, then their knees. Holly realized that the opposite side of the vessel was underwater, and she said to the four, "Grab hands. Hold on tight."

With a grunt, she forced Amanda to her feet and half-walked, half-dragged her to a crew member who stood beside an unlocked bin of life jackets. People were fighting one another for them, grabbing at the orange vests as the beleaguered man tried to pass them out. Holly realized their chances of getting some were next to nothing.

She said, "Keep holding on to one another. We're strongest that way. Concentrate. Keep your eyes open and look into one another's eyes. We're going to see ourselves living through this. We're going to envision survival, embody survival."

Kari's glance ticked to the left, and she let out a terrible scream.

One of the creature's tentacles was whipsawing the crowd. As Holly watched in horror, a man's head was sliced cleanly off his body. Another's arm was severed; blood gushed from his shoulder socket, mingling with the frigid, rising water.

Holly looked left, right; she had no idea what to do. Other people were scrambling onto the side of the wheelhouse, tilted at a frightening angle.

The birds dove at them, screaming.

"Oh, my God. Oh, my God," Amanda panted.

"Stare into my eyes. See yourself surviving," Holly ordered her. "See it."

"I can't. I can't. I can't," Amanda gasped. "Holly, oh, my God . . ."

"You will survive." Holly willed her to feel it, know it.

Then the waters rushed around them, buoying them away like tiny woodchips; they sailed end over end; Holly shut her eyes tight and held on as tightly as she could to Amanda's hand . . . to Amanda's hand . . . to Amanda's hand . . .

She held on for dear life, literally, as they plunged into the black, icy waters; she held on as tightly as she could and tried to kick toward the surface. There were people all around her, grasping, kicking, punching in their terror. She couldn't see a thing, only blackness.

Isabeau, she thought, shifting from praying to the Goddess to begging her ancestress for help. *Please, save us.*

Then miraculously, her head broke the surface. Amanda's too; she saw it by the light of the ferry, which was sinking.

Holly saw what was happening, but it didn't register.

"We need to conjure," she said to her cousin. "We need to focus."

Amanda was sobbing hysterically. Holly gave up, looked around for the others.

"Eddie? Kari?"

"Here," Eddie announced. "I don't know where she is. I can't find her."

"We have to conjure," she repeated to him.

"Kialish," he moaned. "Kialish, I'm gonna die without saying good-bye to him."

"Don't be stupid. We're not going to die."

"It's your curse, Holly. You're cursing us to die."

"You're not going to die," she repeated.

Fresh screams erupted from the other water-bound passengers, announcing a new horror. Holly looked over her shoulder, and that was when she lost it too.

The humanoid creatures were swimming through the throng, raising their talons and chopping randomly into people as they went. Their talons were knife-sharp; the wounds were deep. Most of their victims stopped screaming as soon as they made contact.

And trailing in their wake was the monster.

Holly tried to fight down her own panic, moving down inside herself, finding a place, a center. The rest of her being panicked around it; yet she said, "I abjure thee, I repulse thee, minion of evil. Get thee hence!"

Her words had no effect on it. It rose to a great height as if it were naturally buoyant; she saw its quivering, filthy mass, the tentacles everywhere, the mess that was its head. In its beak it carried a young woman who very quickly stopped struggling and hung limp in its grasp. It chomped her in two; her torso and head hit the water. It tossed away the other half and lumbered ahead, toward Holly.

Eddie swam in front of her, shouting, "Get me! Get me, you bastard!"

"Eddie, no!" It was an unnecessary gesture; if that thing wanted to kill her, it would. She waved at Eddie to stop, and Amanda's grip slackened and went limp.

Amanda let go of Holly's hand, and her head slipped below the surface.

"Amanda!" Holly shouted, and dove underwater to find her.

It was pitch black and crowded, but a faint blue glow guided Holly directly downward. She swam as hard as she could, chasing the glow.

Down she spiraled, and farther down; her lungs were about to explode. She reached the glow, stretched out a hand . . . and it faded and winked out.

No! Holly thought, lunging forward, feeling the

water. Other bodies bumped into her, pieces of sea-weed, and what she hoped were fish.

But of her cousin there was no sign.

Unable to stay below the surface any longer, she rose, sucking in air as she broke the surface.

As if by . . . *magic,* a life ring bobbed beside her. She grabbed it.

And then she panicked at what she saw.

The water was thick with blood, and one of the minion-creatures slashed at her; it was less than a foot away. Its immense companion rushed toward her—

—*game over, I'm dead*—

"Holly," Eddie moaned.

He floated about three feet away to her left. She began to lunge for him . . . until she realized that Amanda had resurfaced, facedown, and bobbed on the waves about five feet away in the opposite direction.

The creatures were bearing down.

"Holly," Eddie said again. He looked at her, reached a hand for her. "I'm hurt."

There was no more time to think, to choose; with a choked sob, Holly pushed the life ring toward Amanda, looped her arm around it and yanked her head out of the water so that her chin was propped up, and began to kick as hard as she could.

She invoked protection spell after protection spell,

begging, pleading with the Goddess and with Isabeau to save her. A talon swiped at her, catching the edge of her heel, and she would have screamed if she could have remembered how. . . .

Then gunfire erupted over her head, someone shooting from in front of her at the monsters. Someone shouting, "Here!"

And Holly managed to look up as she fought for her own life, and for Amanda's, swimming in her icy, sodden clothes; swimming despite the fact that she had no strength left.

A Coast Guard cutter had roared up, followed by another, and another; there was a flotilla of them, and they were shooting at the monsters. Then one of them was throwing her another life ring, but her hands were too numb to catch it. She croaked in frustration—she could no longer speak—and then began to whimper, blinded by panic.

She forced herself to find her calm center again. *I am a Cathers witch,* she thought.

She stared down at her hands, willing them to grab the life ring. Somehow she managed to position Amanda's cold, limp body onto the ring. She gave the line a tug.

"Holly!" Eddie screamed.

She turned to go back to him, but at that moment,

Amanda slipped off the life ring and began to go under. Holly grabbed her, holding on to the ring.

The Coast Guard officer began to reel them in. If she let go of Amanda, her cousin would slide back into the water.

"Holly!" She could hear the terror in Eddie's voice. "Holly, help!"

She turned around; Amanda shifted on the flotation device and she grabbed hold of her.

She couldn't see Eddie anywhere. The water was a swarm of monsters, dying people, and the leviathan that even now moved toward her.

The Coast Guardsman reeled her in; she sobbed as she was pulled onto the deck, as they put a blanket around her shoulders, and as a medic on board gave her something to calm her down.

She saw that Kari had been rescued as well, and tried to be grateful for that.

But she would not be soothed.

Goddess, protect him, she supplicated.

But she knew in the depths of her soul that Eddie was dead.

France, 13th Century

Catherine was dying. Whether through poison or magic or simple bad luck, she could not tell. But she was dying; there was no doubt.

The Deveraux had not won; but then, neither had she. Both covens had lost untold celebrants in the massacre of Deveraux Castle on Beltane, and the resultant reprisals that went on even now, six years later.

She called her new protégé, Marie, to her bedside. The young girl was sixteen and a very good witch. Catherine had imbued her with magical powers, and the girl had understood her role in Coventry: At all costs, the Cahors line must be perpetuated.

Pandion the lady hawk sat on the ornate headboard of Catherine's bed of state. She had slept alone in it for three years, since the death of her second husband, although she had entertained more lovers in it than she could count. They, however, were not allowed to sleep the night there.

But all that was over, and she would soon be dust.

"So many of us are ashes now," she said to the beautiful young girl. Curls tumbled down Marie's back; she was very slender, and her eyes were enormous. She put Catherine in mind of Isabeau, her only child, her dear child.

"To protect you and our coven, I am sending you away," she told the girl. "To England. There are followers of the Circle there who will help you; you will be looked after." She sighed. "I abandoned Jeannette, but I will not abandon you."

"Oui, madame," the girl said feelingly. Her eyes brimmed with tears. "I shall do as you command, in all things, always."

"There's a good girl," Catherine murmured. Then her breath snaked out of her body, and she was dead.

Marie devoutly bowed her head and prayed to the Goddess to lead her through fields of lilies.

"And let her find Isabeau, whom she always loved," she finished.

Then she clapped her hands. Servants appeared instantly, gasping aloud at the sight of their *grande dame*, dead in her bed.

"She shall be burned and put in the garden," Marie informed them.

And I shall not be there to witness it.

I am bound for England, as my mistress wished.

Eli Deveraux: London, Samhain

The innocent called it Halloween.

But in Coventry new marriages were made, old feuds forgotten . . . and sacrifices made.

Eli Deveraux looked up with satisfaction from the

grisly remains of a young woman whose still-beating heart he held in his fist. Her thick, red blood ran down his arm and dripped onto the stone floor of the ancient chamber where he wrought his magic.

"This, my brother's heart," he intoned, showing the heart to the statue of the horned god, who crouched on the altar. "Help me kill him, Great God Pan. Send my familiar to do my work."

There was a great flapping of wings; then the immortal falcon, Fantasme, scowled at Eli and cocked his head. Eli held out the heart, and the bird glided toward it. Fantasme was not a stranger to human sacrifice.

Another young woman, this one very much alive, entered the private chamber and inclined her head. She was dressed in a gossamer robe, and she was here to be his Lady to the Lord, so that he could perform some very high-level magics. He had recruited her to help him during a ritual with Sir William in attendance; Eli was certain she had agreed not because she wanted to, but because she was afraid to refuse him.

"Undress," he said coldly. He wasn't sure why he disliked her now, but he did. He had looked forward to their coupling, which would produce the potent magical energy he required.

I'm just in a bad mood, he told himself. *Learning that*

Jer is alive has put me in a funk. I thought I was rid of him, and now . . . he's like a bad penny.

At least he's in terrible pain and hideously scarred.

Proving that there is a God.

The girl stood undressed. In a voice dripping with hostility, Eli said, "Get ready."

She lay on the altar, waiting for him.

Why did she say yes? he wondered. *Is it some kind of trap?*

And then it didn't matter as he joined her on the altar; he knew then that she had consented because he did something for her. A lot of women liked Eli Deveraux, liked his aura of menace, all that power . . .

That cheered him up a little.

Blue magic began to churn in the room, sweeping over the altar, shining along Eli's athame and the girl's robe. The room began to dance with it. The gray statue's eyes glowed blue; its mouth turned up in a smile.

When it was done, Eli felt stronger, more concentrated, and more focused. Pulling on a green robe decorated with red clusters of holly berries, he picked up the heart again and said, "My lord, I offer this to you, if you will only kill my brother."

The stone jaw of the statue dropped open; the neck extended forward, the eyes rolled downward. In strange, lockstep motions, the statue plucked up the heart, and silently devoured it.

The girl watched in startled fascination.

I'll take that as a yes, Eli thought. He was overjoyed.

My God is going to kill my brother.

So it's a happy Halloween after all.

SIX

HUNGER MOON

(

Cahors witches best beware
As we take to the air
We will kill them where they stand
Everywhere throughout the land

Now we chew upon each bone
Granted us by the Crone
We shall feast with next moon rise
On our victim as he slowly dies

Nicole: Spain, All Hallow's Eve

They had been in the safe house for a week. This particular night, Nicole was asleep as soon as her head hit the pillow. When a hand on her shoulder shook her gently awake, it was dark. Philippe stood beside her, smiling faintly. "Come on. Time to get up."

"What time is it?" she asked.

"Nearly midnight."

"The witching hour?" She smiled.

He laughed low. "You could say that."

He was again dressed in his cloak, but the hood was folded back behind his head. He held out a cloak to her as she sat up. "You can put this on."

She grimaced. "What I'd really like are some clean clothes."

He gestured to the foot of her bed where she saw a shirt and a folded up pair of jeans. "There is a young lady at the villa who is about the same size as you. She donated some clothing."

"Was this your idea?" she asked, surprised.

"Actually it was José Luís's," he conceded. "Come, hurry, *ma belle*. Everyone else is outside; come out when you're dressed."

"*Merci,* Philippe."

Nicole sat up as soon as he left. She spied a water pitcher and a basin on a small table and gratefully discovered that the pitcher had been freshly filled. She peeled off her shirt and splashed some water over her face and shoulders.

She put on the clothes and was pleased to find that they were only a little loose. She ran her fingers through her hair and winced as she tried to pull out the tangles. She must look a fright. *If Amanda could see me now, she wouldn't believe it.* It was a far cry from her days as a beauty queen.

She grimaced as she put on the cloak. The material was thick and course. She lifted the hood up over her head to test the feel. She shuddered slightly as the material engulfed her. Quickly she folded the hood back.

She took a deep breath and opened the door. Outside the five warlocks stood in a loose cluster looking like ghosts in the darkness. As one they turned toward her, the gentle murmur of conversation ceased. She stepped among them, her heart beginning to pound. Dressed as they were it was impossible not to feel a sense of connection, of belonging.

Someone had brought the car up close, and they all piled in except for Armand. As Philippe started the engine, Nicole gestured to the lone figure outside.

"Isn't he coming with us?"

Philippe shook his head. "He will rejoin us soon. For now he has to wipe out the memory of us from this place."

At her look of slight confusion, Alonzo explained, "Have you ever been someplace where you could feel the history, as though the walls were speaking to you?"

She nodded slowly. "I felt that once. My family went to Washington, D.C., to see some old friends. They took us to see the Ford Theatre where President Lincoln was shot. I felt as though if I closed my eyes I could see it all happening. Is that what you mean?"

"*Sí*. People and events leave their imprint upon places. The walls of a building, for instance, record on a psychic level the events that happen within them. It is just like a path in a forest where animals and people leave footprints. The average person never sees these marks, but to an experienced tracker they are clear and reveal much about the creatures that left them.

"In the same way the average person never senses the psychic imprints left on places unless those imprints are unusually strong, and then they often claim that the place has history or is haunted. To a trained tracker, though—"

"The psychic imprints we leave behind are as easily read as tracks on a trail," Nicole finished.

"Yes. Armand is staying behind to cover the traces of our passage, much as though he were scraping a branch along the ground and obliterating footprints."

Nicole shivered. "If he weren't, could someone really find us that way?"

"I could," Pablo answered quietly.

Nicole twisted in the front seat so she could look back at the boy. His eyes shone in the darkness.

"That you could," Philippe affirmed. "So, Armand will catch up with us when he's finished."

"Armand is good at blocking. I can't read him," Pablo said.

She continued to stare at the boy as she thought, *Unlike me?*

He smiled slowly and he looked like a wolf baring its teeth.

Nicole turned back around. She would have to have a talk with Armand later.

They drove in what seemed a winding and circuitous fashion for two hours, skirting at least one village. They pulled off the road and drove for a few more miles. When they finally stopped it was in a large flat field. There were no structures of any kind in view.

"We have several hours yet before dawn. We will wait here for Armand, and when he joins us we will have the ceremony," José Luís announced.

From the trunk of the car the others pulled out firewood and several packets of what looked like herbs. As they began laying the wood out in preparation for a fire, Nicole turned to Philippe.

"Aren't you afraid someone will see the fire?"

He shook his head. "They will enchant it so that only we and Armand can see it. It will help guide him to us. Come, while they are working we will talk."

He led her a little ways away so that they could still see the rest of the coven but they could not be overheard. He sat and motioned for her to do likewise.

Once she was seated facing him he asked, "Who is chasing you, Nicole?"

"I don't know," she stammered, feeling her heart begin to race.

He nodded gravely and took both her hands in his. "Whoever it is is very powerful. Nicole, I fear for you. We must take extra care."

Nicole felt herself crumble. She was tired of all this; she left Seattle to get away from the witchcraft and the danger. At least she wasn't alone.

"I'm glad you found me." She sobbed.

He shrugged and reddened slightly. "I have a confession: Our meeting was no accident. We have been searching for you, Nicole of the Cahors, since we heard that you were in Spain."

She bristled, anxious that they had "heard" of her, hurt that he hadn't told her before. "It's Anderson," she replied icily, not yet sure how she was going to respond to the other.

"Maybe to them," he gestured wide, indicating the world with a sweep of his arm. "But here, with us, and here," he tapped her chest over her heart, "you are Cahors. Yours is an old family, and there is pride to be taken in that."

"My ancestors were murderers and assassins. No pride there."

"Not all," he answered gently. "Some Cahors witches were allied with the covens of the Light and they did much good. Others chose to ally themselves with all the forces of Darkness. And only you, Nicole, can say which side you shall ally yourself with."

She smiled bitterly. "I would be lying if I denied that I was drawn to the dark." She thought of Eli and the excitement she had felt when she was with him. She thought of the things they had done together, how she had let him touch her, and she was filled with mixed emotions. Mainly she felt remorse but there was a small part of her that was defiant, that knew that even with the knowledge she had now, she might not change a thing if given the choice. That was the part that frightened her.

Her scalp began to tingle, and she looked away from him. She glanced toward the others and was unnerved to find Pablo staring straight at her. His eyes bore into hers. Did he know what she was thinking? She fervently hoped not and tried to wipe her earlier thoughts from her mind. He shook his head slowly, whether in disapproval or defeat she did not know. At last he turned away and she felt herself sag with relief.

"Pablito sometimes uses his gifts when he ought not. Unfortunately, discretion is one of those things that only time teaches young men," Philippe observed, having watched the exchange.

Nicole looked back at him guiltily. "Maybe he's right to keep an eye on me."

He smiled. "Time will tell the truth of that. But for now, come. They are ready for the ceremony."

He stood and extended his hand. She took it and he helped pull her to her feet. Together they walked back to the fire.

"What sort of ceremony is it?"

"A seeking ceremony. We are asking for visions of the future."

"So, what, I get to ask to see my future husband?" she joked.

He gave her an appraising look. "Perhaps you will, but it is not for me to say. No one can choose what they are shown."

As they reached the fire, Nicole noticed that Armand had rejoined them. He nodded at her briefly.

"Now that we are together, we shall begin," José Luís announced.

They all seated themselves around the fire. The smoke drifting upward carried the scent of burning wood mixed with something else that was much sweeter. Nicole wrinkled her nose, not sure whether the smell was a pleasing one.

They joined hands, and for one wild moment

Nicole thought they were all going to start singing "Kumbayah." She closed her eyes, willing herself to relax, and took a few deep breaths. The sweet smell wasn't that unpleasant, she decided. It was actually kind of nice.

"We are gathered here to invoke the power of Seeing. We ask for clarity about the path that we are on, where it is leading, and what we must do to uphold the Light. Show us what we must see," Philippe finished.

"Grant us eyes that we might see," Armand added.

"Grant us wisdom to know what we must do," Alonzo said.

"Grant us courage that we might act," Pablo said.

"Grant us strength that we might prevail," José Luís concluded.

On either side of her, José Luís and Alonzo released her hands. Nicole opened her eyes and watched as Alonzo picked up a long, crooked white stick that had been sitting on top of the fire. She gasped as she heard the sizzling wood burning his palm. He held it close to his chest and bent his head over it, eyes squeezed tightly shut.

Nicole watched as the muscle that ran along the left side of his jaw twitched. At last he looked up and his eyes shone brightly. "I see a great evil reaching across Europe, its darkness sweeps everything away before it."

He passed the stick to Armand and picked up a strip of cloth soaking in a bowl of liquid. Gingerly he wrapped it around his burned hand.

Armand bowed his head over the stick reverently. His entire body began to shake. Finally he looked up. "I see myself standing between the Darkness and the Light. We are fighting the Darkness and we are not alone. Others are with us, but there is a great price to be paid."

He passed the stick wordlessly to Philippe and then took a towel from the bowl handed to him by Alonzo and wrapped his hand. Philippe bowed over the stick for only a moment before looking back up. Tears were shining in his eyes.

"I see myself taking up a great burden and lifting it from the shoulders of another. The burden ages me."

He passed the stick to Pablo and took a cloth. The young guy bent over the stick for several minutes quietly before he at last looked up.

"I see an island that has been hidden for centuries. There is a man in chains. A woman watches over him; she has always watched over him. She is afraid. Someone else is on the island, and he frightens her."

José Luís took the stick from Pablo and held it tightly. Nicole could smell his flesh burning as she watched the tendons in his fingers flexing.

At last he looked up. His voice was eerily calm as he spoke. "I see my death."

Shocked, Nicole stared at the stick as he offered it to her. She didn't want to take it, didn't want to be burned, and she certainly didn't want to see anything. Still, she reached out her hand and clasped the stick. Her flesh burned and she knew it, but she could feel nothing. She held the stick in front of her.

She saw Eli's face floating before her, laughing, taunting. It faded and another face was there above her. The features were cruel and twisted beneath a mane of blond hair. She screamed and tossed the stick from her.

Alonzo caught the stick in midair and after saying a few words over it, set it gently down. José Luís began wrapping her burned hand in the soothing cloth. "What did you see?" he pressed.

She looked up at him, gasping for air. She had never seen that face before in her life, and yet now she gasped, clawing for breath as if her head was still under the water in the bathtub at the safe house, "I saw . . . I saw . . . *my husband.*"

She couldn't get warm and she couldn't stop shaking. It was as though she were slowly freezing from the inside out. The ground was hard beneath her and the cloak only kept out the chill of the morning air but did nothing to warm her. Nicole turned onto her side and tucked her knees up into her chest, trying to block out the vision she had had.

She had seen Eli, and a voice inside her had told her that he was still alive. How could that be? Hadn't he, Michael, and Jer died in the fire? If he was alive, Michael might be too. They could be the evil the others had seen sweeping like a plague across the continent.

She should warn Amanda and Holly. They had a right to know. If it was true then they needed to be prepared. *I should be with them.* She pounded her fist against her thigh. *I don't want to go back. I don't want any part of the magic.*

A voice inside her head mocked her, telling her she was a fool to think that she could ever escape the magic. It had followed her. No, it was in her. She couldn't change that no matter how far she ran.

And what of that other face? She had felt the evil oozing from every pore of the lionesque features. And that voice, *"I shall marry you, Nicole Cahors."* Who was he and how did he know who she was?

She stared down at the bandage wrapping her burned palm. Philippe had told her that within twelve hours there wouldn't even be a mark.

A stray cat that had been lurking close by for the

last hour approached quietly. Its fur was dusty and tangled, and its eyes held a feral gleam. It crept close and finally curled up so that it was touching Nicole's chest. She dropped her hand upon the cat's back.

It purred, startling them both. It settled, though, and stared at her with great almond-shaped eyes. "What am I going to do?"

The cat blinked at her once before squeezing its eyes closed and falling asleep.

SEVEN

SEED MOON

🌙

Brains and blood, tissue and bone
Time to reap the death we've sown
Sun above and stones in hand
Help us spread fear throughout the land

Come and see through scrying stone
The plans they make against the Crone
Cast the runes and we shall see
How to triumph, blessed be

Nicole: Outside Madrid, November

Nicole's dreams were wild, vivid. She struggled against
the man she had seen in her vision. He leered at her,
laughing, always laughing. His mouth gaped open
larger and larger like a cavernous yaw. Flames started
shooting out of it, searing her face with their heat. She
tried to scream, to turn away, but her feet wouldn't
move and only a whisper escaped her lips.

"Nicole, come to me," the voice was soft in her mind.

She was finally able to turn, and she saw Philippe standing several feet away, his hand outstretched to her. She reached for his hand.

Now she awoke, and he was saying something to her.

She turned her head toward the door and there he stood, smiling gravely at her. Something warm, like a gentle touch, brushed against her mind, and she smiled. He moved to her and sat down beside her. He took her hand in his and warmth flowed through her.

"We have talked. We will do everything in our power to protect you." He added, "You have a great destiny, Nicole."

Tears stung her eyes. Maybe she had once believed that; it seemed long ago, back when her mother had been alive and they had practiced simple magics together. *But I thought I was going to become a great actress, not a witch!* Now she had nothing. Holly, maybe, had a great destiny, but not her.

"I think you've mistaken me for someone else," she said, dropping her gaze.

With his free hand he tilted her head up so that her eyes met his. "We are not mistaken, Nicole Cahors. You have a great destiny. I know it. I feel it."

She stared deep into his eyes and felt all her barriers falling one by one. She began to cry in earnest, and he wrapped his arms around her, holding her, loving her as all the pain washed through her. His body shuddered slightly at each new wave, as though her pain, memories, and fears were assaulting him as well. When at last she looked up, she saw tears streaming down his face. His lips were moving as though in silent prayer.

He opened his eyes, and she could barely believe, let alone trust, what she saw shining in their depths.

"There's so much I want to tell you," she whispered.

"I know, I can feel it." He bent slowly and kissed her on each cheek.

"I'm not a saint," she said, dipping her head.

He put his hand under her chin and lifted her face back to his. "If you were, we'd have problems. Oh, not that we don't have a few already."

She smiled at his joke even as his touch sent her pulse skittering out of control. She fought down her emotions. There was something she had to do.

"I need to make a phone call."

He nodded as though he had been expecting that. "It has to be short," he warned. "They have been casting their nets trying to find you. We will need to be very fast and very clever."

She nodded and then put her head back against his

chest. All the forces of hell might be looking for her, but for the moment she felt safe.

José Luís had not slept since the vision. When the others had pressed him about it, he had answered in vagaries. Nothing about the vision had been vague, though. He knew even the moment of his death. He also knew there was nothing he could do to avoid it. That didn't mean he wasn't going to try.

This was the fourth place they had been to in search of a phone for Nicole. They needed to avoid the towns, so they had been approaching villas. Within a mile of each they had turned away, sensing something amiss. They were running out of time, though. They could all feel it. Traveling by day was dangerous because of the increased numbers of people, the increased risk of being seen by the wrong person.

He glanced up at the sun as it approached the horizon. Being about during the day, though, had posed less risk than the night would. It was going to be a full moon.

He gazed along the cobblestone street. This tiny village might be their last chance to find a phone before night closed in. Pablo came up next to him. He placed his hand on the boy's head.

"There is a phone next to the café in the square."

José Luís nodded. Something didn't seem quite right here, but he couldn't place his finger on it. He glanced again at the setting sun. There wasn't much time left. They'd have to take the risk.

He began to walk and felt the others falling in behind him. Armand cloaked them so that the villagers would not mark the passage of so many people.

They reached the phone, and Philippe and Nicole began to place the call. The rest of them spread out. José Luís kept one eye on the square and one eye on Philippe and Nicole. He could see the bond that was forming between them and he couldn't help but approve. Philippe was strong and had a stability that Nicole lacked and needed. With his strength and her fire they could make a mark on the world.

It looked as if they had been connected. He smiled tightly. Only magic could allow an international phone call to go through that quickly from a pay phone in a small village.

Nicole's hand shook as she dialed. What was the number? She'd lived in that house all her life, and now when she needed it she couldn't even remember the phone number. Slowly, digit by digit, it came. At last she got through and the phone began to ring.

The answering machine picked up and she hung

up in frustration. She breathed a prayer of thanks to the Goddess when she remembered Amanda's cell phone number. She picked up the phone and dialed.

"Hello?" She nearly wept with joy when she heard her sister's voice on the line.

"Amanda, it's me. Listen carefully."

"Nicole! Nicole, oh, my God! Where are you?"

"In Spain, somewhere, I think. That's not important now, though. You have to listen to me. Eli is still alive."

"Nicki, the *ferry*!"

"Listen to me, Manda." She looked around anxiously. "Eli is still alive."

"But . . . how do you know?"

"I had a vision. It's complicated. But he's alive, and there's big evil happening." Nicole swallowed. "I'm sorry I left, Amanda. Hecate . . ."

"She's fine. Oh, *Nicole*." Amanda was sobbing in earnest now.

Philippe gestured at her to hurry. She took a breath. "Did something happen to Holly?"

"Eddie's dead!"

"What about Holly?" Nicole almost shouted.

"She saved me. I would have died. Nicki, oh, please, Nicki, come home. We need you."

"I—I will," Nicole said firmly. Now Philippe

waved his hands and shook his head, silently urging her to get off the phone. "I have to go."

"No!" Amanda wailed.

"I have to," she said firmly. "I'll try to call again soon."

Hating herself, she hung up.

Nicole looked very upset. José Luís was concerned, watching, unable to hear what she was saying. At last she hung up, and Philippe gathered her close. José Luís took a step toward them. The sooner they left, the better.

Searing pain exploded in his back and chest. He crumbled to his knees, trying to shout. No sound came out. He twisted as he fell, landing on his back and driving the knife further into his punctured lung.

As he stared up into the face of his killer, he could see the moon, pale and full already, visible in the sky above.

As the world went black he thought, *Ay, Dios mío, the visions never lie.*

"I shouldn't have left. I should never have left," Nicole murmured against Philippe's chest as they walked away from the phone booth.

"Ah, petite," Philippe whispered "I am so sorry."

They turned toward José Luís.

Nicole gasped as she saw the dark figure looming behind him.

Then José Luís fell to the ground, stricken.

From everywhere, menacing hooded figures appeared, as though rising from the very earth. Their cloaks were so dark they seemed to absorb the last vestiges of light around them. One rose behind Philippe, and Nicole shouted a warning.

He turned to face it just as the others of the coven exploded onto the scene. Armand shot into motion, a spinning whirlwind of magic and death. The last ray of the dying sun glinted off the sword he wielded. Nicole's shocked mind wondered briefly where it had come from. The man twisted and turned like a fiend, chanting, shouting curses, and swinging the deadly blade. Three dark figures fell. More surged up to take their place.

From the top of a nearby roof, Nicole heard a loud, keening wail. She glanced up to see Pablo. He slowly extended his hands; bright light suddenly seemed to engulf his body. It shot through his fingers and cast the entire square in a blue, unearthly glow. The dark figures squealed and tried to scuttle away from the light.

Suddenly a hand clasped her upper arm and yanked her backward. A moment later another creature appeared where she had been standing. Alonzo kept hold of her arm but took a step forward. He thrust a crucifix toward the creature's face.

"Ego te expello in nomine Christi."

The creature shrieked and dissolved before her eyes. She looked from Alonzo to the cross held in his outstretched hand.

"Hey, whatever works." He shrugged. "It was a demon." He gestured up to where Pablo continued to illuminate the scene. "They have more cause to fear Light than we do. Problem is, not all of these things are demons."

Alonzo spun away at a call from Armand. The younger man was surrounded by cloaked figures brandishing swords of their own. The bluish light flickered for a moment and Nicole glanced upward nervously. Pablo's strength was fading. Maybe she could get up on the roof and help him.

Her scalp began to tingle, and she twisted just in time to sidestep a dark figure rushing her. Demon or something else? She couldn't tell, but she could feel power begin to surge through her. She summoned a fireball. If it was human it would burn. If it was demon it would feel right at home. The thing turned just in time for the fireball to explode in its chest. A deep laugh came from it and set her hair on end. It took a step forward and she braced herself.

A ball of bright blue light burst through the creature's chest, and it stood for only a moment, staring, before it dissipated into smoke. Behind where the creature had stood was Philippe. He gave her a small smile before turning to battle two other demons who had been trying to sneak up on him.

She moved to help him. Just then Pablo's light was extinguished, and the entire square was plunged into darkness. Nicole whispered a spell to help her vision, but it only helped slightly.

Arms wrapped hard around her, lifting her, shrieking into the air. She opened her lips to scream a spell, but a strong hand clamped over her nose and mouth, shutting off her air. She struggled, trying to break free, but her attacker was too strong. As her strength was fading, she managed to twist around. The figure's hood had fallen back to reveal a familiar face, the face she had seen in her dreams.

As the world went black, the last thing she heard was Philippe's voice echoing in her mind. *"I will find you, Nicole. I will track you through heaven and hell if I must."*

Amanda, Nicole, Kari: Seattle, November

Tante Cecile, Silvana, and Tommy—who had not been called to attend the meeting on the ferry—found Holly and Amanda at the hospital. Like so many of the other survivors, they had been herded into a private conference room in the hospital away from the throngs of news media demanding eyewitness accounts, demanding to know exactly what had happened on the dark waters.

The place was in chaos—people in blankets crying, other people shouting, some sitting in numb silence on padded conference chairs or the additional gray metal folding chairs that had been brought in. On the conference room table were urns of coffee and trays of sandwiches.

Ensconced in their own little corner of the room, the two *voudon* enfolded the witches in their arms; all of them wept for Eddie.

Then Nicole called Amanda—whose cell phone, miraculously, had stayed in her jeans pocket and survived the ordeal in the water, as the little case she kept it in was waterproof—and told her about Eli.

Uncle Richard phoned from the hospital parking lot to say that it was a mob scene and that he would get to them as quickly as he could. He had no recollection of his possession, and Holly and Amanda agreed to keep it that way.

Kialish showed. Dan could not be reached. It fell to Holly to deliver the blow of Eddie's death. Kialish fell apart, thanked her, and told her he was so very glad that she and Amanda had survived.

She felt awful; she had not told him that she had abandoned Eddie to the monsters. *That I could have saved him. I picked Amanda . . . and I didn't even know if she was still alive.*

"Why did you tell us to go?" Holly shouted at Tante Cecile, deflecting her guilt on to the other woman. "To meet on *water*?"

Tante Cecile flashed with anger. "Of course I didn't, Holly! You were set up! All of us!"

"But . . ." Amanda wiped her eyes. "But you called me."

Tante Cecile shook her head. "I didn't."

The two witch cousins stared long and hard at each other. "Michael," Holly said, her jaw set.

"It sounded exactly like you," Amanda murmured. "How can he do that?"

"Same way we do so much of what we do," Silvana cut in, her arm around Eddie's stricken lover. His face was gray; in the last five minutes, he seemed to have aged twenty years. "With magic."

"Maybe that's why I wasn't called," Tommy said. "Michael doesn't know I hang out with you guys."

Tears rolled down Kialish's cheeks. "Holly . . ." His

shoulders heaved and he began to sob. "Tell me it was a quick death."

She swallowed hard. "Yes. He didn't even see it."

Oh, Goddess, forgive me.

A woman in bright tropical scrubs scuttled over and put her arm around Kialish, saying, "Do you need something, sir?"

He shook his head, utterly defeated. Like a very old man, he let her lead him to a chair. She bustled off and got him a sandwich and a blanket. He stared down at them as if he had never seen such alien objects in his life.

Silvana put her hands on his shoulders, closed her eyes, and began a quiet incantation.

Tante Cecile turned to Amanda and Holly. "You see how he works against us," she said. "How important it is for us to stick together." She gazed levelly at Holly. "And why you have to remain the High Priestess. Your power is stronger than Amanda's."

"Nicole's coming home," Amanda added. "We'll be the three again."

Holly felt as if she had swallowed a stone. She said, "But Jer and I . . . our power combined is even stronger. It's unbelievably strong."

The others stared at her in disbelief.

"Don't you dare leave us, Holly!" Amanda shouted at her.

Tommy went to Amanda's side, slid his arm around her waist in that defending way boyfriends—not best friends—did. Despite her distraction, Holly took note of that.

"He's going to win if we don't get some help," Holly shot back. She tried to keep her voice calm. Taking a few deep breaths, she said, "I know this so deeply in my soul, Manda. I have to save him. My power merged with his can defeat his father."

"You don't know that! You can't know that!" Amanda shouted. Heads turned in their direction. "You're just like us, figuring all this stuff out as we go along!"

"Shh, Manda," Tommy cautioned. "He might have spies around. We have to be discreet."

Silvana raised a hand. "I'm taking Kialish home," she announced.

That stopped the argument. The three took in Kialish's disheveled appearance, his bereft, lost expression, and the heat among them simply evaporated. Tommy kept his arm around Amanda, and Amanda let it stay there.

"Good," Tante Cecile said, obviously proud of her daughter. "Be careful. Very careful."

"We're not the ones he's after," Silvana said.

Holly felt another rush of shame. *I will kill them one by one. I carry the curse. Will I take it to Jer? Will I kill him, too?*

I have to go to him. I know it. And I know it's not Michael leading me to him. . . .

At the window of the hospital conference room, Fantasme, spirit familiar of the Deveraux, screeched and flapped his wings. He had just come to Michael from England, magically flying to Seattle in a split-second to his master's side.

The bird flew toward the moon, bathing himself in its rays, turning his shiny black body this way and that.

Then he swooped down into the utter confusion of the hospital parking structure, landing on the out-stretched arm of Michael Deveraux, who had been waiting for him.

Bird eye gazed into warlock eye, and Michael saw everything that Fantasme had. He nodded.

"Time for mischief," he told the bird.

With a wave of his hand, he parted the crowd in front of him. They moved without realizing it; he had a clear path that no one else noticed.

He strode down the stairs, disdaining the elevator. Cameras did not aim his way; reporters did not see him. No one saw him, or the huge, magical creature that perched on his arm.

At the foot of the stairs, near a bush, he snapped his fingers.

The imp emerged, its fanged mouth grinning broadly, its eyes shining with glee. Michael was put in mind of Ariel, from Shakespeare's *The Tempest*.

The creature bobbled along beside Michael, gazing up at him with eagerness. It said, "What are we doing?"

"We're up to no good," Michael informed him.

They sauntered along, three figures who could have been alone in the forest, for all the attention anyone paid to them. Then Michael uttered a finder's spell and closed his eyes, seeing in his mind the covenates of Holly Cathers.

The ones named Silvana and Kialish were being escorted by an overly cheerful woman in Hawaiian-motif scrubs, who was vainly trying to get them to take sandwiches with them. Michael shook his head, marveling at her inappropriate behavior. The boy had just lost his lover, for God's sake.

Continuing on his unobstructed walkabout, Michael and his companions began to head toward the same exit, down the side of the hospital, stepping over the cables where TV crews had set up their equipment, observing the emotional after-effects of his attack on the ferry.

It was a good piece of work, he thought. *I'll be censured for it, no doubt, for performing magic in a public place.*

A TV reporter was standing in front of a camera, delivering her version of what had happened.

"A lost gray whale caused an uproar earlier this evening," she began, "when it accidentally tipped over a ferry. Compounding the tragedy, a school of sharks attacked the hapless passengers, all of whom could have been saved by the Coast Guard vessels that sped to the side of the stricken vessel, if only they could have swum more quickly to safety. . . ."

Some will remember what really happened, he thought. *Others will talk themselves out of it.*

Either way, Sir William will not be pleased. But there's not much he can do about it. He wants the Black Fire.

They were almost at the exit door—both he and his companions, and Silvana and Kialish. Grief was making them sloppy; the wards they had set around themselves would be simple to neutralize.

He did so with a few incantations and gestures of his hands.

Then the exit door opened, and he planted himself rather dramatically in front of it.

"Hi," he said to the startled pair.

Silvana opened her mouth; whether to shout or scream—*or say hi back*—he had no idea.

The imp darted forward and leaped at her, both its fists doubled, and slammed them into her face. Kialish would have shouted then, except that Michael aimed a glowing ball of energy at him, and it knocked him out.

The two tumbled to the floor.

Michael stepped around them to an empty gurney pushed against the wall, wheeled it back, and loaded the two on it, Kialish first and then Silvana on top of him, like cord wood.

Whistling to himself, he wheeled them outside.

No one noticed. No one tried to stop him.

She'll be madder than a wet hen, he thought, delighted. *And they won't let her leave to find my son.*

The falcon threw back its head and laughed. The imp joined in, cackling madly. Michael only smiled.

EIGHT

PLANTING MOON

Fear us now our power grows
Strength to vanquish all our foes
Will to crush and might to maim
We'll not rest till they are slain

Growing, swelling, fill the night
Shine upon us with thy light
Blessed moon above us give
Guidance now on how to live

Nicole: En route to London, November

Nicole awoke feeling as if she was going to throw up.
She was lying down and was being bounced all around.
She lay still, trying to suppress the nausea as her brain
raced trying to figure out where she was.

She seemed to be reclining in the back seat of a car;
she tried to sit up but couldn't. Her arms and legs felt
constricted, and she craned her neck trying to look at
her legs and finally caught a glimpse of ropes.

It all came flooding back to her. The battle, the hand over her mouth and nose, the leering face.

And, most of all, Philippe's voice telling her he'd be coming for her.

In a whisper she commanded the knots to loosen. A stabbing pain shot through her skull, but the ropes didn't budge. She blinked hard against the pain and tried again. Nothing except more pain.

A voice laughed hard and low. "Forget about it. You're bound tight both physically and magically."

Eli. A wave of hate washed through her being. Eli was behind this. *Of course.*

But what about the other man, the one from her vision? How did he fit into all of this?

She bounced painfully as the car hit a pothole. Her stomach twisted even more fiercely. The car turned suddenly to the right, and the top of her head smacked against the door. The car stopped hard, and she went flying into the back of the front seats and fell, wedged into the space between them and the back seat.

Disgusted, she lay waiting for assistance. Several minutes passed before the back doors finally opened. Eli chuckled cruelly.

"That can't be comfortable."

She bit back a retort, refusing to rise to his baiting. He picked up her feet and someone else grabbed her shoulders. They threw her up onto the seat. Then Eli grasped her ankles and began to pull her from the car. The friction burned her legs. She was more concerned, though, about her shirt as it began to bunch up around her bra. Finally her feet hit the ground, and with Eli's help she struggled to a sitting position. He grabbed a fistful of her shirt and pulled her up and out of the car to a standing position.

The other man came around the car and his eyes caught and held her. He bent and put his shoulder into her pelvis and rose. She folded in half over his back, feeling helpless and angry as he carried her like a sack of potatoes. Her chin banged painfully against his back, and she felt a little better when he winced.

The small building reminded Nicole of the safe houses she had visited with José Luís's coven. The floor here, though, was covered with dirt, and the furniture was of a cruder make. She'd refused the chair that her captors had offered her, choosing to stand instead. It made her feel more in control, even if it was just an illusion. Eli and the other man conferred together for several minutes, speaking in hushed tones. At last the stranger turned to her.

"Just kill me and get it over with," she said.

Nicole winced as the words sounded hollow even

to her. She'd been trying for defiance, a fierce, fearless declaration of her will. Instead it sounded like the helpless, pitiful cry of a victim who feared her captor's intentions more than death.

His lips twisted in a cruel sneer. He stepped closer to her, so close he was nearly touching her. He met her eyes, and she forced herself to stare back.

"Maybe I will. Probably I won't."

The words hung in the air between them, half-threat, half-promise. Something cold and hard glittered in his eyes: the look of the predator eyeing his prey and imagining the taste of it.

She lifted her chin higher, another instinctive act of defiance. By exposing her throat she showed no fear, at least in theory. A wolflike smile turned the corners of his lips up, and he bared his teeth ever so slightly. His eyes bored deeper into hers, conveying his hate, his contempt, and something more.

He stepped back abruptly and turned away growling, but it was too late. She had seen that which he did not want her to. Aside from the cruelty, the rage, and the evil, she had seen curiosity.

She could work with that.

She quietly tested the ropes that bound her both physically and psychically. There was no give. Holly would be able to escape these bonds. Holly might even be able to take on both Eli and the other man by now, if her strength had grown. But there was something Holly couldn't do that Nicole could.

When he next glanced her way she held his eyes and smiled. His eyes narrowed, but he didn't turn away.

Emboldened, she asked, "Who are you?"

Pride crackled in his voice as he answered, "I am James, son of Sir William Moore, and heir to the throne of the Supreme Coven."

"Supreme Coven? Is that supposed to mean something to me?"

He growled low in his throat. "It should, witch. If you had half a brain you would be trembling in fear from the very mention of it."

She allowed herself a smile. "Sorry. Never heard of it, your dad, or you."

He moved quickly toward her, and for a moment she thought she might have pushed too hard. He raised a hand as though to strike her, but instead twisted his fingers in her hair and yanked her face close to his.

"You'll wish you still hadn't, by the time my father is through with you."

Sleep did not come easily that night. She was stretched out on the hard dirt floor with her cheek to the earth. The two men took turns sleeping, and she could feel their eyes upon her. When at last she did fall asleep, it was only to be awakened minutes later by a rough hand on her shoulder.

"Time to move," Eli informed her gruffly.

At least they permitted her to sit upright in the back seat of the car, although her arms remained tightly bound. She was tired enough that she found herself drifting off to sleep, jarred awake every so often by another pothole in the road.

She was exhausted by the time they stopped for the night. The small shack was little better than the one they'd stayed at the night before. At least this one had cots.

The men produced bread and cheese from somewhere, and Nicole hoped briefly that they might untie her. The hope was in vain, though. Eli fed her while James paced. In between bites she managed to ask, "How come we're taking so long to get wherever it is we're going?"

"This is the quickest way, considering. Our magic's strong, but it would be difficult to keep an entire airport full of people—not to mention plane passengers—from realizing you were our prisoner. Unnecessary, anyway. Two more days and we'll be where we need to go," James answered, barely breaking step.

Eli stuffed another mouthful of bread into her

mouth, and Nicole glanced at him, loathing him as she did herself. She couldn't believe she'd ever been attracted to his dark nature. She had been so foolish to believe that she could tame him. As though sensing her thoughts, he gave her the same twisted smile he used to give her when he was touching her, when he was . . .

He began to undress her with his eyes and she turned away, disgusted. Her eyes fell on the pacing James, and a thought struck her.

Sex is Eli's weakness. Always has been, even before me.

She turned her head slowly, deliberately, back to Eli and batted her eyelashes once, twice. *Easy, don't overdo it.* She smiled and gazed at him suggestively. She gave him her best come-hither look and watched him lick his lips nervously as he glanced toward James.

In the days they'd been together, careful observation had led her to believe that while Eli feared James somewhat, he didn't respect him. Now he glanced back at her, shifting his weight, probably completely unaware of his body language.

Okay, I'm gonna go for it . . . with both of them.

James was an unknown factor, but Eli she knew well. Eli could be counted on to want whatever someone else had. She dropped her eyes to keep him from knowing that the blush mounting her cheeks was not from old days and old memories, but from shame.

She put the whammy on James same as Eli, and he rose to the bait. Soon he was glancing her way, displaying his interest, and Eli was reacting. Without realizing it, the two warlocks were circling her, each with an eye on the other.

She was thrilled, triumphant . . . and a little smug about all those years Amanda had chided her about worrying about what guys thought of her.

When we get back together, I'm going to have to tell Holly and Amanda about this. And we're going to have to read up on sex magic.

That's what all this has been about—Michael seducing Mom, and this whole Jean and Isabeau deal; having a High Priestess and a guy with a "long arm." *Excuse me? A "long arm"?*

After two days the magic bonds had loosened ever so slightly. She had a chance to try something more, a spell small enough that it would not register with the two men. A spell small enough to be covered by the magical energy already flowing about them. Something very small.

She breathed the glamour into life, something to make her even more beautiful and, Goddess willing, completely irresistible.

By dinner James had untied her. And his nearness

excited her; she couldn't deny that. His smoldering looks shot a tingle down to the small of her back.

By breakfast even she was having a hard time remembering that the electricity between them was one of her glamours.

"What is your father going to do to me?" she asked James as they shared a bottle of wine with Eli.

James shrugged nonchalantly. "Kill you, I guess. You are, after all, a Cahors."

"And you are a Moore," she said, "creator of the Supreme Coven chicken sandwich." It had become something of a joke between them.

Grinning, he nodded and took a swig of wine.

"It doesn't have to be this way," she murmured.

He laughed dangerously low as he handed her the bottle. "What's in a name, eh, Rosebud?"

"You're a movie fan." She took the wine and threw some back. Her hands were shaking; she was terrified.

But I'm still alive.

"I'm a movie fan," he said agreeably, but there was flint in his gaze.

I'm not safe, though. I'm not safe at all.

She's a hottie.

James didn't trust her. He'd be lying, though, if he

didn't admit he was attracted to her. Everyone had heard the rumors of Cahors-Deveraux power. It clearly hadn't worked for Nicole and Eli. Maybe it had nothing to do with houses. Maybe it was all about a certain combination of witch and warlock. House Moore was more powerful now than House Deveraux. Maybe leadership was essential. He licked his lips as he imagined an alliance that could bring him even more power.

With Cahors magic aligned with his, he couldn't fail to overthrow his father.

Hmm . . .

He looked into her eyes and couldn't trust what he saw shining there. *She wants me . . . or else she's really good at faking it.*

Okay, maybe the little bitch was playing him. Then again, maybe she wasn't. He wasn't a bad package; and oh, yeah, baby, speaking of packages . . .

He glanced over at Eli and saw the other man eyeing Nicole. A quick burst of anger made him tremble.

You had your shot. Now back off.

A voice from somewhere seemed to be whispering in his ear, *"It's all about the power. That's what she likes. You have it. He doesn't."*

"She wants to feel your power, James.

"That's what she wants. Your power.

"You.

"No need to kill her. . . . No need at all.

"You can have her. She wants you.

"You, James. You can have a Cahors witch."

James smiled slowly as he wrapped an arm around Nicole's waist. She put her hand over his and gave him such a look that it was hard to restrain himself from taking her right then and there.

But that Deveraux nerd Eli was around somewhere, and it wasn't a good idea to provoke a fight with a potential ally, especially while they were traveling together.

We'll be in England soon.

And I think I just might have a little surprise for my father.

King James I: En route to England from Denmark, 1589

Below decks, at the threshold of their royal quarters, the king of Scotland surveyed his bride, whom he was bringing home to Scotland. She was beautiful. She was a few years younger than he, but her mind had been honed by an inquisitive nature, and she had the bearing of someone older. Her heavily embroidered white skirts were lovely, and the black jacket she wore was just as elegant.

He stared down at the decorative roses on his shoes that hid the laces, and lost himself in thoughts of her beauty. Few men had the privilege to marry such a woman, and he would do everything in his power to make her happy.

Finally he looked up and leaned close to Anne, a smile playing across his features. "I think I shall write a poem about your eyes."

She blushed fiercely. "You've already written me a dozen poems."

"Yes, but not one exclusively devoted to those magnificent pools of light that reflect the beauty and purity of your soul."

She laughed in an embarrassed manner, but he could tell by the way she glowed that she was secretly pleased. "We've only half a day until we reach port. Surely the king of Scotland, and one day of England, can find better ways to occupy his time than writing love poetry?"

He took her hand in his and gazed into her eyes. "Nothing is more important to the king than his queen. Has not God commanded us that love is our highest duty? And as a husband I am to care for you as Christ does His faithful ones. Therefore, how could I be trusted to rule a country if I cannot follow God's simplest decrees? How can I rule thousands with compassion if I gaze upon your exquisite face and am not moved to poetry?"

She smiled. "James, I love your poetry. I just wish all you wrote was as pleasant to read."

He patted her hand. "You're referencing the daemonologies that I am penning."

She shuddered. "Such horrible, frightening things."

"Dearest Anne, not all the world is as beautiful as you. This world is filled with terrifying things, both demons and the wretched persons who serve them. It is our duty to dispel the myths and denials surrounding such creatures. We must shine the light of truth upon those that live in darkness."

She shook her head slowly. "Some of it just seems so fantastical."

"Which? Demons or witches?"

She never had a chance to respond. The ship lurched violently sideways. James and Anne were thrown hard against the bulkhead; from the ladderway, water cascaded from the deck and spilled around their ankles.

Shouts of alarm issued from all quarters of the ship.

"Courage, my darling," James shouted as he moved forward toward the ladderway. His thought was to get them on deck, above the water line, where they would be safer.

After listing on its side for what seemed an eternity, the vessel straightened back out.

"Anne, now!" James shouted, slogging through the rising water.

"I can't! My skirts!"

He turned to look at her. Her splendid dress was not only ruined, it was killing her. The skirts held too much water; she could never swim in them. If they had to abandon the vessel, the weight of them would drag her down like a stone to her death.

Barely thinking, he fought his way into the next compartment and picked up his sword from where it had fallen to the floor. The water was waist deep as he made his way back to Anne.

Unsheathing the weapon, he began hacking at her skirts until he was able to cut most of it off. She stood shivering in her undergarments, staring at him with frightened eyes. He grabbed her hand and pulled her out of the cabin. They were halfway up the stairs when the ship lurched again.

He kept going, clinging to her hand, pulling her when he had to. They made it to the deck just as a wave crashed over it. It swept them both into the water. He kicked hard to the surface, Anne still clinging to his hand and kicking along with him. His lungs began to burn from lack of oxygen.

Just when he thought that all was lost, they broke the surface. Air rushed into his lungs, and he gasped and coughed. He twisted around scanning the water. A small boat stood a ways off, and they began swimming toward it, rain pelting their faces.

When they came alongside, hands reached down and pulled them up into the boat. Anxious fisherman scanned their faces and asked them if they were hurt. Slowly James shook his head. He turned to look back toward his ship.

All that was still visible of the royal vessel was her bow, and even as he watched, it slipped beneath the dark waves. As suddenly as it had risen, the storm dissipated.

The captain of the fishing boat crossed himself. "I've never seen anything like it."

"How so?" James questioned sharply.

"The squall. She came out of nowhere. It was like she was alive, passing us to attack your ship. God have mercy."

Eyes hard, James turned back to Anne. "Do you still doubt the presence of witches?"

These Witches . . . can rayse stormes and tempestes in the aire, either upon sea or land, though not universally, but in such a particular place and prescribed boundes, as God will permitte them so to trouble: Which likewise is verie easie to be discerned from anie other naturall tempestes that are meteores, in respect of the suddaine and violent raising thereof, together with the short induring of the same.

The king put his pen down and pressed his fingers to his temples.

His trusted advisor waited patiently. The man knew not to interrupt while James was writing. Finally James looked up wearily. "Any word about the identity of the hags who tried to kill the queen and me?"

After months of negative replies, he had grown to fear he would never discover the responsible ones. He had, however, had some small success in rousting some witches and casting light on the dark places wherein they dwelled.

"Yes, Your Majesty," the man said, clearly pleased with himself. "A gentleman would like to speak with you privately. He claims to have knowledge of the witch who attacked you."

James blinked in surprise. *Could it really be?* His fatigue forgotten, he commanded, "Show him in and make certain no one disturbs us."

His aid bowed and left. Within moments he ushered a tall, dark-haired man into the chamber, then left, closing the door behind him.

"Your Majesty," the stranger greeted, dropping to one knee.

James gestured for the man to rise, leaning forward eagerly to hear what he had to say "Rise, good sir. Tell me who you are and why you have come."

The man did as he was ordered, but bowed his head with great humility and announced, "My name is Luc Deveraux, Your Majesty. I am here because I have come to understand that we have a common enemy."

James lifted a brow. "And who might this unfortunate be?"

"She is called Barbara Cahors."

The king was mildly disappointed. That was no one whom he knew. "The name means nothing to me."

"It will soon, your majesty," Luc Deveraux said earnestly, his expression one of great concern and steadfastness, "for she is the witch that of late tried to kill your good lady and yourself."

James leaned forward farther, eyeing the other man intently. *This is exactly what I have been wanting to hear. And so, I needs must doubt it. Courtiers thrive on pleasing me . . . or rather, appearing to please me.*

With great sternness of tone, he said, "How do I know that you do not have some personal vendetta against this woman and thereby seek to bring her to ruin by my hand?"

"But I *do* have a personal grievance," Deveraux

assured him. "That I do, sir, and I stand by my accusation."

The king and queen both attended the burning of the witches. Barbara Cahors and her handmaid had been lashed to great pyres, found guilty of the crimes of witchcraft and the attempted murder of the royal couple. Luc Deveraux was also present, close enough that Barbara could see him, far enough away that she could not easily identify him to the soldiers guarding her.

A smirk touched his face as he watched the hem of her skirt catch fire. Soon the witch would burn, like so many innocent women had before her. Barbara was far from innocent, though. He had traced her to this place with great effort. Spies and magic spells had revealed to him all the remaining members of the Cahors Coven. Barbara was one of several whom he planned to kill. The destruction of his enemy brought him great joy. Perhaps at last the House of Deveraux would be rid of the House of Cahors.

His victory was not entirely complete, though. Barbara's young daughter, Cassandra, had escaped, and though he had combed the countryside, he had been unable to find the child. Without her mother to train her, though, the girl might never come to fully realize her powers. Regardless if she lived or died, the back of House Cahors was broken, and Deveraux was ascendant.

James: London, November

At the headquarters of the Supreme Coven, Sir William looked up as his son, James, strode into the room. The young man stood before him, barely paying the proper respect. Excitement and arrogance streamed from the young pup like musk.

"Father."

"So, you have returned. Were you successful?"

James smiled. "More than expected."

He turned, and a young woman was escorted into the hall. Though her hands were bound behind her, she bore herself with grace, standing tall. Sir William breathed deeply. He could smell the fear coming off her, but otherwise she masked it well.

"Father, allow me to introduce Nicole Anderson, my fiancée."

Holly: Seattle, November

After Silvana and Kialish left the hospital, Holly, Amanda, Tommy, and Kari stood around awkwardly, angrily, very much at odds with one another. No one spoke. Tommy looked on helplessly, unable to comfort Amanda or the other two.

It fell to Tante Cecile to break the silence. She said to the others, "We must hold a Circle and ask the Goddess our best course of action—whether or not Holly should go to save Jeraud. We have the ability to seek guidance, and we should."

Holly's lips parted to protest. *What if she says no?* It occurred to her that although she had served as High Priestess for months, she had not really yielded herself to the Goddess. She had looked on the success of their magic spells almost the same as if they had been performing successful lab experiments in chemistry class. The thought of laying down her will was terrifying.

Tante Cecile looked straight at her as if she was reading her thoughts. Slowly she nodded. "You have just reached the threshold," she said. "You're on the brink of truly reclaiming your birthright, Holly."

Holly swallowed hard. Her chest was so tight she couldn't breathe. Amanda frowned, puzzled, and Kari said anxiously, "What are you two talking about? You're speaking in secret code."

A great fear washed over Holly. In the midst of the chaos and confusion, she was overwhelmed. *If I do this—agree to really put myself in Her hands—I will be different for the rest of my life. What if my Goddess is a ruthless lady? What if allegiance to her is what made the Cahors before me so brutal?*

"It's still your choice," Tante Cecile said. "You can turn back."

"We'll give Kialish tonight to grieve," Holly said. "Then we'll hold Circle tomorrow night and I'll go before the Goddess." She said to Amanda, "I can't let you lead the coven. It's my responsibility."

"You still can't go to him," Amanda said icily in reply. Tommy put his arm on her shoulder, and this time she shrugged it off, as if she weren't really paying attention to what he was doing and needed to be left alone.

His look of disappointment spoke volumes to Holly.

"We'll ask the Goddess what to do," Tante Cecile soothed. "We'll have a Clearing and a Knowing." She sighed. "If we're lucky."

Amanda and Kari both moved a bit away, Kari folding her arms. She was still an outsider, still not fully committed to sharing her lot with the others. And she loved Jer, and hated Holly for leaving him to burn in the Black Fire.

"Tonight," Tante Cecile said, "we should stick together. Whose house should we sleep in?"

"Girls! Thank God you're all right!"

Uncle Richard hurried across the threshold of the conference room as the ever-helpful woman in bright scrubs pointed the four out to him. His face was radiant with relief; he looked more alive than Holly had seen him since Aunt Marie-Claire's death.

"Daddy!" Amanda cried, and raced toward him.

"I think we should go to their house," Kari said, and Tommy nodded. "Richard won't want Amanda to go out again, and I sure as hell don't want to hold Circle at my place."

Holly nodded, agreeing.

Tante Cecile pulled her cell phone out of her purse and punched in a number. She waited, murmuring, "Come on, Sylvie, pick up. Ah." She brightened. "Sylvie, it's Mom. Listen—"

She caught her breath, her eyes widening. Then she gasped. "No," she whispered. "No!"

Holly grabbed the phone out of her hand and pressed it against her ear.

"If you want to see her again, you'll give up Holly to me," a voice was saying.

Michael. He's kidnapped Silvana.

Tante Cecile sought refuge in Kari's arms, who, though not a warm person, enfolded her in a strong embrace and asked, "What's going on?"

"Do you have Kialish, too?" Holly demanded.

"Oh, no," Kari whispered. "He's kidnapped them?"

Tante Cecile shut her eyes tightly and began to chant in French.

"Why, Ms. Cathers, how nice to hear your voice," said Michael with syrupy sarcasm. "Of course I have Kialish, too. Do you know where his father is? Because I've tried repeatedly to reach him."

"Where do you want to make the exchange?" she said flatly.

Tante Cecile stopped chanting; Kari whispered, "No, you can't do that," but Holly saw the flicker in her eye that said, *Maybe you should, Holly. Maybe that would be payback for Jer.*

"On the water, of course," Michael said, obviously relishing his position.

"When?"

"I would say two nights hence."

"Why not sooner?" Holly asked.

"Patience, Holly." He chuckled. "Oh, and . . ."

"Yes?"

"I probably won't give them back to you alive."

Then he hung up.

Holly and Amanda had still not clued in Uncle Richard, and when the group converged on their house he was unhappy about it. He wanted his daughter and his niece home alone with him, and safe.

After a few minutes of settling in, Tante Cecile wove a spell on him, making him very sleepy. Then she sent him upstairs to go to bed.

Once he was out of the way, she turned to the others.

"We are in a state of siege," Tante Cecile said as she plaited her hair into corn rows, adding beads of silver and turquoise.

The cats patrolled outside, the trio of Cathers witch familiars moving with boldness and stealth. Amanda and Holly had begun to understand what familiars could do, and what they were: magical extensions of a witch's abilities and intentions—confidantes, in a subverbal way, and companions.

As the familiar of a witch who had abandoned her coven, Hecate hung back, deferring slightly to the others. She also tried harder: since then, she hunted birds on the grounds of the Anderson mansion and rodents in their basement with the fervor of a crusader in the Holy Land.

Bast, the familiar of the pivotal witch of the family, reappeared in the living room as if to announce that the perimeter was secured.

It was then that Tante Cecile looked first at her, and then at Holly. Her face clouded; she turned away once, then turned back.

"Holly, in the kitchen?" she asked.

Holly followed her.

Tante Cecile leaned up against the island in the

center of the kitchen and said, "You need to feed the water, child. Your magic will be stronger."

"I'm sorry?" Holly asked, as a chill broke out along her shoulders and up and down her spine. "What do you mean?"

Tante Cecile hesitated. "In the old days, in many religions, there were . . . sacrifices."

"Yes," Holly breathed. "So I've heard."

"Giving something to the water means that you sacrifice it . . . by water."

Holly waited, not getting it. Bast began to weave in and out of her legs, purring and flicking her tail.

"You drown them," Tante Cecile said.

The *voudon* glanced down at Bast, who mewed sweetly at her, then returned to her business of stroking her mistress with her tail.

NINE

NINTH MOON

☾

Nothing now can block our path
The world trembles at our wrath
Murder, kidnap, torture, and lies
Dark hearts beneath darker skies

Crying now within the night
Waiting for the moon's great light
Maiden whispers low and still
Commanding us to go and kill

Holly: Seattle, November

Holly couldn't kill Bast.

So she killed Hecate instead.

She put it from her mind as she did it—the way the beautiful cat stared up at her as she placed her in the bathtub . . .

. . . the way she struggled.

It was as if Holly wasn't really there. She shut herself down completely, neither seeing, nor hearing—not feeling anything. From a hard, dark place in the center of her being, she took the life of Nicole's cat and offered it to darker spirits than she had ever called upon before.

They answered; the act allowed them access, and their presence swept a cold wind through her bones and her heart. From head to toe she was chilled, frightened, and ashamed; she had done something she could never take back, on her knees beside the tub in the darkened bathroom, with one single black candle for company.

Outside the house, Bast and Freya threw back their heads and screamed in fury and despair; they would have wakened the dead, but they could not awaken Amanda and the others, because Holly had put them all into a deep, dreamless sleep. The cats flung themselves at the front door, and at the ground floor windows, livid with her, begging her to stop. Her face a cipher, her heart a stone, she gave to the water something precious, demanding—not asking—the Dark Ones to protect her coven and give her the strength to save Kialish and Silvana.

When it was over, she was different, and she knew she would never be the same again. Her gaze was steadier, her smile less sweet. Ambition and determination had supplanted her goodness; now she had purpose and passion, but she wasn't certain that she was still lovable.

After Hecate was dead, Holly stumbled into her heavily warded bedroom and slept for thirteen hours.

Amanda told her later that she had tried every spell she knew of to awaken her, finally asking Kari and Tommy to go to Kari's for some books she had there, and asking Dan to come and help her and Tante Cecile.

The shaman and the *voudon* had known instantly what she had done, but they didn't tell Amanda. All they told her was to do nothing and let Holly rest.

Holly's dreams were troubled, boiling over with flames and dark waters, monsters that swam out of the chambers of her heart and demons devouring her soul. She dreamed of her parents, waterlogged and dead; she dreamed of Barbara Davis-Chin, still in the hospital and near death. Everyone she loved was cut off from her by a barrier of shiny obsidian black; everyone she hated was pointing at her and laughing.

Then Hecate stared at her from beneath the dirt that Holly had heaped over her in the backyard, the cat whispering, *You crossed the line with my death; you are doomed.*

Over and over the words spilled across her body and crept through her mind: *You sold your soul. . . .*

When Holly awoke, Amanda was standing beside her bed in tears, and a woman with blue-black hair and almond-shaped eyes stood beside her. She was dressed all in black, from a velour turtleneck sweater to a pair of black wool pants. Her skin was very pale and she had on very subtle makeup. Her earrings were silver crescent moons.

Startled to find a stranger in her room, Holly raised herself on one elbow.

Amanda blurted, "Holly, how could you!"

The other woman put a hand on Amanda's arm and said softly, "Amanda, would you get us some tea?"

Amanda frowned, then bobbed her head and dashed from the room.

The woman regarded Holly for a moment. Then she sighed, pulled up a chair, and sat down.

Without preamble, she said bluntly, "You crossed the line."

Holly licked her lips. She was thirsty and still muzzy with sleep. She raked her curls out of her face and sat up against the headboard.

"Who are you?" she asked the woman.

"I'm from the Mother Coven," she told her. "I'm Anne-Louise Montrachet."

Holly looked down at her hands, which were trembling. "No one from the Mother Coven has ever contacted us before," Holly said. "Whatever it is."

"We are a very old and prominent confederation of

covens," she informed her. "We were founded in response to the Supreme Coven." She regarded Holly sternly. "The Deveraux are very prominent within their ranks."

Holly raised her eyes, hopeful that help had come at last. She said, "How do we join up?"

Anne-Louise shrugged. "Your family has always been a member coven since we were founded. We . . . we regret that we did not contact you sooner." She blanched. "Our resources have been stretched."

"We've been fighting for our lives," Holly told her simply. "And we haven't been entirely successful."

Anne-Louise nodded. "Our condolences on your losses." She crossed her arms and legs and added, "All of them, including the death of the familiar, Hecate."

Holly reddened. Then she lifted her chin and said, "Two of my covenates have been kidnapped by Michael Deveraux. I would give anything to get them back."

"We have standards. We have limits," Anne-Louise admonished. "We do not sacrifice coven members, including familiars."

Holly moved her hands. "I didn't know—"

"We have always had problems with you Cahors," Anne-Louise cut in. "You're unpredictable. You're ruthless."

"Until a year ago, I didn't even know I was a witch," Holly protested.

"Witch blood runs in your veins," Anne-Louise cut in, gesturing to her. "Most witches would have been unable to sacrifice a familiar. They would have felt the wrongness of it." She made a fist and placed it over her heart.

"Well, it was wrong of you guys to leave us alone to face Michael Deveraux," Holly said. "I have to go to the bathroom. And I'm dying of thirst."

"Amanda won't be back. Not until I unward your doorway," the woman said. "And you will sit there and listen—"

Holly glared at her. The woman raised her chin. For a few seconds they had a standoff. Then the woman sighed heavily.

"Very well. You aren't my prisoner."

Saying nothing, Holly slid off the bed and walked unsteadily to the door. Truth was, she was shocked that there was such a thing as a Mother Coven to whom she was supposed to answer. And shocked, too, that they had left her and the others to twist in the wind for so long without backup.

But do something they don't like, and they're here in a hot minute.

She went into the bathroom and did her thing, then padded back to her room. The woman was standing and gathering her things: a black shawl, an overnight bag, and a purse.

"You're leaving?" Holly asked. "Aren't you going to help us with Michael Deveraux?"

"Yes. I am," Anne-Louise said in a clipped voice. "I've taken a room at a hotel, and I need to marshal my own powers. Alone," she added pointedly. "I don't want him to realize I'm here. I want him to assume you're still on your own."

Holly wasn't sure what to think about that. She said, "But you're helping, right?"

The woman hesitated. "As much as we can," she replied.

Holly crossed her arms and looked hard at the other witch. "You're afraid of him."

"Any wise witch is."

Holly could practically read her thoughts.

"You didn't want to come here. You asked not to."

The woman inclined her head. "That's also true." She cleared her throat. "I'm going to check in and perform my ritual. I'll get in touch in about six hours."

"We have about a day," Holly pointed out. "He said I had until the full moon." *To save them?*

To die?

The woman exhaled and slung her bag over her shoulder. She began to walk to Holly's door. "I'll be in touch." She added, in a weak tone of voice, "It's the best I can do."

"Pardon me for saying it, but your best sucks," Holly flung at her.

The woman turned her back to Holly and walked out of the room. She murmured something and made a gesture with her hand.

Amanda raced into the room, ignoring the witch. Holly realized Anne-Louise had cloaked herself with invisibility.

"I hate you, Holly!" she shouted. "I hate you for killing Hecate! How could you do that?"

Holly didn't have time to be kind. "If it could have saved Eddie, would you have killed Hecate?"

Amanda's mouth dropped. Holly pressed her advantage.

"Michael Deveraux is planning to kill Silvana and Kialish. He'll come after us next. Don't you think Hecate's death is worth it?"

Speechless, Amanda simply stared at her. Holly felt sick to her soul, and mean, and unlovable.

But she also felt strong.

★ ★ ★

This bears watching, Michael Deveraux thought, as he spied on Holly with a scrying stone from deep within the chamber of spells in his house in Lower Queen Anne, a neighborhood of Seattle.

His imp capered about the room, chattering at the skulls placed on the altar, laughing with mad glee as he glanced into the scrying stone, then darting away, his attention seized by some other object in the room.

Michael had witnessed her sacrifice of the familiar, which he had found both startling and delightful. *I didn't realize she had it in her to do something like that. She's far more blackhearted than I thought.*

He had also heard and seen her side of the conversation with the witch from the Mother Coven; the witch's side of the meeting had been hidden from him. But he knew what that meddler wanted; she was telling Holly to toe the party line: *no deaths among the good guys. But waste all the bad guys you want.*

When Holly had pretty much told her to go to hell, he had silently applauded.

I wonder if I've underestimated her, he thought. *Maybe I can turn her to the darker side. In thrall to me . . . or to Jer, if he regains his sanity. Her union with the Deveraux Coven would assure my rise to power in the Supreme Coven.*

No sooner had he thought those words, than he smelled the stench that often presaged the arrival of

Laurent, Duc de Deveraux, and his ancestor.

Sure enough, as Michael knelt in humble obeisance, the moldering corpse that was his ancestor stepped off Charon's boat as it glided into being in the center of the room. Sulfur mixed with the gut-churning odor of decomposition, telling of the hellfires Laurent had left in order to make the voyage back among the living.

"Laurent, it's been so long since you have made yourself known to me," Michael said. "I have wonderful news. I have two captives, and it looks as though I'll be luring Holly of the Cahors to her death."

"You liar," Laurent said in medieval French. He backhanded Michael, sending him sprawling to the floor. "You are thinking of sparing her. *Cochon.* Don't think it. The entire House must be wiped away from this world and all worlds."

His cheek throbbed as if he'd been branded. Laurent advanced on him, menace in every step.

"You want the Black Fire again, don't you? You want to rule the Supreme Coven. Then you had better kill the witch or you will never be able to conjure it again."

Michael took that in. His heart pounding, he tried to summon his dignity—and his courage—as he got to his feet.

"Then I'll kill her," he said calmly.

Ninth Moon

Anne-Louise had been a practicing witch from the time she learned to speak. She had grown up in the Mother Coven, a ward of it. Her parents had been killed shortly after she was born, so the coven had been both Mother and Father to her.

In her hotel room she meditated, gathering her strength. The coven had sent her because wards were her magical specialty. Diplomacy was her mundane one. Although, one would not have guessed that, given her confrontation with Holly. She shuddered. Being near the younger witch had been an unpleasant experience. Drowning the familiar had tainted her. The evil coming off of her was terrible to feel.

Two tears slid slowly down her cheek. The first was for the familiar, Hecate. The second was for the witch Nicole, whose cat Hecate had been. Anne-Louise prayed to the Goddess that their fates would not be the same.

She took several cleansing breaths trying to regain her focus. She was tired from the long flight and the encounter with Holly. Additionally the ward she had set at the top of the stairs when she left the house had just about drained her. The deep breaths helped refocus her attention, and she resumed her meditations putting the Cahors witch from her mind. Cahors were always such trouble.

Wicked: Curse

"Kill her," Luc Deveraux whispered as he watched the proceedings. He had been tracking Cassandra Cahors ever since he had arranged for her mother, Barbara, to be burned at the stake. Now finally Cassandra would die as well and by another fine witch-hunter's tradition.

Dunking.

Onlookers gathered at the water's edge while the witch-finders in charge of her case spread across London Bridge to watch her drown, and drown she would. The commonly held belief was that witches floated. So, a woman accused of witchcraft was often thrown into a small body of water to see if she floated. The only way to prove that one was innocent was to drown and die. Much good innocence did for one.

Of course the common superstitions were all wrong. Witches didn't float. Cassandra Cahors would drown and everyone would believe she had been innocent of witchcraft. Nothing could be further from the truth.

He smiled, savoring the irony.

Tied to the ducking stool, she struggled beneath the water, then was pulled up in case she wished to make a confession. She looked like a drowned cat, all huge eyes, her hair beneath her mob cap plastered to her head. She was wearing down; her breath was very labored, and he was overjoyed.

Cassandra was dying, and as she looked out at the crowd, all the fires of hell burned in her eyes.

"I curse you, all of you!" she shouted. "You shall all drown, every one of you! As I die, so shall you."

Luc waved his hand and whispered a few incantations. He changed the spell, twisting it back toward Cassandra. At last he smiled triumphantly. "No, Cassandra. But all who love your descendants shall. I curse your house for all time.

"The loved ones of Cahors shall die by drowning."

Michael and Laurent: Seattle, November

Laurent, the mighty duke of the House of Deveraux, watched his descendant Michael attempting to hide his fear as he got to his feet, and his entire being flooded with rage. *To see my house reduced to this: a modern-day playboy who tries to play the game as the Cahors did.* . . .

Laurent possessed a ferocity and passion that, quite literally, had taken him beyond the grave. Catherine of the Cahors, his rival in life, had not managed to make that transition, and she spun through the universe as ashes.

Jean was dead because of them. True dead.

I will not have this. I have found the living Cahors witch, and I will see her dead.

Thus far, he had only been able to appear to Michael and to touch only him. But as he stood livid and furious, he felt strength rushing through his being.

Energy crackled around and through him; his head snapped back, and it was as if lightning had jolted through him.

Michael's eyes widened, and the duke realized that something was happening to himself; he glanced down at his hands and watched the gray, rotten flesh drop from his bones and soft new skin appear. He touched his face; the same thing was happening there.

In large clumps, his old body fell away.

He was becoming a man again—vigorous, filled with life.

At last. At last!

"Whoa," Michael whispered, impressed. Michael's imp chittered and pointed, leaping about the room.

"Did I not tell you that I would come back to this plane a full man?" Laurent chided Michael, although his heart was overflowing with shock. He had not realized it would ever really happen.

He took a step forward, and another. His ancient clothing fell away, leaving him naked.

He said to his many-times-great-grandson, "Fetch me clothing."

Michael raced off to do as he was told, his imp bounding after him.

Then Laurent closed his eyes and raised his arm; he whispered, "Fantasme."

The great falcon took shape and weight as he landed on the arm of his lord and master. His bells tinkled; he screeched softly.

Laurent opened his eyes and looked fondly at the bird.

"*Ma coeur,*" he said. "My heart. Come with me, my beauty, and we'll hunt as we once did."

The bird cawed in reply.

Michael returned with clothing for him—a black sweater, black trousers, boots—and Laurent savored the sensation of fresh, new attire on his new body. He realized he was hungry. But that hunger would have to wait.

He had a witch to kill.

He strode past Michael, who called, "Where are you going?"

"To do your work," he flung over his shoulder, not even breaking stride.

His strong thighs propelled him up the stairs. He hesitated, unsure of his bearings, when the falcon lifted from his arm and fluttered down a corridor. Within a minute Fantasme had shown Laurent the way to the front entrance of the Deveraux home.

He moved his wrist and the door opened. As he crossed the threshold, he was tempted to turn the entire house into a raging inferno, be done with Michael Deveraux once and for all. But he reminded himself that, after all, Michael was a strong warlock who knew his family's proud history and longed to restore the family honor.

He's not all bad, Laurent thought.

He's just not me.

The moon was nigh full as its beams glowed over him. Michael was right to set the meeting with Holly Cathers on the full moon, which was on the morrow. His power would be greater for killing her then.

But Laurent was not going to wait that long.

He snapped his fingers and shouted, *"Magnifique!"*

Clouds roiled and scudded over the yellow moon, and stars blinked and shuddered. An arc of flame shot across the sky, and upon it, the mighty hooves of Laurent's warhorse, Magnifique, took form. They were followed by his legs and then his body. Flames shot from his nostrils, his mane, and his tail, and he cantered down from the sky to the ground, stomped his left foot, and dipped his head to Laurent.

"By the Horned One, I have missed you," Laurent said fervently. Then he climbed on the back of the horse, sans saddle. Fantasme rode on his shoulder, and the trio galloped down the streets of Michael's town, Seattle.

The skies cracked open and rain poured down. Steam rose off Magnifique's heavily muscled body, and Laurent threw back his head and laughed. Then he put his heels to the horse and they picked up speed, until the warhorse's hooves made the street sizzle and melt.

Fantasme showed the way; the dark lord of the Deveraux rode for hours; and then . . .

. . . he stood before the house where the witch resided.

Without a moment's hesitation, he galloped up the walkway toward the porch.

He fully expected there to be wards, and he conjured as he rode, breaking each one as he did so. He was surprised when he had disabled them all, expecting more fight in the young woman, and with a wave of his hand, flung open the door. Magnifique trotted inside.

He smelled smoke and remembered the night Michael had attempted to conjure the Black Fire through the sacrifice of Marie-Claire, the lady of this house. How livid Laurent had been that night! Michael had disobeyed him, putting that lady in thrall to himself—that minor Cahors witch, that adversary— after Laurent had expressly forbidden it.

He had materialized here and cuffed Michael, and hated him for his duplicity.

But would I respect a man who did not push, take chances? When has obedience mattered to the Deveraux? I would rather he take the initiative and accomplish great things than allow fear of me to limit him.

He raced through the living room. The hot winds of anger rose with him; Magnifique's body sizzled and burned from the speed at which he ran. Laurent reveled in all the sensations, and he laughed in anticipation of what he was going to do to that little witch, either carry her off and kill her slowly, or allow Magnifique to trample her as she ran.

He started up the stairs and—

—was blocked.

A powerful ward shimmered between him and the top of the stairway. Roses shimmered in it, and lilies, suspended as if in crystal.

He lips curled back in utter hatred. He changed spells and created from his hands an enormous fireball, which he lobbed at the ward.

Nothing he did had any effect.

The Mother Coven has been here. This is one of their wards.

He urged Magnifique on; the horse reared, as frustrated as his master. His large hooves slammed at the barrier, the magical energy shocking them both. Magnifique reared again and again, coming down hard on the ward. It would not give. Fantasme struck at it with claws and beak, and still it remained intact and in place.

And then, standing inside the barrier, a woman's shape shimmered and blurred. She looked at him with eyes he knew, with a sneer he knew too well. . . .

She lives on. I had not known that.

That threw him . . . but he found his composure as he regarded the ghostly image of his dead daughter-in-law.

"Isabeau," he proclaimed, "get thee hence. I abjure you!"

Her image wobbled but did not fade. She was staring at him with the same degree of hatred he felt for her. Tearing her apart with his teeth would be too good for her.

"You murdered my heir," he said to her. "It's only just that I take the life of the Cahors descendant."

She made no reply, but a strange smile ghosted across her lips, then was gone.

She raised a hand and pointed toward the front door, contemptuously dismissing him.

Laurent clapped his hands three times . . .

. . . and he, Magnifique, and Fantasme were magically transported back to Michael's chamber of spells.

Michael looked startled, but the two young people who lay tied up on the floor were terrified. The girl began to scream; the young man closed his eyes and began to chant. Laurent felt his attempt to send him back into the ether as a mild tickle across his sternum.

He dismounted and slapped the horse on the hindquarters. Fantasme perched on his shoulder, then glided over the two prone figures, screeching in anticipation. The bird had been taught to love tidbits of human flesh.

"You couldn't get to her," Michael guessed.

Laurent nearly hit him again for embarrassing him in front of mere captives, but he put his hands on his hips. He said, "The Mother Coven is here. Did you know that?"

Michael exhaled with contempt. "Who cares? A bunch of withered old nuns who are ineffectual at best."

"Tomorrow, the witch dies," Laurent ordered him, trying another tack. He smiled evilly at the two on the floor. "So you might as well kill them now."

"She's a *voudon;* he's a shaman. I'll get more power tomorrow if I kill them on the full moon."

"Very well," Laurent said, conceding the point. Then he touched his stomach and said, "I want to eat."

Michael nodded. "I'll take you upstairs and make you a steak."

They went upstairs.

Jer: Avalon, November

It was a freezing cold day, and Jer was starving. Healing took a lot of energy. James had jumpstarted the process, but it was far from over. He was still horribly scarred.

Bundled in a pea coat, a blanket over his knees, he sat on a stone bench and looked out to sea. He wondered what Holly was doing; if she dreamed of him. He would be surprised if she didn't. He knew that in his dreams, he called out to her.

I have to try harder not to do that. I will be the death of her.

There was a soft pad of footsteps. Jer looked up to see one of the servants cautiously approaching with a silver tray. Silver covered dishes gleamed on its surface.

Jer signaled for her to come closer. She was afraid of him, whether because he was a powerful warlock or because he was so horrible-looking, he had no idea.

He said to her, "What do you want to know today?"

She was shy; she said, "How to find money."

"All right."

She handed him the tray. They had a deal going. She told him any news she heard, and in return, he taught her simple spells.

"What do you have for me?" he asked her.

"James is back," she said. "He's got a girl with him. A witch."

That caught his attention. His hair stood on end; his cheeks grew hot as he wondered, *Have they taken Holly?*

"What's her name?" he demanded.

She cocked her head. "I want to learn how to find money and how to make someone I hate lose her glasses."

On any other day, he might have laughed. But today he said, *"What is her name?"* He lifted a finger and pointed it at her, an ominous threat.

She backed up. "Nicole."

Holly's cousin. She used to date my brother.

This could not be good.

He nodded and said, "Okay. I'll teach you. But first . . ." He took the cover off one of the dishes and smiled appreciatively. Fish and chips. He loved them.

He picked up a fry and began to pop it in his mouth when a terrible smell hit his nose. He froze, staring down at the fry.

Green energy shimmered around it, and its manifest aspect was that of a shriveled piece of rotting garbage.

Poison, he realized. *From Eli . . . or James?*

The girl watched him; she was curious, but there was no sign about her that she knew she had brought him food designed to harm him, if not kill him.

He put it back down. He looked at her and said, "Get me something else. Something you've had some of."

Her eyes widened at the implication.

Without another word, she took the tray and hurried away, as if she was afraid he would blame her.

He stared out to sea.

Nicole's with James. Are they upping the stakes, trying to get Holly to come here, to Avalon?

"Don't do it," he said aloud. "Holly, don't."

TEN

STRAWBERRY MOON

Catch them now as they run
Kill the moon with the sun
We will take what they won't give
Cahors die so Deveraux live

Try to fight the sun god's power
Call on Goddess every hour
Fight them, kill them, don't give in
House Deveraux must not win

Seattle, November

In her hotel off Pioneer Square, Anne-Louise snapped wide awake. She lay still for a moment, allowing her memories of the past day to flood back in. One of her wards was under assault. It was the one she had placed in Holly's home. She closed her eyes, feeling the ward, feeling the energy assaulting it. Who was it? It was a Deveraux. Michael? No. She gasped and reached for her cell phone.

London, September, 1666

Giselle Cahors paced before the altar in the great house that was home to the Mother Coven in London. She was skeptical of the High Priestess's decision to move the Temple from Paris to this place, and not shy to state her opinion on it.

"London is barely large enough to hide one coven, much less two," Giselle observed.

"What would you have us do, child? Abandon the city to the Supreme Coven?" the High Priestess of the Mother Coven asked, raising her brows.

Giselle stopped pacing and put her hand on the carved folds of the wooden wall panel as she touched the athame tucked in the girdle of her full, black skirts.

"No, Priestess. I would have us *destroy* the Supreme Coven, not try to dwell in its stated territory."

"And with its destruction, destroy your Deveraux enemies?" The High Priestess sat back in her curved-back chair and folded her arms over her chest. She looked so like a nun, in her white wimple and robes, that Giselle had to remind herself that they were of the same tradition. "Is your concern for the Mother Coven or for your own house?"

"For both," Giselle protested.

The woman cocked her head. "My child, if your loyalties are divided, then you are not to be trusted.

The strength of your purpose must outweigh the call of your blood. We shall fight the Supreme Coven in our own time on our own terms. When our power grows to surpass theirs, then we can rid the world of their evil."

Evil. The word flowed silkily off the older woman's tongue, and Giselle could not help but shiver. Standing there in the inner sanctum, she stared at the altar and the blood stains on the floor all around it. It was a fine line that divided the Mother Coven's evil from that of the Supreme Coven.

"Very well, *ma mère*," Giselle bit off. "I will be the coven's obedient daughter."

"There's a good girl," the High Priestess said patronizingly. She reached out her arms to receive a ritual embrace. "Now, leave us. We have much to do."

With a hot heart, Giselle embraced her, dipped her head, and left the room.

This may have been a mistake, she thought.

Realizing she could not battle the entire Deveraux family alone, she had joined the newly formed Mother Coven, which was made up of witches who claimed to practice "whiter" magic than those of the more powerful Supreme Coven. Over the last few months Giselle had been given reason to question that claim.

Still, the leadership of the Mother Coven said all

the proper things about the superiority of white magic and made all the appropriate gestures to Coventry at large. To hear them, it was *she* who was the problem, she who was the bloodthirsty one. It was her Cahors blood that was tainted and evil and to be reigned in.

For the thousandth time she wondered what her grandmother, Barbara, had been like, and if she, Giselle, would have a different view of magic had the older witch lived to influence her offspring.

Thanks to Luc Deveraux she would never know the answer. He had been responsible for her grandmother being burned at the stake and for her own mother's life of running and hiding before he had finally caught her and had Cassandra Cahors drowned. He thought he had finally succeeded in wiping them out and had risen through the ranks of the Supreme Coven based on that accomplishment.

He didn't know that one Cahors still eluded him.

He would, though, soon enough.

She had seen him in her scrying stones. He was near. For weeks she had read the signs. They all pointed to the next few days. If she was to finally kill Luc Deveraux, she might never have a better opportunity.

Despite what she promised the High Priestess, she did not intend to let this chance pass her by.

I've made a few close friends among the other covenates, she thought as she strode down the corridor and away from the inner sanctum. *They might aid me in the coming battle.*

Luc Deveraux was older than he looked. Some shred of vanity prodded him to maintain his appearance. The magic kept his body alive, and with a little effort he could look well when he chose. His family had grown even more powerful under his tutelage, and their alliance with the Supreme Coven had only brought them more power. Within a couple of generations they might even be leading it.

Only the House of Moore posed a threat. The warlocks of that family seemed to grow more powerful by the day. House Deveraux needed to be focused in order to outwit House Moore and claim the throne of the coven, the seat of power. House Deveraux could suffer no distractions, no barriers. He had systematically removed all that he could think of. All but one.

She thinks I don't know about her, he thought, *but I do. I have always known about her.*

The signs were right. He would wipe the last descendant of the Cahors from the earth.

He has called me.
He has challenged me.

Giselle was thrown. She had thought to have the

element of surprise in her armory. She had also thought to have one more moon before she challenged Luc Deveraux to battle.

But he had thrown down the gauntlet first.

Drawn by his magics, Giselle and her two sister witches found themselves in Pudding Lane.

He was there, waiting, and he was not alone. The two groups approached each other slowly, silently.

They were met on the street as though on a battle-field. Luc and Giselle locked eyes, warriors about to do battle.

Without warning Luc pulled a wicked dagger from beneath his cloak and threw it with deadly accuracy toward her head. She lifted a hand and the dagger stopped in midair. It slowly spun in a half-circle till it was facing its master. She sent it back with all the ferocity she could muster.

It was the signal the others had been waiting for. The battle was fierce, the opponents equally matched. Dark forms spun and twirled by the light of the moon, dancing to their own macabre tune with steps only those attuned to dark magics could accomplish.

Around Luc and Giselle the others slowly fell away. A warlock turned to melt into the night and a witch followed him. Another couple's struggles carried them into a nearby street. At last the two of them were alone.

Slowly they circled each other, searching for weaknesses. Both were tired, both were running out of strength.

"I shall kill you as I killed your mother and grandmother before you."

"And I swear by the Goddess that this Cahors will avenge all whom you have slain. You shall not kill another of my kin."

She was exhausted and shaking, but Giselle could feel the rage rising in her, filling her and giving her strength. Her hands began to shake with the power that coursed through her. At last she let it out in a single shout.

"Incendia!" Fireballs appeared in the air before her. She hurled them at the old man, one after another.

Luc batted them out of the sky as if they were children's playthings. Several landed at his feet, sputtering and dying in the dirt. Two plummeted into a nearby watering trough. One flew through a window into the home of the king's baker. The last one he sent back to her.

She threw her hand up and the ball of flame stopped in midair. It vibrated for a moment, humming as each applied more and more force to it. At last it exploded in a shower of sparks that rained down in the street between them.

"I've seen better tricks from charlatans, my dear child," he sneered.

"Poor Luc. Did you think that you had ended the House of Cahors then? You didn't take into account that she had a daughter."

"Ah, but I did," he riposted. "And you will certainly not escape me now."

Before she could respond, flames erupted from the window of the baker's house and shouts came from within. A woman screamed in anguish, and around the Coventry witches and the warlock, houses stirred to life with flickering candles as sleepy residents rushed to see the problem.

Giselle and Luc stared at each other for a long minute. At last he gave a mocking bow before wrapping himself in a cloak of darkness and vanishing.

As the first faces started peering out of doors, she realized that she had no time to be discreet. She picked up her skirts and ran down the street yelling, "Fire!"

People burst from their homes and ran toward the blaze upon hearing her shout. Not a single one of them gave her a second glance.

* * *

The fire moved like a living thing, terrible in its ferocity as it swallowed houses, shops, and churches alike without discretion. As if the destruction caused by the licking flames was not enough, houses were pulled down one after another, destroyed in an attempt to stop the fire's path. The fire just laughed and leaped across the ruins of people's homes and lives.

Ministers preached farewell sermons as the flames approached their churches. Thousands of people fled, many with only the clothes upon their backs. Still the relentless flame pressed on. Many claimed that it was the hand of God, that His face had been set against London because of its great wickedness.

For days the inferno blazed its way across London. When at last it seemed to die out at Temple Church, it was only gathering its strength for one last savage run. The smoke and debris clogged the air until it seemed the whole world was on fire.

In the end, the fire killed many people and destroyed thousands of buildings. When the last flame had died, Giselle stood in Pudding Lane, surveying the damage. She could scarcely believe that she had been standing in the exact same spot a few nights before.

Tears stung her eyes. So much carnage, so much death. Luc Deveraux had not come looking for her, and as she stood staring at the chaos they had caused, she vowed not to hunt for him. It was too dangerous.

There was a ship sailing in the morning for the New World. She and her daughter and infant sons would be on it. In the Americas she would start over. A new life with a new name. The old one reeked of death.

Gwen Cathers would be on that ship. Giselle Cahors had died in the fire.

Luc Deveraux tried in vain to still the trembling of his limbs as he stood before the Supreme Coven. Any warlock would be a fool not to fear the judgment of the coven under the circumstances.

The coven leader, Jonathan Moore, could not hide the smirk on his face as the coven delivered its proclamation.

"Luc Deveraux, you have willfully disobeyed the law of the coven by making your battle with the House of Cahors a public one and thereby endangering us all." It was significant that the coven did not care so much about the fire and the destruction it had caused except as it might lead to exposure.

"Already several have been arrested in connection with the conflagration. Two of them are warlocks, members of this coven who foolishly followed you. The other is your manservant. This reckless disregard for the safety of the coven cannot be overlooked. House

Deveraux shall hold no place in the leadership of this coven, and you must step down as the head of your house."

Luc was stunned. Death he expected and would have accepted, but he had not expected them to censure his entire family. He opened his mouth to protest. "My actions are mine alone. Do not punish House Deveraux for what I alone have done."

Moore was having none of it. "It is no secret that House Deveraux and House Cahors have feuded for many years. These public uses of magic will stop here and now. House Deveraux must regain the trust they once enjoyed in this coven."

So there is hope. Luc's agile mind began to consider strategies. He asked humbly, "How might we prove our loyalty?"

There were a few murmurs that were quickly silenced. Moore narrowed his eyes and thought for a few moments.

"House Deveraux must cease all displays of public magic immediately and forever. Also, your coven may eventually redeem itself by bringing the secret of the Black Fire to the Supreme Coven."

Luc felt sick in the deepest recesses of his twisted soul. The secret of the Black Fire was lost. House Deveraux could never redeem itself without it.

Philippe: On the Spanish border, November

They were going to burn José Luís's body.

They had waited the requisite three days to see if he would rise. But the warlock was truly dead.

Philippe wondered for a brief moment if it had been the death José Luís envisioned. He shook his head slowly, grief stricken.

Mon vieux, he thought fondly, *the battles we fought!*

Pray for me in Paradise that I will fight one to save Nicole, and win that one.

Several feet away the others huddled. Armand sat on the ground, too injured to stand. Seated beside him, Pablo was shaking with exhaustion. Philippe felt his throat constrict as he gazed upon José Luís's little brother, who looked so much like him. Alonzo crouched, eyes alert and probing the darkness, a cross in one hand and a crystal in the other.

He looked back down at the shell that had housed his friend and mentor. José Luís was dead, Nicole taken, and the battle against darkness had been well and truly joined.

He passed his hand over José Luís's face, blessing him. "We lost this time, old friend. But I swear to you, we shall prevail in the end."

He bowed his head briefly—half-praying, half-meditating. When he was finished he stood up slowly, his face set. He felt old and tired, but he knew what he had to do.

The others stared at him, seeking guidance, direction. He would give it to them. "We are going to find Nicole and battle this evil before it spreads farther."

"Where do we go?" Alonzo asked.

"Pablo?"

Pablo raised his head and in a weak voice answered, "London. They're taking her to London."

Philippe nodded. "Then that is where we shall go."

The others nodded agreement as he locked eyes with each of them in turn. Armand held his eyes the longest, and Philippe winced at the pain reflected there. Armand was more seriously injured than he had let on.

Philippe knelt beside him and placed a hand on his chest. Slowly he exhaled as his heart sped up to match the rapid beating of Armand's. Blinding pain surged through his body as his nervous system linked with Armand's. His body was trying to help heal the other warlock.

Suddenly the pain lessened dramatically, and Philippe opened his eyes to see that Alonzo was beside him, also working to heal Armand.

At last the most dangerous injuries were healed and the three broke contact. Philippe rocked backward on his heels.

From the torch stand, he plucked the flaming torch and touched the wood beneath José Luís's body. "As soon as he is ashes, we leave."

Seattle, November

The full moon was drowned by the heavy rains that fell from the sky in large, gulping cascades. Pioneer Square was awash; the twinkling funk of Hill Street was inundated; the bay was gorged and overflowing. It was not a fit night for anything, much less a battle. But it was the full moon, and witches were at their strongest.

Warlocks, too, but there was nothing to be done about that. Holly had called the Circle together at Dan's house. It was a beautiful, hand-built cabin in the woods, almost too small for the gathering that had assembled: Holly, Amanda, Tommy, Tante Cecile, Kari, Dan himself, and Uncle Richard.

"We have to get him out of town," Holly said to the group. "He won't be safe here no matter the outcome. He hasn't been safe here for months." She was speaking of her uncle, who was seated beside Dan's cast-iron stove in a state of shock. Back at the Anderson home, she and Amanda had revealed the truth about everything that was going on: the reality of Coventry, the fact that they were witches, that Michael

Deveraux, who had been his wife's lover, had also probably murdered her.

"But . . . but she had a heart attack," Richard had protested weakly. He looked so upset, Holly was afraid he himself might have a heart attack. So they performed for him, she and Amanda, conjuring the equivalent of witch parlor tricks. They conjured fire and wind, and they levitated objects in the room.

Then Holly produced a scrying stone, and asked him to look into it. He saw Michael Deveraux in robes, bowing before what looked very much like a Black Magic altar covered with skulls and black candles and a large book bound in black leather. The stone also showed Silvana and Kialish bound with ropes, their faces wan and bloodless. They might have been dead, except that at one point Silvana's eyes opened, and she stared in the direction of the stone's field of view, as if she knew it was focused on her.

Perhaps it was then that he began to believe. At any rate, he agreed to accompany them to Dan's, sitting in stunned, exhausted silence. Holly and Amanda had agreed not to tell him about the imp they had pulled from him and drowned, nor the fact that they had tied him up in case he tried to kill the two of them. He didn't remember any of it, and they thought it best to leave him ignorant of those recent dark days.

At Holly's request, Dan was going to purify each one of them for the coming rescue attempt. Each would go into his sweat lodge alone, hopefully to have a vision. Then he would speak to her of the shadow she had seen, and help her to use it to fortify herself in the coming battle.

At her request, everyone had dressed in the colors of the ancient House of Cahors: silver and black. She and Amanda were dressed in black sweaters and black leather pants, with silver hoops in their ears and silver chain necklaces from which dangled amethysts and silver. Dried herbs had been braided into their hair. Tante Cecile had plaited their hair, Amanda's into French braids and Holly's into corn rows.

Kari was swathed in a silver-and-black shawl over a black silk blouse and black jeans. Tante Cecile had on a form-fitting black dress embroidered with gold and silver leaves at the hem. Tommy wore black slacks and a T-shirt. He had borrowed a silver bracelet from Amanda, and he wore it awkwardly.

We used to be so many more, Holly thought. Then she reminded herself, *We defeated them on Beltane, on the 600th anniversary of the massacre of Deveraux Castle. We can defeat them again.*

"We have to assume Michael may launch an attack on us at any moment," Holly reminded the others.

"He has spies and scrying stones too. So I should go first. I'm point."

The others agreed.

Holly took off her clothes in Dan's bedroom, then wrapped herself in a large beach towel and followed him into the sweat lodge. Dressed in a T-shirt and buckskins, he stoked the alder smoke for her, sitting on his haunches while she inhaled the scent and began to sweat. The combination of smoke and heat made her dizzy; she allowed the sensations to take her over, and then the spirits showed her Pandion, the lady hawk, perched on her arm. Isabeau was riding Delicate, her mare, and the sun was shining gloriously down on her dark, unruly hair. She was galloping; her skirts of velvet were flying behind her, and Jean was shouting, "Slow down, wench! You'll break your neck!"

She cast a glance over her shoulder at her husband, laughing at him because he was having trouble keeping up with her. They were in the forests outside Deveraux Castle, and she was in love with him.

Never mind politics and magic spells, she was young and beautiful, and he was likewise young and very handsome . . . and the day was filled with joy. Above Jean's head the Deveraux falcon circled and soared in wild abandon, as exuberant as the witch and warlock. Then he screeched and dove into the thick underbrush. A battle ensued.

"He's caught something," Isabeau said delightedly, pulling on the reins. Delicate slowed.

"As have you," Jean replied, trotting up beside her. "My heart."

And then she was Isabeau, cradled beneath Jean as her kinsmen burned his castle to the ground; as his own kinsman Laurent conjured the Black Fire and sent it sweeping through the bailey. She could hear Jean screaming; could hear herself begging him to forgive her.

Through centuries they had searched for one another, locked in love and heat . . .

. . . and then a lady hawk flew above a misty island, dropping down, down, to land on the arm of a man who was so horribly, terribly scarred:

Jer.

Then overhead something wheeled, but it was not a bird; it was an Orca, a black-and-white whale, and it floated and swam. *I'm underwater. I'm drowning.*

She was beneath the waters of the bay, and as she turned to the right, she saw Eddie in the grip of the hideous monster that had killed him; and to the left, the rest of her coven, caught in the grip of its minions, each struggling to make it to the surface, their eyes bulging, unable to move as the creatures held them down.

They will drown.

She was spinning as if someone had tossed her out of a window headfirst; the vertigo made her sick and she crouched forward to vomit . . .

. . . and that was when she opened her eyes and came back to herself. She was back in the sweat lodge.

To one side of the sweat lodge was a shower; Holly rinsed first in warm water, and then in cool, allowing her mind to sharpen. Tommy went in next.

While she was there, Holly dressed and emerged from Dan's bedroom, facing her coven sisters, Kari and Amanda. Dan, who had finished helping Tommy get started, came out of the sweat lodge and regarded her soberly. It was he who spoke first.

"You want to go alone."

She replied, "I don't want to. I have to."

"No," Tante Cecile insisted, rising. "He has my daughter. I'm going with you."

"We all go together, or we all die here and now." Amanda spoke, pale and shaking with the force of her convictions. "He hurts us only when we are weakened by the absence of one or more. If we all stay together, we can all protect each other. It is our only chance of survival."

"I can't protect you," Holly protested, weakening under the onslaught.

"Who made you queen of the universe?" Kari asked sharply. "No one's asking you to protect us. If anything, I'm here to make sure you don't screw up again and hurt anyone else I care for."

Her reference to Jer and the fire that had nearly killed him was like a slap in the face. Holly took it, though she felt a growing animosity toward Kari that she knew she would not always be able to quell.

Anne-Louise watched from a safe distance as the members of the coven one by one entered the sweat lodge and took part in the ritual. Things were about to get very ugly. She could feel it with every fiber of her being. The only question was: What should she do to stop it?

Part Three
Waning

☾

"And when Lithia has passed and the year is waning there will be a great
pall that settles upon the earth. Some will be given in marriage whom should not and
others will wield a power unforeseen and uncontrolled. Then the earth will tremble
and the skies will rain fire."

—Lammas the Elder

ELEVEN

BLESSING MOON

🌙

Fill us now, Lord, with your might
Help us now to end this fight
And we will defile the head
Of the Cahors Coven dead

Evil about, evil without
Don't let it turn you inside out
But as we turn from their sin
We find it naught to the evil within

Michael Deveraux: Seattle, November

In the day, Michael mused as he held his athame up to the candlelight and admired the very, very sharp blade, *a Deveraux warlock facing battle would have received last words through runners or carrier pigeons. Deveraux warlocks even conjured with smoke signals, back in the Wild West. Phones are much more magical, carrying our disembodied voices across space, and yet they seem far more mundane. The romance is lost, somehow.*

No matter that I have magically enhanced the connection, because of the rain.

November in Seattle was not a kind month. It was harsh and wild and angry—warlock weather. Samhain—Halloween in the parlance of humanity— had passed by without the proper obeisance from him. For the first time in his memory, he had not run his life by the esbats and sabbats of his tradition. Instead he had focused his energies on the Cahors and on regaining leadership of the Supreme Coven—an internally driven calendar based on ambition . . . and revenge.

"Why *not* try for a hostage exchange?" Eli asked. He was still in England keeping an eye on the Moores for his father. And watching his brother.

Jer, my errant son.

And if truth be known, my pride and joy. . . .

"She won't sacrifice herself to save two people who aren't even related to her," Michael said. "She's a Cahors, after all. The best I can hope for is that her coven will put the screw to her to make a rescue attempt."

"It's gotta happen, Dad," Eli murmured, lowering his voice. "You've got to kill her. Sir William's got them all totally freaked out. Some of them want to take you out."

Because of the attack on the ferry, Michael knew. *There's some flaw in me,* he thought. *I could've been more subtle. So why wasn't I? Deveraux rush in where angels fear to tread.*

"Don't sweat it," he drawled. "I'm this close to conjuring the Black Fire again. Then past history won't matter a damn."

Just past ancestry.

Everyone knows the Deveraux should rule the Supreme Coven.

He changed the subject. "What's the situation with Jeraud?"

"He's still on Avalon. James has done a lot to make him feel better, but he sure looks gross."

"So you've seen him."

"From afar. I'm at the headquarters in London."

You've probably been trying to kill him from afar too, Michael thought. *If you manage it, you'll be sorry. Jer's the one who has made the connection with Jean and has the power to show for it. Not you.*

There's some reason we were able to conjure the Black Fire last Beltane, and we have to find out why we haven't been able to repeat our success. And I don't think the answer lies with you, Elias.

"So, are you, like, challenging her to a duel? Inviting her over for hot wings and a Mariners game?"

"I thought I'd let her come to me," Michael told his son. He added, "I'll be in touch."

"But—"

"Good-bye, Eli."

He hung up and put the cell phone on the altar.

Michael was one of the premier architects of Seattle, and as such, quite a wealthy man. He had a lot of disposable income—not an unusual situation for a warlock of his stature—and much of it he had spent on a beautiful yacht, which he had christened *Fantasme*. When he took friends out, they were piloted around the bay by Michael's captain, a man named Hermes. But when he was alone, Hermes revealed his true aspect: He was a fiend, a servant of Hell, and had been in the employ of the Deveraux family for sixty years. He had taken quite a liking to Michael's little imp, and the two were having a grand time above deck, navigating the yacht through the black waters of Elliott Bay.

There had been discussion about closing the bay down entirely, then shutting it down to pleasure craft, then the entire matter had been dropped simply because the Coast Guard did not possess enough manpower. Michael had worked many obscuring spells and chants of forgetting, and the majority of the population had decided that there had not been monsters in Elliott Bay, but a renegade Orca and a school of sharks.

Also, as with any warlock of means, Michael's yacht was equipped with a fine altar to the Horned

God. His personal grimoire was placed next to the skull of Marc Deveraux, his father and a worthy warlock in his own right, and the cell phone next to that. A statue of the God loomed over the bowls and candles of the Rite, it being very similar to the one back in the chamber of spells in his home.

He bowed low, making obeisance, naked beneath his red and green robe, which was covered with signs and sigils. They matched the ritual scars with which he had decorated his body as a testament to his art. The blood from the original cuts had fed his blade well.

Now he turned to his two distraught prisoners. Propped up back-to-back on the floor, they were both bound and gagged without ceremony, he cut off one of the braids of the female and nicked the left cheek of the male. His athame sucked greedily at the young man's blood, and he shivered with delight, feeling the power as it built up in the blade.

He flicked his finger at the Hand of Glory on the altar—the shriveled hand of a dead man, from which five black candles glowed. Then he loosened his robe and drew a long line down the center of his chest with the tip of his athame. The blood poured freely.

"I call upon the God," he said in a loud voice. "I summon the powers at my disposal to aid me in battle. I seek revenge against the House of Cahors, and I call upon my imps and my demons, my fiends and my kinsmen, to aid me. I call this three, three, three; I call this seven, seven, seven, seven, seven, seven, seven. Abracadabra."

He could feel the power rushing through him and around him. Memories of long dead kinsmen filled his mind, and he began to chant in an ancient tongue that not even he knew.

Swirls of green, blue, and red materialized along the wooden floor, rolling like carpets of mist and smoke, gathering momentum and tumbling upon one another. From the porthole window, the flash of lightning illuminated the terrified faces of Kialish and Silvana as the mist crept around them, slithering up their bodies and dancing along their skin. Thunder rumbled, joining the bass roar of the yacht as Hermes opened her up.

Then the sound changed. There was a deeper bass line, which gradually took on a rhythm—*ka-thun, ka-thun*—as the mist grew thicker, folding in upon itself repeatedly until it reached Michael's knees and came up to the chests of his victims.

"I call upon my forebears," he yelled above the noise.

Ka-thun, ka-thun . . . the distant pounding of horse hooves. Inside the mist, prone skeletons began to form and take shape, solidify, and rise to their feet. Shields appeared, strapped to their arms, and swords. Others materialized with rifles and six-shooters. Then more— the modern Deveraux—took shape as moldering corpses, machine guns and Uzi's slung over their arms.

Ka-thun, ka-thun . . . Michael smiled as the mist completely filled the cabin, engulfing the two young people. Eagerly he crossed to the ladderway, his athame in his fist, and climbed up to the deck.

He beheld a glorious sight: the phantom hundreds of his kinsmen, riding on horseback down from the sky, driving up from the depths in sleek cars, cantering and racing to join the battle.

At the head of the skyriders, his standard bearer to his left, Laurent, Duc de Deveraux, rode astride Magnifique. His armor gleamed in the mist; Magnifique was armored as well and wearing the skirt of a warhorse, decorated in green and red.

The dead wailed with glee and a thirst for vengeance; as the Deveraux assembled, horned demons and imps popped into being. Red-skinned, long-knuckled fiends joined them, and the hellhounds bayed and globbered for witch blood.

Then came the falcons—hundreds of them.

All ready to gouge out eyes and pluck hearts from chests.

The duke rode down onto the deck, and Michael lifted his chin as he saluted him. In response, the duke took off his helmet and held out his hand.

"Well done," he said to Michael. "Perhaps you'll pull this off."

Surrounded by her coven, Holly stood underneath a black umbrella at the water's edge and watched hell fill Elliott Bay. Kari was staring through binoculars and muttering, "No freaking way."

Beside her, Tante Cecile murmured a spell and Dan slowly shook his head, looking stricken.

Amanda left Tommy's side, sidled up to Holly, and put her hand in hers, joining the two parts of the lily that they two bore as brands.

"Where's the Coast Guard?" she asked.

"Hell with the Coast Guard," Kari said. "Where's the National Guard?"

Dan shook his head in a perverse sort of admiration. "He was cleverer this time. He's cloaked everything. I doubt anyone else can see it. This show is for us and us alone."

"Then he knows we're here." Kari's voice was shrill.

"He wouldn't be much of a warlock if he didn't," Dan ventured.

"Then why not attack?" Amanda asked, licking her lips. "Why stay out there?"

Holly closed her eyes. "Because he's surrounded by water."

And he wants my covenates to drown.

Leaving me alone to face him.

I can't let that happen.

She watched as the dead army of the Deveraux continued to mass; they were thousands against six.

Holly closed her eyes.

Isabeau, I call upon thee, she pleaded. *I can't fight them like this. I need your help. I am a Cahors. Bring on my kinsmen and their allies and their servants in the arts. Save us . . . and I will give you whatever sacrifice you wish.*

Something churned inside her; she felt herself falling and tumbling; she was going into a very cold, very dark place. All around her, stars danced; there was no ground, there were no walls. She was in space. The stars stretched and glowed.

She was outside time.

Vivid colors swirled around her, blacklight and silverflash; purple, scarlet, cyan. Bursts of light danced and flamed out; stars fell by the hundreds.

She heard screams and wailing; she heard a single woman's voice whispering, "My daughter, my daughter, my daughter . . ."

Mom? she wondered excitedly.

But it was not her mother who called.

It was Isabeau's.

In a cloud of glowing rainbows, a woman shimmered into being. She was tall and imperious, wearing a double-horned headdress and clutching a bouquet of lilies to her breast. Her gown was black and silver, bunched up in yards of fabric around her feet. Her mouth was bound shut; she was a corpse being prepared for burial. Her eyes opened and she looked straight at Holly.

Are you worthy? she asked without speaking.

Holly swallowed hard. She raised her chin.

I have to be, she replied.

Are you worthy to carry the mantle? the ghost demanded. *They have all failed me, all. No one has ever taken Isabeau's place; brought our house back to its former glory . . . Are you the one? Should I bother sparing you?*

"Yes," Holly said.

She opened her eyes.

In the driving rain, Holly was surrounded by phantom warriors from other times and places, some carrying the standard of the lily, others waving swords. There were Cahors with crossbows and Cahors with spears.

When they saw that Holly had opened her eyes,

they raised their halberds and their maces and their swords and shouted, "Holly, Queen!"

Holly gasped and looked around for the others. They had moved about one hundred yards farther down the beach. She was alone in the tornado that was her army.

A lady hawk fluttered down and hovered beside her; Holly raised her arm and the bird landed with ease. Then a young man materialized in front of Holly. He was wearing a tunic and leggings, and he led a massive warhorse by its reins. He knelt down and offered her the stirrup.

Holly understood; she put her foot in the stirrup, and somehow she had the wherewithal to hoist herself up and onto a boxy saddle made of bone and metal. The bird stayed firmly perched on her arm.

Armor magically covered her; the world narrowed through the slits of a helmet.

"Vive la Reine!" the army chorused, hoisting their weapons into the air. *Long live the Queen!*

Holly took a deep breath. *I have absolutely no idea what I'm doing.*

The other members of her circle scrambled toward her; she hurtled them away with a bolt of magic from her fingertips. Falling end over end, they managed to get to sitting positions, looking quite astonished.

"You'll drown," she said, but she knew they couldn't hear her because of the wild war cries and cheers around her.

"*Alors, mes amis!*" Holly cried, though she had never spoken French in her life. "We shall kill the Deveraux once and for all!"

"*Deveraux, la-bas!*"

Her squire handed her a lance, just like in the movies about tournaments. Banners fluttered from the shaft; the head glowed a poisonous green. Though it was massively heavy, she hefted it into the air as if she would spear the rainclouds themselves.

Thunder rumbled; lightning flashed. The dead of the Deveraux wailed and shrieked. Their falcons were more numerous than raindrops.

"Holly!" Amanda shouted. "Holly, take us with you!"

Holly paid her no mind. *Live,* she thought to her cousin.

Then she put her heels to the flanks of her warhorse and cantered toward the water. Cheering wildly, her soldiers followed her.

As soon as the horse's hooves hit the water, it galloped on top of the waves, sending out flumes of water as it hastened to the battle. Steam issued from its nostrils; tiny flames danced along its back and mane.

Holly's entire being tingled and jittered as if she had been plugged into a huge machine. She felt the connection between her and each member of her army . . . and she saw Isabeau on one side of her, and Catherine, Isabeau's mother, on the other side, although she knew they were invisible and what she was seeing was a sympathetic vibration in her mind.

Like volleys of cannon, she and her troops flew across the water. The Deveraux falcons began to dive-bomb at them; Holly raised her lance and conjured a spell. Fireballs issued from her lance, taking out dozens of the birds; then another fireball followed, and more.

Others of her army did the same. Corpses of dead falcons plummeted into the water.

From the center of the Deveraux storm—the yacht—horsemen and soldiers took a cue from their leader and raced toward Holly and her hordes. The sound was deafening; Holly could hear nothing; and yet, she could hear the thundering of her heartbeat—

—and someone else's—

Her lance crossed the lance of a Deveraux whose face was a skull. Though she had never jousted before, she pushed hard against her enemy's lance, and to her astonishment, he dropped it. In her left hand a sword materialized. She raised herself in the saddle, leaned over the horse, and stabbed the skeleton in the rib cage.

It exploded.

She blinked, but had no time to process what she'd seen as more Deveraux converged on her. She swung her sword and aimed her lance as if she had been born to battle; the lady hawk fluttered at her ear, chirruping as if she were giving Holly directions. It felt to Holly as if she were actually guiding her arms and legs; she had no idea how to fight like this, and yet she was doing a superb job.

Down the Deveraux fell, and down, exploding into nothingness; her army was astonishing in its daring and skill. Whooping and yodeling with pure wanton battle lust, her warriors attacked with fearless abandon.

Holly fought just as well as they; and when she realized that she was actually making headway toward the yacht, she was so amazed, that she was nearly taken out by a hideous creature dressed in skins and a helmet topped with a human skull.

But it was there! She could see the navigation tower and the thing inside it, an imp larger than the one she had drowned seated on its head. The yacht was flying through the water as if Michael were retreating, but Holly knew that would be too good to be true.

"Allons-y!" she shouted, gesturing to half a dozen of her ghostly companions. She pointed with the tip of her sword at the yacht. "We'll board her!"

"Non, non," a voice sounded in her head. "Below decks."

Her horse galloped at an angle, its hooves working underwater. A line of portholes gleamed with magical energy at Holly's eye level.

She knew deep in her soul that Silvana and Kialish were inside.

"Attack!" she shouted.

All around her, her fighters launched themselves at the line of portholes, smashing them with sheer bodily mass—startling, for they were phantoms—and Holly's horse flew into the gash. It was pitch black inside.

The vessel immediately listed and began taking on water.

Holly leaped off her horse into the icy bay, slogging waist-deep, shouting, "Silvana! Kialish!"

Her right knee hit something; she reached down and grabbed a head of hair. There were two of them.

They're tied together.

She felt down farther and found ropes, gathered her hands around them, and began to struggle back toward the gash.

The yacht was going down.

"Horse!" she shouted.

Her horse chuffed at her, and she dragged the nearly dead weight toward it.

How long have they been under? Goddess, protect them, keep them alive. . . .

Then, with strength she knew she did not possess, she hoisted them up out of the water.

In the moonlight she saw the faces of Silvana and Kialish, slack and empty, and she feared the worst. But there was no use worrying about that know.

With her sword she cut them free, trying to position them so that they would be able to stay on the horse. But they were too limp.

"Help here!" she bellowed.

Two phantoms rode up. One was a skeleton; the other was dressed in the soggy clothing of a Jamestown Puritan. Each took one of the stricken comrades without comment, laying them in front of them over their saddles.

Holly slapped the horses' flanks and said, "Back to shore."

The horsemen complied.

Then all at once, the yacht went down.

Coughing and vomiting water, Kialish regained consciousness. He was staring straight at the yacht when it sank beneath the surface. That was shock enough; what was worse was that Laurent, the ghostly leader of the Deveraux, dove in after it astride a huge black horse.

In his right hand he carried a wicked-looking sword. In his left, a magic wand.

The water he dove into glowed blood red.

Kialish closed his eyes. *He's after Holly.*

By the change in the troops around him, he knew he was right. Those who still had faces looked stricken; skull jaws dropped open. Heads tilted back. There was screaming such as Kialish had never heard before. Fear boiled around him.

The Deveraux saw their panic and redoubled their fight . . . and Holly's army began to falter.

All this Kialish saw with a strange, lockstep clarity. He knew what was happening almost before it occurred.

He also knew that Laurent was going to kill Holly . . . unless something could be done.

Something can be done, said a voice inside his head. *You can do it.*

Though he was being carried along at breakneck speed, a woman's figure shimmered in front of him. She was holding a mirror, and she gestured for Kialish to look into it.

He saw Holly drowning Hecate. He knew why she had done it.

She needs to give something more to the water, the figure said. *Something of value.*

The figure faded, then vanished, her mirror with her. The red glow where he had last seen Holly bloomed and spread like blood on the water.

Kialish thought of Eddie, and his heart ached.

You will see him again. I swear it.

He thought of all the things he had planned to do with his life.

You will do other things, on another plane.

And then quickly as he could, so that he couldn't be saved, Kialish heaved himself into the water.

It was black, and filled with energy and things that moved; as something dove into the water above him— his rescuer, perhaps—something else grabbed on to his ankles and began to pull him down into the water, too far down to breathe, ever again, even though within seconds, his lungs were screaming for air . . .

. . . and then in a shimmering sphere, he saw Eddie, his arms outstretched; he stretched out his own, or thought he did; his mind was fuzzy and he was starting to die. But there was Eddie. . . . Yes . . .

. . . and he loved him, and he would be with him. Yes.

And the Goddess took what had been offered her, upon the water.

TWELVE

HARVEST MOON

☾

We savor all the death we cause
Tear the bodies with teeth and claws
Drink the blood and eat the flesh
Quickly now while they're still fresh

Cahors now have too much power
We glory in our unholy hour
Twisting, turning they will writhe
As we harvest them with scythes

Holly: Seattle, November

The coven went to Dan's, though the shaman had taken Uncle Richard to San Francisco to keep him from harm.

Now, facing her covenates, Holly couldn't meet their eyes. She had done something horrible. She could feel it in the weight of the stares on her. Still, in her very core, defiance stirred. She had done what she had to, what was necessary to save them, all of them.

Except Kialish.

She couldn't stop the tears that burned the back of her eyes. Kialish was her failing, though she knew he had chosen to sacrifice himself to save her. Had she not needed saving, had she been more powerful, then he would still be alive.

She closed her eyes, remembering what it had felt like when he died. There had been one intense moment of pain followed by a surge of power unlike everything she had ever felt before. Even the water seemed to push back from her as though in awe of the energy crackling through her veins.

Holly has lost it, Tommy thought as he stared at her. She swayed slightly, and he wondered what she was seeing, what she was feeling. Beside him Amanda sat and he could feel her anger and her fear. Holly was beyond them now.

He would never forget the terrible things he had seen the night before, watching, helpless, from the shore.
It shouldn't be this way. It isn't right.

He stared around at the others and knew they were thinking the same. He knew that Kari was thinking of leaving the group; she had all but said it. He would go if he could, but he was bound. Still, his loyalty was to Amanda, not Holly. If Amanda chose to follow Holly then he would too.

★ ★ ★

Anne-Louise could still feel her heart pounding in her chest. It seemed as though it had not slowed since the battle's end. The news she had to deliver to the Cathers witches from Mother Coven had done nothing to soothe her nerves. The thought of breaking that news to Holly just made her heart pound harder.

Holly was unlike anything she had ever seen. The young witch's power was tremendous, greater than she even guessed. In time she would learn how to use and harness her power. She would be nearly unstoppable then. Now, though, she was still too wild, too untrained. She wasted much of her strength, and she had no idea of the unplumbed depths within her.

Anne-Louise could not help but wonder what Holly would be like had she also been raised in the coven. She would be more skilled, stronger, certainly more controlled. *And maybe none of this mess with the Deveraux would have happened.*

She shook her head. That wasn't true. As long as there were Deveraux and Cahors alive there would be a blood feud. It was a shame, such a waste of time and magic. The rift between the two families was too great, though, for even her to mend. Some things couldn't be fixed with words. Some truce's couldn't last and sometimes peace could not be forged.

She smiled wryly. Not that anyone was even trying to do those things. No, the feud between the two families was permitted, perhaps even secretly encouraged by both the Supreme Coven and the Mother Coven. The power of House Deveraux and House Cahors was too fearsome, and the only way either coven had truly found to control it was to keep it focused elsewhere. As long as Deveraux and Cahors were fighting each other neither could take over one of the covens . . . or the world.

She cleared her head of such thoughts; it would not do to have them read by others. She took a deep breath. Time to face Holly and her coven.

She passed through the wards without needing to break them. It was a trick that, so far as she knew, she alone in Coventry could do. It was a lost art, mentioned only once in one of the ancient texts. It had taken her fifteen years to learn to do it. It came in handy, though, whenever she wanted to arrive unannounced.

Holly and company stared up at her in shock as she lifted her veil of invisibility and appeared in their midst. She surveyed the ragtag group, noting their injuries, both the physical ones and the mental ones.

She wished that she was bringing them comfort. Unfortunately it was quite the opposite.

Nicole: London, November

Nicole had to admit that it felt good to bathe. She had been given some privacy, or at least she thought she had. As she disrobed she couldn't put from her mind the thought that someone might be spying on her. She had fought the urge to dive into the bathtub, clothes and all. Instead she had forced herself to undress slowly.

She was enough of a performer to make a good show of it, even if her hands were shaking. Now, as she lay in the steaming bath, she scrubbed away all the dirt with a loofa and vanilla-scented soap. Rose petals floated in the water.

She felt more like a virgin about to be sacrificed than a bride. She shivered despite the warmth of the water. As she sunk lower in the water, she thought of how she had nearly drowned in the last bathtub she had been in. She vaguely remembered a foolish vow never to take another bath and only to shower. But that was before the dirt.

Her mind drifted back over the past twenty-four hours. Sir William had been furious when James had presented her. She hadn't needed any special powers to sense that. Not half as furious as Amanda and Holly would be if they knew. She couldn't help but smirk weakly at the thought.

Would they think that she had lost her mind, or worse, her heart? Amanda would probably think the worst. After all, in the good old days hadn't Nicole gone out with Eli, attracted to his darkness?

What would Amanda and Holly think when she didn't come home? Would they look for her? Were they okay? Amanda had tried to tell her something, something about a ferry, but she had had no time to listen. *She said that Eddie was dead.* Nicole had not known him well enough to mourn him, but still she shuddered. Things could not be good back home. They probably needed her, and now she couldn't go to them.

I'm not flaking on you, Amanda. I just can't get out of this one.

She closed her eyes and fought the urge to explode into giddy hysteria. Amanda didn't know her anymore. She barely knew herself.

No, in the old days she would probably have been attracted to James. She freely admitted it. That was back when she confused dark with strong, before she had felt the power of the Light. Before Philippe had held her while she cried.

Her heart ached at the thought of him. She knew he would be coming for her, but he didn't know when. Her job was to stay alive until he did, no matter the cost, no matter that she had to marry the devil to survive.

The Cathers/Anderson Coven: Seattle, November

"What do you want?" Amanda asked, breaking the silence.

In the shaman's house, Anne-Louise stared unblinkingly from one to another. "You, all of you. Holly has been summoned to meet with the Mother Coven in Paris, and everyone is to come along."

"Why should we?" Holly asked.

"Because we can help you." Anne-Louise continued to hold the room a moment longer. Finally she stepped backward, and everyone started talking all at once.

She waited patiently for several minutes. At last everything had been discussed and Holly rose to her feet. Anne-Louise stepped back to the group.

"We will go, but not all of us. Tante Cecile and Dan are taking Uncle Richard to San Francisco. There they will protect him and also look out for an old friend. Amanda, Kari, Tommy, Silvana, and I will go with you."

Anne-Louise nodded understanding. She disguised her relief. The discussion had gone better than she had dreamed.

* * *

The private jet was standing by at the airport, and Holly could not help but gawk. They were ushered inside by Anne-Louise and were soon seated in the softest of leather chairs.

"Drinks and food are in the galley," Anne-Louise informed them, pointing. "Help yourselves."

Tommy, eager to be of help, jumped to his feet and raced off. He was back in moments with sodas for all and little bags of nuts.

"Ever think of becoming a flight attendant?" Kari quipped.

"Travel, meet interesting people, gain unique life experience? Sorry, I think I've had my share of those," he answered good-naturedly.

Holly gazed at Tommy. The young man was not a warlock, not truly, but he tried so hard. When he handed Amanda her soda, his smile brightened and he brushed her hand.

Holly stared in turn at Amanda, wondering if her cousin knew how Tommy felt about her. If she did, she didn't let on. *Either break his heart or give him some bit of hope,* Holly thought.

As though she had heard her, Amanda turned and gave her a tight smile. Holly smiled weakly in return before settling back in her chair. It was going to be a long flight.

Gwen: Atlantic Ocean, 1666

The storms had raged for days all around the ship. Everywhere, people were sick and dying. Giselle, now Gwen, had gathered her children—she had three—and left London. The Mother Coven was furious with her, and she had no use for them.

Now she chanted spells of protection over her twin boys, Isaiah and David, and Marianne, her daughter. The four of them were still healthy, Goddess be praised. The people needed fresh air, needed to get away from each other. At last one of the crew informed her that the rain had stopped.

She gathered up her children and went up on deck. Around them the ocean churned, but a pale stream of sunlight cut through some of the clouds. She breathed in deeply and urged the children to do the same.

Marianne scampered away from her across the deck. Gwen did not stop her. The child needed the exercise, needed the freedom.

When Marianne walked over to the side of the ship and peered over into the water, though, Gwen felt her heart move into her throat.

"Come away!" she shouted.

But it was too late.

A massive wave swept over the side of the boat and sucked the child with it back into the sea.

Gwen lurched forward, screaming. The captain had seen, and he stopped her, pushing his body between her and the side of the boat.

Two crewmen ran over to the side and peered into the dark waters. Slowly they straightened, shaking their heads grimly.

"I am sorry, madam. She is gone," the captain told her in a gruff voice. His eyes, though, gleamed with sympathy.

She screamed and tried to throw herself after her daughter. Maybe she could still save her. She could at least join her.

"Madam! Think of your other children!"

The words brought her to her senses. She turned, sobbing, and ran back to her two small boys. They looked up at her with fear shining in their eyes. She crushed them to her and wept.

By the time the forests of the new land came into view, she had resigned herself to the death of Marianne. Her heart was broken, but she was a Cahors, and broken hearts had little to do with what must be done.

Now we are three, we "Cathers." I have no daughter to carry on the family line, but the boys have at least some magic. Mayhaps 'tis just as well. Perhaps it is a sign from the Goddess that House Cahors is truly dead . . . and that the magic should die with me.

Gwen of the Cahors looked down at her boys and felt only love for them. She wanted them to grow up knowing only love. And peace. No, she wouldn't teach them the magics. She wouldn't tell them of the Goddess and their sworn enemies, the Deveraux.

It would all die with her. The cycle would be broken.

Her daughter was the last sacrifice. "No one else shall die because of our family," she swore to herself.

She gathered the children in her arms and took them to the rail.

"Look, my children. We are coming to a new world. A new place. It is called Jamestown."

A cloud passed over her joy.

Jamestown had been named for King James, the monarch who had so detested witches.

No matter, she reminded herself. *All that is over.*

The Mother Coven: Paris, November

"It was nothing short of miraculous," Anne-Louise told the High Priestess as they sat together in the

Moon Temple. The circular room glowed with luminous paintings and holograms of the moon, graced with golden-yellow candlelight and verdant pools of fragrant water. Ancient mosaics to Artemis decorated the floors; the walls were covered with murals and sacred writings to the Moon Lady, who was the Goddess in all her aspects.

Acolytes moved soundlessly, tending the flames of the many candles and braziers, heaping lilies and roses at the feet of the statues of the Goddess in her many incarnations: Hecate, Astarte, Mary of Nazareth, Kwan Yen, and others.

The Moon Temple was the most sacred space of the Mother Coven.

They were sipping covenate wine; Anne-Louise had requested and been granted rites of purification upon her return. She still wasn't certain if she had been cleansed of Holly's taint. She didn't feel as whole and strong as she had upon her arrival in Seattle.

"Miraculous is an odd word for a witch to use," the High Priestess observed. She was an older woman, still very beautiful, with long red hair tumbling around her shoulders. She was dressed in the white robes of her office, with a moon tattooed onto her forehead. Anne-Louise also wore white flowing robes.

"The Deveraux disappeared," Anne-Louise continued, waving her hand so violently that she almost spilled her wine. "The entire army simply disappeared." She leaned forward. "The Mother Coven *must* protect her . . . no matter what she does."

The High Priestess looked thoughtful. "But she's a Cahors . . . blood will out. That boy who died . . ."

Anne-Louise shook her head. "Would you rather that she joined the Supreme Coven? They highly prize ambition and power. What if they facilitated a truce between her and the Deveraux?"

The High Priestess scoffed. "Sir William Moore would never allow that. It would pose too great a threat to his leadership."

"Sir William has many enemies," Anne-Louise said reasonably. "Our only hope is to stand by Holly, let her know that we are her friends."

The High Priestess regarded the other woman for a full minute. Then she said simply, "So mote it be."

They raised their glasses of wine in salute, took a sip of wine, and smashed them on the tiled floor.

Paris, November

The room was humbling; even Holly felt the power of it and dropped her eyes reverently. The Moon Temple was beautiful and filled with peace and light. The High Priestess had greeted them briefly and then withdrawn. Anne-Louise stood to the side.

There were half a dozen other women spread throughout the room, all staring at the new arrivals. One of them moved toward Holly. Her silver hair cascaded to her knees.

It was the woman from her dream. She moved with the same grace in the flesh that she had in Holly's vision. She strode forward and very solemnly kissed Holly on each cheek.

"Who are you?"

The woman gave her a ghostly smile. "My name is Sasha. I am Jer and Eli's mother."

Beside her Kari gasped. Sasha turned toward her. "And you, my friend, know me as Circle Lady."

Holly was shocked to see Kari throw her arms around Sasha and begin to sob.

THIRTEEN

DARK MOON

Darkness covers all we do
Fills our souls through and through
Death and evil lurk in our wake
What Deveraux want Deveraux take

Goddess guide us through the night
Fill us with your will and might
Grant us will to carry on
And chase away the fateful dawn

The Cathers/Anderson Coven: Paris, November

In her white temple robes, Holly walked by the light of the waning moon in the robe garden, savoring the tranquility of the Moon Temple compound. It was amazing to Holly that such a vast complex could be located within the city limits of noisy, busy Paris. But the place was very peaceful, warded against the hubbub and the chaos, and part of her wished she could become an acolyte and live here for the rest of her life.

They have no idea what it's like beyond these walls, she thought. *They've forgotten. Or is it that we're more jacked into reality, aware of the evil in the world because we're fighting Michael Deveraux?*

Someone was following her; she sensed a vibration in the air, the soft pad of footfalls on the smooth-stoned path that meandered like a snake through the garden. She closed her eyes and murmured a spell of Seeing, then relaxed as she saw that it was her cousin.

She walked slowly so that Amanda could catch up. Amanda's white robe was a little long on her, and she had gathered up the extra fabric in her fists; she looked like a little girl playing dress-up. Holly smiled wistfully for younger days, happier days.

"They sent me to find you," Amanda said by way of greeting. "They're getting ready for a strengthening ritual for us."

Holly took that in. *They know we're leaving.* They had only been there one day and one night, but she knew too that they could spend no more time recuperating from their battle with Michael and the long flight to Paris.

"Tommy and Silvana are already there," Amanda went on, then added, smirking, "Kari says she's not going to participate, and she wants the High Priestess to get someone to drive her to the airport."

"*So* not a team player," Holly observed, then realized that she was hardly one to talk.

A beautiful-sounding gong rang three times. Amanda turned to Holly, who said, "Let's do it."

They walked the serpentine path together, turning along a hedgerow to face the entrance to the Moon Temple. The entrance was a fat arch of stone, the building topped with a dome shaped like half a grapefruit. Beautiful plane trees, commonplace in France, flanked the entrance; before each tree stood an oversized white marble statue of the Goddess in one of her aspects, as within the temple: Astarte, Diana, Jezebel, Mary of Nazareth, and Mother Teresa.

Amanda stopped abruptly. She put a hand on Holly's forearm and whispered, "Look, Holly."

The statue of the Goddess as Hecate was crying. Tears streamed in rivulets down the stone face.

Holly swallowed. Moved, she slowly knelt on both knees and bowed her head. Amanda watched, her features soft, and Holly said silently, *My cousin thinks I'm begging your forgiveness, Goddess Hecate. But I only did what you wanted, and I refuse to believe that the familiar's death is my sole responsibility.*

The statue's tears stopped.

Holly had no idea what that signified, only that some sort of response was implied.

"Oh, Holly," Amanda whispered as she stared at the statue. She took Holly's hand and helped her to her feet. "Holly, I . . . I'm sorry I've been so mean."

Holly was sorry too, but not in the way Amanda meant. She was sorry that Amanda's apology meant nothing to her, except that it was proof that Amanda wasn't strong enough to lead the coven.

I've changed so much, she thought. *After I sacrificed Hecate, I got tougher. And with Kialish's death . . . my heart has hardened.*

Well, so be it. If this is what I have to become in order to keep my coven alive and save Jer, then that's fine with me.

They entered the temple together, moving through the foyer to stand beneath the rotunda, which was made of alabaster and allowed the moonlight to shine through. Then they walked through another smaller arched entrance to the temple proper, and they both drew back.

There were probably two hundred women dressed in white robes lounging throughout the temple room. They reclined gracefully on white satin pillows or rested beside the pools, which were floating with roses and lilies. There were no chairs, no rows of seats—the seating was very casual, haphazard, and fluid.

They look like cats, Holly thought.

A large stone table had been erected in the center

of the temple under a second dome not visible from the exterior of the building. The High Priestess stood behind it, opening her arms in welcome to Holly and Amanda. She wore a headdress of silver topped by a crescent moon sparkling with diamonds. Moons had been tattooed with henna on the backs of her hands and on her cheeks.

"Welcome, Cahors. We salute you."

Amanda glanced sideways at Holly and whispered, "Why is she using the older version of our name?"

Because in Coventry it's who we are, Holly wanted to tell her. *We're not Cathers and Anderson.*

We are the House of Cahors. For all we know, you, Nicole, and I may be all that is left of the line.

"Welcome, Cahors," the white-robed women chorused throughout the temple.

"Come forward, Circle," the High Priestess intoned.

Silvana and Tommy rose from beside a statue of the Goddess and came toward the High Priestess. Like everyone else, they wore white temple robes, but Silvana's dark hair hung free over her shoulders. Tommy looked awkward in the white robes among all the women, but he gave them a brave smile.

At her urging, Holly and Amanda came forward as well.

The High Priestess kept her arms held out and pivoted in a circle as she continued.

"We are here, sisters, to strengthen and protect this, our daughter coven, as they prepare to leave these walls."

Holly couldn't help her reaction of disdain, lifting her chin and frowning as she thought resentfully, *We are not a daughter coven. We're a separate, independent entity. We haven't agreed to let them boss us around.*

But the other women in the room murmured, "Blessed be," signifying their approval of the High Priestess's sentiment.

She motioned for Holly and the others to kneel. They complied, Holly bracing herself for whatever came next.

A lovely young girl with delicate Asian features glided to the High Priestess's side. She was carrying an alabaster bowl; the scent of lavender wafted from it.

"We anoint you with oil," the High Priestess intoned. She dipped her fingertips in the bowl and lifted them up. Lavender-scented oil dripped from them.

She and the girl moved first to Silvana.

"Goddess, protect this girl's eyes." Silvana blinked, and the High Priestess placed her fingertips on Silvana's closed eyelids.

"Goddess, protect her lips."

She touched oil to Silvana's mouth.

"Protect her heart."

It went on. Holly's mind began to wander.

I don't belong here. The Mother Coven is out of touch, out of date. I need to work with a stronger group; people who aren't afraid to use the hard magics to fight the Deveraux and the Supreme Coven.

She pictured harder, tougher women, not so soft and anxious.

Amazons, Holly thought. Her mental image expanded to include herself, astride her ghostly warhorse, commanding the ghost army back on Elliott Bay.

I need to find more women—correction, more people— who have the guts to fight like that.

". . . and aid them on their quest to save the third Lady of the Lily from the clutches of our enemies. . . ."

Lady of the Lily?

"Blessed be," the women lifted up in heartfelt prayer.

"So as they go from this place to save their sister witch, Nicole Anderson—"

"No."

Holly stood, forcing the girl holding the alabaster bowl to step anxiously back. Some of the oil spilled out of the bowl onto her sleeve.

There was a collective gasp.

"Holly?" Amanda murmured.

"We will go to Nicole," Holly assured her cousin, "but first—"

"No," Amanda cut in, rising to her feet. She said to the High Priestess, "You know what she wants to do."

The priestess nodded, then said to Holly, "Nicole is of your blood. Your duty is to her."

"I have no duty!" Holly thundered.

Then it was as if someone had placed a kind of shimmering, projected field in front of her. From her perspective, everything and everyone in the temple was bathed in blue light. She looked down at her hands and saw that they, too, were covered in blue.

"Isabeau," Amanda said, staring open-mouthed at Holly.

Holly's mouth opened, but it was not her voice that spoke.

"*Alors*, we came to you for courage, for strength. But you are so weak! This one and this one alone will save the Mother Coven and prevent the Supreme Coven from enslaving all humanity! And she will do it with the aid of our enemy's own son, Jeraud Deveraux!"

The High Priestess moved directly in front of Holly, as if shielding everyone else in the temple room from her.

She's afraid of us, Holly thought with glee.

Amanda spoke next.

"Isabeau," she said, her voice faint but steady. "I know why you want to go to him. Your husband can take him over, just like you're doing with Holly."

"Silence!" Isabeau launched into a barrage of what Holly, standing aside as Isabeau took her over, assumed to be medieval French.

Then Isabeau forced Holly to press both her hands together. A glowing sphere of blue energy formed between her hands. It tingled and sizzled, teasing the skin on her palms. She slowly rolled and shaped it into a ball, and it burst into flame.

The women in the temple reacted instantly. Some cried out; some ducked. All except for one who stood slightly off to the side, her face obscured by her hooded robe. Holly's eyes were drawn to her. There was something about her. . . .

Her attention moved back to the others as they scurried out of the way. Holly was exhilarated by their expressions of fear and of respect. Even the High Priestess withdrew, putting at least fifteen feet between them.

I'm with you, Lady Isabeau, she silently told her ancestress.

Ma brave, Isabeau replied. *What a fine witch you are!*

"Don't push us!" Holly cried, savoring the moment. And with a rush of pure joy, she raised her hand menacingly over her head, aiming the fireball at the nearest statue of the Goddess—

—*Hecate again!*—

—and as with the statue in the garden, the statue in the temple began to weep.

Holly was instantly jerked out of her reverie.

What am I doing?

Do it, do it, Isabeau urged her. But her dominion of Holly had ebbed.

Flamed-cheeked, Holly lowered her arm. The fireball vanished.

Then Isabeau was gone. Holly felt the connection break as surely as if someone had disconnected from a phone call.

Aghast at what she had said and done, she rushed into Amanda's arms and murmured, "I'm sorry, Manda. I'm sorry." She burst into tears.

"It's all right," Amanda murmured. But the fear that lingered in her tone gave the lie to her words.

Her face against her cousin's shoulder, Holly said, "We'll go to Nicole. We'll save her."

Sir William, James, and Nicole:
The Supreme Coven headquarters, November

Sir William looked on with great pleasure—and wistful envy—as Nicole Anderson, bewitched into mute obedience, placed her hand in his son's. Sir William himself bound them together with herb-soaked rope and cut their palms to mingle their blood.

He'll bed her, take her power, lure the remaining Cathers witches here, and then I'll have all three of them burned alive on Yule.

The news had just come in: Holly Cathers and what was left of her coven had just snuck into London for the express purpose of saving Nicole.

He was amused by how cautiously they skulked about; José Luís's coven had done the same. Didn't they realize that London was the home base of the Supreme Coven? That nothing that went on here escaped notice?

Nothing. *Surely James knows I'm aware of his many plots and schemes to depose me,* he thought as he beamed at his son the bridegroom. *Michael Deveraux must realize that as well.*

The Deveraux are such wonderful loose cannons. One never knows which way they'll aim . . . and once their fuses are lit, whom they will hit.

It makes life interesting. And when one has lived as long as I have, that's a rare and precious gift—precious enough to keep dangerous foes alive when they should be rotting in the garden with their eyes gouged out.

Before him, the little bride, swathed in black from

head to toe, swayed slightly and blinked her eyes. In those eyes he read her horror and dismay to find herself utterly powerless to stop the marriage. She could not speak, could not refuse to marry James.

Happy to rub salt in that wound, Sir William lifted up the cup into which their blood had been dripping and toasted them, saying, "It's done. You're married."

Then, almost in the same breath, he turned to a very young and very ambitious warlock named Ian, whose real ambition was to become a producer-director in Hollywood, and said, "Search for Holly Cathers and her followers and take them down. If you can't contain her, destroy her on the spot."

Michael, Eli, and Laurent: Seattle, November

The moon had waned and waxed, and now it was full again. The Anderson family mansion was deserted. Polite inquiries had yielded the information that Richard Anderson had relocated, at least temporarily, although neither the phone company drone, the utility minion, or the travel agent Richard usually used could tell Michael where they had gone.

None of his scrying arcana in the house could tell him either.

No matter. I'll find him soon enough . . . if I need him.

He stood in the backyard of the fine mansion with Laurent and Eli, who was newly back from London with the news that James had married Nicole.

Eli had gotten the distinct vibe that it might be time to step well away from all the intrigues in London and reassess his position. He had not been able to kill Jer—*yet*—and he had figured out that before he managed it he'd better have a significant peace offering to give his father, or he might end up dead as well.

"There it is," Michael said, pointing to a rosebush in the backyard. Roses did not normally bloom in November, at least not in Seattle, and yet the bush was bursting with color, despite the fact that moonlight usually bled red to gray.

Then Fantasme the spirit-falcon appeared in the sky and flew down to join the party. Michael smiled in greeting, and Eli nodded. Laurent sighed with pleasure and held out his arm. In his living days, Fantasme had been his boon companion on many a day of hunting.

Then Michael got down to business. He took a deep breath and found his center, then spread his arms wide and spoke to the earth.

"I bid thee, rise, and become one of mine," he commanded.

Thunder rumbled in the distance and it began to rain.

Michael did not move, but repeated the incantation a second time. "I bid thee, rise, and become one of mine."

The rain came down harder.

"We should have brought umbrellas," Eli muttered. Laurent silenced him with a harsh glare. But that was all he did. The great lord of the Deveraux had already started adjusting to the realities of modern life . . . including mouthy young many-times-great-grandchildren.

Lightning flashed again.

"I bid thee, rise, and become one of mine."

The rosebush shook and an ungodly howl of fury echoed from beneath the ground.

As the three looked on, the muddy earth from which the rosebush grew began to shift.

A yowl issued from the mud, followed by a low, menacing hiss.

"I command thee, live," Michael said, flinging wide his arms.

A single paw shot up from the mud. Then the mud heaved; in the pouring, hard rain, the dead familiar,

Hecate, wobbled onto her four legs and blinked her golden eyes.

"I have given you back your life," Michael said to her, "which was taken from you by the witch Holly Cathers. Will you serve me now?"

Hecate opened her mouth.

"I freed you from death," he reminded her. "Will you serve me now?"

She shuddered.

"I will," she said.

That done, Michael wheeled around in a circle, inundated by the storm. The winds howled and screamed; lightning flashed and crackled.

"Who else?" he demanded.

The rain poured down and clouds raced across the moon. "Who enters my service? Who joins my coven?"

"I will," came a chorus.

Hecate jumped into his arms. He petted her fondly as, all around him, forms took shape: dead men, dead women, gnomes and spirits, disfigured demons, and imps bearing the scars of torture.

Michael understood. They were who had come up against the Cahors before and been cut down, often savagely. The Cahors had never shown their enemies any mercy—a fact which Isabeau had conveniently ignored, in her so-called "plan" to spare Jean from burning to death. The need for revenge was so great in these who had answered his summons that it had kept them earthbound—a kind of living, if one stretched the definition.

"We'll find her together," he promised them. "And we will make her and her coven pay for everything every Cahors has ever done to any of us."

"For everything," the bled, gray dead chorused.

Michael smiled at them and at Laurent, who looked on approvingly and said, *"Bien.* Well done."

Michael replied, "I promised her I would kill her by midsummer. And I will."

Jer: Avalon, December

On Avalon, Jer paced his cell, listening to his informant as she told him, "The Cathers/Anderson Coven is said to be in London. Sir William and James are searching for them everywhere."

I must not send my spirit out to her, or they might track her, Jer thought, stricken by the news. *I told her to stay well away from me . . .*

. . . but she isn't in London searching for me. She's looking for her cousin.

He was both glad and disappointed. But that was not important.

She must live.

Dark Moon

Isabeau and Jean: Beyond Time and Space

Isabeau ran to Jean, her arms outstretched, but the hatred on his face made her legs give way. She crumpled to the ground before him, murmuring, "Forgive me, my darling. I tried to save you. I did not want you to die by my hand."

"Yet obviously you swore to another to do so," he riposted, "and so we chase one another through time, locked in hatred."

"*Non, non.* In love," she insisted. "In love, *mon* Jean."

The look on her face entrapped him, charmed him, hexed him. She was his Isabeau; she was his love. . . .

"*Ma vie, ma femme!*" Jean cried. *My life, my woman.*

He fell onto his knees before her, gathered her up in his arms, and kissed her.

Jer kissed Holly in his dreams. . . .

In her dreams, Holly kissed him back.
"Jer," she whispered, sleeping. "I will find you."

USA Today bestselling author **Nancy Holder** has received four Bram Stoker awards for her supernatural fiction. She has served on the board of trustees for the Horror Writers Association. Her work has been translated into more than two dozen languages, and she has more than seventy-eight books and two hundred short stories to her credit. Her books for Simon Pulse include the Wicked series and the novel *Spirited*. She lives in San Diego with her daughter, Belle, and far too many animals. Visit Nancy online at nancyholder.com.

Debbie Viguié is the author of several Simon Pulse books, including the Wicked series, *Midnight Pearls*, *Scarlet Moon*, and *Violet Eyes*. Debbie has been writing for most of her life and holds a degree in creative writing from UC Davis. When Debbie is not busy writing, she enjoys traveling with her husband, Scott. They live in Florida. Visit Debbie online at debbieviguie.com.

Witches
Secrets
Alliances
Destiny

The new and final volume to a magnificent series

wicked

Resurrection

Nancy Holder & Debbie Viguié

A series by
Nancy Holder and
Debbie Viguié

The first two novels in the captivating series . . .

wicked

Witch & Curse

Nancy Holder & Debbie Viguié

The third and fourth novels in the captivating series . . .

wicked 2

Legacy & Spellbound

Nancy Holder & Debbie Viguié

From Simon Pulse
Published by Simon & Schuster

The Cursed Ones have made their presence known,
and the world will never be safe again....

From the *New York Times* bestselling authors of the Wicked series
NANCY HOLDER AND DEBBIE VIGUIÉ

COMING FALL 2010

From Simon Pulse

Published by Simon and Schuster